BY THE AUTHOR OF "JOHN HALIFAX."

From the North British Review.

She attempts to show how the trials, perplexities, joys, sorrows, labors, and successes of life deepen or wither the character according to its inward bent.

She cares to teach, *not* how dishonesty is always plunging men into infinitely more complicated external difficulties than it would in real life, but how any continued insincerity gradually darkens and corrupts the very life-springs of the mind; *not* how all events conspire to crush an unreal being who is to be the "example" of the story, but how every event, adverse or fortunate, tends to strengthen and expand a high mind, and to break the springs of a selfish or merely weak and self-indulgent nature.

She does not limit herself to domestic conversations, and the mere shock of character on character; she includes a large range of events—the influence of worldly successes and failures—the risks of commercial enterprises—the power of social position—in short, the various elements of a wider economy than that generally admitted into a tale.

She has a true respect for her work, and never permits herself to "make books," and yet she has evidently very great facility in making them.

There are few writers who have exhibited a more marked progress, whether in freedom of touch or in depth of purpose, than the authoress of "The Ogilvies" and "John Halifax."

HANNAH. 8vo, Paper, 50 cents ; 12mo, Cloth, $1 50.

MOTHERLESS ; or, A Parisian Family. Translated from the French of Madame De Witt, *née* Guizot. For Girls in their Teens. Illustrated. 12mo, Cloth, $1 50.

FAIR FRANCE. Impressions of a Traveller. 12mo, Cloth, $1 50.

A BRAVE LADY. With Illustrations. 8vo, Paper, $1 00; Cloth, $1 50; 12mo, Cloth, $1 50.

A FRENCH COUNTRY FAMILY. Translated from the French of Madame De Witt, *née* Guizot. Illustrated. 12mo, Cloth, $1 50.

A HERO, AND OTHER TALES. 12mo, Cloth, $1 25.

A LIFE FOR A LIFE. 8vo, Paper, 50 cents; 12mo, Cloth, $1 50.

AGATHA'S HUSBAND. 8vo, Paper, 50 cents; 12mo, Cloth, $1 50.

A NOBLE LIFE. 12mo, Cloth, $1 50.

AVILLION, AND OTHER TALES. 8vo, Paper, $1 25.

CHRISTIAN'S MISTAKE. 12mo, Cloth, $1 50.

FAIRY BOOK. Illustrated. 12mo, Cloth, $1 50.

HEAD OF THE FAMILY. 8vo, Paper, 75 cents; 12mo, Cloth, $1 50.

JOHN HALIFAX, GENTLEMAN. 8vo, Paper, 75 cents; 12mo, Cloth, $1 50.

MISTRESS AND MAID. 8vo, Paper, 50 cents; 12mo, Cloth, $1 50.

NOTHING NEW. 8vo, Paper, 50 cents.

OGILVIES. 8vo, Paper, 50 cents; 12mo, Cloth, $1 50.

OLIVE. 8vo, Paper, 50 cents; 12mo, Cloth, $1 50.

OUR YEAR. Illustrated. 16mo, Cloth, Gilt Edges, $1 00.

STUDIES FROM LIFE. 12mo, Cloth, $1 25.

THE TWO MARRIAGES. 12mo, Cloth, $1 50.

THE UNKIND WORD, AND OTHER STORIES. 12mo, Cloth, $1 50.

THE WOMAN'S KINGDOM. Illustrated. 8vo, Paper, $1 00; Cloth, $1 50; 12mo, Cloth, $1 50.

BOOKS FOR GIRLS. Written or Edited by the Author of "John Halifax." Illustrated. 16mo, Cloth, 90 cents each. Now ready:

LITTLE SUNSHINE'S HOLIDAY.
THE COUSIN FROM INDIA.
TWENTY YEARS AGO.

☞ HARPER & BROTHERS *will send either of the above works by mail, postage prepaid, to any part of the United States, on receipt of the price.*

THESEUS AND ARIADNE.

THE

WOMAN'S KINGDOM.

A LOVE STORY.

BY THE AUTHOR OF

"JOHN HALIFAX, GENTLEMAN," "HANNAH," "A BRAVE LADY,"
"MISTRESS AND MAID," "OLIVE," "THE OGILVIES,"
"THE HEAD OF THE FAMILY," &c., &c.

"Queens you must always be: queens to your lovers; queens to your husbands and your sons; queens of higher mystery to the world beyond. . . . But, alas! you are too often idle and careless queens, grasping at majesty in the least things, while you abdicate it in the greatest!"—JOHN RUSKIN.

NEW YORK:
HARPER & BROTHERS, PUBLISHERS,
FRANKLIN SQUARE.
1872.

Dedication:

TO

MONA MARGARET PATON.

My little girl! sweet uncrowned queen
Of a fair kingdom, dim and far;
Whose budding life 'neath rosy screen
Scarce recognizes yet, I ween,
What lives of other women are;

Child, when the burden we lay down,
Thy tender hands must lift and bear;
The household sceptre and love-crown,
Green-wreathed, or hung with dead leaves brown—
Take courage. Both are holy wear.

Better to love than to be loved:
Better to serve, and serving guide,
Than wait, with idle oars unproved,
And flapping sail by each breath moved,
The turning of life's solemn tide.

Live, work, and love; as Heaven assign
For heaven, or man, thy sacred part;
Ancestress of a noble line,
Or calm in maidenly decline;—
But keep till death the woman's heart.

THE WOMAN'S KINGDOM.

"*Queens you must always be: Queens to your lovers: Queens to your husbands and your sons: Queens of higher mystery to the world beyond. ...... But, alas! You are too often idle and careless Queens, grasping at majesty in the least things, while you abdicate it in the greatest.*"—JOHN RUSKIN.

THE TWO SISTERS.

CHAPTER I.

"OH, Edna, I am so tired! And this is the very dullest place in all the world!"

"Do you think so, dear? And yet it was the place you specially wanted to go to."

Edna spoke in the soothing yet cheerful tone which all people—that is, people like Edna Kenderdine—instinctively use towards an invalid; and, laying down her work—she rarely was without some sort of work in her tiny hands—looked tenderly and anxiously at her sister. For they were twin-sisters; though, as sometimes happens with twins, so excessively unlike that they would scarcely have been supposed akin at all.

"You know, Letty dear, that as soon as you began to get better the Isle of Wight was the place you fancied for a change."

"Yes; but we might have found many a nicer spot in the Isle of Wight than this—Ryde, for instance, where there are plenty of houses, and a good pier, and probably an esplanade. Oh, how I used to enjoy the Brighton esplanade in the days when I was a little girl, and we were rich and happy!"

"Were we happy then? I don't remember. But I know I have been quite as happy since."

"You always are happy," returned the invalid, with a vexed air. "I think nothing in the world would make you miserable."

Edna winced a little, but she was sitting in the shadow of the window-curtain, and was not seen. "Come, come," she said, "it is of no use quarrelling with me because I will not see the black side of things; time enough for that when we go home to Kensington. Here we are, out on a holiday, with beautiful weather, comfortable lodgings, no school to teach, and nothing in the wide world to do but to amuse ourselves."

"Amuse ourselves! How can we? We don't know a soul here. In-doors there is nothing to do, and nobody to come and see us; and out-of-doors there is not a creature to look at or to speak to."

"I thought we wanted to get out of the way of our fellow-creatures. Besides, they would not care for us just now. It is not every lodging-house, even, that would have taken us in, and we lately out of scarlet-fever."

"We need not have told that."

"Oh, Letty! we must have told."

"Edna, you are so ridiculously conscientious! I have no patience with you!"

Edna made no reply; indeed, it was useless replying to the poor convalescent, whose thin face betrayed that she was at the precise stage of recovery when every thing jars against the irritable nerves, and the sickly, morbid fancy changes its moods twenty times a day. Otherwise, to people in the somewhat dreary position of these two young school-mistresses—driven from their labors in the midst of the half-year by a dangerous fever which had compelled the shutting up of the school, brought the one sister nearly to death's-door, and the other not far from it by the fatigue of sick-nursing—even to them the parlor they sat in was not uncheerful. It was very neat and clean, and it had a large bay-window looking out on a verandah; beyond that a little garden; farther, a narrow strip of bright, green, grassy cliff, fringed with a low hedge, where the "white-blossomed sloe" was in full glory, and a pair of robin-redbreasts were building and singing all the day long. Below, at the cliff's foot, the unseen sea was heard to tumble and roll with a noisy murmur; but far away in the distance it spread itself out in sleepy stillness, shimmering and glancing in the sunshine of early spring. The sight of it might well have gladdened many a dull heart; and the breath of it, which came in salt and fresh, though not cold, through the half-open window, might have given health to many a sick soul, as well as body—granting that soul to be one of those whom Nature can comfort. It is not every one whom she can.

Poor Letty was not of those thus comforted. Her eyes looked as sad as ever, and there was a sharp, metallic ring in her voice as she said:

"I can't imagine, Edna, why you make so much fuss about the fever. You would drive every body away from us as if we had had the plague. This morning I overheard you insisting that the gentleman who wants the opposite parlor should be told distinctly what had been the matter with me. It is very foolish, when I am quite well now."

"Yes, dear, quite well, thank God!" returned Edna, soothingly. "And the gentleman said he was not in the least afraid; besides, he was a doctor."

"Was he, indeed? A real gentleman, then!"

"Supposing that a doctor is—and he certainly ought to be—a real gentleman."

"Nonsense! I mean a professional man; not one of those horrid shop-keepers whose children we have to teach —how I hate them all! And we must go back and begin again after midsummer. Oh, Edna, I wish I were dead!"

"I don't, and I doubt if you do—not just this very minute. For there is your dinner coming in—and you like fish, and you declared you were so frightfully hungry."

"You are always making fun of me," said the sick sister, half plaintively. Nevertheless she yielded to the influence of that soft, caressing, and yet encouraging tone; her gloomy looks relaxed into a faint smile, and she fell to her simple invalid meal of fried sole and rice-pudding with an appetite that proved she was really getting well, in spite of her despondency and fretfulness. Edna sat by her and ate her own cold mutton with an equal relish; and then the sisters began to talk again.

"So, after to-day, we shall not be the only lodgers in the house. How very annoying!"

"I don't think the new-comers will harm us much. They are likely to be as quiet as ourselves. Besides, they will have a fellow-feeling for us. One of them is also an invalid, and a great deal worse than you, Letty."

"The doctor?"

"No; his brother, whom he has brought here for change of air."

"Did you see them? Really, you might have told me all this before. I should have been so glad of any thing to interest me. And you seem to have inquired all about them."

"Of course I did. It was very important to us whom we had in the next parlor, and probably to them also, in the young man's sickly state. I dare say the brother took as much pains as I did to find out all about his opposite neighbors."

"Did you see him?"

"No; except his back, which was rather round, and the coat very shabby at the shoulders."

"He isn't a gentleman, then?"

"I can't tell. If he happened to be a poor gentleman, why should not his coat be shabby at the shoulders?"

"I don't like poverty," said Letty, with a slight shrug; and drawing round her the soft, rich shawl, relic of the "happy" days she regretted, when the little twins were expected to be co-heiresses, and not school-mistresses. Those days were dim enough now. The orphans had been brought up for governesses, and had gone out as governesses, until difficulties arising, from Letty's extreme beauty on the one hand, and Edna's fond clinging to her sister on the other, they had resolved to make themselves a home by setting up one of those middle-class day-schools which are so plentiful in the immediate suburbs of London. It had done well, on the whole; at least it had sufficed to maintain them. They were still young women—only twenty-six—though both, Edna especially, had a certain air of formality and authority which all school-mistresses seem gradually to acquire. But they were, as could be seen at a glance, well-bred, well-educated women; and, besides, Letitia was one of those remarkably handsome persons of whom one scarcely sees half a dozen in a lifetime, and about whose beauty there can not be two opinions. You might not fancy her style; you might have some ideal of your own quite contrary to it; but if you had eyes in your head you must acknowledge that she was beautiful, and would remain so, more or less, to the last day of her life. Hers was a combination very rarely to be met with; of form and color, figure and face—enough completely to satisfy the artist-eye, and indicate to the poetical imagination plenty of loveliness spiritual beneath the loveliness external. Even her illness had scarcely clouded it; and with her tall figure shrouded in shawls, her magnificent brown hair cut short under a cap, and her graceful hands, white and wasted, lying on her lap, she was "interesting" to the last degree.

Indeed, to tell the truth, Letty Kenderdine's beauty had been the real hindrance to her governess-ship. Wherever she went every body fell in love with her. Mothers dreaded her for their grown-up sons; weak-minded wives were uneasy concerning their husbands. Not that Letty was the least to blame; she was so used to admiration that she took it all quite calmly. Too cold for passion, too practical for philandering, there was no fear of her exciting any unlawful jealousies; and as for regular love-affairs, though she generally had one or more on hand, it was a very mild form of the article. She never "committed" herself. She might have married twenty times over—poor tutors, country clergymen, and struggling men of business; even a few younger sons of good families: but she had, as she said, a dislike to poverty, especially matrimonial poverty.

> "Will the flame that you're so rich in
> Light a fire in the kitchen,
> Or the little god of love turn the spit, spit, spit?"

was the burden of her sweet, smiling refusals, which sent her lovers away twice as mad as they came. But, though she smiled, Letty never relented.

So, though she had been once or twice on the brink of an engagement, she had never fallen over the precipice; and as she confided all her difficulties to Edna, and Edna (who had never any of her own) helped her out of them, they came to nothing worse than "difficulties." True, they had lost her a situation or two, and, indeed, had determined Edna to the point which she carried out—as she did most of her determinations, in her own quiet way—the setting up of a school; but they never weighed seriously upon either sister's mind. Only sometimes, when the school duties were hard, Letty would sigh over the comparatively easy days when she was residing in "high" families, well-treated, as somehow she always had been, for there was a grace and dignity in her which compelled respectful treatment. She would regret the lost luxuries—a carriage to drive in and a park to walk in with her pupils, large rooms, plenty of servants, and dainty feeding—recapitulating all the good things she used to have, balancing them against the ill things she had now, until she fancied she had made a change for the worse; complained that her present life was not half so pleasant as that of a resident governess, and lamented pathetically over the cause of all—what she called "my unfortunate appearance."

Still the fact was patent—neither to be sighed down nor laughed down—and it had a laughable side—Letty was much too handsome for a governess. Too handsome, indeed, for most of the useful purposes of life. She could not pass anywhere unnoticed; to send her out shopping was a thing difficult enough, and as for her taking a walk alone in pleasant Kensington Gardens, or the lonely Brompton Road, it was a thing quite impossible. Edna often said, with a queer mixture of perplexity and pride, that her beautiful sister was as much trouble to her as any baby. And, invalid as Letty now was, it must be confessed that not without a secret alarm had Edna heard of and made inquiries about the impending lodgers.

Letty half guessed this, though she was not very vain; for she had long become used to her "unfortunate appearance;" and, besides, your superlatively handsome people generally take their universally-acknowledged honors as composedly as a millionaire takes his money, or a poet-laureate his crown. When, after Edna's communication respecting the gentleman's shabby shoulders, the two sisters' eyes met, Letty broke into an actual smile.

"How old is he? Are you afraid that something will happen?"

"Perhaps. Something of that sort always is happening, you know," said Edna, dolefully; and then both sisters burst out laughing, which quite restored Letty's good-humor.

"Come, dear, don't be alarmed. He will not fall in love with me—I'm getting too ugly and too old. And as for myself, no harm will come to me. I don't like shabbiness, and of all people alive, the person I should least like to marry would be a doctor. Only fancy having one's husband at every body's beck and call—out at all hours, day and night; never able to take me to a party—or give me a party at home without being fetched away in the middle of it; going to all sorts of nasty places and nasty people; bringing home fevers, and small-pox, and the like—oh! what a dreadful life!"

"Do you think so?" said Edna. "Why, when I was a girl I used to fancy that had I been a boy, and could choose my profession, of all professions I should choose a doctor's. There is something in it so grand, and yet so useful. He has so much power in his hands. Such unlimited influence over souls as well as bodies. Of course it would be a hard life—nothing smooth or pleasant about it—but it would be a life full of interest, with endless opportunities of usefulness. I don't mean merely of saving people's lives, but of putting their lives right, both mentally and physically, as nobody but a doctor can do. Hardly even a clergyman could come so near my ideal of the perfect existence—'he went about doing good.'"

Edna spoke earnestly, as sometimes, though not often, she was roused to speak, and then her plain little face lighted up, and her tiny form took an unwonted grace and dignity. Plain as she was—as noticeably so as her sister was handsome—there was a certain character about her in her small firm mouth, and babyish yet determined little chin—in her quick motions and active ways, and especially in her hands, the only decided beauty she possessed—which, though they flitted hither and thither, light as snow-flakes and pretty as rose-leaves, had an air of strength, purpose, and practicability which indicated fully what she was—this merry, busy-bee-like little woman—who

> "Gathered honey all the day
> From every opening flower;"

but yet, on occasions, could be the very soul of the household—the referee, and judge, and decisive voice in all matters, great or small.

"Edna, you are preaching me quite a sermon," said Letty, yawning. "And I really don't deserve it. Did I ever say I wouldn't marry a doctor?—even this very doctor of yours, if he wishes it particularly. I am sure," she added, plaintively, with an anxious glance towards the mirror, "it is time I should make up my mind to marry somebody. Another illness like the last would altogether destroy my appearance."

"What nonsense you talk!"

"No, it isn't nonsense," said Letty, with a queer humility. "It is all very well for you, who are clever and can talk, and do things prettily and practically, and make yourself happy in your own way, so that, indeed, it is little matter whether you are ever married or not. But if any body marries me, it will be only for my appearance. I must make my hay while the sun shines. Heigh-ho! I wish something would happen—something to amuse us in this dull place. Do tell me a little more about the new lodgers."

"I have nothing to tell; and besides—there they are!"

At that moment, coming round the corner of the house (the Misses Kenderdine's parlor-window had to be passed in reaching the front door), appeared a porter and two portmanteaus, and immediately afterwards a Bath chair. Therein sat a figure so muffled up, in spite of the sunshiny day, as to awaken a feeling of compassion in any beholder.

"Do come away, Letty. It is the sick brother. He may not like to be looked at."

"But I must look at him. I have not had the least thing to interest me all day. Don't be cross. He shall not see me. I will hide behind the window-curtains."

And curiosity quite overcoming her languor, she left her easy-chair, and crouched down in a very uncomfortable attitude to watch the proceedings outside.

"Do come and look too, Edna. I wonder—is he a man or a boy? He has got no whiskers, and he is so very thin. He looks a walking skeleton beside his stout brother. Do say if that big, awkward man is the brother, the doctor,

I mean, whom you are so extremely anxious for me to marry."

"Letty, what foolishness!"

"Well, I'll promise to think about him if he ever gives me the chance. He does look like a gentleman, in spite of his shabby coat. But, as for the other, you need not be alarmed about him. He seems to have one foot in the grave already. Just come and peep at him. No one can see you, I am sure."

Edna looked—she hardly knew why, unless out of pure compassion. It was a face that any woman's heart, old or young, would have melted over—white, wan, with heavy circles under the large eyes, and a drawn look of permanent pain round the mouth. One of those faces, so delicately outlined, so almost feminine in contour, as to make one say, instinctively, "He must be very like his mother," and to wish likewise that he might always have his mother or his wife close at hand to take care of him. For it was undoubtedly one of those sensitive yet passionate faces which indicate a temperament that requires incessant taking care of—the care that only a woman can take. Though the big brother seemed tender enough. He wrapped him, and lifted him, and talked to him gently, as if he had been a child. Something touchingly child-like—the poetic nature is always young—was in the poor fellow's looks, as he wearily obeyed; doing all he was told to do, though every movement seemed a pain.

"I wonder what his illness has been," said Edna, won into a sympathy that deadened even her sense of propriety. "Not consumption, I fancy. I should rather say he was just recovering from rheumatic fever."

"Never mind his illness. What do you think of himself?"

"I think it is one of the most interesting faces I ever saw. But if ever I saw death written in a face— Poor fellow—and so young, too!"

"Not much above twenty, certainly."

"There, he has turned, and is looking right in at our window. Come away—you must come, or he will certainly see you, Letty!"

It was too late. He had seen her; for the poor sensitive youth started violently, and a sudden flush came over his wan cheek. He drew back hastily, and pulled his fur cap closer down over his face.

Edna rose quickly and shut the Venetian blind. "It is cruel — absolutely cruel—to stare at a person who is in that sickly, nervous state. How angry I should have been if any body had done it to you when you were ill! and I am certain he saw you."

"POOR FELLOW—AND SO YOUNG, TOO!"

"Never mind: the sight is not so very dreadful; it won't kill him, probably," laughed Letty, whose spirits had quite risen under this unwonted excitement. "Perhaps it will even do him good, if he wants amusement as much as I do; and he need not excite your sisterly fears: he won't fall in love with me. He is too ill to think of any body but himself."

"Poor fellow!" again said Edna, with a sigh.

She was too well accustomed to her sister's light talk to take it seriously, or indeed to heed it at all. People cease to notice the idiosyncrasies of those they have been accustomed to all their life. Probably, if any other young woman had talked as Letty did, Edna would have disliked it extremely; but she did not mind Letty—it was her way. Besides, she was her sister—her own flesh and blood, and the two loved one another dearly.

Shortly the slight bustle in the hall subsided, the Bath chair was wheeled empty away, and a confusion of footsteps outside indicated that the sick man was being carried up stairs by the brother; then the house sank into silence.

Edna drew up the blind, and stood gazing out meditatively upon the sunshiny sea.

"What are you thinking of?" Letty asked.

"Of that poor fellow, and whether this place will do him any good—whether he will live or die."

"The latter seems most likely."

"Yes; and it seems to me so sad, especially—" and her voice sank a little—"especially since, thank God! we have passed through our time of terror and are safe again. So very sad, with every thing outside bright and happy; trees budding, birds singing, the sky smiling all over, and the sea smiling back at it again, as if there was no such thing as death in the world. How the brother's heart must ache through it all!"

"The big brother—the doctor you mean?"

"Yes; and, being a doctor, he must know the truth—that is, if it is to be—if the young man is not likely to recover."

"Yet the doctor seems cheerful enough. As it sounded outside in the hall, I thought I never heard a more cheerful voice."

"People often speak cheerfully—they are obliged to learn to do it—when—" Here Edna suddenly stopped. It was not wise to enlighten Letty, still an invalid, upon her own sad sick-room experience. "But things may be more hopeful than we suppose. Nevertheless, I am very sorry for our new neighbors—for them both."

"So am I. We must ask the landlady all about them when she brings in tea."

But though, in her extreme dearth of outside interests, Letty's curiosity became so irresistible that she hurried on the tea by half an hour, her inquiries resulted in very little.

Mrs. Williams knew no more of her new inmates than most sea-side landladies do of their lodgers. The gentlemen had come from the inn; they were named Stedman —Dr. and Mr. Stedman—and she rather thought they were from London. "As the ladies also lived in London, perhaps they might know something about them," suggested the simple island woman, who was quite as eager to get as to give information, for she owned to being rather sorry she had taken them in.

"Why?" asked Edna.

"I do believe the young gentleman is only brought here to die; and death is such a bad thing to happen in any lodgings."

"Nay, we will hope for the best. This fine, pure air may restore him. See how strong my sister is getting."

"Yes, indeed, miss; and so I told his brother. I wished he could have seen how wonderfully the young lady had picked up since she came. And he said, 'Yes, she didn't look a bit like an invalid now.'"

"Had he seen me?" asked Letty, half smiling.

"I don't know, miss; but he has got sharp, noticeable eyes—real doctor's eyes."

"Oh!" said Letty, and subsided into silence.

"Does he seem very anxious about his sick brother?" Edna inquired.

"Ay, sometimes, to judge by his look. But he talks quite cheerful-like. Just hark! you can hear 'em a-laughing together now."

"How I wish we had any thing to make us laugh!" sighed Letty, when the door closed; and the important event of tea being over, she relapsed into her former dullness, leaned back again in her easy-chair, letting her hands fall drearily on her lap—such soft, handsome, idle, helpless hands.

"Shall I read?" said Edna, with an anxious glance at

A DAUGHTER OF THE GODS.

the clock. It was too late to go out, and it was many—oh! so many hours till bed-time.

"You know I never cared for reading, especially poetry books, which are all you brought with us."

"Shall I try to get a novel from the library?"

"Threepence a volume, and you'll grumble at the extravagance, and I shall be sure to go to sleep over it too. Well, I think I will lie down and sleep a little, for I am so tired I don't know what to do."

She rose, walked once or twice across the room, looking most majestic in her long, soft, flowing draperies—for it was twenty years ago, and women's draperies were both graceful and majestic then: with her large lovely form and classical face she was the personification of Tennyson's line—

> "A daughter of the gods: divinely tall,
> And most divinely fair."

And when she lay down, she idealized the common horsehair lodging-house sofa by an outline most artistically beautiful—fit for a sleeping Dido or dying Cleopatra. Such women nature makes rarely, very rarely; queens of beauty, crowned or uncrowned, who instinctively take their places in the tournament of life, and "rain influence," whether consciously or not, to an almost fearful extent upon us weak mortals, especially men mortals, who, even the best of them, are always prone to reconstrue the dogma that the good is necessarily the beautiful, and to presuppose the highest beauty to be the highest good.

But this is wandering into metaphysics, of which, however she might be the cause of them in others, there certainly was no trace in Letty Kenderdine. She lay down and made herself comfortable, or rather was made comfortable by her sister, with shawls and pillows; then she fell sound asleep, like any other mortal woman, breathing so peacefully and deeply that, if it would not utterly destroy the romance about her, I feel bound to confess she *almost* snored.

Edna sat beside her till certain of her repose, and then crept softly away. Not for idleness, and not for pleasure, though the sweet evening tempted her sorely, with its sunset of rose and gray, its fresh sea-breeze, and, as is found along most of the south coast of England, and, especially the Isle of Wight, its delicious mingling of sea and country pleasures. Above the lapping of the tide on the beach below was heard the good-night warble of the robins and the deep note of the thrush; and besides the salt sea smell there was an atmosphere of trees budding and flowers blossoming, giving a sense of vague delight, and tender foreboding of some unknown joy.

It touched Edna; she could not tell why, except that she loved the spring, and this was the first April she had spent out of London for several years; scarcely since those dimly-remembered years of their country house in Hampshire, which, to her, balanced Letty's memories of the Brighton esplanade. One had been the summer, the other the winter residence of the rich merchant, who, absorbed in money-making, and losing fortune and life together, had left no remembrances to his motherless twin-girls but these.

They recurred at times, each in their turn, and to each sister according to her nature. To Edna at this moment came a rush of the old child-life—the pony she rode—a pretty little gentle thing, loved like a human companion; a certain stream, which danced through a primrose wood, and over which dragon-flies used to skim, and where endless handfuls of king-cups grew; an upland meadow, yellow with cowslips—Edna could smell the odor of it yet.

"How I should like to make another cowslip-ball! I believe I could do it as well as ever. I wonder if cowslips grow anywhere about here!"

And then she smiled at the silliness of a school-mistress wanting to make cowslip-balls, and wondered at the foolish feeling which came over her in her monotonous life; and why it was that, just rising up out of the long strain of anxiety, her heart was conscious of a sudden rebound—a wild longing after happiness: not merely the busy content of her level life, but actual happiness. In picturing it, though it was very vague too and formless, she, however, did not picture the usual sort of happiness which comes most natural at her age. Unlike her sister, no lovers had ever troubled Edna's repose. In the dull city family where she had been governess ever since leaving school no such things were ever thought of; besides, Edna was plain, and knew it—felt it too—perhaps all the keener for her sister's beauty and her own intense admiration of the same. No; Edna Kenderdine was not a marrying woman. She herself was convinced she would be an old maid, and had laid her plans accordingly; and mapped out her future life with a quiet acquiescence in, and yet a full recognition of—alas! what woman was ever without that?—its sad imperfectness.

Thus her ideal of happiness was not love, or, at least, not consciously, and certainly not love on her own account. This golden dream — this seeming height of complete felicity — was thought of with reference to Letty alone. For herself, she hardly knew what she wanted; perhaps a better school, more pupils, and these of a higher class, for it was hard and thankless work trying to make little common girls into little gentlewomen. Or possibly—though to that El Dorado Edna scarcely dared to lift her eyes—some extraordinary windfall of fortune—a legacy, or the like—which would forever lift her out of the necessity of keeping school at all, and enable her to set up a cottage in the country—ever so small, she did not care, so that it was only in the country, and had a garden to it, and fields around it, where she might do as she liked all day long, without being haunted by the necessity of school-teaching, or by that dread of the future, of breaking down helpless in the midst of her career, which, since the fever time, had often painfully pursued her. She herself, though not exactly ill, had been very much enfeebled; and probably it was this weak condition of body which made the little woman mentally less brave than usual; caused her to long, with a sore yearning, not merely to be sheltered from evil, but to have her dull life turned into brightness by some absolute tangible good.

So, while Letty slept—the sound, healthy sleep of which her easy temperament never made any difficulty—Edna stood looking out on the twilight sea, still thinking—thinking—till the tears came into her eyes, and rolled slowly down.

They were soon wiped away—not dashed off, but quietly wiped away with a resolute hand. She could not have repressed them, they would have choked her; but she could help indulging in them, taking a sentimental pleasure over them, or exalting them into a real grief. Alas! she knew what real grief was when Letty was at the crisis of scarlet-fever.

"No! I'll not cry—it's wicked! What have I to cry about? when my sister is nearly well, and we shall be able to gather the school together very soon, and meantime we have enough money to last us, and no other cares. There is much more to be thankful for than afraid of. And now, before she wakes, let me see exactly how we stand."

She took her little writing-desk to the window, that she might catch the utmost of the fading light, and with one anxious glance at the sofa, set herself to a piece of work which always fidgeted Letty—the balancing of her weekly accounts. Nominally the sisters kept these week and

a fortnight's butter, or a pair of gloves for Letty, or something else that otherwise would require to be done without. She racked her brains to remember how she had spent it, added up the conflicting columns of figures again and again, and counted and re-counted the contents of her two purses—one for current coin, the other the grand receptacle of the family income.

Vain, vain! Poor Edna could not make matters right. Her head burned, her brow throbbed—she pushed her hair back from it with trembling fingers—she was very nearly crying.

It was a small thing—a silly thing almost; but then she had been weakened by anxiety and fatigue, and do what she could, the future rose up before her darker, and reasonably darker than it had ever done before. What if the pupils, scared by fever, should not readily return? What if she and her sister were to be left with a house on their hands, the rent to be paid, the servant to be kept, and nothing to do it with? That morbid dread of the future—that bitter sense of helplessness and forlornness which all working-women have at times, came upon Edna, and made her think with a strange momentary envy of the women who did not work, who had brothers and fathers to work for them, or at least to help them with the help that a man, and only a man, can give.

And then looking up, for the first time for many minutes, Edna became aware of two eyes watching her, resting on her with such an expression of kindliness and pity, the sort of half-amused pity that a man would show to a troubled and perplexed child, that this poor child—she was strangely young still in many ways—looked fearlessly back into them, almost with a sort of appeal, as if the observer had been an authorized friend, who could have helped her did he choose. But the moment after she drew back, exceedingly annoyed; and the gazer also drew back, made a slight apologetic half-bow, then blushed violently all over his face, as if conscious that he had been doing a most unwarrantable and ungentlemanly thing, rose from his bench by the window, and walked hastily away.

As he turned, by the broad stooping shoulders and well-worn coat rather than by the face, which she had not seen until now, being so attracted by the face of the invalid brother, Edna recognized the doctor, Dr. Stedman.

CHAPTER II.

THIS will be a thorough "love" story. I do not pretend to make it any thing else. There are other things in life besides love; but every body who has lived at all knows that love is the very heart of life, the pivot upon which its whole machinery turns; without which no human existence can be complete, and with which, however broken and worn in part, it can still go on working somehow, and working to a comparative useful and cheerful end.

An author once wrote a book of which the heroine was supposed to be painted from a real living woman, whose relations were rather pleased than not at the accidental resemblance. "Only," said they, with dignified decorum, "in one point the likeness fails; our Anastasia was never in love with any body." "Then," replied the amused author, "I certainly can not have painted her, for she would have been of no use to me; such an abnormal specimen of humanity is not a woman at all."

No. A life without love in it must of necessity be an imperfect, an unnatural life. The love may be happy or unhappy, noble or ignoble, requited or unrequited; but it must be, or have been, there. Love absolute. Not merely the tie of blood, the bond of friendship, the many close affections which make existence sweet; but the one, closest of all, the love between man and woman—which is the root of the family life, and the family life is the key to half the mysteries of the universe.

And so, without disguise of purpose, and rather glorying in the folly, if folly it be, I confess this to be a mere love-tale, nothing more. No grand "purpose" in it, no dramatic effects—scarcely even a "story;" but a few pages out of the book of daily life, the outside of which looks often so common and plain; and the inside—but One only reads that.

Under Mrs. Williams's commonplace unconscious roof were gathered these four young people, strangers to one another, and ignorant of their mutual and individual destinies, afterwards to become so inextricably mingled, tangled, and crossed. The like continually happens; in fact it must, in most cases, necessarily happen. The first chance-meeting, or what appears chance; the first indifferent word or hap-hazard incident—from these things do almost all love-stories date. For in all true marriages now, as in Eden, the man and woman do not deliberately seek, but are brought to one another; happy those who afterwards can recognize that the hand which led his Eve to Adam was that of an invisible God!

But this only comes afterwards. No sentimental premonitions weighed on the hearts of any of these, the two young men and two young women, who had, each and all, their own lives to live, their own separate cares and joys. For even if blessed with the closest bonds of fraternity, every soul is more or less alone, or feels so, till the magic other soul appears, which, if fate allows, shall remove solitude forever. There may or may not be a truth in the doctrine of love at first sight, but it is, like the doctrine of instantaneous conversion, too rarely experienced to be much believed in. Ordinary men and women walk blindfold to the very verge of their fate, nor recognize it as fate till it is long past. Which fact ought to be, to both young folks and their guardians, at once a consolation and a warning.

Edna, when, immediately after the doctor's disappearance, the entrance of candles awakened Letty, told her sister frankly, and with considerable amusement, of the steadfast stare which for the moment had annoyed her.

"At least, I should have been annoyed had it been you, Letty. But with me of course it meant nothing; merely a little harmless curiosity. Certainly, as Mrs. Williams says, he has thorough 'doctor's eyes.' They seem able to see every thing. As a doctor ought to see, you know."

"And what color were they, and what sort of a face was it altogether?"

"I really can not tell. A nice, kindly sort of face, and that is all I know."

"But, Edna, if I am to marry him you ought to know. So look hard next time, and tell me exactly what he is like."

"Very well," said Edna, laughing; thankful for any little joke that lightened the heavy depression which was the hardest thing to contend with in Letty's present state. And then she took to her work and forgot all about it. Not until, after putting her sister to bed, she came down again for one quiet hour, to do some needful sewing, and institute a last and finally successful search among the odd corners of her tired brain for the missing half-crown, did Edna remember the doctor or his inquisitive stare.

"I wonder if he noticed what I was doing, and whether he thought me silly, or was sorry for me. Perhaps he is good at arithmetic. Well, if there could be any advantage in having a man belonging to one, it would be to help in adding up one's weekly accounts. I shall advise Letty to make that proviso in her marriage settlement."

While the sisters thus summarily dismissed the question of their new neighbors, their neighbors scarcely thought of them at all. Dr. Stedman sat by his brother's bedside, trying by every means he could think of to make the weary evening slip by, without forestalling the burden of the still heavier night. He talked; he read a little out of an old *Times*—first the solid leaders, and then a criticism on the pictures forthcoming in the Royal Academy Exhibition, till, seeing the latter excited his patient too much, he ingeniously shortened it, and went back to the heavy debates and other masculine portions of the newspaper. But in all he did, and earnestly as he tried to do it, there was something a little clumsy, like a man—and one who is altogether a man—not accustomed to women's society and influence. There was nothing rough or untender about him; nay, there was exceeding gentleness in his eyes and voice; he tried to do his very best; but he did it with a certain awkwardness that no invalid could help feeling in some degree, especially such a nervous invalid as this.

The two brothers were very unlike—as unlike as the two sisters who sat below stairs. And yet there was a curious "family" expression; the kindred blood peeping out, pleadingly, amidst all dissimilarities of character and temperament. The younger was dark; the elder fair. The features were not unlike, but in one face delicate and regular; in the other, large and rugged. The younger had apparently lived altogether the student's life; while the elder had been knocked about the world, receiving many a hard hit, and learning, in self-preservation, to give a hard hit back again if necessary. Besides, an occasional contraction of the brow, and a slight projection of the under lip, showed that the doctor had what is called "a temper of his own;" while his brother's expression was altogether sweet, gentle, and sensitive to the last degree.

As he lay back on his pillow—for he had been put to bed immediately—you might have taken him for a boy of seventeen, until, looking closer into the thin face, you read there the deeper lines which rarely come under the quarter-century which marks the first epoch in a man's life. No; though boyish, he was not a boy; and though delicate-looking, not effeminate. His was the temperament which we so ardently admire in youth, so deeply pity in maturer years—the poetic temperament—half masculine, half feminine—capable of both a man's passion and a woman's suffering. Such men are, as circumstances make them, the angels, the demons, or the martyrs of this world.

He lay—restless, but trying hard to be patient—till the light failed and his brother ceased the reading, which was not specially interesting, being done in a slightly formal and monotonous voice, like that of a person unaccustomed to, and not particularly enjoying the occupation.

"That will do, Will. It's really very good of you to stay in-doors with me all this evening; but I don't like it.

I wish you would go out. Off with you to the beach. Is there a good beach here?"

"A very fine one. You shall see it by-and-by."

"Nay, my Bath chair could never get down these steep cliffs."

"Do you think I mean you to spend all your days in a Bath chair, Julius, lad?"

"Ah, Will, shall I ever do without it? Tell me, do you really, candidly, in your honest heart—you're almost too honest for a doctor, old boy—believe that I shall ever walk again?"

The doctor turned and gave him a pat on the shoulder—his young brother, five or six years younger than himself, which fact had made such a vital difference once, and the fatherly habits of it remained still. There was a curious twitching of his mouth, which, though large and firm, had much lurking softness of expression. He paused a minute before speaking, and then said, earnestly:

"Yes, I do, Julius. Not that I know it for certain; but I believe it. You may never be quite as strong as you have been; rheumatic fever always leaves behind great delicacy in many ways; but I have known cases worse than yours which ended in complete recovery."

"I wish mine may be, if only for your sake. What a trouble I must have been to you! to say nothing of expense. And you just starting for yourself too."

"Well, lad, it didn't matter—it was only for myself. If I'd had a wife, now, or half a dozen brats. But I had nobody—not a single 'responsibility'—except you."

"And what a heavy responsibility I have been! Ever since you were fifteen I must have given you trouble without end."

"Pleasure, too, and a deal of fun—the fun of laughing at you and your vagaries, though I couldn't laugh you out of them. Come, don't be taking a melancholy view of things. Let's be jolly."

But the mirth came ponderously out of the big fellow, whose natural expression was evidently grave—an enemy might have called it saturnine. And Dr. William Stedman looked like a man who was not likely to go through the world without making some enemies, if only from the very honesty which his brother spoke of, and a slight want of pliability—not of sympathy, but of the power of showing it—which made him a strong contrast to his brother, besides occasionally jarring with him, as brothers do jar against brothers, sisters against sisters, friends against friends—not meaning it, but inevitably doing it.

"I can't be jolly, Will," said Julius, turning away. "You couldn't, if you had my pains. Ah me! they're beginning again—they always do at night. I think Dante would have invented a new torment for his Inferno if he had ever had rheumatic fever. How mad I was to sit that week painting in the snow!"

"Let by-gones be by-gones, Julius. Never recall the past except to mend the future. That's my maxim, and I stick to it, though I am a stupid fellow — you're the bright one of us two."

"And what good has my brightness done me? Here I am, tied by the leg, my profession stopped—so far as it ever was a profession, for you know nobody ever bought my pictures. If it had not been for you, Will, what would have become of me? And what will become of me now? Well, I don't care."

"'Don't care' was hanged," said the elder brother, sententiously; "and you'll be hung, and well hung, I hope, in the Royal Academy next year."

The threadbare joke, so solemnly put forward and laughed at with childish enjoyment, effected its purpose in turning the morbid current of the sick man's thoughts. His mercurial and easily-caught fancy, which even illness could not destroy, took another direction, and he began planning what he should do when he got well—the next picture he should paint, and where he should paint it. His hopes were much lower than his ambitions, for his bias had been towards high art, only his finances made it impossible to follow it. And, perhaps, his talent — it scarcely reached genius — was more of the appreciative than the creative kind. Yet he loved his art as well as he loved any thing, and in talking about it he almost forgot his pains.

"If I could only get well," he said, "or even a little better, I might find in this pretty country some nice usable bits, and make sketches for my next year's work. Perhaps I might do a sea-piece: some small thing, with figures in it—a fisherman or a child. One could study from the life here without ruination to one's pocket, as it used to be in London. And, by-the-bye, I saw to-day a splendid head, real Greek, nearly as fine as the Clytie."

"Where?"

"Here—at the parlor-window."

The elder brother smiled. "You are always discovering goddesses at parlor-windows, and finding them very common mortals after all."

"Oh, I have done with that nonsense," said Julius, with a vexed air; adding, rather sentimentally, "my day is over—I shall never fall in love again."

"Not till the next time. But this head? I conclude it was alive, and had a woman belonging to it?"

"Probably, though I only saw the head. Are there any lodgers here besides ourselves?"

"Two ladies—possibly young ladies; but I really did not think of asking. I never was a ladies' man, you know. Shall I make inquiries on your account, young Lothario?"

"Well, you might, for I should like a chance of seeing that head again. It would paint admirably. I only wish I had the luck of doing it—when I get well."

"When I get well"—the sad, pathetic sentence often uttered, often listened to, though both speaker and listener know by instinctive foreboding that the "when" means "never." Dr. Stedman might have shared this feeling in spite of his firm "I believe it" of ten minutes before, for in the twilight his grave face looked graver still. Nevertheless, he carefully maintained the cheerful, even jocular tone of his conversation with his brother.

"You might ask the favor of taking her likeness. I am sure the young lady could not refuse. No young ladies ever do. Female vanity and your own attractions seem to fill your port-folio wherever you go. But to-morrow I'll try to get a look myself at this new angel of yours."

"No, there is nothing angelic about her face; not much, even, that is spiritual. It is thorough mortal beauty; not unlike the Clytie, as I said. It would paint well—as an Ariadne or a Dido; only there is not enough depth of sadness in it."

"Perhaps she is not a sad-minded young woman."

"I really don't know, or care. What nonsense it is our talking about women! We can't afford to fall in love or marry—at least I can't."

"Nor I neither," said the doctor, gravely. "And I did not mean to talk any nonsense about these two young women—if young they are—for the landlady told me they had just come out of great trouble—being school-mistresses, with their school broken up, and one sister nearly dying through scarlet-fever."

"That isn't so bad as rheumatic fever. I remember rather enjoying it, because I was allowed to read novels all the time. Which sister had it? the Clytie one? That rare type of beauty runs in families. Perhaps the other has a good head too."

"I don't think she has."

"Why not?"

"Because I suspect I saw her just before I came up stairs to you—a little, pale, anxious-looking thing—not at all a beauty—sitting adding up her accounts. Very small accounts they were, seemingly; yet she seemed terribly troubled over them. She must be very poor or very stupid—women always are stupid over arithmetic. And yet she did not look quite a fool, either."

"How closely you must have watched her!"

"I am afraid I did, for at first I thought her only a little girl, she was so small; and I wondered what the creature could be so busy about. But I soon found she was a woman, and an anxious-faced little woman too. Most likely these two school-mistresses are as poor as we are; and, if so, I am sorry for them, being only women."

"Ah, yes," said Julius, absently; but he seemed to

weary of the conversation, and soon became absorbed in his own suffering. Over him had evidently grown the involuntary selfishness of sickness, which Letty Kenderdine had referred to; probably because she herself understood it only too well. But her sufferings were nothing to those of this poor young fellow, racked in every joint, and with a physical organization the very worst to bear pain. Nervous, sensitive, excitable; adding to present torment by both the recollection of the past and the dread of the future; exquisitely susceptible to both his own pains and the grief and anxiety they caused to others, yet unable to control himself so as in any way to lessen the burden of them; terrified at imaginary sufferings, a little exaggerating the real ones—which were sharp enough—the invalid was a pitiable sight, and most difficult to deal with by any nurse.

But the one he had was very patient—marvellously so for a man. For hours, until long after midnight—for Edna told her sister afterwards she had heard his step overhead at about two in the morning—did the stout, healthy brother, who evidently possessed in the strongest degree the *mens sana in corpore sano*, devote himself to the younger one, trying every possible means to alleviate his sufferings; and when all failed, sitting down by his bedside, almost like a woman and a mother, saying nothing, simply enduring; or, at most, holding the poor fellow's hand with a firm clasp, which, in its mingled strength and tenderness, might have imparted courage to go through any amount of physical pain—nay, have led even to the entrance of that valley of the shadow of death which we must all one day pass through, and alone.

Help, as far as mortal help could go, William Stedman was the one to give; not in words, but in a certain atmosphere of quiet strength, or rather, in that highest expression of strength which we call fortitude. It seems easy to bear with fortitude another person's sufferings; but that is, to some natures, the very sharpest pang of all. And with something of the same expression on his face as once (Julius reminded him of the anecdote about one in the morning), in their first school, he had gone up to the master and begged to be flogged instead of Julius—did William Stedman sit by his brother's bedside till the paroxysms of pain abated. It was not till nearly daylight that, the sufferer being at length quietly asleep, the doctor threw himself, dressed as he was, on the hearth-rug before the fire, and slept also—suddenly, soundly, and yet lightly; the sleep of a sailor or a mastiff dog.

Morning broke smilingly over the sea—an April morning, breezy and bright; and Edna, who had not slept well —not nearly so well as Letty—being disturbed first by the noises overhead, and then kept wakeful by her own anxious thoughts, which, compulsorily repressed in daytime, always took their revenge at night—Edna Kenderdine welcomed it gladly. Weary of sleeplessness, she rose early, and looking out of her window, she saw a man's figure pacing up and down the green cliff between her and the sea-line. Not a very stylish figure—still in the old coat and older wide-awake hat; but it was tall, broad, and manly. He walked, his hands folded somewhat ungracefully behind him, with a strong and resolute step, looking about him sometimes, but oftener with his head bent, thinking. Undoubtedly it was the doctor.

Edna watched him with some curiosity. He must have been up all night, she knew; and as she had herself lain awake, listening to the accidental footfall, the poking of the fire, and all those sick-room noises which in the dead silence sound so ominous and melancholy in a house, even to one who has no personal stake in the matter, she had felt much sympathy for him. She was reminded keenly of her own sad vigils over poor Letty, and wondered how a man contrived to get through the same sort of thing. To a woman and a sister nursing came natural; but with a man it must be quite different. She speculated vaguely upon what sort of men the brothers were, and whether they were as much attached to one another as she and Letty. And she watched with a vague, involuntary interest the big man who kept striding up and down, refreshing himself after his weary night-watch; and when at last he came in and disappeared, probably to his solitary breakfast, she thought, in her practical, feminine soul, what a dreary breakfast it must be; no one to make the tea, or see that the eggs were boiled properly, or do any of those tender duties which help to make the day begin cheerily, and in which this little woman took an especial pleasure.

As she busied herself in doing them for Letty, who was always the last down stairs, Edna could not forbear asking Mrs. Williams how the sick lodger was this morning.

"Rather bad, miss. Better now; but was very bad all night, his brother says; and he has just started off to Ryde to get him some new physic."

"To Ryde—that is nine miles off!"

"Yes; but there was no help for it, he said. He inquired the short way across country, and meant to walk it, and be back as soon as he could. I asked him about dinner; but he left that all to me. Oh, miss, how helpless these men-folk be! He only begged me to look after his brother."

"Is the brother keeping his room?"

"No; he dressed him and carried him down stairs, just like a baby, before he went out. Poor gentleman, it's a heavy handful for him; and him with no wife or mother or sister to help him; for I asked, and he said no, they had none; no relations in the world but their two selves."

"No more have we; but then women are so much more used to sickness than men are, and more helpful," said Edna. Yet, as she recalled her own sense of helplessness and entire desolation when she and Letty were landed in this very room, wet and weary, one chill, rainy afternoon, and the fire smoked, and Letty cried, and finally went into hysterics, she felt a sensation of pity for her neighbors—those "helpless men-folk," as Mrs. Williams called them, who, under similar circumstances, were even worse off than women.

"How is the poor fellow now?" she asked. "Have you been in again to look at him? He should not be left long alone."

"But, miss, where am I to get the time? And, besides,

he don't like it. Whenever I go in and ask if I can do any thing for him, he just shakes his head and turns his face back again into the pillow. And I don't think any thing will do him much good; he isn't long for this world. I wish I hadn't taken 'em; and if I can get 'em out at the week's end—not meaning to inconvenience—and hoping they will get as good lodgings elsewhere, which no doubt they will—"

"You wouldn't do it, Mrs. Williams," said Edna, smiling, and turning upon her those good, sweet eyes, which, Miss Kenderdine's pupils declared, "frightened" all the naughtiness out of them.

The landlady smiled too. "Well, miss, maybe I wouldn't; for I feels sorry for the poor gentleman; and I once had a boy of my own that would have been about as old as him. I'll do what I can, though he is grumpy and won't speak; and that ain't pleasant, is it, miss?"

"No."

This little conversation, like all the small trivialities of their life, Edna retailed for Letty's edification, and both sisters talked the matter over threadbare, as people in seaside lodgings and out on a holiday have a trick of doing; for holiday-making to busy people is sometimes very hard work. They even, with a mixture of curiosity and real compassion, left their parlor-door open, in order to listen for and communicate to Mrs. Williams the slightest movement in the parlor opposite, where the sick man lay so helpless, so forlorn, that the kindly hearts of those two young women—certainly of one of them—forgot that he was a man, and a young man, and wished they could do him any good.

But, of course, under the circumstances, it would, as Letty declared, be the height of indecorum; they, unmarried ladies and school-mistresses, with their credit and dignity at stake, how could they take the slightest notice of a young man, be he ever so ill?

"Yet I wish we could," said Edna. "It seems so heartless to a fellow-creature to let him lie there hour after hour. If we might go in and speak to him, or send him a book to read, I can't believe it could be so very improper."

And when they came back from their morning stroll she lingered compassionately in front of the closed window and drawn-down blind behind which the sick man lay, ignorant of, or indifferent to, all the glad sights and sounds abroad—the breezy sea, the pleasant country, rejoicing in this blessed spring morning.

"Do come in," sharply said Letty, who had in some things a keener sense of the outward proprieties than Edna. "Don't be nonsensical and sentimental. It would never do for us to encourage, even in the smallest degree, these two young men, who are certainly poor, and, for all we know, may be scarcely respectable. I won't allow it, sister."

And she passed hastily the opposite door, which Edna was shocked to see was not quite closed, and walked into their own, with Letty's own dignified step and air of queenly grace, which, wherever she went, slew men, young and old, in indiscriminate massacre.

She was certainly a rare woman, Letitia Kenderdine—one that, met anywhere or anyhow, would make one feel that there might have been some truth in the old stories about Helen of Troy, Cleopatra of Egypt, and such like—ancient queens of history and fable, who rode rampant over the necks of men, and whose deadly beauty proved a fire-brand wherever it was thrown.

"Yes," replied Edna, as she took off her sister's hat and shawl, and noticed what a delicate rose-color was growing on the sea-freshened cheek, and how the old brightness was returning to the lustrous eyes. "You are quite right, Letty, dear. It would never do for us to take any notice of our neighbors, unless, indeed, they were at the very last extremity, which is not likely to happen."

"Certainly not; and even if it did, I must say I think we ought not to trouble ourselves about them. We have quite enough cares of our own without taking upon ourselves the burden of other people's."

This was only too true. Edna was silenced.

CHAPTER III.

"L'HOMME propose, et Dieu dispose," is a saying so trite as to be not worth saying at all were not its awful solemnity, in mercy as often as in retribution, forced upon us by every day's history; more especially in those sort of histories of which this is openly one — love-stories. How many brimming cups slip from the lip, according to the old proverb! how many more, which worldly or cruel hands have tried to dash aside, are nevertheless taken and guided by far diviner and safer hands, and made into a draught of life all the sweeter for delay! And in lesser instances than these, what a curious path Fate oftentimes seems to make for mortal feet, leading them exactly whither they have resolved not to go, and shutting up against them those ways which seemed so clear and plain!

For some days Fate appeared to be doing nothing as regarded these four young persons but sitting invisibly at their mutual threshold with her hands crossed, and weaving no web whatever for their entanglement. They went out and came in — but their going and coming chanced to be at different hours; they never caught sight of one another. Edna, moved by her kindly heart, every morning made a few civil inquiries of Mrs. Williams after the invalid; but Letty, seeing that no interesting episode was likely to occur, ceased to care at all about the newcomers. Indeed, as she was now rapidly getting well, blooming into more than her ordinary beauty in the rejuvenescence that sometimes takes place after a severe illness, how could she be expected to trouble herself about a sick young man in a Bath chair, and a stout brother who was wholly absorbed in taking care of him? Except for Edna, and her occasional inquiries and remarks concerning them, Letty would almost have forgotten their existence.

But Fate had not forgotten. One morning the grim

unseen Woman in the door-way rose up and began her work.

The "last extremity" of which Edna had spoken suddenly occurred.

They had seen Dr. Stedman start off, stick in hand, for his evening walk across the cliffs—which was the only recreation he seemed to indulge in—he took it while his brother slept, Mrs. Williams said, between twilight and bedtime; otherwise he rarely left him for an hour. This night it was an unfortunate absence. He had scarcely been gone ten minutes when the landlady rushed into the Misses Kenderdine's parlor in a state of great alarm.

"Oh! Miss Edna, would you come? You're used to illness, and I don't know what's the matter. He's dead, or dying, or something, and his brother's away. Please come!—this minute—or it may be too late."

"Don't go!" cried Letty. "Mrs. Williams, it's impossible—impertinent of you to ask it. She can't go."

But Edna had already gone without a word.

She was not surprised at the landlady's fright. One of those affections of the heart which so often follow rheumatic fever had attacked the young man; very suddenly, as it seemed. He lay not on the sofa, but on the floor, as if he had slipped down there, all huddled up, with his hands clenched, and his face like a dead man's face. So like, that Letty, who, after a minute, had, in spite of her opposition, followed her sister, thought he really was dead; and, having a nervous horror of death, and sickness, and all kinds of physical unpleasantnesses, had shrunk back again into their own sitting-room, and shut the door.

Edna knelt down and lifted the passive head on to her lap. She forgot it was a young man's head; she scarcely even saw that it was beautiful—a poet's face, like that of Shelley or Keats. She only recognized that he was a sick human creature who lay there needing her utmost help; and, without a second thought, she gave it. She would have given it just the same to the ugliest, coarsest laborer who had been brought injured to her door, and have shrunk as little from dirt and wounds as she did now from the grace of the curly black hair and the gleam of the white throat, which she hastily laid bare to give him a chance of breath.

"No, he is not dead, Mrs. Williams. I can feel his heart beat. He has only fainted. Bring me some smelling-salts and a glass of water."

Her simple restoratives took effect — the patient soon opened his eyes.

"Go into our room; tell my sister to send me a glass of wine," whispered she; and the frightened woman at once obeyed.

But the glass was held to his lips in vain. "Don't trouble me," said the poor fellow, faintly, and half-unconscious still. "Don't, Will! I'm dying—I would rather die."

"You are not dying, and we can not allow it," said Edna from behind. "Drink this, and you will be better presently."

Instinctively he obeyed the cheerful, imperative voice, and then, coming more clearly to his senses, tried to discover whence it came, and who was holding him.

No vision of beauty; no princess succoring a wounded knight; or queen of fairies bending over King Arthur at the margin of the celebrated lake; nothing at all romantic, or calculated to fix a young man's imagination at once and forever. Only a little woman—a rather plain little woman too — who smiled down upon him very kindly, but without the slightest confusion or hesitation; no more than if she had been his aunt or his grandmother. He did not even think her a young woman—not then—for his faculties were confused; the only fact he was sensible of was her womanliness and kindliness.

The conversation between them was also as common-place as it could be.

"You are very good, madam; I am sorry to have troubled you — and all these women," looking round on Mrs. Williams and the servant with an ill-concealed expression of annoyance. "I am quite well now."

"You will be presently. But please don't talk. Drink

this, and then lie down again on your sofa till your brother comes back. Will he be long?"

She had scarcely said it before the brother himself appeared. He stood a minute at the parlor-door. To say he looked astonished at the scene before him is needless; but his penetrating eye seemed to take it all in at a glance.

"Don't move, Julius. I understand. I wish I had not gone out," said he; and kneeling beside him, felt his pulse and heart.

"Never mind, Will; I am better now. Mrs. Williams looked after me; and this lady, you see."

"Mrs. Williams fetched me, knowing I was accustomed to illness," explained Edna, simply, as she resigned her post to the doctor and rose to her feet. "I do not think it was worse than a fainting-fit, and he is much better now."

"So I see. Thank you. We are both of us exceedingly indebted to you for your kindness," said Dr. Stedman, rather formally, but in a manner which proved he was—as Edna had said every doctor ought to be—really a gentleman. . And then, taking advantage of his complete absorption in his brother's state to the exclusion of all standers-by, she quietly slipped out of the room; thereby escaping all further thanks, explanations, or civilities.

Letty, having recovered from her fright, and being reassured that there was not that dreadful thing "death in the house," nor likely to be at present, became, as was natural, mightily interested in the episode which had taken place in the opposite parlor.

"Quite a scene in a play. You must have felt like a heroine of romance, Edna."

"Indeed I didn't; only rather awkward and uncomfortable—that is, if I felt any thing at all, which I am not sure I did, at the time. He was a very sad sight, that poor young fellow. Fainting in the reality is not half so picturesque as they make it on the stage and in books. Besides, I fear it is only an indication of worse things. Heart-disease almost invariably follows rheumatic fever. I know that."

"Of course. You know every thing," said Letty, with

the slight sharpness of tone which was occasionally heard in her voice, and startled a stranger by the exceeding contrast it formed to her beautiful classical face. "But, for all you say, it was a charming adventure. A sick young man lying unconscious, with his head in your lap, and his brother coming in and finding you in that romantic attitude."

"Nonsense!" cried Edna; a slight color, half shamefaced, half-indignant, rising in her honest cheek.

"It isn't nonsense at all. It's very interesting. And pray tell me every word they said to you. They ought to have overwhelmed you with gratitude; and one or both brothers — both would be better — ought to fall in love with you on the spot. The result—rivalry, jealousy, fury, and fratricide. Oh! what fun! To have two brothers in love with one lady at the same time! I wonder it never happened to me; but perhaps it may some day."

"I earnestly hope not," said Edna.

But at the same time a horrible foreboding entered her mind concerning these two brothers, who must inevitably live under the same roof with Letty for some days, possibly weeks; who would have many opportunities of seeing her—and nobody ever looked at the beautiful Letty who did not look again immediately. For her charms were not those recondite and variable ones of expression and intellect; they were patent—on the surface—attractive at once to the most refined and the coarsest masculine eyes. Hitherto no young man had ever cast the merest glance upon Letty Kenderdine without trying to pursue the acquaintance; and the anxious sister began to wish that her own sympathies had not led her into that act of kindly civility which might prove the "open, sesame" to a hundred civilities more, were the opposite lodgers so inclined. Should it appear likely, she determined to make a dead stand of opposition, and not allow the least loop-hole through which they could push their way to any further acquaintance.

This determination, however, she wisely kept to herself; for in Letty's last little love-affair they two had held divided opinions, and, with all her affection for her sister, she had begun to find that sisters do not necessarily think alike. Their twelvemonths' living together, after an almost total separation since their school-days, had taught Edna this fact—one of the sad facts which all human beings have to learn—that every one of us is, more or less, intensely alone. Before marriage—ay, and after any but the very happiest marriage—absolutely and inevitably alone.

"Don't speak so seriously," said Letty, laughing. "You are not vexed with me?"

"Oh no!"

Where, indeed, was the use of being vexed with her? or of arguing the point with her? Edna knew that if she were to talk to her sister till doomsday she could no more make her understand her own feelings on this subject than if she were preaching to a blind man on the subject of colors. To Letty love merely meant marriage, and marriage meant a nice house, a respectable, good sort of man as master to it—probably, a carriage; and at any rate as many handsome clothes as she could possibly desire. She did not overlook the pleasantness of the preliminary stage of love-making, but then she had already gone through that, in degree; in truth, her lovers had of late become to her more of a worry than an amusement, and she was now disposed to take a thoroughly sensible and practical view of things.

Nevertheless, there was in her a lurking love of admiration *per se*, without ulterior possibilities, which had grown by what it fed on—and there was no lack of provender in Letty's case, for every man she met admired her. Also, she had in her a spice of feminine contradictoriness, which, had she discovered any lack of admiration, would have roused her to buckle all her beauty's armor on, and remedy it, thus marring, by one fortuitous glance or smile, all her sister's sage precautions.

Edna knew this; knew it by the way in which, while protesting that she hoped no further acquaintance with the two Stedmans would ensue through this very imprudent step on Edna's part, she talked all evening about them, and insisted on hearing every particular concerning them: what they did, said, and looked like; what sort of a parlor they had, whether it was very untidy and bachelor-like.

"For, of course, neither of them is married, though the doctor is old enough to be; but doctors never can afford to settle early, especially in London. These people live in London, don't they?"

"I really don't know. I have never inquired."

"Do inquire, then; for if Dr. Stedman should take it into his head to call—and it would be the least thing he could do, in acknowledgment of your kindness to his brother—"

"Oh, I hope not."

"So do I; for it might turn out exceedingly"—Letty cast a half-amused glance at herself in the mirror—"exceedingly awkward—for him, poor fellow; of course, it couldn't affect me. Though big and rough—as he is, you say—he seems decidedly the most interesting of the two. And depend upon it, Edna, if we should happen to make acquaintance with these two brothers, he is the one that will fall in love with me."

"Why do you think so?" asked Edna, internally resolving that, if she could possibly prevent it, the poor honest-looking doctor should be saved from that dire calamity.

"Why? Because he's ugly, and I'm—well, I'm not exactly ugly, you know; and I always notice that plain people are certain to fall in love with me—probably just by the law of contrast. For the same reason you'll tell me, I suppose, that I ought to marry some very wise, grave fellow, possibly such an one as this doctor of yours, who would altogether look after me, take me in and do for me—admire me excessively, no doubt, but still save me all trouble of thinking and acting for myself. Heigh-ho! what a comfort that would be!"

"It really would!" said Edna, seriously, and then could not help smiling, for the hundredth time, at Letty's very matter-of-fact style of discussing her loves and her lovers. Her extreme candor was her redeeming point. She was not a wise woman, but she was certainly not a hypocrite. No need to fear that with Letty Kenderdine it would be "all for love and the world well lost," or that if she married she would make otherwise than what even Belgravian mothers would call "a very good marriage," and afterwards strictly do her duty to her husband and society, or rather to society first, and then, so far as was practicable, to her husband. And, Edna sometimes thought, judging by the sort of lovers that came after Letty, with whose characters and feelings she, Edna, was fully conversant—for her sister had no reticence whatever concerning them—men marry for no higher, perhaps even a lower, motive.

"I am rather glad," said she, suddenly, apropos of nothing, "certainly more glad than sorry, that I shall be an old maid."

"Well, as I always said, you will be an extremely happy one," returned Letty; "and you ought to be thankful to be saved from all the difficulties which fall to my lot. There! don't you hear the opposite door opening? He is stopping in the lobby—speaking to Mrs. Williams. Of course, I knew what would come of all this. I was certain the young man would call."

But, in spite of Letty's tone of indignation, her countenance fell considerably when the doctor did not call, but shut his sitting-room door again immediately, apparently without taking the slightest interest in, or manifesting the smallest desire to communicate with, his fair neighbor. And another night fell, and another day rolled on, bright, sunshiny, calm; it was most glorious weather; just the "fullness of the spring," when

> "A young man's fancy lightly turns to thoughts of love;"

and still Fate sat motionless at the threshold—nor approached a step nearer to make these young hearts beat or tremble with premonitions of their destiny.

It was not until the last evening of the week, and three days after Edna's act of unacknowledged, and, Letty declared, quite unappreciated kindness, that the four inmates of Mrs. Williams's lodgings really met, face to face, in a rencontre unplanned, unexpected, and impossible to be avoided on either side. Yet it came about naturally enough, and at the most likely place—the garden gate.

Just as the two sisters were setting out for the latest of their three daily strolls, and the doctor was bringing his brother home from his, the Bath chair stopped the way. Letty, walking in advance, as she usually did, being now as restless for going out as she had formerly been languid and lazy in stopping in, came suddenly in front of her fellow-invalid.

She drew back—as has been said, Letty had an instinctive shrinking from any kind of suffering—and Julius, lifting up his heavy eyes, saw this tall, beautiful woman standing with one hand on the wicket gate, and her hat in the other, for she rather liked to go bareheaded in the sea-breeze. Now it freshened her cheek and brightened her eyes, until she seemed a vision of health as well as beauty in the sight of the sick man, who was turning homeward after a long afternoon's stroll, weary of himself, of life, of every thing.

His artistic eye was caught at once; he recognized her with a look of admiration that no woman could mistake; though it puzzled Letty Kenderdine a little, being different from the bold, open stare she was so well used to. It was a look, respectful and yet critical; as calmly observant as if she had been a statue or a picture, not a living woman at all, and he bent upon investigating her good and bad points, and appraising her value. Yet it was a gaze of extreme delight, though delight of a purely artistic kind—the pleasure of looking at a lovely thing; the recognition, open and free, of that good gift—beauty; when, or how, or upon whomsoever bestowed. Therefore it was a gaze that no gentleman need have blushed to give, nor any lady to receive; even Edna, who, coming behind her sister, met and noticed it fully, could not take offense at it.

And at sight of Edna the sickly face broke out into a smile.

"It is you. I hoped I should see you again. I wanted to thank you for your kindness to me the other day. I told Will— Here, Will, I want you."

Dr. Stedman, who had been pushing the Bath chair from behind, also stood gazing intently at the beautiful vision, which, indeed, no man with eyes could possibly turn away from.

"Will, do come and thank this lady—I forget her name; indeed, I don't think I ever heard it."

This was a hint which Edna did not take; but, to her surprise, it was unnecessary.

"Miss Kenderdine, I believe" (and he had got the name quite pat and correct, which strangers seldom did), said the doctor, taking off his hat, and showing short, crisp, brown locks, curling tight round what would, ere many years, be a bald crown. "My brother and I are glad to have an opportunity of thanking you for your kindness that day. It made a strong impression on him; he has talked of you ever since."

"Yes, indeed; it was such a charitable thing for a stranger to do to a poor sick fellow like me," added Julius, looking up with a simplicity that had something almost child-like in it. "Such a frank, generous, womanly thing! I told Will he ought to go in and thank you for it, but he wouldn't; he is such a shy fellow, this brother of mine."

"Julius, pray—we are detaining these ladies."

But Julius never took any hints, and often said and did things which nobody else would ever think of; and yet, coming from him, they were done in such a pleasant way as never to vex any body.

"Nonsense! we are not stiff in our manners here: we are at the sea-side; and then I am an invalid, and must be humored, must I not, Miss Kenderdine? You don't mind my detaining you here for two minutes, just to thank you?"

"No," said Edna, smiling. She wondered afterwards that she had responded so frankly to the young man's greeting, and allowed so unresistingly the introduction which soon brought them all to speaking terms, and drew Letty also into the quartette who, for the next five minutes or so, paused to talk over the garden gate. But, as she was forced to confess—when in their walk afterwards Letty reproved her, laying all the blame upon her, whatever happened—she could not help it. There was a charm about Julius Stedman which made every body do as he wished, and he evidently wished exceedingly to make acquaintance with these two young ladies. Not an unnatural wish in any man, especially in dull sea-side lodgings.

So he detained them as long as he civilly could, chatting freely to the one, and gazing silently at the other — the owner of that wonderful Clytie face. He put himself, with his unquestioned prerogative of illness, much more forward than his brother—though the doctor, too, talked a little, and looked also; if not with the open-eyed admiration of Julius, with a keen, sharp investigation, as if he were taking the measure, less artistically than morally, of this lovely woman.

Nevertheless—or, perhaps, consequently—the conversation that went on was trivial enough: about the sea, the fine coast, the lovely spring sunset, and the charming weather they had had these two days.

"Yes, I like it," said Julius, in reply to Edna's question. "It warms me through and through—this glorious sunshine! I am sure it would make me well if it lasted; but nothing ever does last in this world."

"You will speak more cheerfully by-and-by," said Edna. "I was pleased at this change of weather, because I knew it would do you and all sick people so much good."

"How kind of you to think of me at all!" returned Julius, gratefully. "I am sure you must be a very nice woman."

"Must I?" Edna laughed, and then blushed a little, to find herself speaking so familiarly not only with strangers, but with the very strangers whom she had determined to keep at arm's-length under all circumstances. But then the familiarity was only with her—Edna, to whom it signified little. Neither of the brothers had addressed Letty, nor offered her any attention beyond a respectful bow; and Letty had drawn herself up with considerable *hauteur*, adding to the natural majesty of her beauty a sort of "fall-in-love-if-you-dare" aspect, which, to some young men, might have been an additional attraction, but which did not seem to affect fatally either of these two.

They looked at her; with admiration certainly, as any young men might—nay, must have done—would have been fools and blind not to have done; but that was all. At first sight neither seemed disposed to throw himself prone under the wheels of Letty's Juggernaut chariot; which fact relieved Edna's mind exceedingly.

So, after some few minutes of a conversation equally unembarrassed and uninteresting, the young people parted where they stood, all four shaking hands over the gate, Julius grasping Edna's with a grateful pressure that would decidedly have startled her, had she not recognized by instinct the impulsive temperament of the young man. Besides, she was utterly devoid of self-conscious vanity, and accustomed to think of her own relation to the opposite sex as one that precluded any special attentions. Her personal experience of men had been solely in the character of confidante to Letty's lovers. She used to say, laughing, "She was born to be every body's sister, or every body's maiden aunt."

And so the ice was broken between these four young people, so strangely thrown together in this solitary place, and under circumstances when the world and its restrictions—whether needed or needless—were, for the time being, more or less set aside. They met, simply as four human beings, through blind chance, as it seemed, and wholly ignorant that the innocent wicket gate, held open so gracefully by Letty's hand for the Bath chair to pass through, was to them an opening into that enchanted garden which is entered but once. Which most of us—nay, confess it! all of us—dream about continually before entering; and passing out of—even for happier Edens—seldom leave without a sigh of regret. For it is the one rift of heaven which makes all heaven appear possible; the ecstasy of hope and faith, out of which grows the Love which is our strongest mortal instinct and intimation of immortality.

CHAPTER IV.

It is an undoubted fact, that when that event happens, the most vital in human life—the first meeting of two persons who are to influence one another's character and destinies in the closest manner, for good or ill, happiness or misery, nay, even for virtue or crime—the sky does not fall, no ominous signs appear in the outside world; nay, the parties concerned, poor puppets as they are, or seem to be, are usually quite unconscious of what has befallen them, and eat, drink, and sleep just as composedly as ever.

Thus the two Misses Kenderdine, after shaking hands with the two Stedmans over the gate, went calmly on their usual stroll along the cliffs, discussing in feminine fashion their new acquaintances, and speculating about them with an indifference that was perfectly sincere; for though these school-mistresses were young enough to have the natural lot and future of womanhood running a good deal in their heads, especially at holiday time, when they had no more serious business in hand, and Letty's continual "difficulties" always kept the subject alive, still they were neither of them silly school-girls, in love with every man they met, or fancying every man in love with them. Letty, perhaps, had a slight tendency in the latter direction, which her experience rather justified than not; but Edna was free from all such folly, or only regarded the question of love and matrimony in its relation to her sister.

So they discussed freely and openly the two young men.

Edna had been most interested in the invalid, as was natural; her heart warmed towards every kind of suffering; while her sister had chiefly noticed the big healthy-looking brother, who was evidently "a man with no nonsense about him," by which Letty meant no sentiment; for she, who had been haunted by sentimental swains, poets addressing verses to her, and artists imploring to sketch her portrait, disliked sentiment above all things.

"Besides, this doctor does really seem a gentleman, in spite of his shabby coat. He might be spruced up into a very good-looking fellow if he had somebody to see after him. You are quite sure he is not married, Edna? And where did you say he lived? I wonder if it is in a respectable street, and what sort of a practice he has got."

"Letty," cried Edna, turning sharply round, half amused, half angry, "you are not surely going to—"

"No, you foolish child; not being quite a simpleton. I am not surely going to—to marry him—your friend with the shabby coat. Nor even to let him fall in love with me, if I can help it. But if he does, you can't blame me. It's all my unfortunate appearance."

Edna attempted no reply—where was the use of it? Indeed she shrank back into total silence, as was her habit when the sense of painful incongruity between herself and her sister, their thoughts, motives, and actions, rose up more strongly than usual. She wished there was no such thing as falling in love—as Letty put it—or that Letty would fall in love honestly and sincerely, once for all, with some good man—she began not to care much who it was, if he were only good—marry him and have done with it. These perpetual "little affairs" of her sister's could not go on forever. Edna was rather weary of them; and wished, more earnestly than she liked to express, that she could see Letty "settled"—fairly sheltered under the wing of a worthy husband who would at once rule her and love her—pet her and take care of her; for indeed she needed taking care of more than most women of six-and-twenty. Perhaps Dr. Stedman might be the very sort of man to do this. He looked like it. There was a steadfast honesty of purpose in his eyes, and a firmness about his mouth, which seemed to imply sterling worth. But, though a good man, his expression was not exactly that of an amiable man; and Letty was a person likely to try a husband's temper considerably at times. Besides, what if he were poor? Indeed the fact seemed self-evident. A poor man—as she said herself, and Edna confessed the truth of this—would never do for Letty Kenderdine.

Edna's thoughts had galloped on thus far in a perfect steeple-chase of fancy, when she suddenly pulled up, reflecting how exceedingly ridiculous it was. She almost despised herself for speculating thus on so slender a foundation, or no foundation at all, and bent her whole attention to the outer world.

Every thing was so beautiful in the still evening—the sea as calm as the sky, and the cliff-swallows skimming airily between both. Even Letty, whose thoughts there is no need to follow, for she never thought much or long about any thing, noticed them, and called them "pretty little things;" while Edna, who had a great love for birds, watched them with a curious tenderness—the creatures that came so far from over the waters—guided unerringly—to make their nests here; as (Edna still firmly believed in her deepest heart, though her twelvemonths' life with Letty had somewhat shaken the out-works of that girlish faith) Heaven guides all true lovers that are to be husband and wife—leads them from farthest corners of the world, through storm and trial, danger and death, to their own appointed home in one another's arms.

So she left her sister's lot—her own she never thought of—in wiser hands than hers; trusting that He who mated the swallows and brought them hither from across the seas, and made them so content and happy, hovering about in the spring twilight, would in time bring Letty a good husband, and relieve her sisterly heart from the only real care it had—the unknown future of this beautiful, half-foolish, half-worldly-wise woman, who, though her very flesh and blood, was so unlike herself that it puzzled Edna daily more and more both to understand her and to guide her.

The two sisters went back to their dull lodgings, which, in common with all lodgings, looked especially dull and unhome-like at this hour. They sat down to their innocent milk supper, and the one glass of wine which Letty still indulged in, as a last relic of invalidism, though saying each day she would give it up. And then they settled themselves to sewing, at least Edna did, Letty declaring she never could sew with the poor light of two mould candles. She amused herself with lying on the sofa and talking, or chatting, the sort of desultory chat which people who live together naturally fall into—it is only strangers who maintain "conversation." Besides, Letty's talk was never conversation; it rarely rose beyond ordinary facts or personalities; generally of a trivial kind. Clytie-like though her lips were, they did not drop pearls and diamonds; but then they never dropped toads and adders. She was exceedingly good-natured, and never said sharp or unkind things of any body; in this having the advantage of Edna, who sometimes felt sorely tempted to be severe and satirical, then blamed herself, and took refuge in mild generalities, as now.

The two brothers would have been more amused than flattered had they known that on this momentous evening of their first rencontre with the two young ladies, which meeting had conveyed to both an impression of undefined pleasantness, as the society of all good women ought to give to every good man, their fair neighbors' conversation was, from the time of re-entering the house, strictly on the subject of clothes.

"Alas!" Letty broke out, almost as soon as supper was over, declaring the matter had been on her mind all day—the spring weather was coming on fast, and they had only their winter garments with them, and no possibility of getting more.

"For we can't buy every thing new, and our last summer's things are locked up at home; and besides, I almost forget what we have."

"Nothing very much, I fear."

"We never have," said Letty, in a melancholy voice. "When I was in situations I was obliged to dress well; but now? Just think, Edna, to-morrow is Sunday, and we have only our brown bonnets and our winter cloaks; and it will likely be as hot as to-day, and the sunshine will show all their shabbiness. It is very provoking; nay, it it is exceedingly hard."

"It is hard, especially for you, Letty."

And Edna glanced at her beautiful sister, upon whom any thing looked well; yet whose beauty would have borne the most magnificent setting off that wealth could furnish. How splendid she would have looked in silks, laces, and jewels—the prizes that in all ages there have been found women ready to sell their souls for! Was Letty one of these? Edna could not believe it. Yet she knew well that dress, and the lack of it, was a much severer trial to her sister than to herself—that Letty actually suffered, mentally and morally, from a worn-out shawl or an old-fashioned bonnet; while as to herself, so long as she was neat and clean, and had colors matching—no blues and greens, pinks and scarlets, which poverty compelled to be worn together—it did not materially affect her happiness, whether she had on a silk dress or a cotton one.

This catastrophe of the winter bonnets was annoying; but it was a small annoyance—not worth fretting about, when they had so many more important cares, and many a blessing likewise. Her mind, which had been wandering alternately back to the house and the school to which in a short time they must return, and dwelling on a few pleasant fancies left by the evening walk, felt suddenly dragged down into the narrow ways of ordinary life—made narrower than they need to be by this hopeless way of looking at them. She did not like it; for, monotonous and commonplace as her life had been—ever since she was twelve years old—first school life, then governess life in a dull country city family, there was in this young school-mistress's soul a something which always felt like a little bird that would stretch its wings, feeling sure there must be a wide empyrean waiting for it somewhere. In her long pauses over her needle-work this little bird usually sat pluming its feathers and singing to itself, till some chance word of Letty's silenced it—as was wisest and best. For Letty would not have understood the little bird at all.

Edna fastened its cage-door, and determined to make the best of things.

"Yes, as you say, it is hard; but be patient this one Sunday, and before the next I will see what can be done. Suppose I take the coach to Ryde, and choose two plain straw bonnets and trim them myself—with green, perhaps. You always look so well in green. Then we should be quite respectable while here, and they would last us as second-best all summer."

Letty brightened up amazingly. "That is a capital thought, Edna. You are the very cleverest girl! I always said, and I will say it, a great deal cleverer than I am, if the men could only find it out."

"They never will, and I don't want them," said Edna, laughing. "And now let us come to bed, for it is quite time."

As the sisters passed up stairs, both cast a glance on the shut parlor-door opposite, behind which was complete silence, as usual of evenings. The brothers did not seem to have such long tongues as the sisters.

"I wonder how they contrive to amuse themselves, these two young fellows," said Letty, yawning. "I hope they are not as dull as we are sometimes."

"Men never are dull, I suppose," replied Edna, in her glorious maiden ignorance. "They have always something to do, and that alone makes people cheerful. Besides, they don't dwell on trivial things, as we do; their minds are larger and clearer—at least, the best of them must be so," she corrected herself, reflecting that she was speaking more out of her ideal than her actual experience of the race. And with a feeling of weariness at the smallness into which her daily gossip with Letty sometimes degenerated, Edna thought she would really like, just for a change, to have a good, sensible talk with a man. She wondered what those two men down stairs talked about when they were alone, and whether their chief conversation, corresponding with that in the next parlor, was on the subject of clothes. And the idea of Dr. Stedman discussing the shape of his new hat, or Mr. Stedman becoming confidential with his brother on the question of coats and trowsers, proved so irresistibly ludicrous that Edna burst into one of her hearty fits of laughter—her first since Letty was ill—which did her so much good that she was sound asleep in five minutes.

And what of the two men fated to influence, and be influenced by, these two young women, in the way that human lives do act and react upon one another, in a manner so mysterious that all precautions often seem idle—all plans vain—all determinations null and void—and yet we still go on working, planning, and resolving—deliberately laying out the pattern of our own and others' future, of which we can neither forecast, nor control, nor, alas! recall, one single day.

They did not talk over their neighbors; it is not man's way, or not the way of such men as, with all their faults, these two Stedmans were—honest young fellows, from whom neither sin nor folly had rubbed off the bloom of their youth, or led them to think and talk of women as, God forgive them! men sometimes do—men, who were born of women, who once hung as innocent babies at some woman's breast.

They came in-doors, Julius with evident reluctance.

"Why didn't you give me another turn on the cliff, Will? I wanted two or three more minutes to study that head."

"Miss Kenderdine's?"

"Isn't it grand, now? Bring me my sketch-book, and I'll have a try at the profile. Finest profile I ever saw. It might be useful some day, when I get well."

"You'll be well sooner than you think, old boy."

And that was literally all which passed concerning the two sisters.

The brothers spent their usual silent evening, Julius drawing, and William immersed in a heap of medical literature which lay on a table in the corner, into which he plunged at every possible opportunity. For he knew that time was money to him, in these early days when he had more leisure than fees; and besides, he had a genuine love of acquiring knowledge, all the stronger, perhaps, that he was of too cautious, modest, and self-distrustful a temperament to strike out brilliant ideas of his own. But he had the faculty, perhaps safer for ultimate success, of acquiring and assimilating the ideas of other men. And consequently he had a keen delight in what is called "hard reading."

His head, as he bent it over the chaotic mass of books, had a finer expression than its ordinary one, which was a little heavy, and sometimes a little cross. But both these expressions originated in a sort of undeveloped look he had, as if in him the perceptive and the practical had been well cultivated, while the fancy lay dormant. A strong contrast to that sweet, sensitive, poetic head of his brother's, where the balance lay in precisely the opposite direction. Any superficial observer would have wondered how they got on together at all, except for the patent fact that people sometimes fit into one another precisely because they differ, when the difference is only difference and not contrariety.

"There! I think I've got it at last!"

"Got what?" said the doctor, rousing himself and rubbing his fingers through his short curly locks till they stood out all round his head like a *chevaux de frise.*

"That profile, of course. Come over and tell me if you think it like. Pretty well, I think, for a study done from memory. I must get her to sit to me. Will, couldn't you manage it somehow? Couldn't you cultivate their acquaintance?"

"I? Nonsense! I never knew what to say to women."

"Then how, in the name of fortune, do you mean to make yourself into a London physician? If a doctor can't be sweet to women he never earns even salt to his porridge."

"As probably I never may. And then I'll keep on being a poor hospital doctor, or doing a large practice gratis, as I do now."

"More's the pity."

"Not at all. It is practice. And it saves one from rusting to death, or eating one's heart out in disappointment before the good time comes, as I suppose it will come some time. And now give me your sketch to look at."

He examined it minutely, deliberately rather than enthusiastically, taking exception to certain points of feature both in it and the original, but, on the whole, very laudatory of both.

Still, Julius put up the port-folio half dissatisfied.

"You are so confoundedly cool about things. Why, Will, it's the finest subject I ever had. A perfectly correct face. Not a feature out of its place, and the coloring glorious. What a blessing to have such a model always at hand! I could understand Raffaelle's carrying off the Fornarina, and Andrea del Sarto marrying his beautiful Lucrezia, if only for convenience."

"You scape-grace!" cried the elder brother, laughing. "If I thought you were going to make a fool of yourself—"

"No, no; my fool-days are done. I'm nothing but an artist now. Don't make a mock of me, Will!—a poor, helpless fellow that can't even walk across a room."

"Yes, you could if you tried. I told you so yesterday. Will you try?"

Julius shook his head. "That was always your motto —'Try!' You should paint it on your carriage when you hunt up the Heralds' College to get arms for your two-horse brougham, in which you come to visit me in a two-pair back in Clipstone Street, or Kensal Green Cemetery. I don't know which, and don't much care."

The elder brother turned away. He was used to these sort of speeches—hardened to them, indeed; yet they could not fail slightly to affect him still, with the sort of feeling—half pity, half something less tender than pity—with which we are prone to regard weaknesses that we ourselves can only by an effort comprehend.

"Well! in the mean time, as to your walking. I have often told you, Julius, some of your ailments are purely nervous. I mean, not exactly imaginary," seeing that Julius winced, "but in the nerves. And the nerves are queer things, my boy: very much guided by the will, which is a queerer thing yet."

"What do you mean? That I could walk if I tried?"

"Not precisely. But that if you were forced to walk—if some strong impulse came—say a fire in the house, and you were compelled to escape for your life—you would find you could do it. At least that is my opinion."

"Opinions are free, of course. I wish for your sake I could gratify you, William. I would not then be detaining you here from your practice, your profession, and all the enjoyments of your life, in waiting upon a miserable fellow who had much better be in his grave."

The quick, irritable pride—the readiness to take offense—William Stedman was familiar with these vagaries too. But the next minute they were gône, as they always were. In the sweet nature no bitterness ever lingered long. Julius held out his hand to his brother with a child-like expression of penitence.

"I beg your pardon, Will. You're the best old fellow alive. Give me your hand, and I'll try to walk, or at least to stand."

"That's right."

"Will it—will it be very painful?"

The doctor hesitated; and as he looked at his brother there came into his face that deep tenderness—wholly a man's tenderness—which none but strong men ever feel, and rarely feel except to women.

"Painful, lad? Yes, it may be painful. I am afraid it will be, at first. I wish I could bear it for you. Which is a silly speech, because I can't. Still, won't you try?"

"I will—with somebody to help me."

Ay, that was the key to his whole nature—that sensitive, loving, delicate nature. He could do almost any thing with somebody to help him; without that, nothing.

The brother held out a steady hand; and then slowly, shrinkingly, trembling all over with nervous apprehension, Julius tried to raise himself in his chair and stand upon his stiff limbs. So far he succeeded; but when he attempted to move them, the pain, or the dread of pain, was too much for him. He fell back white and exhausted.

"It won't do, Will; it won't do."

"Not this time. Wait a few minutes, and then—"

"Must I try again? Oh, couldn't you be kind to me, and let me rest?" said the poor fellow, piteously.

"If I did, it would not be real kindness. Let me talk to you a little common sense—you're not an invalid now, nor a baby either. Will you listen to me?"

Julius opened his eyes from the sofa where his brother had tenderly laid him down, and saw Will sitting on the table opposite, playing with a paper-cutter, but keenly observant all the while.

"Yes, I'll listen. But it will be useless; you can't give me my legs again. Oh, Will, it's easy for you to speak—such a big, strong, healthy fellow as you are! And I was the same once, or nearly so, till I threw my health away. It's too late now."

"Too late, at twenty-five? Bosh! Look here, lad. As I told you before, a doctor has a pretty severe handful with fellows like you. He has to fight against two things—the reality and the imagination. You are ill enough, I know—at least, you were when you were down with that rheumatic fever."

"By George, I was ill! Never suffered such a horrible pain in all my life. Don't tell me that was fancy."

"No; but the pain has left you now. Your last bad attack was the night you came here. I do not believe you will have any more. Your feet don't swell now; your joints are supple; in fact, your legs are as sound as my own. Yet there you sit, and let them stiffen day by day; or rather, I'm such a fool as to let you, because I happen to be brother as well as doctor. Once for all, Julius, do you wish to be a cripple for life?"

"No. Oh, my God, no!" replied Julius, with a shudder.

"Then try once more, before it is too late, and you really do lose the use of your limbs. Walk, if only three steps, to prove to yourself that walking is possible."

Julius shook his head mournfully.

"It is possible," cried Will, almost angry with earnestness. "On my honor as a doctor, there is no physical reason why you should not walk. I am sure of it."

"Of course it is only my 'fancy,' which you are always throwing in my teeth. I suppose I could jump up this minute and run a hurdle-race across the cliff for your amusement. I only wish I could, that's all! If you are right—and of course you always are right—what an awful humbug I must be!"

"I never said that—I never thought it," replied the elder brother, very patiently—far more patiently than his looks would have given reason to expect. "You are no humbug: no more than was a certain patient of mine, who fancied he could not use his right arm; went about with it in a sling; won unlimited sympathy; learned to write with his left hand; for he was an author, poor fellow!"

"Ah! according to you, half the 'poor fellows' in the world are either authors or artists."

"He would come to me," William went on, "with the saddest complaints and the most hopeless forebodings about his arm. Yet if I got him into an argument, and made him forget it, he would slip it out of the sling, and clench and flourish it in his own excitable manner; nay, I have seen him hammer it on the table as orators do. And when I smiled he would suddenly recollect himself, pull a pitiful face, and slip it back into its sling as helpless as ever."

"The hypocrite!"

"Not a bit—no more a hypocrite than you or I. He was an exceedingly honest, good fellow, but he was afflicted with nerves. He had not the sense to fight against them manfully at first, till afterwards they mastered him. He had a great dread of pain: his imagination was so vivid, and he yielded to it so entirely, that at last he could not distinguish between what he felt and what he feared, until his fancies became only too sad realities."

"How did he end?" said Julius, roused out of the contemplation of himself and his own sufferings.

"I can not tell, for I lost sight of him."

"But how do *you* think he would end?"

William was startled by the excessive earnestness of

the question. "I could not say—indeed, I should hardly like to speculate. In such cases, these delusions are only the beginning of the end."

"Isn't it a strange thing," said Julius, after a long pause, "that we none of us know, have not the dimmest idea how we may end? Here you and I sit, two brothers, brought up together, or nearly so; living together, with one and the same interest, and—well, old fellow! with a decent amount of what folk call brotherly love—yet how shall we both end?"

He put his thin hand on William's arm and looked at him, or rather looked beyond him into vacant space, with that expression of sad foreboding constantly seen in faces like his, which is at once cause and effect, prevision and fulfillment.

But it fell harmlessly on the unsuperstitious doctor.

"How shall we end? I trust, lad, as we began — together. And that is as much as either of us knows, or ought to know. I don't like to look far ahead myself; it does no good, and is often very silly. Come, we both have preached quite enough, let us practise a little. Will you walk back to your arm-chair?"

"You are the most obstinate, determined fellow. I do think, if I were lying dead, you would coolly walk in with your galvanic battery to galvanize me to life again."

"Perhaps I should, because I should never believe you dead. Fellows of your temperament take a vast deal of killing. Besides, I don't want you to be killed. There's a deal before you yet. Will Stedman can never set the Thames on fire, but perhaps Julius Stedman may."

Julius again shook his head, but smiled, and made an effort to rise.

"Give me your hand, Will. It's just like learning to walk again, as if I were a baby. And you did teach me to walk then, you know. You'll have to do it again now."

"Very well. Here is a finger; now toddle away, and don't be frightened, you old baby."

Julius tried, walked two or three steps with difficulty, and many an expression of suffering, then he succumbed.

"I can't, Will, I can't do it; or, at least, it isn't worth the pain—'*Le jeu ne vaut pas la chandelle*,' as I used to say so often. It wasn't true then; it is now. Never mind me: let me be a cripple for life, or let me die."

"Neither the one thing nor the other. It isn't likely, and I'll not allow it. Cheer up, my boy! You've made a beginning, and that was all I wanted. You have had plenty of exercise for to-night, and now for a sound sleep till morning."

So saying he took his brother up in his arms, lifting the thin, slight figure as easily as if it had been a woman or a child, and carried him off to bed.

CHAPTER V.

A BRIGHT, cheery, sunshiny Sunday morning, such a Sunday as makes every honest heart glad, down to the young 'prentice-boy who sings, in that pleasant old English song—

> "Of all the days throughout the week
> I dearly love but one day,
> And that's the day that comes between
> The Saturday and Monday:
> For then I'm dress'd in all my best
> To walk abroad with Sally."

And though not dressed in all her best, and having no one (save Edna) to walk abroad with, even Letty Kenderdine enjoyed this Sunday; ay, though she had to attire herself for church in the obnoxious brown bonnet and well-worn cloak—the cloak of two winters. But under it her tall figure, now lithe and upright with renewed health, looked so exceedingly graceful, and above the brown bonnet-strings, carefully tied, bloomed such apple-blossom cheeks, that when she saw herself in the glass even Letty was contented. Perhaps all the more so because her beauty had not been quite unbeheld.

Passing through the hall, Dr. Stedman, who chanced to open his door at the same moment, had bowed to her with a courteous "good-morning," not pausing to say more;

though she declared to Edna he looked as if he should have liked it, and she was certain he blushed. However, he had given the mere salutation and walked rapidly on ahead, till the sisters lost sight of him.

"Very good manners. He evidently does not wish to intrude," observed Letty.

"No gentleman would," said Edna, "unless quite sure that we desired his company."

"I wonder where he is going? Probably to church—so you see he must be quite respectable."

A little lurking devil in Edna's spirit inclined her to begin and argue that question, and prove how many bad people went to church, and how many good people conscientiously staid away; but she restrained it, and soon forgot the evil spirit in the delicious calm of their walk, through lanes green with budding hedge-leaves and sweet with the scent of primroses, to the tiny old village church. Such a contrast it was to their London church—so different was this day to their terrible London Sundays, with the incessant stream of feet pattering along the dusty, glaring pavement, church-goers and holiday-makers all hurrying on to their worship, their amusement, or their vice, with much the same countenance, and perhaps with not such a vital difference in their hearts! Edna often used to think so, and then rebuked herself for her uncharitableness.

But, in truth, she hated London—she hated, above all things, London Sundays. Her Sundays here, in the gray little church, with a green vision of the outside world showing through its unpainted windows and open door, recalled to her the sweet peaceful Sabbaths of her childhood, when she was a little country girl in Hampshire, and was taken across fields and woods to just such a village church as this. As she sat there, in the free seats (which Letty did not like at all), there came back into her head a poem which, in her dreary school-days at St. John's Wood, she had learned, and the school-mistress had reproved her because there was "love" in it. But Edna had fancied it because there was in it a feeling like those country Sundays; and oh! how unlike the Sunday at St. John's Wood! It was something about—

"There the green lane descends,
Through which I walked to church with thee,
O gentlest of my friends!

"The shadow of the linden-trees
Lay moving on the grass,
Between them and the moving boughs,
A shadow, thou didst pass.

"Thy dress was like the lilies,
And thy heart was pure as they:
One of God's holy messengers
Did walk with me that day."

And so on, and so on—sweet stray verses, which all the service long "beat time to nothing" in Edna's brain. A strangely simple, yet acute and tenacious brain—a strangely young heart, that in the midst of all its cares could go back upon lots of silly childish poetry. Yet she did so, and recalled the exact state of mind she was in when she learned it—poor little sixteen-year-old girl, brimming over with romantic dreams, none of which had ever come true. No, not one; nor did she expect it now; yet they were to this day vivid as ever. And as, with a half-comical application to the present, her fancy went over the lines—

"Long was the good man's sermon,
But it seemed not so to me;
For he spake of Ruth the beautiful,
And still I thought of thee.

"Long was the prayer he uttered,
Yet it seemed not so to me;
For in my heart I prayed with him,
And still I thought of thee."

—she still felt, as she remembered to have done then, that it would be the summit of earthly happiness to go peacefully to church—just such a village church as this, and on just such a summer Sunday morning—and sit there, with the beloved of one's heart, worshipping and loving, with the prayer that has its root in love, and the love that is worth nothing unless it is a perpetual prayer.

"What a dear little church this is!" she whispered to her sister as they went out.

"Very; but a rather common congregation. I saw scarcely any one above the class of farmers, except in the rectory pew. And did you notice a bonnet there—straw, with a green trimming and a wreath of pink daisies all round the face? That is how I should like my bonnet, Edna. Please, remember."

"Very well."

"Dr. Stedman did go to church. He sat just behind us. Didn't you see him?"

"No. In truth, I had forgotten all about him."

"Hush! there he is."

He might have overheard the remark, for he passed close by the sisters, passed again with only a bow—not manifesting the slightest intention of stopping and speaking, like the rest of the congregation, who lingered in friendly groups all the way between the church-porch and the lich-gate. Presently his long strides took him far away down the road.

"What very odd manners!" remarked Letty, a little annoyed.

"I think they are the manners of a gentleman who has the sense not to intrude upon two ladies who have neither father nor brother to make his acquaintance desirable—or even possible," said Edna, determined to hold to her resolution, and allow no loop-hole of civility through which the enemy might assault their little encampment, and bring about that passage of arms for which Letty was evidently accoutring herself—making ready for a tournament which, in Edna's mind, was either foolish child's play, or a battle royal for life and death.

Not that any idea of so serious a crisis struck her on that bright Sunday morning. She simply thought that her sister wanted a bit of flirtation, and was resolute she should not have it. At which Letty sulked a little all the afternoon, and spent a long, leisurely, lazy Sunday, without referring again to either Doctor Stedman or his brother.

After tea she insisted she was strong enough to go to church a second time, but recalled her wish when she looked out on the sweet Sabbath evening. "We'll take a walk instead, if you are not too good, Edna."

Edna was not in the least too good. She longed to be out in the green lanes, enjoying the birds' Sunday hymns, and the incense of the Sunday flowers, and the uplifting of the elm-trees' tall arms, in a dumb thanksgiving for being again clothed with leaves: all creatures, great and small, seeming to feel themselves happier and merrier on a Sunday than on any common day. So she brought down Letty's hat—deposing the obnoxious brown bonnet—wrapped her up well in a warm shawl, and went out with her, having first cast a glance to see if the opposite door were shut. It was, and the blinds were down. The brothers seemed seldom or never to go out of evenings.

The sisters crossed the threshold with light steps and lighter hearts. But as they did so the grim invisible Woman, sitting there, laughed at them, knowing she had her will—not they.

And what of the two divided from them by just a wall on this momentous, monotonous Sunday—the two young men, about whom, whether they thought or not, they said nothing?

Julius Stedman had been terribly depressed all day. There came upon him one of those moody fits to which, even in health, he had been subject, and which now were so severe as to try to the utmost both body and mind; and the cloud did not lift off for hours. Except during church-time, his brother never left him, but hovered about him with a tenderness, less brotherly than sisterly, alternately reasoning and jesting, reproving and persuading, but all in vain. He lay silent, shutting out daylight and cheerfulness, refusing to do any thing, or to suffer any thing to be done for him. At last, *apropos* of nothing that William could discover, unless it was the ringing of the bells and the closing of the hall-door, indicating the departure of somebody to evening church, Julius said, "I should like to go out."

The doctor remonstrated. It was late—the dew would soon be falling.

"What do I care? What need I care? It will do me no harm. Or if it did, what matter? You can't cure me, Will, with your cleverness. You had better kill me off quick."

"How? Mention the easiest way."

"Oh, any thing. I hate this shilly-shally work — one day better, the next day worse. Your prognostications were all wrong. This place does not cure me, and never will."

"Shall we go back to London?"

"Horrible! No. Besides, didn't you tell me you wanted a fortnight's quiet reading before your hospital lectures began?"

"I'll manage about that, if you would like to go home. In fact, though it isn't much of a home we have, I think we should be better off there than here."

Then, with the contrariness of sickness, Julius veered round, and argued energetically, almost irritably, on the other side.

Dr. Stedman could not repress his annoyance. He was a man who always knew his own mind, and his brother's indecision tried him severely.

"Have it which way you like," he said, sharply. "You are as bad to deal with as any woman. Stay or go—which you choose; only let me know, that I may take my measures accordingly."

"As bad as a woman," repeated Julius, mournfully. "Yes, I suppose I am. Not half a man, and never shall be. Ah! I wish I had some woman about me; she would pity me; she would understand me. Nay, Will, don't look savage. I didn't mean to vex you."

"Nor did you vex me; so don't be fancying that among other nonsense," returned Will, with some impatience. "Just let us try to have an ounce of common sense between us. The larger matters we can settle to-morrow.

At present the question is, Will you or will you not go out this evening? Say yes, and I'll go and fetch the chair."

"Thank you. But it's late, and it's Sunday evening."

"Pshaw!" The doctor rose, searched for his hat, and was off in a minute.

In ten minutes more the brothers were out on the cliffs, in their accustomed mode of progression, along the familiar way. Doubtless, a weary life for them both; an unnatural life for two young men, in the very flower of their age, and both in the most critical time of their career; a time when to most men every week, every day is of moment as regards their future. Yet here they were, passing it in compulsory idleness. No wonder both were silent, and that the lovely evening did not steal into their hearts as it did into those of the two young women. Nay, their forced companionship seemed to throw the brothers wider apart than it had done the sisters. True, Will and Julius never quarrelled, as Letty and Edna sometimes did—bursting into a thunder-storm of words, ending in tears and kisses of reconciliation—womanish but safe. On the contrary, each fortified himself behind his masculine armor of steely reticence, smooth and cold, feeling all the while that within it he was a dull fellow—a solitary fellow—even with his own brother beside him. Such lonely moments come to all people—before marriage (Heaven help them if they come after marriage!)—and it would be well if brothers and sisters, fathers and mothers, recognized this fact—as a law of God and necessity—that all the love of duty never makes up for the love of choice.

What poor Julius was thinking of as he sat, helplessly propelled along, and looked listlessly on the sweet landscape that he had neither strength nor heart to paint—what William felt as he expended in pushing the Bath-chair the manly strength that would have enjoyed a good twenty-mile walk across the island, geologizing, botanizing, and what not—must remain alike unknown. Certainly, neither brother communicated his feelings to the other. They were uncommonly dull company this evening, and that was the truth of it.

The cliffs were deserted—all the good people at church. Only, just as they were returning home, Julius pointed out two figures standing on the cliff-top, sharp against the sky.

"Two ladies, I think they are—a very tall one and a very short one."

"It is probably the Misses Kenderdine. They were out, for I saw their door open as we passed."

"Hurry back then, Will. Don't let us meet them. They will only look at me with their confounded pity. I hate being pitied. Make haste!"

The doctor did his best, but there were some steep little ascents and descents which required all his skill and strength. In one of these his pilotage failed. In turning past a large stone the wheel came off, and the chair toppled over, landing its occupant ignominiously on the grass.

A slight, almost ridiculous accident, if it had not happened to an invalid, and to such a nervous invalid as Julius Stedman. As it was, his brother was seriously alarmed. But Julius, whose state could never be counted on with certainty for five minutes at a time, seemed to take his disaster easily enough. Nay, the little excitement roused his mobile temperament into healthy vitality. He sat on the grass, perfectly unhurt, and laughing heartily.

"I never knew such a 'spill.' Done as cleverly as if you had done it on purpose—perhaps to attract the attention of those ladies. They evidently think we have had a frightful accident. See how they are running to the rescue—that is, the little one; the other is too majestic to run. She stalks down, Juno-like, to offer her benign aid to me, miserable mortal! And, by Juno, what a gait she has! Never did I see such a handsome creature! No, I thank you, Miss Kenderdine," added he, when, a second time led away by her impulse of kindness, Edna came hastily down to the scene of disaster. "No, I'm not killed—not this time. But I seem always destined to fall into sudden misfortune and have you appearing to me as my guardian angel."

Edna did not laugh, for she caught sight of Dr. Stedman's anxious face, and guessed at once that the position of affairs was rather serious—the chair useless, no carriage attainable, the dews beginning to fall heavily, and they on the cliff-top, at least a quarter of a mile from home, with an invalid who could not walk a step, and was too heavy to be carried.

"What is to be done?" said she, in a low tone, to the elder brother, while the younger, oblivious of his disaster, became absorbed in conversation with Letty, who, arriving stately and slowly, had just begun to hope, with condescending interest, that he had not hurt himself. "I see how things are. What must we do?" repeated Edna, in unconscious fraternity. "Shall I run and fetch assistance?"

"No; it would only annoy him. Besides, there is no need. We must get him to walk home. I know he could walk if he tried."

Edna looked amazed—a little indignant.

"You think me cruel, I know; but we doctors are obliged to be so to some sort of patients. And it is the real truth. He is quite capable of walking a short distance, and I shall be rather thankful for any thing that forces him to acknowledge it. Am I very hard-hearted, Miss Kenderdine?"

"I can not say. I suppose you know best."

This little conversation was carried on in confidence over the broken wheel, but there was no time for discussion. Every minute the air grew more chill and the grass more dewy; the tide was rising, and the wind that came in with it began to blow freshly from over the sea. To healthy people it was delicious—intoxicating in its pure saltness; but to the invalid, though apparently he did not notice it, being engaged talking to Letty, who was sympathizing with him in the most charming manner—to a person in Julius Stedman's condition, Edna felt that it might be most dangerous.

"We must get him home somehow at once, and I see but one way," said the doctor, with a professional air, decisive and dictatorial, which at any other time would have amused Edna. "Will you help me, Miss Kenderdine? If I support him on one side, will you let him lean on you at the other? I am sorry to trouble you—very sorry; but it is a case of emergency. And if, as you said, you are accustomed to sick-nursing—"

"Yes; and I think I can do this. I have almost carried Letty many a time. Though I am small, I am very strong."

"I can see that."

"But how will you persuade him to walk?"

"Will you suggest it? It might come better, coming from a stranger. Try, please; for we have not a minute to lose."

Nobody knew exactly how it was done—probably by the invalid's being taken by surprise, and left no chance of refusing; but it was done. Between his two supporters Julius was marched remorselessly on, half in jest, half in earnest, across the smooth down. And then, no doubt, it was rather pleasant to be assisted in his steps by one charming girl, and have his progress watched and encouraged by another. Be that as it may, Julius did walk, with the assistance of his brother and Miss Kenderdine, the whole quarter of a mile; and when he reached the garden gate, so far from being exhausted, as they had expected, he turned, with his countenance all beaming—

"How cleverly I have done it! I do think I shall get back the use of my limbs. Will said so—but I never believed him. I say, old fellow, don't be too conceited—but you were right, after all."

The doctor smiled. Edna saw something in his face that touched her even more than the delighted excitement in that of the invalid.

"Oh, if you knew what it feels like!" said Julius to Edna. "To have been tied and bound for weeks to that chair—to feel as if one should never walk any more; and now, I do believe, if you would let me, I could walk quite alone."

"Try," said the doctor, composedly.

"Oh, do try!" cried Edna, eagerly.

The young man did try, and succeeded. Very tottering steps they were, and not many of them, for his brother would not allow it; but he did really walk—alone and unassisted. And only those who know what it is to be deprived for a season of the power of locomotion, or of any power which we use so commonly and thanklessly that we need to lose it before we fully recognize its blessing, can understand the ecstasy which lit up every feature of the poor fellow's face, and was reflected in the faces round about him.

"I declare I am just like a baby—a baby first learning to walk," said Julius, viewing first one leg and then the other—patting them and looking down upon them as if they were quite new acquaintances or lately-recovered friends. "Don't laugh at me, please, you two young ladies. Will, there, won't; he knows I always was a simpleton. And then I have been so ill, and the future has looked so terrible. Don't laugh at me."

"We are not laughing," said Letty, whose good-nature had really been roused—so much so as to forget herself, her "unfortunate appearance," and the sense of dignified propriety due to both, in the warm human interest of the moment. "Indeed, we are exceedingly glad to see you better—are we not, sister?"

But Edna was so moved that she was actually crying.

"How good you are!" said Julius, taking her hand and pressing it warmly. While the whole four stood silent, something—they knew not what—seemed to come creeping round them like an atmosphere of peace, and kindliness, and mutual sympathy—compelling them into friendliness, whether they willed it or not. And as they stood at the front door, the soft, gray, misty twilight was drawing a veil over the sea, and the robin-redbreast, from his nest at the cliff's edge, gave one or two good-night warbles over his mate and his little ones, and the first star came out, large and bright, in the zenith. This sunshiny Sunday was making a good end.

"Come in, now," said the doctor, for nobody seemed disposed to stir. "At least, we must. Julius, say good-night, with many thanks, to these two ladies. Are you quite warm, lad? I wish I had ordered a fire."

"Ours is lit," said Edna; and, with a glance at her sister, she did on the impulse of the moment what seemed a simple thing enough, yet was the very last thing which, an hour ago, she would have thought of doing—the thing of all others she had determined not to do—she invited the brothers into their parlor.

"It will prevent all danger of a chill," said the little woman, turning to Dr. Stedman with quite a grandmotherly air. "Your room will be warm in half an hour; and meantime he can lie down. We have a capital sofa; indeed, Mrs. Williams told us it was better than yours, and we offered to exchange."

"Do not think of such a thing," said Julius. "I shall soon be well; indeed, I feel myself well now. It is astonishing what good this evening has done me; or rather, not astonishing—a little society cheers one up so much. Well, I may go in and sit by that nice blazing fire?"

"By all means, since these ladies are so kind."

The doctor helped his brother in, made him comfortable on the sofa ("and how cleverly he did it too—wouldn't he be uncommonly good to his wife, that great big fellow!" remarked Letty afterwards), and then was about departing, as if he hesitated to consider any one but Julius included in the invitation.

Letty said, in her most stately but most fascinating manner, "she hoped Dr. Stedman would remain." So he remained.

It was the first evening they ever spent together—these four; indeed, it could scarcely be called an evening, for Dr. Stedman carried his brother away remorselessly at the half-hour's end. Its incidents were unimportant, and its conversation trivial, as is usually the case with first acquaintance. Only in books, seldom or never in real life, do youths and maidens dash into the Romeo-and-Juliet passion of the instant. Nowadays people—even young people—rarely fall in love; they walk into it deliberately and open-eyed, or slip into it gradually unawares. It is all one.

"Come he slow, or come he fast,
It is but Love that comes at last."

The only notable fact in the evening's entertainment

was that, ere he sat down, Dr. Stedman pointedly took out his card and laid it before the sisters.

"I think, Julius, before we intrude upon these ladies' hospitality, we ought to tell them who and what we are. Miss Kenderdine, my brother is an artist, and I am a doctor. There are only we two; our parents are long dead, and we never had a sister. We live at Kensington, where I have taken the practice of the late Dr. Young."

"We knew Dr. Young," replied Edna, with very considerable relief; "and we heard he had a high opinion of the gentleman who afterwards succeeded him. That must have been yourself?"

Dr. Stedman bowed. "Then," he added, smiling, and in his smile the not quite good-tempered look before spoken of certainly disappeared—"then I may be considered to have given in our certificates of character?"

"Not mine," observed Julius from the sofa. "I may be a most awful scape-grace for all these ladies know; a ne'er-do-weel, hanging round the neck of my respectable brother like a millstone on an old man of the sea; a poor artist—disreputable, as most poor artists are. Nobody can expect the luxury of a character unless he is rich; and I am as poor as a church mouse, I assure you, Miss Kenderdine. All our money came to Will there; his grandfather's pet he was, and he left him his heir, but he halves it all with me, and—"

"Julius, what nonsense you are talking!"

"I always do talk nonsense when I'm happy; and I am so happy to-night I can't think what has come over me. So now you know all about us, Miss Kenderdine; and you may either make friends of us or not, as you choose."

"Say, rather, acquaintance; friendship does not come all in a minute," said the doctor, regarding his brother, who sat looking so handsome and bright, pleasant and lovable, with something of the expression, deprecating yet proud, with which a parent regards a spoiled child, for whom he feels bound to apologize, but can not quite see the necessity, and thinks every body must secretly be in as admiring an attitude as he himself. In fact, the big brother's evident admiration of the sickly one struck the sisters as something quite funny—if it were not so touching and so unusual in its way.

"Well, then—we being two lonely brothers, and they two sisters, thrown together in this not too lively abode—will they kindly permit our acquaintance, after the pattern of Queen Elizabeth's celebrated letter—'Yours as you demean yourselves, Edna Kenderdine and—' I have not heard your sister's Christian name."

"Letty—Letitia," said the owner of it, looking downward.

This was the only information vouchsafed to the two guests by their hostesses. As Letty said, after they were gone, the two brothers, who were evidently gentlemen, must have seen at a glance that she and her sister were gentlewomen; and any further facts were quite unnecessary.

Edna thought so too; still, with her exceeding candor, and perhaps a lurking pride, she would have liked them—the doctor especially—to know that Letty and herself were only school-mistresses.

CHAPTER VI.

Why do people take to loving one another—or liking, the customary and safe preliminary to loving? And how does the love first come? Through what mysterious process do young folks pass, by steps rapid or slow, according to circumstances and their own idiosyncrasy, out of the common world—the quiet, colorless, everyday world—into that strange new paradise from which there is no returning? No, none! We may be driven out of it by an angel with a flaming sword—out into the wilderness, which we have to till and keep, changing its thorns and thistles into a respectable ordinary garden—we may pass out of it, calmly and happily, into a new earth—safe and sweet, and homelike; but this particular paradise is never found again—never re-entered more.

Why should it be? All life is a mere progression—a pressing on and on; and death itself—we Christians believe—but a higher development into more perfect life. Yet as nothing good is ever lost, or wholly forgotten, one can imagine even a disembodied spirit sitting glorious before the great white throne, recalling with a tender sweetness the old earthly heaven which was first created by that strange state of mind—that intoxicating idealization of all things within as without, as if every thing were beheld with new eyes—the eyes of a creature new-bound; the condition which silly folk call being "in love."

It has its sillinesses—no one will deny; its weaknesses and madnesses; but it has its divine side too, chiefly because then, and not till then, comes the complete absorption of self into some other being dearer and better, higher and nobler than one's self, or imagined so; which is the foundation of every thing divine in human nature. If men or women are ever good at all—ever heroic, unselfish, self-denying—they will be so when they first fall in love; and if the love be worthy, that goodness will take root and grow. As a tree is known by its fruits, so a noble love, be it happy or unhappy, ennobles a whole life. And I think no friends—no parents especially—if they are real friends, real parents, true as tender, generous as wise, can see two young people standing at the enchanted gate without a prayerful thankfulness—ay, thankfulness. For it is the gate of life to them, whatever be the end.

Neither friends nor kindred stood by these four to watch or warn them, to help or to hinder their footsteps, in entering this unknown paradise; they walked into it deliberately, day by day and hour by hour, from that first Sunday night when Julius Stedman lay on the Misses Kenderdine's sofa, talking to one and gazing at the other, with all his heart both in his lips and eyes.

He was the grand foundation of the acquaintance, the corner-stone which seemed to make it all safe and right and natural. The sacredness of sickness was upon him and around him; for after the exertion of that night he fell back considerably, and for some days made his brother and his friends—in the anxiety they grew into friends—very miserable about him. The Misses Kenderdine were by no means strong-minded women, to fly in the face of the world, and make acquaintance with, or suffer themselves to be made acquaintances by, any stray young man they happened to meet. They had a keen sense of decorum; but then it was the decorum of true womanliness, the pure simplicity of soul which sees no harm in things not really harmful; the sweet dignity of maidenhood, which, feeling that, known or unknown, met or unmet, there can be to any woman but one man alive who is a possible husband, regards the rest of the sex with a gentle kindness—a placid indifference—nothing more.

At least such was Edna's condition, and by the strong influence of her character she turned Letty into the same, or an imitation of the same, for the time being. After a long consultation between themselves, the sisters agreed that it would be ridiculous in them to stand aloof from the poor sick fellow in the next room, and his grave, anxious brother, who seemed wholly absorbed in nursing him, because these happened to be young men, and they themselves young women; and no regular introduction in society had taken place between them.

"But we know all about them, nevertheless," argued Edna. "I quite well remember that when I was urged to send for Dr. Young to you, and found he had died suddenly, his successor was very highly recommended. It must have been the same Dr. Stedman. Had I sent, and had he attended you in the fever, how very funny it would have been!"

"Yes, indeed. Suppose we tell him what a near escape he had of either killing or curing me!"

"I think not, dear. As you say, there is no necessity for them to know any thing about us. I do not mean even to tell them that we live at Kensington; but it is a satisfaction to know something about Dr. Stedman, and it warrants us in being kind and civil a little to that poor sick lad—he looks no more than a lad. And how very ill he seemed this morning!"

So Edna reasoned with herself, most simply and sincerely; as she drifted—they all drifted—into that frank association, which, the first barrier being broken, was sure to come to people living in the same house, having nothing in the wide world to do but to go out and come in, and watch each other's goings out and comings in, innocently enough; but yet with a certain interest that appeared to waken up into new life the whole party, especially the invalids.

For Letty was a little of an invalid again. She took a slight chill; and Dr. Stedman prescribed for her in a very reticent, formal, but still pleasant and friendly way, which further helped on the intimacy between them. And as for Edna, her chief friend, as she openly declared, was Julius. He took to her suddenly and completely, with a kind of child-like dependence, so affectionately persistent that there was no withstanding it. Soon it became quite natural for him to send for her in to sit with him when his brother went out, to beg her to accompany them and "see that nothing happened to them" in the daily walk that Will shortly began to insist upon, first round the garden, and gradually lengthening, to the total abolition of the Bath-chair. He talked and jested with her alternately, for she was a merry as well as earnest little woman; he tyrannized over her, making her see to his little comforts, which she did in quite a motherly, or, rather, as he declared, a "grandmotherly" way; sometimes he even presumed to tease her, but all in such frank, boyish, and yet perfectly gentlemanly fashion, that the result was inevitable—Edna grew exceedingly fond of him.

"Fond of" is the word—that gentle tenderness which almost invariably, though not always, precludes the possibility of any thing more.

This firm alliance, open and free, between Julius and Edna, made things progress amazingly, and threw the two others together more than Letty's sister would, a week ago, have dared to risk. But then Dr. Stedman, the more she knew of him, seemed the more unlikely to fall into the ranks of Letty's victims, being exceedingly sedate and middle-aged for his years, and apparently not at all disposed to make the best of his opportunities. He would walk by Letty's side for hours without detaching her from the others, or talking to her very much himself; he seemed to like looking at her as any man might, and that was all. Obviously he was incapable of flirtation, did not seem to understand what it meant, carried on all conversations with the sisters in the most open, grave, and courteous earnest; as Letty declared, it would have been quite impossible for her to set up a flirtation with him, even had she tried.

To do her justice, she did not try. She too was subdued by the shadow of heavy sickness, which she had so lately escaped, and which still hung over the two brothers. Her sympathy was aroused; she thought less of herself and her charms, and was consequently more charming than she had ever been in her life.

Did the young men see and feel it? This extraordinary fascination, half of soul, half of sense, which breathes in the very atmosphere of a beautiful woman, if she has any thing womanly in her at all. And Letty had a good deal. There was in her not a particle of ill-nature, that "envy, malice, and all uncharitableness," which women have sometimes sore need to pray against. She was always gentle and lady-like, and extremely sweet-tempered. If, taken altogether, her character was chiefly made up of negatives, her beauty was a thing so positive that it supplied all deficiencies, at least for a long time. In the eyes of men, probably for always.

Julius had his wish, and made sketches innumerable, sometimes open, sometimes surreptitious, of her flexible figure and lovely face. Of evenings he used to repeat them from memory, and make compositions out of them. Dr. Stedman was called out of his medical researches for endless criticism upon Miss Kenderdine — they always called her Miss Kenderdine, and her sister Miss Edna, though why, nobody knew—as the gardener's daughter,

> "Gowned in pure white that fitted to the shape,
> Holding a branch to fix it back,"

Miss Kenderdine in mediæval costume, as Kreimhild in the Niebelungenlied, and Miss Kenderdine with her hat off, and sea-weeds in her hair, standing with the tide rolling in upon her feet, musing pensively with head bent forward —a veritable Ariadne of Naxos.

"That's the best, I think," said Will, whose comments were always sharp, short, and decisive.

"I think so too," replied the other, lingering over his work with an artist's delight. "There is a wonderful deal of the Ariadne in her face naturally."

"Yes. The features are of the true Greek type—sensuous without being sensual, pleasure-loving, but not coarse. She ought to marry a rich man, and then she would do uncommonly well."

"Probably; so would most women," said Julius, with some sharpness.

Will did not notice that, but still gazed in keen criticism on the sketch.

"Ay, it's like her; a true Ariadne face—that, Theseus lost, would take up very comfortably with Bacchus."

"Horrible!" cried the artist. "I never knew such a matter-of-fact, abominably blunt fellow as you. You might as well say that if Miss Kenderdine were disappointed in love she would take to drinking."

"She might. I have seen some terrible cases of female Bacchants under similar circumstances. But I beg your pardon. You need not tell her I said so. Besides, she is never likely to be disappointed in love," added the doctor, as he put down the sketch-book, and ceased the conversation.

It was the only conversation that during the first fortnight the brothers held concerning their new acquaintances. Indeed, there was not time, for, excepting the late working hours — after nine or ten o'clock — scarcely an hour passed when the occupants of the two parlors did not meet, or sit waiting, expectant of the chance of meeting. Not that any walks or talks were purposely or systematically planned — still they always seemed to come about, and at length both sides seemed to make reasons or excuses for them.

"We are just a lot of children out on a holiday," said Julius one day, when they were all sitting eating their combined lunch on a primrose bank, with larks singing madly overhead, the salt wind freshening all their faces, and far away the outline of white cliffs and blue sea stretching into infinite brightness—infinite peace. "Just mere children, Miss Edna, and oh, do let us enjoy ourselves as such. We shall have hard enough work when we get home."

"That is true," said Edna, with a half sigh; and she too gave herself up to the enjoyment of the moment.

None the less enjoyable that it was, strangely enough, the first time in their lives that these two young women had had any frank association with men—good, pleasant, clever men. To Letty the opposite sex had always come in the form of lovers—not always satisfactory, especially in the amazing plurality with which they had blessed Letitia Kenderdine; while Edna knew nothing about men at all. That cheerful, frank intercourse—social, moral, and intellectual—which, within limits, does both sexes a world of good, was to her not only a novelty, but an exceeding pleasure. She was not a stupid woman—indeed it sometimes dawned upon her that she might have a few brains of her own, since she could so readily enter into the talk of these two men, who both, in their way, were undoubtedly clever men—thoughtful, original, and with no folly or coarseness about them, such as would at once have repelled these maidenly gentlewomen. Neither of the brothers attempted in the slightest degree to make love to Letty, and both treated Edna with a grateful politeness, a true heart courtesy, that did her own heart good. For, she argued to herself, it was not like the civilities shown to Letty; it must be sincere, since it was shown to a poor, plain little school-mistress. She had taken care to let their new friends know they were only school-mistresses, teaching tradesmen's daughters in a London suburb—so much, no more; and she had noticed with approbation that neither brother had made the slightest further inquiry; nor had their respective positions in life, or pecuniary affairs, or family connections, been again referred to.

Thus they spent day after day, these four young people, in as complete an Arcadia as if there were no such a place as the common, working-day world, no sound of which ever reached them. This little Isle of Wight, which was not then what it is now, but far simpler, far lonelier, far lovelier—though it is lovely yet—might have been an enchanted island of the sea—an Atlantis, such as weary mariners sailed after in vain—where no one toiled and no one suffered; no one hated, or quarrelled, or betrayed; but all within was as sweet and peaceful as without, and where these young people seemed to live a life as innocent as the birds, and as peaceful as the primroses.

Letty even forgot her new bonnet, Edna never took that expedition to Ryde; it seemed a pity to waste a day thereon; and for two Sundays more the sisters went contentedly to church in their winter's clothes. But it was spring in both their hearts all the while.

This was, they agreed, the most wonderful spring they had ever seen. The primroses were so large; the hyacinths so innumerable and intensely blue, and the trees came into leaf with such especial luxuriance—all in a minute, as it seemed; some days you could almost see them growing. The twenty-ninth of May the oaks were full enough to shelter a moderate-sized King Charles; and on a certain country walk Edna discussed eagerly with Julius that celebrated historical fact, which he had tried to illustrate by a large cartoon in the previous year's exhibition at Westminster Hall.

"Did you compete for the prizes?" she asked, walking along by his side, while the others went on ahead, this being their usual way, because Letty disliked being hindered with Julius's still feeble steps.

"I tried, but I failed. I always do fail, somehow."

"That is hard. I wonder why it should be so, when you are so very clever," said Edna, innocently.

"Perhaps other people—Will especially—think me cleverer than I am. I don't know how it is," added he, mournfully, "but I always seem to miss the exact point of success. I get near it, but I never touch it. I am afraid my life has been—always will be—a failure."

"Many lives are, that do not show it outside," replied Edna, more sadly than her wont. For she too, on that sunshiny day, with all things luring her to enjoyment, had become slightly conscious of something lacking. Did the others feel it, she wondered? Was Letty, there, as happy as she looked, when stopping with Dr. Stedman on the summit of the steep cliff, up which she herself had managed to climb with Julius, indulging him with the fancy that he was helping her, while, in reality, she supported him—a common fiction.

"My brother and your sister have got on ahead of us," said Julius, pausing, breathless. "They seem capital friends. He admires her extremely, as, indeed, every body must do. She is the most beautiful person we ever saw."

"Yes; all people say that. I am quite used to hearing it now."

"Of course you are, which must be my apology for making the remark. The fact is so patent that it ceases to be either a compliment or an impertinence."

"It would never be an impertinence, said as you say it," replied Edna, gently, for she saw that the young man was a little annoyed in some way. "Yet, I will confess, you are the first person whom I ever heard call my sister handsome without its making me angry."

"What an odd observation to make! How it might be misinterpreted!"

"How? That it meant I was jealous of her? Oh, how very funny! What an altogether ridiculous idea! Me jealous of my sister because she is so beautiful, while I myself am—well—"

"Never mind what you are," interrupted Julius, blushing, for he felt he was treading on the very bounds of incivility.

"Oh, but I do mind a little. I confess I should like to have been handsome, too. But as it can't be, it can't be; and I have now grown quite used to being plain."

Julius was fairly puzzled. It had been his trial, and a not inconsiderable one, in his acquaintance, or friendship, or whatever it was, with this sweet little woman, that she was so plain. To his keen artist eye her want of complexion, of feature, and general brilliancy of effect, was sometimes really annoying. She would have been so attractive, so original, so altogether charming—if only she had been a very little prettier.

Of course he would not betray this, and yet he did not like to tell an untruth, or to pay a silly compliment, which the candid Edna could at once have discovered and scorned. A bright thought struck him, and he compromised with it.

"Plain, are you? Every body doesn't think so; Will doesn't. The very first night he saw you, when you sat adding up your accounts, he told me what a nice face you had."

"Did he? I am sure I am very much obliged to him."

"And your sister?" continued Julius, still watching the other two with an intentness that might have seemed peculiar had not Edna now become accustomed to his artist way of staring—"quite in the way of business," as he took care to explain. "What does your sister think of Will?"

"I really can not tell," replied Edna, smiling. "In truth I have not the slightest idea."

She might have added—once she thought she would, and then despised herself for such an unsisterly betrayal—that Letty's thoughts did not much matter, as she was not in the habit of thinking long or seriously about any thing. So she held her tongue, and the brotherly earnestness of her companion's next speech shamed her still more.

"I hope she likes him; she ought—you both ought, for I am sure he likes you, which is a great deal to say for Will, as he does not usually get on with young ladies. Yet he is a wonderfully good fellow, Miss Edna; a fine fellow in every way, as you would say if you knew him."

"I have no doubt of it."

"Brothers don't often pull together as well as we do, yet we are very unlike, and I have tried him not a little. When I get strong—if I ever do get strong—"

"You certainly will. Dr. Stedman said so to me only yesterday."

"What was he saying about me? You see, Will and I don't talk much either of or to one another, and I should like to know what he could find to say."

Edna hesitated a moment whether or not to repeat this, the only bit of confidence that had ever passed between herself and the doctor, and which had at once amazed and puzzled her for the time: it seemed so very uncalled for. Then she thought she would tell it, for it could do no possible harm out of its anxious brotherly affectionateness. And it might even do good, by rousing Julius out of that languid indifference to the future, that loose grasp of life, with its duties and pleasures alike, which was such a sad, nay, a fatal thing to see in a young man of his age.

"It was very little your brother said; only he told me his firm conviction that you had no real disease or feebleness of constitution. You would be all right if you could once be roused out of your melancholy and moody fits by any strong feeling of any kind: made to take care of your health, work hard, though not too hard, and finally marry and settle."

"Did he say that? Did he want me to marry?"

"Very much indeed," replied Edna, laughing. "No match-making mother was ever more earnest on the subject. He said that a good wife would be the best blessing that could happen to you, and the sooner it happened the better."

"Were those his words? Exceedingly obliged to him!"

From the tone Edna could hardly tell whether the young man was pleased or vexed, but he blushed extremely: so much so that she began to blush too, and to question within herself whether she had not gone a little too far, and in her sublime grandmotherly indifference had overstepped the boundary of maidenly propriety. But at this instant the other two returned, and the conversation became general.

Edna was glad Dr. Stedman had called hers "a nice face." It showed that he liked her, and she had rather thought the contrary. Scarcely from any expression or non-expression of the fact, but because he did not seem a person who would easily like any body: but once liking, his fidelity would be sure for life. Or so at least fancied Edna in her simple speculations upon character, in which she was fond of indulging—as most people are who do not take very much trouble in thinking about themselves. She must think about something, and not being given to lofty musings or abstract cogitations, she thought about her neighbors; and, for the remainder of that walk, about that special neighbor who had been her first acquaintance of the two; since Dr. Stedman had more than once declared, when they were jesting on the subject, that his acquaintance with the sisters dated from the moment when he had been moved to such deep sympathy by Miss Edna's arithmetical woes.

She was glad he liked her, for she liked him; his keen intelligence, less brilliant than Julius's, but solid, thorough, and clear; his honesty of speech and simple unpretending goodness—especially his unvarying goodness to his brother, over whom his anxiety and his patience seemed endless; and Edna could understand it all. In the few private talks she and Dr. Stedman had together, their conversation seemed naturally to turn upon the nearest subject to both their hearts—their respective sister and brother.

Was he falling in love with Letty, or fearing Julius would do so? Either chance was possible, and yet improbable; nay, in the frank pleasure of their intercourse, Edna had almost ceased to dread either catastrophe. Now, as they turned homeward along the cliff, she noticed that Dr. Stedman looked exceedingly thoughtful—almost sad—that he either walked beside Letty, or, when she was walking with his brother, he followed her continually with his eyes.

No wonder. Edna thought she had never seen her sister so irresistibly attractive. If half the men in the world were on their knees at Letty's feet, it would have scarcely been unnatural. And yet—and yet—

Edna did not like to own it to herself—it seemed so unkind, unsisterly; still, if, as a perfectly unprejudiced person, she had been asked, was Letty the sort of girl likely to carry away captive Dr. Stedman, she should have said no. She should have thought a man with his deep nature would have looked deeper, expected more. With all her love for Letty, Letty would have been the last person in the world whom, had she been a man, she, Edna, would have fallen in love with; if Dr. Stedman had done so, she was a little surprised and—it must be confessed—just a trifle disappointed.

Chiefly so, she argued internally, because she felt certain that Letty would never look at him, and then it might turn out such an unlucky business altogether—the worst yet; for the doctor was not a person to take things easily, or to be played fast and loose with, as was unfortunately rather Letty's way. Edna felt by instinct that he would never be made a slave of—much more likely a tyrant. And if he should be very miserable—break his heart perhaps—that is, supposing men ever do break their hearts for love—Edna would have been so very sorry for him.

She watched him closely all the road home. She did not even ask him to come in to tea, as both brothers seemed half to expect, and as had been done more than once before the quartette started together for their evening ramble. Nevertheless, one was arranged—to look at a wreck which had been washed ashore the previous winter, and which Julius wished to make into a sketch for a possible picture. And though there was some slight opposition from Edna, who thought the walk would be too long for Letty, and from Dr. Stedman, for the same reason as regarded his brother, Julius was obstinate, and carried his point.

So they parted; for the brief parting of an hour or two, which scarcely seemed such at all.

Letty threw off her hat and lay down, with both her arms over her head, in an attitude exquisitely lovely.

"I am quite tired, Edna; that doctor of yours does take such gigantic strides, and he talks on such solid subjects, it quite makes one's head ache to follow him. I wonder why he chose me to walk with, and not you; but these wise men like silly women. I told him so. At least I owned I was silly; but of course he didn't believe it."

"Of course not. But what was he talking about?"

"Oh, nothing particular," said Letty, with a slightly conscious air. "Men all talk alike to me, I fancy."

Edna asked no more questions.

DOCTOR STEDMAN.

CHAPTER VII.

"WILL, do you mean to sit over your books all evening? Because if you do I'll not wait for you any longer, but take myself off at once."

"Where? Why, were you waiting?"

"Don't pretend that you have forgotten." Julius spoke with some of his old irritability. "We were to walk as far as the wreck; and unless we start in good time the tide will have risen, and we shall not be able to pass the point; which would be uncomfortable for ladies."

"Did the ladies decide to go? I thought Miss Edna rather objected."

"Miss Edna's objections were overruled. I arranged the matter."

Will smiled.

"Yes—I did. I'll not have her and you always getting your own way. I must have mine sometimes. I'm not your patient now, Will, and I have just as much right to enjoy myself as you have."

"Did any body say you hadn't, my boy? Who hinders you? Carry out any plans you fancy, provided they do you no harm."

The doctor rose, put a mark in his book, and prepared to clear his "rubbish" away.

"So, Will, you are going. I thought you would go, though you made believe to be so indifferent about it."

The elder brother flushed up, for there was an undertone of rudeness in the younger's speech not exactly pleasant. But Will was too well accustomed to the painful irritability of illness to take much heed of it. He only said:

"For many reasons, I don't consider the expedition very wise; but if these young ladies are determined to go, they will be all the better for having a man to take care of them."

"They will have one in any case. I am going. No need for you to trouble yourself concerning them."

The sharpness of this speech made Dr. Stedman turn round. He was not a man of many words, nor yet a very sensitive man — that is, he felt deep things deeply and strongly, but the small annoyances of life passed harmlessly over him. He had always had something else to think about than himself, and the way people treated him. For this reason he often did not even see when Julius was annoyed; but he did now, and turned upon the brother a full, frank, good-natured smile.

"What are you vexed about, lad? Do you want to have your friends all to yourself? If so, I'll stay at home and read. I dare say Miss Edna—"

"Stop there. Yes, Will, I am vexed with you, and I have good reason to be."

"Out with it, then."

"What business had you to go talking to Miss Edna about me? Why open up to her my weaknesses and follies, which nobody knows but you, and you only too much? Why should these two girls—for whom, mind you, I care not a straw, except that they are pleasant companions—be taught to criticise me and pity me?"

"Pity you?"

"Of course they do—a poor fellow with not a half-penny of money, and no health to earn it—wholly dependent upon you."

"That is not quite true."

"Yes, it is; and they must despise me—any girls would. There are times when I despise myself."

This outburst was so sudden, vehement, and inconsequent, as it seemed, that Will Stedman, though tolerably used to the like, scarcely knew what to answer. When he did, he spoke gently, as to a passionate child who was talking at random.

"Indeed, Julius, I had no thought of annoying you in what I said, which was, in truth, very little; and I felt I was saying it to a friend of yours, who was quite welcome to repeat it to you if she chose."

"But why talk to her at all about me? What are my concerns to her? If a friend, she isn't an old friend. Three weeks ago we had neither of us set eyes on either of these women. I wish we never had. I wish to Heaven we never had!"

Will replied a little seriously:

"I can not exactly see the reason of that. They are both pleasant enough, and, so far as we can judge, very excellent women."

"I hate your excellent women!"

"You don't hate these, though, I am sure of that, lad," said the doctor, smiling. "Be content; I have done you no harm. I said not a word against you to Miss Edna—quite the contrary."

"But, I repeat, why speak of me at all?"

"Perhaps I had my own reasons."

"What are they? I insist upon knowing!" and Julius rose and walked up to his brother with a dramatic air.

Will was comparing his watch with the clock on the mantel-piece. He paused to wind up and set both before he replied:

"Since you compel me to speak—and perhaps after all it's best—it has struck me more than once, Julius, that you would very well like—and, moreover, it would not be a bad thing for you—to spend your life, as you have pretty well spent the last fortnight, with such a sweet, good, sensible little woman as Edna Kenderdine."

Julius threw himself back into his chair, and burst into shouts of laughter.

"Was that it? And so you were saying a good word for me to her! What a splendid idea! You are the queerest old fellow that ever was."

"But, Julius—"

"Don't interrupt. Do let me have my laugh out. It's the best joke I've ever heard. You dear old boy! What on earth have I ever done or said to make you take such a ridiculous notion into your head?"

The doctor looked a little bewildered.

"It did not seem to me so ridiculous; and, at any rate, it is hardly civil to the lady to suppose so. She is about your own age—perhaps a year older; but that would not signify much. She is healthy, bright, active, clever—"

"But oh, so plain! Now, Will, in the name of common sense, do you think I ever could fall in love with a plain woman?"

The child-like directness and solemnity of the appeal broke down Will's gravity; he, too, laughed heartily.

"Never mind. I've made a mistake, that's all. I don't know whether I'm glad or sorry. But still, it is a mistake; and I beg your pardon—Miss Edna's too—for mixing her name in such talk. I am certain no idea of the kind has ever entered her head."

"I trust not—nay, I am sure not," replied Julius, warmly. "She's not an atom of a flirt—quite different from any girl I ever knew—the best, kindliest, sweetest little soul.

But I would as soon think of marrying her—or, indeed, of marrying any body—"

"Wait till your time comes. Meanwhile, shake hands, and forget all this nonsense. Only, if ever you do fall seriously in love, come and tell it to your brother. He'll help you."

"Will he?" said Julius, eagerly.

But at that moment, sweeping past the window, plainly visible beneath the half-drawn Venetian blind, came the violet folds of Letty Kenderdine's well-known gown—the much-abused winter gown which had in its old age been complimented, and sketched, and painted, as making the loveliest bit of color, and the most charming drapery imaginable.

"There they are: we must not keep them waiting," said Dr. Stedman, as he took his hat and went out at once to the sisters.

The three sat talking very merrily on the bench at the cliff edge for several minutes, till finding Julius did not appear, his brother went in to look for him. He had started off alone, leaving word that they were not to wait—he might possibly join them on their return.

"Perhaps he wants to make a sketch or two alone," said the doctor, apologetically. "We will go without him."

"Certainly," said Letty, who was a little tenacious of the disrespect of delay. "Dr. Stedman, your brother is a most peculiar person; and I can never understand peculiar people."

"He is peculiar in the sense of being much better than other people," replied the doctor, who—whatever he might say to Julius—never allowed a word to be said against him, which idiosyncrasy at once amused and touched Edna. With the new idea she had taken concerning him, she resolved to watch William Stedman rather closely, and when, before they had gone half a mile, Julius turned up, and attached himself very determinedly, not to her side, but her sister's, she fell into the arrangement with satisfaction. It would give her opportunities of observing more narrowly this big, quiet, grave man, who was not nearly so easy to read as his volatile, impulsive, but clever, affectionate brother.

So they descended the steep cliffs, and walked along underneath, just below high-water mark, where the wet sand was solid to their feet: a little party of two and two, close enough to make neither seem like a *tête-à-tête*, and yet sufficiently far apart to give to each a sense of voluntary companionship. But the conversation of neither seemed very serious; for Letty's gay laugh was continually heard, and Edna made, ever and anon, sundry darts from her companion's side to certain fascinating islands, formed by deeper channels intersecting the damp sand, and which had to be crossed through pools of shallow sea-water, crisped by the wind into wavelets pretty as a baby's curls. Edna could not resist them; but whenever Dr. Stedman fell into silence—which he did pretty often—she quitted him, and ran with the pleasure of a child to stand on one or other of these sand islands, and watch the long white rollers creeping in, each after each, as the tide kept steadily advancing upon the solitary shore.

Very solitary it was, with the boundless sea before, and the perpendicular wall of cliff behind, and not an object to break the loneliness of the scene, except that loneliest thing of all—the stranded ship. She lay there, fixed on the rock where she had struck, with the waves gradually reaching her and breaking over her, as they had done night and day, at every tide, for six months.

Julius regarded her with his melancholy poet's eyes.

"How sad she looks—that ship! Like a lost life."

"And what a fine ship she must have been! How very stupid of the sailors to go so near the rocks!"

"How very stupid of any body to do any thing which is not the best and wisest thing to do! Yet we all do it sometimes, Miss Kenderdine."

"Eh, Mr. Stedman? Just say that again, for I did not quite understand. You do say such clever things, you know."

"That was not clever, so I need not say it again. Indeed I'd better hold my tongue," replied Julius, looking full at Letty Kenderdine, with the sudden thirst of a man who is looking for perfection, has been looking for it all his days, and can not find it. And Letty, with those blue eyes of hers—the sort of azure blue, large and limpid, which look so like heaven, except for a certain want of depth in them, discoverable not suddenly, but gradually —Letty

"Gave a side glance and looked down,

in her long-accustomed way, thinking of nothing in particular, unless it was that the evening was coming on, misty and gray, and the sands were wet, and she had only her thin boots on.

She meant no harm, poor girl! She was so accustomed to be admired, to have every body looking at her as Julius Stedman looked now, that it neither touched nor startled her, nor affected her in any way—especially as the look was only momentary; and the young man returned immediately to his ordinary lively talk—the chatter of society—in which he was much more *au fait* than his brother, and which Letty could respond to much more easily. Indeed she had felt the change of companionship to-night rather an advantage, and had exerted herself to be agreeable accordingly. Though no one could say she smiled on one brother more sweetly than on the other; for it was not her habit either to feel or to show preference. She just went smiling on, like the full round moon, on all the world alike, as she had nothing to do but to smile. Did any hapless wight fall, moon-struck—who was to blame? Surely not Letitia Kenderdine.

And, meanwhile, Edna too had been enjoying herself very much, in a most harmless way, clambering over little rocks, and trampling on sea-weed—the bladders of which "go pop," as the children say, when you set your feet upon them — a proceeding which, I grieve to say, had amused this young school-mistress as much as if she had been one of her own pupils. Finally, by Dr. Stedman's assistance—for the rocks were slippery, and she was often glad of a helping hand—she gained the farthermost and most attractive sand island, and stood there, with her hat off, letting the wind blow in her face, for the sake of health and freshness; she was not solicitous about bloom or complexion.

Yet Edna was not uncomely. There was a fairy grace about her tiny figure, and an unaffected enjoyment in her whole mien, which made her interesting even beside her beautiful sister. While she was looking at the sea, Dr. Stedman stood and looked at her, with a keen observation —inquisitive, and yet approving—approving rather than admiring; not at all the look he gave to Letty. And yet, perhaps, any woman, who was a real woman, would rather have had it of the two.

"You seem to enjoy yourself very much, Miss Edna. It does one good to see any person past childhood who has the faculty of being so thoroughly happy."

"Did I look happy? Yes, I think I am: all the more so because my happiness, my sea-side pleasure, I mean, will not last long. I want to get the utmost out of it I can, for we go home in three days."

"So soon? When did you settle that?"

"At tea-time to-day. We must go, for we have spent all our money, and worn out all our clothes. Besides, it is time we were at home."

"Have you taken all precautions about fumigating, whitewashing, etc., that I suggested?" (For she had told him about the fever, and asked his advice, professionally.)

"Yes; our house is quite safe now, and ready for us. And most of our pupils have promised to come back. We shall be in harness again directly after the holidays. Ah!" she sighed, hardly knowing why, except that she could not help it, "I have need to be happy while I can. We have a rather hard life at home."

"Is it so?" Then, after a pause, "Forgive me for asking, but have you no father living, no brothers? Are there only you two?"

"Only us two."

"It is a hard life, then. I have seen enough of the world

to feel keenly for helpless women left to earn their livelihood. If I had had a sister I would have been so good to her."

"I am sure you would," said Edna, involuntarily. And then she drew back uneasily. Was it possible that he could be thinking of her in that light—as a sister by marriage, who might one day take the place of a sister by blood? Was that the reason he was so specially kind to her?

She could not have told why—but she did not quite like the idea, and her next speech was a little sharp, even though sincere.

"Yet, on the other hand, however kind a brother may be, it is great weakness and selfishness in a sister to hang helplessly upon him—draining his income, preventing him from marrying, and so on. If I had ten brothers, I think I would rather work till I dropped than I would be dependent on any one of them."

"Would you? But would that be quite right?"

"Yes, I think it would be right—for me, at least. I don't judge others. Let all decide for themselves their own affairs, but, as for me, if I felt I was a burden upon any mortal man—father, brother, or—well, perhaps husbands are different, I have never thought much about that —I believe it would drive me frantic."

"You independent little lady!" said Dr. Stedman, laughing outright. "And yet I beg your pardon," he added, seriously. "I quite agree with you. I don't see why a woman should be helpless and idle any more than a man. And a woman who, if she has to earn her daily bread, sets bravely to work and does it, without shrinking, without complaining, has my most entire respect and esteem."

"Thank you," said Edna, and her heart warmed, and the fierceness that was rising there sank down again. She felt that she had found a friend, or the possibility of one, did circumstances ever occur to bring them any nearer than now. Which, however, was not probable, since, as to these Stedmans, she had determined that when they parted—they parted; that this brief intimacy, which had been so pleasant while it lasted, should become on both sides as completely ended as a dream. Indeed, it would be nothing else. The sort of association which seemed so friendly and natural here, would, in their Kensington life, be utterly impossible.

"Things are hard enough even for us men," said Dr. Stedman, taking up the thread of conversation where Edna had dropped it. "Work of any sort is so difficult to obtain. There is my brother, now. He drifted into the career of an artist almost by necessity, because to get any employment such as he desired and was fitted for was nearly impossible. Even I, who, unlike him, have had the advantage of being regularly educated for a profession—would you believe it?—I have been in practice three years and have hardly made a hundred pounds. If I had not had a private income—small enough, but just sufficient to keep Julius and me in bread and cheese—I think we must have starved."

"So he has told me. He says he owes you every thing—more than he can ever repay."

"He talks great nonsense. Poor fellow! if he has been unsuccessful it has neither been through idleness nor extravagance. But he has probably told you all about himself. And you, I find, have told him what I yesterday said to you concerning him."

"Was I wrong?"

"Oh no. If it had been a secret I should have said so, and you would have kept it. You look like a woman who could keep a secret. If I ever have one I will trust you."

What did he mean? Further hints on the matter of sisterhood? Edna earnestly hoped not. Perhaps the fatal time had passed over, since the people who fell in love with Letty usually proposed to her suddenly—in two or three days. Now Dr. Stedman had been with her a whole fortnight—every day and all day long—and, so far as Edna knew, nothing had happened. If the sisters went away on Thursday nothing might happen at all.

She dismissed her fears and went on with her talk, in which the two others soon joined—the pleasant, desultory talk, half earnest, half badinage, of four young people allied by no special tie of kindred or friendship, bound only by circumstance and mutual attraction—that easy liking which had not as yet passed into the individual appropriation which, with the keen delights of love, creates also its bitter jealousies. In short, they stood, all of them, on the narrow boundary-line of those two conditions of being which make hapless mortals—especially men—either the best or the worst company in the world.

They strolled along the shore, sometimes two and two, sometime falling into a long line of four, conversing rather than looking around them—for there was nothing attractive in the evening. A dull, gray sky, and a smooth, leaden-colored sea, had succeeded those wonderful effects of evening light which they had night after night admired so much; yet still they went on walking and talking, enjoying each other's company, and not noticing much beyond, until Dr. Stedman suddenly stopped.

"Julius, look there; the tide is nearly round the point. We must turn back at once."

Letty gave a little scream. "Oh, what will happen! Why did we go on so far? Edna, how could you—"

"It was not your sister's fault," said Dr. Stedman, catching the little scream and coming anxiously over to Letty's side. "I was to blame; I ought to have noticed how far on the tide was."

"But oh, what will happen? Edna, Edna!" cried Letty, wringing her hands.

"Nothing will happen, I trust, beyond our getting our feet wet. Perhaps not that, if we walk on fast. Will you take my arm?"

"No, mine," said Julius, eagerly, and his brother drew back.

"Do not be alarmed, Miss Edna; but indeed I see you are not," said the doctor, striding on, while she kept pace with him as well as she could with her little, short steps. "We two will just walk on as fast as we can. There is no real danger. At worst we shall only get a good wetting; but that would be very bad for our invalids."

"Very bad. Letty—Mr. Stedman—please come on as fast as you can."

"Will!" shouted out Julius, "is it spring or neap tide?"

"I do not know; only get on. Don't lag behind."

"Get on yourself, and leave us alone."

"That isn't your habit, I'm sure, Miss Edna," said Will Stedman.

"What isn't my habit?"

"To get on by yourself and leave others to get on alone, as my brother has just advised my doing."

"Oh, he did not know what he was saying."

This was all that passed between them, as walking as rapidly as they could, though often turning uneasily back to watch the other two, the elder brother and sister reached the point where a "race," that is, a line of rocks reaching right up to the cliff, made the sea more turbulent, and where the cliff itself, jutting out a considerable way, caused the distance between it and high-water mark to be scarcely more than a foot—in spring-tides nothing at all. It was not exactly a dangerous place—not in calm weather like this. At most, a wade up to the knees would have carried a wayfarer safely beyond the point; but still it was an uncomfortable place to pass, and when Dr. Stedman and Edna reached it, they found the worst had come to the worst—there was no passage remaining, or merely a foot or two left bare, temporarily, at each ebb of the wave.

There were no breakers, certainly; nothing more threatening than the long slow curves of tide that came creaming in, each with a white fringe of foam, over the smooth sand; but whenever they met not sand but rocks, they became fiercer, and dashed themselves about in a way that looked any thing but agreeable, and rendered footing among the sea-weed and sharp stones extremely difficult.

Edna and Dr. Stedman exchanged looks—uneasy enough.

"You see?"

"Yes, I see. It is very unfortunate."

"Will she be frightened, think you? Your sister, I mean. She seems a timid person."

"Rather, and she dislikes getting wet. How fast the

tide comes in! Is there no chance of climbing a little way up the cliff?"

"No, the cliffs are perpendicular. Look for yourself."

But the doctor looked uneasily back, his mind full of the other two.

"How slow they are! If they had only been here now we might cross at once, and escape with merely wet feet. There would be just time. Julius!" he shouted, impatiently—"Julius, do come on!"

"He can not," Edna said, gently. "Remember, he can not walk like you."

"Thank you; you are always thoughtful. No; I suppose there is no help for it. We may as well sit down and wait." He sat down, but started up again immediately. "I beg your pardon, Miss Edna, but would you like to go on? I can easily take you past the point, and return again for them. Will you come?"

"No, oh no." And she, too, sat down on the nearest stone; for she was very tired.

It was full five minutes before Julius and Letty reached the point, and by that time the sea was tumbling noisily against the very foot of the cliff. Julius at once saw the position of things and turned anxiously to his brother.

"Will, this is dreadful! Not for us, but for these ladies. What shall we do?"

Letty caught at once the infection of fear.

"What is so dreadful? Oh, I see. Those waves, those waves! they have overtaken us. I shall be drowned! Oh, Dr. Stedman, tell me—am I going to be drowned?"

And she left Julius's arm and clutched the doctor's, her beautiful features pallid and distorted with fear. Also with something else besides fear, which shows plainly enough in most faces at a critical moment like this, when there awakes either the instinct of self-preservation, said to be nature's first law, or a far diviner instinct, which is not always—yet, thank God! it is often—also human nature.

Dr. Stedman was an acute man. No true doctor can well be otherwise. He said little, but he observed much.

Now, as he looked fixedly down upon the lovely face a curious change came over his own. More than once, without replying, he heard the piteous cry—sharp even to querulousness—"Shall I be drowned?" and then gently released himself from Letty's hold.

"My dear Miss Kenderdine, if any were drowned, there would be four. But I assure you nothing so tragical is likely to happen. Look at the line of sea-weed all along the shore; that is high-water mark; farther the tide will not advance."

"But the point—the point."

"Even at the point the water is not more than six inches deep. It could not drown you."

"But it will spoil my boots, my dress—every thing. Oh, Edna, how could you be so foolish as to let us come?"

Edna, indeed, did feel and look very conscience-smitten, till Dr. Stedman said, rather abruptly,

"There is no use regretting it, or scolding one another; we were all equally to blame. Don't let us waste time now in chattering about it."

"No, indeed. Let us get home as quickly as we can. Letty, take hold of me, and try to wade through."

But Letty, tall as she was, shrank in childish terror from the troubled waters, and several more precious minutes were wasted in conquering her fears, and finding the easiest passage for her across the sands. Meantime the line of sea-weed began to be touched—nay, drifted ominously higher and higher by each advancing wave, until Dr. Stedman noticed it.

"Look!" he said in an under-tone to Edna; "last tide may have been neap, but this is evidently a spring-tide. It makes a great difference. We must go on without losing more time. How shall we divide?"

"I'll help Letty."

"No, that is scarcely safe—two women together. Shall I take your sister, and you my brother? You can assist him best! Poor fellow! this is more dangerous for him than for any of us. Julius!" he called out, "don't waste more time; take Miss Edna and start."

Julius turned sharply upon his brother:

"Excuse me, but we have already made our plans. Come, Miss Kenderdine."

Will Stedman once more drew back, and would not interfere, but he looked seriously uneasy.

"What must be done?" he said again to Edna. "I wanted you to walk with Julius. She can not take care of him—she is too timid. She will only hang helplessly upon him, and drag him back when he ought to get on as fast as possible."

"Is there danger—real danger?"

"Not of drowning, as your sister thinks"—with a slight curl of the not too amiable mouth—"but of my brother's getting so wet and exhausted that his illness may return. Look! he is staggering now, the tide runs so strong. What can I do?"

"Go and help them. Get them safe home first."

"But you?"

"I can not cross by myself. I see that," said Edna, looking with a natural shiver of dread at the now fast-rising waves. "But I can stay here. I should not be afraid, even if I had to wait till the tide turns."

"That will be midnight. No, about eleven, I think."

"Even so, no harm will come to me; I can walk up and down this beach, or else I could clamber to that ledge on the cliff where the cliff-swallows are building. The highest tide could not reach me there. I'll try it. Good-bye."

She spoke cheerfully, reaching out her hand. Dr. Stedman grasped it warmly.

"You are the bravest and most unselfish little woman I ever knew."

"Then you can not have known many," said she, laughing; for, somehow, her courage rose. "Now, without another word, go."

He went, but returned again in a minute to find poor Edna clambering painfully to her ledge in the rock. He helped her up as well as he could, then she again urged him to leave her.

"I can not. It seems so wrong—quite cruel."

"It is not cruel—it is only right. You and I are far the strongest. We must take care of those two."

"I have taken care of him all my life, poor fellow!"

"That I can well believe. Hark! is Letty screaming? Oh, Dr. Stedman, never mind me. For pity's sake go and help them safe home."

"I will," said he, "and then I'll come back for you in a boat, if possible, only let me see you safe. One step more. Put your hand on my shoulder. You're all right now?"

"Quite right, and really very comfortable, considering."

"This will make you more so, and I don't need it."

He took off his coat and threw it up to her, striding off before she had time to refuse.

"Miss Edna!" and to her great uneasiness she saw him looking back once more. "You'll not be frightened?"

"Not a bit. Oh, please go!"

"Very well, I am really going now. But I'll never forget this day."

Edna thought the same.

CHAPTER VIII.

EDNA sat on her ledge of rock, to the great discomfiture of the cliff-swallows, for a length of time that appeared to her indefinite. She had no means of measuring it, for the very simple reason that the sisters had only one reliable watch between them, and, when it gave her no trouble, Letty usually wore it. Now, in her long, weary vigil, Edna's mind kept turning regretfully and with a childish pertinacity to this watch, and wishing she had had the courage—she did think of so doing once, and hesitated—to borrow Dr. Stedman's. It would have been some consolation, and a sort of companion to her, during the hour or two she should still have to wait before the tide went down. That was, supposing Dr. Stedman found it impossible to get the boat; which, when the evening began to close in, and still there was no sign of him, she thought must have been the case.

EDNA WAITING.

She was not exactly alarmed: she knew that the highest spring-tide could never reach the ledge where she sat—where the birds' marvellous instinct had placed their nests. Her position was safe enough, but it was terribly lonely; and when night came rapidly on, and she ceased to distinguish any thing except the momentary flashes of foam over the sea—for the wind had risen, and the white horses had begun to appear—she felt sadly forlorn—nay, forsaken. The swallows ceased their fluttering and chattering, and becoming accustomed to her motionless presence, settled down to roost; soon the only sound she heard was the waves breaking against the cliff beneath her feet. She seemed to hear them quite close below her: so the spring-tide must have been a high one; and she felt thankful for this little nook of safety—damp and comfortless as it was: growing more so, since, with the darkness, a slight rain began to fall.

Edna drew Dr. Stedman's coat over her shoulders, as some slight protection to her poor little shivering, solitary self: thinking gratefully how good it was of him to leave it, and hoping earnestly he had got home safely, even though in ignominious and discreditable shirt-sleeves. And, amidst all her dreariness, she laughed aloud to think how funny he would look, and how scandalized Letty would be, to see him in such an ungentlemanly plight, and especially to walk with him through the village. But while she laughed the moral courage of the thing touched her. It was not every gentleman who would thus have made himself appear ridiculous in a lady's eyes for the sake of pure kindness.

And then, in the weary want of something to occupy her mind and to pass the time away, she fell into vague speculations as to how all this was to end: whether Dr. Stedman really wished to marry Letty; whether Letty would have him if he asked her. One week would show; since, after Thursday, circumstances would be so completely changed with them all that their acquaintanceship must, if mere acquaintance, die a natural death. No "gentlemen visitors" could be allowed by the two young schoolmistresses; so that even though the Stedmans lived within a mile of them—which fact Edna knew, though they were not aware she knew it—still they were not very likely to meet. People in and near London often pass years without meeting, even though living in the next street. And if so—if this association, just as it was growing quite pleasant, were thus abruptly to end—would she be glad or sorry?

Edna asked herself the question more than once. She could not answer it, even to her own truthful heart. She really did not know.

But she soon ceased to trouble herself about that or any thing; for there came upon her a feeling of intense cold, also—let it not disgrace her in poetical eyes, this healthy-framed and healthy-minded little woman!—of equally intense hunger: during which she had a vision of the bread-and-cheese and beer lying on the parlor-table, so vivid and tantalizing that she could have cried. She began to agree with Dr. Stedman that it was rather cruel to have left her here—at least for so long—so much longer than she had anticipated.

Surely they had all got home safe by this time. Nothing had happened—nothing was likely to happen; for she had seen them with her own eyes cross safely the perilous point and enter upon the stretch of level sand. With a slightly sad feeling she had watched the three black figures moving on—two together and one a little apart—till they vanished behind a turn in the cliff. Beyond that nothing could be safer, though it was a good long walk.

"And that young man is weak still," thought Edna, compassionately. "Of course he could not walk quickly; and Letty never can. Besides, when she learned I was left behind she might have been unwilling to go home without me."

But while making this excuse to herself Edna's candid mind rejected it as a fiction. She knew well that, with all her good-nature, Letty was not given to self-denial: being one of those theoretically-virtuous people who are content to leave their heroisms to be acted out by some one else. But the doctor: he was a man—a courageous and kindly man, too. He surely would never leave a poor, weak woman to spend the night upon this dreary ledge of rock.

"He said he would bring a boat; but he may not be able to get one, or to pilot it in this darkness and among all these rocks. It would not be safe." And this thought conquered all her personal uneasiness. "Oh, I hope he will not try it. Suppose he did, and something were to happen to him! I wish I had told him I would wait till the tide went down. Rather than any risk to him I would have sat here till daylight."

And with a kind of vague terror of "something happening"—such terror as she had never felt concerning any one except Letty—nay, with her very slightly, for in their dull, peaceful lives had occurred none of those sudden tragedies which startle life out of its even course, and take away forever the sense of security against fate—Edna sat and listened for the sound of oars, of voices—of any thing; straining her ears in the intense stillness until the sensation became actual pain.

But she heard nothing except the lap-lap of the tide going down—either it was going down, for it sounded fainter every minute, or else she herself was sinking into a state of sleepy exhaustion, more dangerous than any danger yet. For if she fainted or dropped asleep she might fall from her narrow seat and be seriously hurt. She thought, should he come and find her there, lying just at his feet, with a limb broken, or otherwise injured, how very sorry Dr. Stedman would be!

All these fancies came and went, in every form of exaggeration, till poor Edna began to fancy her wits were leaving her. She drew herself as far back against the rock as possible, crouching down like a child, leaned her head back, and quietly cried. Then excessive drowsiness came over her: she must, for some minutes at least, have actually fallen asleep.

She was roused by hearing herself called: in her confused state she could not think where or by whom; and her tongue was paralyzed and her limbs frozen just as if she had the nightmare.

"Miss Edna—Miss Edna!" the shouting went on, till the cliffs echoed with it. "Where are you? Do answer—only one word!"

Then the voice ceased, and a light like a glow-worm began to wander up and down the rocks below. Edna tried to call, but could not make herself heard. The whole thing seemed a kind of fever-dream.

At length, sitting where she was, she felt a warm hand touch her. She uttered a little cry.

"You are alive," some one said. "Thank God!"

Though she knew it was Dr. Stedman, and tried her utmost to appear the brave little woman he had called her, Edna's strength failed. She could not answer a word, but fell into a violent fit of sobbing, in the which the doctor soothed her as if she had been a child.

"There now. Never mind crying—it will be a relief. You are quite safe now; I have come to fetch you home. Oh, if I could but have got back here a little sooner!"

And then Edna was sufficiently her natural self to ask eagerly if no harm had befallen Letty or his brother—if they were both safe at home?

"Yes, quite safe. But it was a long business. Twice I thought Julius would have broken down entirely."

"And my sister?"

"Your sister is perfectly well, only a good deal frightened."

"Was she very uneasy about me?"

"Not overwhelmingly so," said Will Stedman, with that slight hardness, approaching even to sarcasm, which came occasionally into his voice as well as his manner, giving the impression that if very good he was not always very amiable. "But come! we are losing time; and I have to get you safe home now. I have no boat. I was delayed; they were so long in reaching home that when I went after a boat the water was too shallow to make it available—the men refused it."

"How did you come, then?"

"I waded. But the tide is down now. We may easily walk—that is, if you can walk. Try."

Edna stretched her poor cramped limbs, and attempted to descend. But she grew dizzy; her footing altogether failed her.

"I can't stand," she said, helplessly. "You will have to leave me here till morning."

"Impossible."

"Oh no! Indeed, I don't much mind."

For in her state of utter exhaustion any thing—even to lie down there and die—seemed easier than to be forced to make a single effort more.

"Miss Edna," said the doctor, with all the doctor in his tone—calm, firm, authoritative—"you can not stay here.

You must be got home somehow. If you can not walk, I must carry you."

Then Edna made a violent effort, and succeeded in crawling, with both hands and feet, down the cliff-side to the level sands. But as soon as she stood upright and attempted to walk, her head swam round and consciousness quite left her. She remembered nothing more till she found herself lying on the sofa in their own parlor, opposite a blazing fire, with Letty—only Letty—sitting beside her.

"Mrs. Williams! oh, Mrs. Williams! come here! She's quite herself now. My sister—my dear little twin-sister! Oh, Edna, I thought you were dead. I have been near breaking my heart about you."

And Letty hugged and kissed her, and hung over her, and gave her all manner of things to eat, to drink, and to smell at—with an affection the genuineness of which was beyond all doubt. For Letty was no sham; she had a real heart, so far as it went, and that was why Edna loved her. All the better that it was a keen-eyed love, which never looked for what it could not find, and had the sense not to exact from the large, splendid, open-bosomed *Gloire de Dijon*, the rich depths of perfume that lie hidden in the red moss-rose.

"Yes, Letty dear, I must have frightened you very much," said she, clinging to her sister, and trying to recall, bit by bit, what had happened. "It must have been a terrible suspense for you. But indeed I could not help it. It was impossible for me to get home. How did I ever get home at all?"

"I don't know, except that Dr. Stedman brought you. You were quite insensible when he carried you in, and he had a deal of trouble to bring you to. Oh, it was such a comfort to have a doctor in the house! and he was so kind!"

"Where is he now?" And as Edna tried to raise her head a faint color came into her white face.

"He has just gone away. He said it was much better that, when you came to yourself, you should find nobody beside you but me—that he had to sit up reading till about three in the morning; and if you were worse I was to send for him—not otherwise. He told me not to frighten myself or you. He was not uneasy about you at all; you would soon recover, you were such an exceedingly healthy person. Indeed, Edna, he must be a very clever doctor: he seemed to understand you as if he had known you all your life."

Edna smiled, but she felt too weak to talk. "And you —how did you get home?"

"Oh, it was terrible business. I was so frightened. And that young Julius Stedman—he was no help at all. He is but a poor stick of a fellow for all practical purposes, and gets cross at the least thing. Still, when we reached home, and his brother started off again to fetch you, he was very kind also."

"I am sure he would be."

"He sat with me all the time we were waiting for you; I sent for Mrs. Williams, so it was quite proper—but, indeed, I was too miserable to think much about propriety. I only thought, What if you were drowned, and I were to lose my dear little sister—my best friend in all this world? Oh, Edna, Edna!"

And once again Letty kissed and embraced her, shedding oceans of tears—honest tears.

Mrs. Williams, too, put her apron to her eyes. She had grown "mighty fond" (she declared afterwards) of these two young ladies. She was certain they were real ladies, though they had only one bottle of wine in the cupboard, and their living was as plain as plain could be. So she, too, worthy woman! shed a few glad tears over Miss Edna's recovery, until Edna declared it was enough to make a person quite conceited to be thought so much of. And then, being still in a weak and confused state, she suffered herself to be carried off to bed by Mrs. Williams and Letty.

It was a novelty for Edna to be taken care of. Either she was very healthy—though so fragile-looking—or she did not think much about her own health, which is often the best method of securing it; but for years such a thing had not happened to her as to lie in bed till noon, and have Letty waiting upon her. It was rather pleasant than otherwise for an hour or two, until Letty began to weary a little of her unwonted duties, and Edna of the dignity of invalidism. So she rose, and, though still feeling dizzy and strange, crept down stairs and settled herself in her usual place, with her work-basket beside her.

There Dr. Stedman found her, when, having sent a preliminary message through Mrs. Williams, he came, in the course of the afternoon, to visit his patient.

His patient he seemed determined to consider her. He entered the room with a due air of mental gravity—nay, a little more formal than his customary manner—touched her pulse, and asked a few unimportant questions, after a fashion which quite removed the slight awkwardness which Edna felt, and was painfully conscious she showed, towards him.

"Yes, she will soon be quite well," said he, turning to Letty. "Your sister is thin and delicate-looking, Miss Kenderdine, but she will take a great deal of killing, she has such a thoroughly pure constitution. You need not be in the least alarmed about her. Still, I will just look after her for a day or two, professionally—I mean in an amateur professional way—if she will allow me."

Letty was overflowing with thanks. Edna remained silent. She disliked being Dr. Stedman's, or indeed any doctor's patient; but her position would have been still more difficult had he appeared to-day in the character of her brave preserver, who had waded through the stormy billows like a Norse hero, and carried her back in his arms—as she now was sure he had carried her, for he could have got her home in no other way. But he had said nothing about this, and, apparently, nobody had asked him. Nor did he refer to it now, for which reserve Edna was very grateful. She would not have known what to say, nor how to thank him, but his delicate silence on the matter made all things easy.

Likewise Letty, who was not given to penetrate too

deeply below the surface of things, seemed blessed with a most fortunate lack of inquisitiveness. She made no reference to last night, but sat talking sweetly to the doctor in the character of affectionate nurse and sister, looking the while so exquisitely lovely that Julius, who, on his brother's suggestion, had been invited in to see Edna, was driven to beg permission to make a sketch of her on the spot, in the character of a guardian angel.

Nobody objected—for the young artist was treated like a spoiled child by them all. And, as it was a wet day—so wet that nobody could think of going out, and every body would be dull enough in-doors—they agreed to share their dullness and spend the afternoon together; for, as some one suggested, their time was drawing short now.

So Julius brought in his sketch-book and fell to work. After a long discussion as to what sort of an angel Miss Kenderdine was to be made into, it was finally decided that she would do exactly as one of the Scandinavian Valkyriæ, who wait in the halls of Odin to receive the souls of the departed slain.

"Is that the business of guardian angels?" asked Will Stedman. "I should have thought they would have done better in taking care of the living than making a fuss over the dead."

Julius looked annoyed. "Pray excuse Will, Miss Kenderdine. He is not at all poetical; he always takes a matter-of-fact view of things. Now, just the head bent, with a pitying sort of expression, if you can manage it. Thank you—that will do exactly."

And Julius, with that keen, eager, thirsty look, which for the last few days had begun to dawn in his face, gazed at Letty Kenderdine, who smiled as usual, calm and moonlike. Even as Andrea del Sarto's Lucrezia might have smiled on him, and as dozens more as lovely women to the end of time will continue to smile, maddeningly, upon the two types of men with whom such charms are all-powerful—the sensualist, who cares for mere beauty, and it alone; the poet, who out of his own nature idealizes physical perfectness into the perfection of the soul.

But there is a third type which unites both these. Was it to this that William Stedman belonged?—that is, in his real heart, though his eyes might have been temporarily no wiser than his neighbors'.

He seemed a little changed in his manner since yesterday—graver, and yet franker and freer. He made no attempt to interfere with his brother's complete engrossment of Letty, though he watched the two very closely at intervals. This Edna saw, and drew her own conclusions therefrom; but they were erroneous conclusions. Nevertheless, they made her resolve more strongly than ever that with next Thursday this intimacy should entirely cease. That one or both of these brothers should fall in love with Letty was a catastrophe to be avoided, if possible. They were two good men, she was sure of that, and they should neither of them suffer if she could help it. No: just two days more, and the acquaintance with the Stedmans should come to a natural and fitting close.

This being decided, Edna threw herself unresistingly into the pleasures of it while it lasted. For it was a pleasure—she had ceased to doubt that. No good, simple-hearted, sensible woman could help enjoying the society of two such men, each so different, and yet each acting as a set-off to the other. Julius, when he flung himself into conversation, was not only clever but brilliant; William said little, but whatever he did say, he said it to the point. True, as his brother had accused him, he did now and then take a matter-of-fact view of things; but his matter-of-factness was neither stupid nor commonplace. He might be slow, or obstinate, or hard to please, but he was not a fool—not a bit of it; in spite of his grave and solid temperament, most people would have considered him an exceedingly clever man, in his own undemonstrative way.

So Edna thought. And since he chose to talk to her, she talked to him back again, and enjoyed the exercise. For there could hardly have been a greater contrast than these two. Edna Kenderdine, though so quiet, was not a passive, scarcely even a calm woman. Whatever she felt, she felt acutely. Life and energy, feeling and passion, quivered through every movement of her small frame, every feature of her plain but sensitive and spiritual face —more so to-day than usual, through the excitement left behind by her last night's peril. Also by another sort of excitement, for which she could not at all account, but which seemed to make her whole being thrill like a harp newly tuned, which the lightest touch causes to tremble into music.

She could not think how it was: she ought to have been miserable, leaving that pleasant place to go back to London, and work, and endless anxieties. Yet she was not miserable; nay, she felt strangely happy during the whole of this day, wet as it was, and through great part of the next day — except the hour or two that she occupied in packing.

There, in the solitude of her own room — for Letty, whose back was quite too long for packing, was sitting on the bench outside, between the two Stedmans—poor Edna felt just a little sad and dull. They had had such a happy time, and it was now over, or nearly over: ay, forever! —such times do not return. People say they will, and plan renewed meetings of the same sort; but these seldom come about, or if they do, things are different. Edna, in her level existence, had not known enough either of happiness or misery to feel keenly the irrecoverableness of the past; still she had sense enough to acknowledge that a time such as she and Letty had had for the last fortnight, so exceptional in its circumstances and its utter unworldliness of contentment, was never likely to occur twice in their lives.

First, because two hard-working, solitary women were never likely again to be thrown into such close yet perfectly harmless and blameless relations with two such young men as the Stedmans—thorough gentlemen, refined in act and word, never by the slightest shadow of a shade crossing the boundary of those polite and chivalric attentions which every man may honorably pay to every woman; men, too, whom they could so heartily respect, who apparently led a life as pure and simple as their own. At this time it was with the young men, as with the young women, such an innocently idle life. When they met again, if they ever did meet, they would all be in the whirl of London, absorbed in work—the restless, jarring, selfish work of the world—in which they might both seem and be quite different sort of people, both in themselves and to one another.

So thought Edna, as she hastened her packing in order to go down to the others—who did not seem to want her much, she fancied. Still, she wanted them: there were several things she would like still to talk about to Dr. Stedman, and why should she not talk to him as long as she could?

As she closed her trunk the heavy fall of the lid felt like closing a bright chapter in her existence. She had an instinct that such seasons do not come often, and that when they do they are brief as bright. She did not weep—this cheerful-hearted Edna, who had, and was always likely to have, enough to do and to think of to keep her from unnecessary grieving. She locked her box, having placed inside it the little mementos they were carrying home—a pebble which Letty had picked up on the beach, supposed to contain the possibility of a valuable brooch, if they could afford to have it cut and set; a piece of some queer sort of sea-weed which Dr. Stedman had given her, telling her that, if hung up in a dry place, it would prove a faithful barometer for months and years; also, pressed between her blotting-book's leaves, the very biggest of primroses, a full inch in diameter, which she had gathered in a competition with Julius Stedman. All these trifles, and a few more, which were nobody's business but her own, she locked up fast: but as she did so Edna sighed.

CHAPTER IX.

In this love-tale I find I am telling the story of the women more than of the men—which is not unnatural.

But, in truth, of the men there is as yet little to be told. Their passion had not arrived at the demonstrative stage.

Every thing they did was done quite as usual. No doubt they seized every opportunity of joining their fair neighbors—watched them out and in; met them constantly on the cliff and down the shore; contrived in short, by some means or other, to spend with them nearly the whole of the last three days; but beyond this they did not go. And even this was done by tacit understanding, without prior arrangements. Men are much more delicately reticent in love-affairs than women. Many women, even good women, will chatter mercilessly about things which a man would scorn to reveal, and think himself a brute to pry into.

On the Wednesday night the brothers had sat till ten o'clock in the Misses Kenderdine's parlor—the visits were always there. On no account would the sisters have penetrated into that bachelor sanctum, of which, in its chaos of bachelor untidiness, they had sometimes caught a glimpse through the open door—to Edna's pity and Letty's disdain. The young men themselves felt the contrast between their masculine chamber of horrors and the feminine sitting-room opposite, which, humble and bare as it was, looked always cheerful, neat, and nice.

"What a muddle we do live in, to be sure!" said Will, when they returned this last evening to their own parlor. But he sat down to his books, and Julius to his drawing, and there they both worked away till nearly midnight, without exchanging ten words.

At length Will rose and suggested his brother's going to bed.

"We have to be up early to-morrow, you know."

"Have we?"

Will smiled. "Didn't I hear you settling with the Misses Kenderdine to see them off by the coach? It starts at seven A.M."

"I said I would go; but that does not imply your going."

"Oh, I should like to go and see the last of them," said Will.

"It may not be the last. There is no necessity it should be. They live in London, and so do we."

"Do you know their address?" Will asked, abruptly.

"No. Do you?"

"Certainly not. They did not tell me, and I should have thought it a great piece of impertinence to inquire."

"Should you? Perhaps you are right. I assure you I have never asked them—though I intended to ask to-morrow. But one wouldn't do the ungentlemanly thing on any account. So I suppose, if they give us no special invitation to call on them, they will drift away like all the pleasant things in this world, and we shall never see them more."

Julius spoke sentimentally—nay, dolefully; but with a complete resignation of himself to fate, as was his character. He never struggled much against any thing.

Will moved restlessly among his books—piling and re-piling them in a vain effort at order. At last he let them be, and lifting up his head, looked his brother steadily in the face.

"Yes, I suppose at seven to-morrow morning we shall see the last of them. And I think it ought to be so."

"Why?" said Julius, sharply, taking at once the opposition side, as was also his character.

Dr. Stedman paused a minute before speaking, and the blood rose in his rugged brown face as he spoke.

"Because, Julius, in plain English, two young men can not go on in this sort of free-and-easy way with two young women—at least, not in any place but here, and not here for very long—without getting talked about, which would be very unpleasant. For the men it doesn't matter, of course, which makes it all the more incumbent on us to be careful over the women."

"Careful! What nonsense!"

"No, it isn't nonsense, though perhaps my speaking about it may be. But I've had it on my mind to speak, and it's better out than in."

"Very well, then. Preach away."

And Julius stretched himself along the sofa, his arms over his head, listening with a half-vexed, half-contemptuous air.

F

"Well, lad," said Will, stoutly, "I think that for a man, because he likes a girl's society, to daunder after her and hang on to her apron-strings till he gets her and himself talked about, is a piece of most arrant folly—not to say knavery; for he gets all the fun and she all the harm. It's selfishness—cowardly selfishness—and I won't do it! You may, if you choose; but I won't do it!"

"Do what?" said Julius, with an irritable and most irritating laugh. "What's the use of blazing up and striking your hand on the table as if you were striking me—which, perhaps, is what you're after? Come on, then!"

"Do you suppose I'm an idiot?"

"Or I either? What harm have I done? Was I going to offer myself on the spot to either of your fair friends? A pretty offer it would be! A fellow who has not a half-penny to bless himself with. Why, she'd kick me out of doors, and serve me right, too. No—no!" and Julius laughed again very bitterly: "I know women better than that. Pray compose yourself, Will. I'm not going to be a downright fool."

"You quite mistake me," said Will, gravely. "Any man has a right to ask the love of any woman—even if he hasn't a half-penny. But he has no right to pay her tender attentions, and set people gossiping about her, and perhaps make her fancy he likes her, when he either does not like her, or doesn't see his way clear to marry her. It's not to be done, lad—not to be done."

"And have I any intention of doing it? You foolish old fellow—what crotchets you take up! Why—hang it—if I had never flirted more than I have here—"

"I hate flirting," broke in Will, tearing a sheet of foolscap violently in two. "Women may like it; but men ought to have more sense. What's the use of philandering and fooling when you mean nothing, and it all ends in sheer waste of time? If ever I marry, I vow I'll go up to the woman and say, 'Mary' or 'Molly'—"

"Her name is Molly, then? That's information."

"I mean, I'd ask her point-blank to marry me. If she said 'Yes,' well and good."

"And if 'No?'" said Julius, with a keen look.

"I'd walk off, and never trouble her more. If a girl doesn't know her own mind, she isn't worth asking—certainly not asking twice. She never would be asked twice by me."

"Wait till your time comes—as you once said to your obedient, humble servant. Go on, Will. I'm waiting for another sermon, please. Plenty more where that last came from, I know."

Julius seemed determined to turn the whole into a laughing matter; and at last his brother was fain to laugh too.

"One might as well preach to a post—it always was so, and always will be! Come, I've said my say, and it's done. Let us dismiss the subject."

"Not a bit of it," replied Julius, who, with his other womanish peculiarities, had a most provoking habit of liking to have the last word; "only just tell a fellow what you are driving at. What do you want us to do about these girls? Shut ourselves up in our rooms, and stare at them from behind the key-hole without ever daring to bid them good-bye?"

"Rubbish! We'll just meet them, as you said, at the coach, wish them a pleasant journey, and there it ends."

"Does it?" said Julius, half to himself; while his soft, sad look wandered into vacancy, and he leaned his arm behind his head, in his favorite listless attitude, in which there was something affected and something real; his small, slight figure, dark, meagre face, and brilliant eyes, making equally natural to him both languor and energy. A true Southern temperament—made up of contrarieties, if not contradictions, and never to be reckoned on long together in any way.

But he ceased to argue, either in jest or earnest; and soon the two brothers parted for the night; quite amicably—as, after all their little warfares, they were in the habit of doing; for neither of them were of the sullen sort; and, besides, Will had a doctrine—learned at the big public school where he had been educated, fighting his way of necessity from bottom to top—that sometimes after a good honest battle, in which either speaks his mind, men, as well as boys, are all the better friends.

Julius went to bed. But far into the small hours Will's candle burned in the parlor below, as was his habit whenever he had spent a specially idle day.

Edna, too, sat up late, for to her always fell the domestic cares of packing, arranging, and settling every thing. Not that Letty did not try to help her; but she helped her so badly that it was double trouble—every thing had to be done over again. Letty's unconscious, good-humored incapacity was one of the things which tried her sister most, and caused her to hope that whenever the of-course-certain husband did appear, he might be a man sensible and practical, and sufficiently rich to make his wife independent of those petty worries which a cleverer and braver woman would breast and swim through, and perhaps even gain strength and energy from the struggle.

As it was, whenever they had any thing to do or to suffer, Edna's first thought was, how to get Letty out of the way. She had sent her to bed early, and, creeping in tired beside her, was only too thankful to find her sound asleep. And Letty slept still when in the gray dawn of the morning Edna woke, with the consciousness that something had to be done, or something was going to happen, which came with a sharp shock upon her the minute she opened her eyes.

She took her watch to the window to see the time correctly, and stood gazing out upon the sea, which lay so lonely and quiet—dim and gray—just brightened in the eastward by those few faint streaks in the sky which showed where the sun would rise ere long.

A strange unquietness came into Edna's spirit—hitherto as placid as that sea before the sun rose—a sense of trouble, of regret, for which she could not account. For though she was of course sorry to leave this place, still she might come back again some day. And now she was going home with Letty quite strong again, and herself also ready to begin their work anew. Why should she grieve? She ought to be very glad and thankful.

Perhaps she was only tired with the excitement of last night—when the two Stedmans had staid later and talked more than usual; pleasant, refreshing talk, such as clever, good men can make with good, and not stupid women; talk difficult to be detailed afterwards, if indeed any conversation written down does not seem as tame and lifeless as yesterday's gathered roses. But it had left a sweet aroma behind it, and while it lasted it had made Edna feel happy, like a creature long pent up in horrible cities, who is set free upon its native mountain, and led cheerily up the bright hill-side, at every step breathing a fresher and purer air; at every glance seeing around prospects wider and fairer; the sort of companionship, in short, which makes one think the better of one's self because one can appreciate it and enjoy it. How keenly she had enjoyed it Edna knew.

And now, with a slight spasm or constriction of the heart, she recognized that it was all over, that this morning was the very last day. She should probably never meet the Stedmans more.

She was not "in love." She did not for a moment fancy herself in love with either of them, being no longer of that unripe age when girls think it fine to be in love with somebody; but she was conscious that all was not right with her; that the past had been a delicious time, and that she began to look forward to her school-life, and her home-life, alone with Letty, with a sense of vacancy and dreariness almost amounting to dread. Be sorry for her, you who can understand this state of mind! And ye who can not—why, she had need to be sorry for you!

She stood looking at the sombre sea—at the smiling, hopeful dawn, then went back to her bed, and, hiding her face in the pillow, wept a few tears. But there was no time for crying or for sleeping; she had still a great deal to do, and they must leave soon after six; so, early as it was, she rose.

Her neighbors were early stirring too, though it was, after all, Will who accomplished this, rousing his brother into sufficient energy to be in time. The impulse of overnight had faded out, and Julius now seemed very indifferent whether or not he wished the sisters good-bye.

"If we are never to see them again, what does it matter to see them now?" said he, carelessly. "Or, indeed, what does it matter in any case? Women only care for fellows with lots of money."

"In one sense, perhaps—the matrimonial; but I thought we had decided that this was not the sense in which your civilities were to be construed."

"Our civilities, Will. You have been quite as sweet upon them as I have."

"Then there is no reason why our civilities should not be continued to the end. Get your hat, man, and let us start to the coach-office."

"Now?"

"Yes, now. We are better out of the way here. We'll not bother them with any last words."

And the doctor, who looked a little jaded, as if he had sat up most of the night—which indeed he had—contrived to stay out, and keep his brother out, on the breezy cliffs during the half hour that there was any chance of staircase meetings, or interference, for good or ill, with the proceedings of the Misses Kenderdine. But all this half hour the young men never once referred to their friends—or regretted their departure. They lounged about, read the newspaper, and talked politics a little, until, suddenly taking out his watch, Will said:

"Now, if we mean to be in time, we had better be off at once."

They walked up to the coach-office. In those days, and at that early season of the year, there was only a diurnal coach which passed through the village, taking up any chance passenger by the way. It was just the usual old-fashioned stage, with outside and inside places, and was rarely full; still, to-day, as it came lumbering up the hilly street, it looked to be so.

"Suppose they can't get seats," suggested Julius.

"Not impossible. I wish I had suggested their booking places over-night."

Small, trivial sentences about such a trivial thing!—save that all the manifold machinery of life hangs pivoted upon trifles.

The brothers found the two sisters standing waiting amidst a conglomeration of boxes, at which Julius shrugged his shoulders and winked aside at Will in thankful bachelorhood. But the four met and shook hands as usual, just as if they were starting for their conjoint walk this merry, sunshiny, breezy morning.

"What a fine day! I am glad you have good weather for your journey. We thought we might be allowed to come and see you off. Can we be of any use, Miss Kenderdine?"

Dr. Stedman addressed himself to Letty, who looked nervous and fidgety.

"Thank you, thank you. It is so troublesome, travelling; especially without a gentleman to take care of us. Edna, are you sure the boxes are all right? Did you count them? Two trunks, one bonnet-box, one—"

"Yes, all are right. Don't vex yourself, dear," said Edna, in her soft *sotto voce*, and then she was aware that Dr. Stedman turned to look at her earnestly, more earnestly than usual.

"Let me help you! you are carrying such a heap of cloaks and things, and you look so tired. Are you able for the journey to-day?"

"Oh yes, quite able. Besides, we must go."

Will made no reply, but he took her burdens from her, arranged her packages, and stood silently beside her till the coach came up.

Julius too, his languor and indifference dispersed as if by magic, placed himself close to the blooming Letty, paying her his final politenesses with remarkable *empressement*.

"Yes, I am sorry to leave this place," she said, in answer to his question. "We have had a pleasant time; and we are going back to horrid school-work. I hate it."

"No wonder. Still, your pupils are somewhat to be envied."

"Eh?" said Letty, not detecting the compliment, her

mind being divided between Julius, the boxes, and the approaching coach. "Look, Edna, it is quite full. We shall have to go inside—nay, the inside is full too. What must we do? Oh, Edna, what must we do?"

"It was my fault," said Will Stedman. "I ought to have told you it was better to secure places. Coachman, is there no chance whatever for these ladies?"

Coachman shook his head, remorseless as Fate; and Fate, laughing from under the coach-wheels, and making mouths at them from the dickey, set at naught all the excellent schemes of these four young people.

The two sisters regarded each other in mute consternation.

"How very, very foolish I was!" said Edna, in extreme vexation. "Can nothing be done? Dr. Stedman, will you think for us? We *must* go home to-day."

"Po'-chay, ma'am—po'-chay to Ryde," suggested the landlord.

"How much would that cost?"

A serious sum was named. Edna looked at and counted her money. No, it was not to be done. She saw Dr. Stedman watching her, and blushed crimson.

He came near her, and said, almost in a whisper, "Excuse me, but at a journey's end one sometimes runs short. If—"

Edna shook her head, and set her little mouth together, firm as Fate—whom she fancied she was thus resisting: at which Dr. Stedman blushed as deeply as herself, and retired.

There was no help for it. Several boats crossed daily from Ryde; but to get to Ryde from this out-of-the-way place was the difficulty.

"No, Letty," said Edna, "not being able to travel about in post-chaises, we must e'en put up with our misfortune. We can go by the coach to-morrow morning. I dare say Mrs. Williams will take us in for one night more. Things might be worse, you see."

But as she watched the coach roll away, Edna, though she spoke cheerfully, looked a great deal more annoyed and troubled than her sister did; and Dr. Stedman saw it.

"You have a tell-tale face," said he. "This has vexed you very much, I perceive."

"Of course it has. Many reasons made it important for us to go home."

"Your sister takes it easy enough, apparently."

"She always— " and Edna stopped herself. Why should she be discussing Letty with a stranger—with any body?

"I beg pardon," said Dr. Stedman, abruptly, and disappeared.

But when they had all escaped out of the condolences of the little crowd round the inn-door, and were ignominiously retracing their steps to Mrs. Williams's lodgings, he overtook them, breathless.

"Stop, Miss Edna. I have found a way out of your difficulties. There will be a post-chaise here at noon, bringing a wedding-couple from Ryde. It will take you the return-journey for merely coach-fare. If you cross at once you will be able to start from Portsmouth to London to-night. Will that do?"

"Admirable," said Edna, turning back. "Let me go and settle it at once."

"It is settled—I took the liberty of settling it with the landlord, whom I know. Always provided you were satisfied. Are you?"

"Quite."

"Thank you. And now you have only to repay me the coach-fare—inside places for two," said the doctor, holding out his hand with a smile.

Edna laughingly and, as it occurred to her long after, most unsuspiciously, gave him the money; and he walked on beside her, receiving silently her expressions of gratitude. She did indeed feel grateful. It was so new to her to have the burdens of daily life thus taken off her, and in such a considerate way, simply a man doing a man's part of kindness to a woman—nothing more. It made her remember his words: "If I had had a sister I would have been so good to her." Though while Edna recalled them, there was a strange sting in the remembrance.

At the familiar door they all stopped, rather awkwardly, till Dr. Stedman said, with something beyond his usual formality:

"I wonder, Julius, if these ladies would consider it presumption in us to offer them our bachelor hospitality for the next few hours? It might be more convenient, and they would at least get a dinner."

"Oh, they must—they must," cried Julius. "Say you will, Miss Edna," and he caught hold of her hand in his boyish, affectionate way. "Come and dine with us; it will be such fun. And we will go a long walk before then. Oh, I am so much obliged to Fate and that grim coachman! We'll have such a jolly day!"

He was evidently in a state of considerable excitement, which relieved itself in almost puerile pranks, and incessant flow of talk, and a pettish assertion of his own will, which was, as Edna declared, "exactly like a baby." Nevertheless, she and the others only laughed, and gave way to him.

Evidently the catastrophe about the coach had produced in none of the little party any permanent depression; and it was with almost exuberant spirits that they prepared to make the very most of this sweet, stolen day—all the sweeter, Julius insisted, because it was stolen—a clear robbery out of the treasure-house of Destiny, who had not many such.

"At least not for us," added he, with the dash of melancholy which ran through his merriest moods. "So I'll take the residuum of my pleasures as I used to take the spoonful of sugar at the bottom of an emptied coffee-cup, which I was always told it was such ill-manners to touch, though it was the best bit of the draught. And yet we have had a good draught of happiness this fortnight—have we not, Miss Edna? Our coffee of life was thoroughly well-made—strong and clear, with plenty of milk in it."

"The milk of human kindness?"

"Yes; and some water too. We had only too much water on Monday night. But I beg your pardon." For Edna still turned pale, and then red, whenever there was the slightest allusion to her painful adventure; so that now all reference to it had tacitly ceased.

"I think," said Dr. Stedman, "since our friends have gained an extra day of sea-air they had better make use of it. So come away all of you down to the shore."

There they wandered for hours, as merry as children, tossing the shingle at one another, or entombing themselves in it as they sat; writing names and sentences with umbrella-sticks on the sand, or building out of it castles and moats for the incoming tide first to fill and then to wash away. Some mixture of seriousness there was; for sea-side folly has always a touch of solemnity in it; and there is but a step between the babyish pranks on the sand and the awfulness of the silent ocean beyond. But still, whatever they did, or whatever they talked about, these four were very happy. It was a day—one of those single, separate days which stamp themselves upon the memory for years, both from their heavenly beauty, externally, and their moral atmosphere of pleasantness and peace. A day never to be forgotten in its innocent Arcadian enjoyment, to which all things seemed natural; and they themselves felt not like modern work-a-day men and women, but creatures of some perfectly ideal world—shepherds and shepherdesses of some long-past golden age.

They dined, nevertheless—upon cold mutton and suet dumplings, which was the best Mrs. Williams could provide; and they dined heartily and merrily. It might have been a little "incorrect," this bachelor entertainment to two young maiden ladies. In the midst of the meal a grave doubt of this struck Edna; but it was a merry meal, for all that, with not one bit of sentiment about it, or regret that it was the first and last. For still, with all their mutual friendliness, the sisters withheld their address, and the brothers were too courteous to ask for it.

Suddenly, in midst of the gayety, Dr. Stedman said, "It is nearly three. Your carriage will be at the door in five minutes." And for that five minutes every body was rather silent.

Edna sat at the window, taking a farewell look at the

beautiful sea; and Dr. Stedman came and looked at it with her.

"You are better now than in the morning, I hope?"

"Yes, the salt air always does me good."

"It will be very late before you reach home to-night. Are you afraid?"

"Oh no."

"You seem afraid of nothing."

"Not of many things—outside things. Why should I be? And it would do no good. I am not like a carefully-guarded young lady; I am a poor school-mistress, who, whether she likes it or not, must face the world."

"Do you find that very hard?"

"Sometimes—only sometimes; for I am young and strong, and not given to despondency. It may be otherwise when I get older."

And a vague cloud came over Edna as she spoke; a fear that it not only might but would be thus; that the days would come when her strength would fail, and her courage sink, beaten down; when she would be dull, weary, lonely, and old.

"Are you afraid of growing old?" said Dr. Stedman again. "I am—a little."

"Why should you be?" said Edna, forgetting the question in the confession, and turning to look inquiringly at him. "Old age can have no terrors for you. A man is so different from a woman."

"He is—horribly different—in some things. Miss Edna—I would give the whole world if I were more like you."

These words, spoken in a tone that seemed at once appealing, apologizing—nay, almost caressing, so low and soft was it, quivered through Edna from head to foot. But before she had time to answer or think of answering, the post-chaise was at the door—a goodly equipage—all in its bridal splendor—white favors and all.

Letty jumped up in delight. "Oh, how nice! We shall get to Ryde so comfortably. And think of our starting from the very door. So kind of you to order it, Dr. Stedman. It is almost as good as if we had our own carriage. Ah, Edna! shall we ever have our own carriage?"

"Possibly—I should say not improbably," said Dr. Stedman, dryly, as he handed the beautiful woman, with careful courtesy, to the chaise, which she seemed to step into as if she were born to a carriage.

Julius hung back, and made his adieux with a cynical air.

"Mrs. Williams thinks the white favors a lucky omen, Miss Kenderdine. She hopes to see one or both of you two young ladies back again ere long—in a similar equipage. I trust the owner may be a duke at least."

"Eh?" said Letty, not comprehending, but smiling still.

"Mrs. Williams says, next time you come here, she hopes it will be in your own carriage, and married to some rich gentleman—possibly a duke."

Letty bridled. "Oh, Mr. Stedman, you are so funny! Good-bye!"

So they parted—all four with the smile on their lips, shaking hands cordially, and keeping up their jests even to the last moment; expressing all manner of mutual good wishes, but not a hint or hope of future meetings. They parted—as completely as two ships that had crossed one another's track in the mid-ocean—paused alongside for a short space of kindly greeting—then divided, steadily and finally, to sail on round the world their several and opposite ways.

Edna knew it must be thus—that it was best it should be. Some instinct, forestalling experience, warned her of the fact—proved fatally by how many wrecked lives!—that men ought to be nothing to women, and women nothing to men, except in the merest ordinary friendship—unless they are either akin by blood, or deliberately choose one another in love and marriage: that all so-called "Platonic attachments," sentimental compromises which try to steer clear of both, and institute pseudo-relations which nature never meant, almost always end in misery—blameless, but still heart-deep, life-long misery. Edna wished to avoid every thing of the kind—both for herself and her sister. Nothing had happened; nobody had proposed to Letty, and she was thankful thus peacefully, friendly, and kindly to close all associations with the Stedmans.

Yes, they had parted just as (she said this to herself again and again during the long drive)—just as she most desired them all to part—like ships on the ocean, never to sail in company again. Still, she felt that for some days to come her own little vessel would sail rather drearily, and flap its canvas idly in the breeze, scarcely noticing whether or not there was sunshine on the sea, which looked so limitless, and yet which she must cross—and cross alone.

"I wonder," she thought to herself, "which of us will grow old the fastest or live the longest—Dr. Stedman or I?"

CHAPTER X.

KENSINGTON twenty years ago was not like the Kensington of to-day. It seemed much quieter and farther from London. No great Exhibitions had beaten down the smooth grass of Hyde Park and stamped out the green lanes of Brompton, which then formed a barrier between "the old court suburb," as Leigh Hunt tenderly calls it, and the metropolitan vortex. Down the long, dusty miles of the Knightsbridge road crawled a few uncomfortable omnibuses—forming the chief communication with London—except for those fortunate people who had carriages of their own. Consequently, to middle-class respectability, Kensington was a rather retired place. Townified, certainly, but then its queer winding streets, its old-established shops and old-fashioned houses, above all, its palace and ancient church, gave it a dignified quaintness which half atoned for the want of the country. And but a little way beyond it were many ruralities: lanes and gardens, haunted by larks in the day-time and nightingales at eve; here and there a real field—not yet become a brick-field; and several "lovers' walks," where, between the tall hedge of May or wild roses, young people thus circumstanced might exchange a kiss safely and unobserved.

About half a mile from where the Misses Kenderdine lived was a canal, along the banks of which ran a slip of waste ground, where bloomed as if by stealth many a real country flower: bind-weed—the little pink creeping sort and the large white one, that in late summer mounts the hedges and stars them with its dazzling, short-lived bells; abundance of those flowers which grow on commons and waste ground—bright yellow hawk-weed, and the delicate primrose-tinted kind; with various tiny plants, pleasant enough to observant eyes, and of which there used to be plenty in these regions, till London, gradually growing, has forced them to give place to coarser weeds.

To this place Edna often came, between or after school-hours, to fancy herself in the country and get a breath of air, for the sisters' house was somewhat small and close. Not that it was an ugly house; creepers, jasmine, and grape-vine half covered it, and it was open, front and back, to a view of market-gardens. Nobody can find it now—it has been completely swept from the face of the earth; pulled down and built upon, with all its surroundings. Year by year genteel terraces and squares are growing where the cabbages—acres of them—once grew. So if I say, with the lingering tenderness that its inhabitants also learned to speak of it, that it was not an ugly house, there is no one who can contradict me.

It boasted three stories, of two rooms each, the most important of which were the sitting-room, the drawing-room above, made into a school-room, and a large (or they called it large) bedroom overhead, where the two sisters slept. Thus, at a glance, may be seen their small establishment, of which the only other inmates besides themselves were one servant and a cat. A very microscopic, maidenly establishment, simple even to poverty, and yet it had its happiness—to Edna at least—for it was their own. Every atom of furniture had been bought with their own money—bought and paid for—which is more than can be said of many magnificent mansions. Every corner, from attic to basement, was theirs to do with as they liked. And to these governesses, who had lived for years in other people's houses, any nook they could call their own and do what they chose in, possessed a certain charm, of which the novelty was not even yet exhausted. In this nest of theirs, narrow as it was, the two sisters had not been unhappy—Edna especially had been the merriest little bird —till now.

It chanced that after the pleasant spring came a very hot summer; weeks of settled drought. By August the leaves were almost burnt off the trees, and the dusty, languid air that seemed to creep, or rather to stagnate, over the lanes and market-gardens, and the line of road between Kensington town and Holland House, was almost stifling, even at twilight, when Edna insisted on their going out, just for health's sake.

"Oh, Edna," Letty would say, drearily, as she crawled along the heated pavement and looked up at the handsome houses, nearly all with closed windows—"every body is gone out of town. Why can't we go too? It's very hard for us to be teaching school here when all the world is away at the sea-side. I wish we were there also. Don't you?"

"No," replied Edna. "One holiday is enough for one year. No."

But she knew she was telling a falsehood; that in her heart of hearts she had a frantic longing for the sight of the sea, for the sound and smell of briny waters, lapping on shingle and sand, for even a handful of sea-weeds, damp, salt, and living—not like that poor dead mummy of a sea-weed that still hung up in a corner of the room, though Letty had begged her more than once to take it down, it looked so "nasty," for its meteorological powers had signally failed. Yet still she let it hang there—a thing that had missed its destiny, and was of no mortal use to any body—except as a memento of a very pleasant time.

That pleasant time had passed out of all memories. Even Letty scarcely mentioned it now—three months was far too long for Letty to remember any thing or any body. At first she had found home extremely dull, had talked incessantly of the Isle of Wight and of the two Stedmans, wondering whether they had come home—if when they did come they would make any effort to renew the acquaintance.

"It would be possible, nay, easy, to find out our address, for our boxes were marked 'Kensington,' and there is the post-office to inquire at. If I were they I would hunt us out, and call. In which case, Edna, you know, we must be polite to them. They might mean nothing."

"Probably not. What would you wish them to mean?"

"How sharp you are with me! Of course, if Dr. Stedman did call upon us two single ladies, he could have but one intention in doing so. Not that he ever gave me any reason to suppose any thing," added Letty, looking down with her half smile, that implied an expectation of being contradicted in her assertion. But no contradiction came.

"Of course, a man so poorly circumstanced couldn't be expected to come forward at once; but then you see—"

Edna would see nothing. Every time the conversation took this turn she resolutely avoided it: to speak her mind, or to open her heart to this her only sister, became every day more impossible. Not that there was less affection between them, but there was a clearer perception and a sadder acceptance of the great difference in thought and feeling, which sometimes happens—that alienation of nature which no nearness of blood can atone for, or prevent, or cure.

Sometimes, when in the long bright June evenings Letty persisted in walking out regularly—not down the actual street where Dr. Stedman lived (Edna knew it well, and kept half a mile from it always), but up and down the long green alleys of Kensington Gardens, looking round at every corner, and fancying every tall figure—or two figures, a taller and a shorter—must surely be the two Stedmans—the patient elder sister would grow excessively irritable, and then Letty, who was invariably good-tempered, would wonder at her, and fear she was not well, and pet her and caress her in a fashion harder to bear than the interminable talkativeness.

But when week after week crept by, and the Stedmans gave no sign, Letty's interest in her lost admirer or admirers died out. Besides, school-time began, and the small worries of the present completely extinguished the past. Then, when her sister seemed quite to have forgotten them, poor Edna's memory of those happy sea-side days woke up with a vividness quite horrible in its pain, and in its sharp consciousness of what that pain was, whence it arose, and to what it tended.

I will tell no untruth about my poor Edna, nor make any pretenses concerning her, which she herself would have been the first to scorn. I believe that no woman, gifted with common sense and common feeling, ever "falls in love," as the phrase is, without knowing it: at least not when the love comes suddenly, and for one who heretofore has been a stranger, so that no gradual previous relations of intimacy have disguised the true state of things for a while, as sometimes occurs. She may refuse to acknowledge the fact, even to herself; but she knows it—knows it at the very core of her heart—in all its sweetness, and in all its bitterness too.

Long before those three months had gone by, Edna Kenderdine, who had met so few men, and had never taken the smallest interest in any man, began to find out that she was never likely again to meet such an one as Dr. William Stedman—never likely, in all her future life, to have such a happy fortnight as that she spent in the Isle of Wight, when her anxiety for her sister was over, and she and Letty were roaming about the sweet country and pleasant sea-shore, and meeting the two Stedmans every day and all day long.

Only a fortnight—fourteen days—a short time on which to build—or to wreck—a life's happiness; yet many have done it before now, and will do it again. Fate sometimes compresses into a few days the events and experience of years. People love in divers ways, and marry under infinitely varied circumstances, concerning which no person can judge, or has a right to judge, any other; yet there is but one true love—leading to the one perfect marriage, or else leading through dark and thorny yet sacred ways to that perpetual virginity of heart and life which is only second to marriage in its holiness and happiness.

This love had come to Edna, and she knew it.

She did not fall into romantic ecstasies of joy or grief over it, though let not even these be condemned; they are natural in the time of passionate youth—the Juliet-time. But Edna was a woman—not a girl, though her heart was as fresh as if she were sixteen. She said nothing—she betrayed nothing; externally she was the school-mistress only; but within she was conscious of the great change which only comes once in a lifetime, and after which no woman is ever quite the same again.

Of her lover—or her love, a tenderer and nobler name—she did not sit and think all day long—her days were too busy for that; but she thought of him in every idle or solitary minute, and often when neither idle nor alone; till day by day she learned to mingle him in all her doings and all her dreams. Him—the one "him" in the world to her now, whom by a magic sympathy she seemed already to understand, faults and all, better than any other human being she had ever met.

For she did not think Dr. Stedman faultless; she had seen in him a good many things she would have liked different, and had to apologize for—shortcomings of temper, roughness, and hardness, which seemed the result of circumstances. Still he was himself drawn to her, or rather she to him, by a strange attraction, and, as a whole, very near her ideal of what a man should be.

But it is idle reasoning about such things, and soon Edna ceased to reason, and was content only to feel. All the stronger because in her intense humility it never occurred to her that the feeling could be reciprocated. She accepted with a strong, silent courage the lot which had befallen her—a great misfortune, some would say. But she did not call it so, though she recognized to the full its sadness, hopelessness, and — no, she was not so cowardly as to add, its humiliation.

She had done nothing wrong in loving, even though she loved a man who had never asked her to marry him, who had apparently no intention of asking her, whom, in all human probability, she would never meet again. Well, let it be so; she had met, for once in her life, the man who she felt could have satisfied her whole heart, reason, conscience—whom, had he asked her, she would have married, and whom otherwise she would remember tenderly to the day of her death. This is, next to a thoroughly happy marriage, the best lot which can befall any woman.

I linger over Edna Kenderdine because I like to linger over her, just here: the picture of a woman who is brave enough to love, unloved, the best and highest; embodied to her, as it was to her mother Eve, in a man. For Milton's celebrated line,

> "He for God only, she for God in him,"

is so far true that no woman can love either lover or husband perfectly, unless—in a sense—she sees God in him, and sees in him, beyond herself, the desire for God only. And if so, her love is neither an unhappy nor an unfortunate love, however it may end.

One fact proved incidentally how utterly removed from the selfishness of all personal feeling was this ideal admiration, this self-existent, up-looking, and outloving love which had taken such sudden and strong hold of Edna's heart, and after lurking there awhile, sprung up, forced into being not by the sunshine of hope, but by the warm darkness of complete though quiet despair. The possibility—which Letty's vanity had taken for granted—of Dr. Stedman's attentions being to herself, awoke in her sister's mind no jealousy or dread—indeed no sensation of any kind. In those early days—when she was so ignorantly happy—Edna had thought the matter over in all its bearings, and set it aside as a mistake. For had he really fallen in love, there was no reason why he should not have spoken, nor why afterwards he should not have hunted

Letty out and followed her to the world's end. Edna thought, if she were a man, she would have done so. She could imagine no hinderance strong enough to prevent a man who really loved a woman from seeking her out, wooing her, and carrying her off triumphant—like one of the old Paladins—in face of all the world.

Yet all these three months William Stedman had lived close by them, and given no sign of his existence. Therefore, of course, there was but one conclusion to be drawn. Letty, she supposed, had come to it likewise, or else had forgotten the whole matter—Letty could so easily forget!

Still, this summer was a dull time with poor Letty Kenderdine. After the fever, pupils were naturally slow of returning; the sisters were likely to be very poor this half year. Edna did not care much for the fact; but she tried to make things as easy as she could to Letty, whom want of money always affected keenly with a hundred small wants and petty humiliations, which her sister, if unable to sympathize with, felt heartily sorry for. She taxed her ingenuity to lighten Letty's school-duties, and out of school to invent inexpensive amusements for her; but still the dullness remained. Only dullness; certainly not disappointed love, for Letty spoke more than once of accepting her latest offer from an Australian sheep-farmer, once the boy-brother of one of her pupils, whose ardent admiration had gone so far as to entreat her to come out to Geelong and marry him. And so Edna, who, in her simplicity, could not conceive the possibility of liking one man, and in the remotest degree contemplating marriage with another, became quite satisfied as to the state of her sister's affections.

Thus they went on, teaching school daily, and spending the time as well as they could after school-hours, generally in the arduous duty of making ends meet, until the leaves which had budded out in that happy, merry springtime in the Isle of Wight began to change color, wither, and fade.

"How fast the year slips by!" said Letty, drearily, one half-holiday when she sat at the window, with nothing to do but to look over the long flat of market-gardens, and wish she was anywhere but where she was. "I declare, to-day is the last day of the band playing in Kensington Gardens, and we have never yet been to hear it. It is your fault, Edna. Why wouldn't you let us go?"

The question was not easy to answer. There was, of course, the obvious reason that Letty was too beautiful a person to promenade much in so public a place without father or brother; but Edna's conscience told her this was not the only reason why she had so persistently resisted such a very harmless amusement.

She knew quite well, that if by walking twenty miles she could, herself unseen, have caught one glimpse of William Stedman — resting her weary, thirsting eyes on his brown face, which might not be handsome, yet was so manly, gentle, honest, and good—she would eagerly have done it. That even the dim remote possibility of seeing him — his tall, sturdy, erect figure, turning round some street corner—a common Kensington street—sanctified to her even those dusty pavements and ugly roads. Sometimes the craving only to know that he was alive—alive and well—pursuing his duties, which she knew were so close to his heart, working at his profession, and carrying out nobly his useful, beneficent life, without the remotest thought of herself, came upon poor Edna with a force that was almost maddening in its pain. But, at the same time, the chance of really seeing him, of meeting face to face, and being obliged to bow, or to shake hands and speak to him, in the visible flesh—him of whom she thought night and day—was to her an apprehension almost amounting to terror. The mere thought of it often, in her walks, made her heart stand still a minute, and then go on beating so violently that she scarcely knew where she was or what she was doing. Therefore she had contrived always to avoid that band promenade, where Kensington young men might naturally take an afternoon lounge, and where Julius Stedman had once said he was rather fond of going.

But this day Letty was so persistent, that, with a kind

of fear lest her secret reason should be betrayed, Edna ceased resistance, and they went.

Only, however, for one or two turns, during which she looked straight before her, and deported herself as grimly as possible towards the fops and fashionable idlers who never failed to stare at the tall beautiful woman and her unobtrusive companion. Only two turns; but even these were one too many. At the second, Fate came, dead front, to meet the sisters.

"There they are! Don't look, Edna; don't let them fancy we see them; but there are the two Stedmans."

Edna's heart gave a wild leap, every thing seemed turning round and round for a minute, then she gathered up her senses, and recovered her strong self-control, which had never failed her yet. Happily, her veil was down; but Letty's careless eyes roved everywhere rather than to her sister's face. Had it been different, still Edna would have been safe. Usually tears and blushes came readily to that sensitive little face, which changed its expression half a dozen times in a minute; but when any thing smote her hard, Edna neither blushed nor wept, but grew perfectly white, and as quiet as a stone. She did so now.

"The Stedmans, is it? You are right, Letty, we will not look. They are not likely to see us. They are passing on."

And they did pass on, their attention being caught by some acquaintance on the other side of the promenade, to whom they stood talking for some time.

That while, the eyes Dr. Stedman did not see—the sad, fond, lingering eyes—had seen him—vividly, distinctly; had noticed that he was a good deal thinner, paler, graver—very unlike his former self; until in talking he chanced to smile, and then Edna recognized it again fully—the face stamped indelibly upon her memory.

Perceiving he was fully occupied, and that there was no possibility of his noticing her, she looked at him once again, with a quiet, sad feeling—"God bless him; no man is any the worse for a woman's loving him"—and turned away.

As soon as she could she lured Letty out of the crowd into one of those green alleys that abound in Kensington Gardens, in sight of the queer old red brick palace, with its Dutch garden, where, long ago, the courtiers of William and Mary, and the maids of honor of Queen Anne, and the first two Georges, may have strolled and coquetted and made love—the old, old story! In their long-effaced footsteps walked the lovely Letty Kenderdine, as fair as any of them, and talking, perhaps, not greater nonsense than they had talked.

"Well, I must say it was strange," said she. "It only shows how easily men forget. To pass me by within a few yards, and never even see me!"

"They were talking to some gentlemen."

"Oh, but people always see those they want to see. Perhaps I ought to have bowed. You know they could not come and speak to us unless we bowed first. And how nice and gentlemanly they both looked, especially Julius! Really Julius is a very handsome young fellow, now he is quite well. I suppose he is quite well by this time."

"He looked so." And Edna felt glad partly for his own sake, but more for his brother's. That anxiety at least was over. And then she let her imagination wander wildly as to what could be the secret trouble which showed plainly on Dr. Stedman's face, and had altered him so much. The desperate longing to comfort him, to take part of his burden, whatever it might be, came upon her, sad and sore.

So much so, that she never heard footsteps behind, nor guessed what was going to happen, until Letty called out in her loud whisper:

"Goodness me! There they are."

And at an angle of the path the two brothers and two sisters met, face to face, abruptly and unexpectedly, so as to make non-recognition, or the half-recognition of a formal bow, impossible. They were all evidently taken by surprise. Involuntarily they stopped and shook hands. Not without a certain awkwardness in the greeting, probably caused by the suddenness of their rencontre; but after the first minute it passed off. In spite of all the good resolutions on both sides, every body seemed unfeignedly glad to meet.

The two young men turned back with them in the old familiar way; Julius by Edna, Dr. Stedman by Letty, until with some slight excuse Julius crossed over to the latter, and his brother fell behind with Edna. Thus they went, walking slowly, the whole way up the broad walk to the Bayswater Gate. The younger brother and sister began laughing and talking immediately, Julius making himself agreeable in his old light way, as if it were but yesterday that he had carried on the same pleasant badinage on the Isle of Wight shore; but the two others were rather silent.

Dr. Stedman asked Edna a few questions as to her sister's health and her own; if they had had no return of scarlet-fever in the house, and if their pupils had come back; to all of which she replied quietly, briefly, and categorically; then he seemed to have nothing more to say. And, far in the distance, they heard the faint sound of the band playing, and one or two straggling groups of gayly-dressed people passed them, chattering and flirting—a great contrast to this quiet, silent pair.

Very silent, very quiet outside, but beneath that—?

Many people might call it wrong for an unsought woman—a tender, sweet, reticent maiden—to feel as Edna felt, walking along beside him who, she now knew, was the lord of all her life. But there was no wrong in her heart. She had no hope of being wooed or married by Dr. Stedman; she only loved him. She only felt that it was heaven to be near him—to catch again the sound of his voice—to rest again in the protection of his honest goodness. Oh that protection! the one thing a woman needs—even a woman so brave as Edna Kenderdine. As for herself, she thought if she could only serve him, tend him, do him good in any way; ay, in the pathetic way of some ballad-heroine she had read of—making the house ready for his bride, and helping to rear and cherish his children

—it would have been not hard, but happy to have done it; for he seemed, now she saw him again, just as heretofore—unlike all others, simplest, noblest, best; truest man and most perfect gentleman—one worth living for—worth dying for.

She idealized him a little: women always do that; but William Stedman was a great deal that she believed; and for her idealizing, perhaps it did no harm. Men so loved not seldom grow to be as good as the fond women believe them.

At the Bayswater Gate Dr. Stedman paused.

"This is our best way home. Will you come, Julius?"

"Certainly not; I have not half talked out my talk. Do you turn? Then so shall we—with your permission, Miss Kenderdine."

Letty bowed a smiling assent. After her long fast from flirtation she was all graciousness, even to the "boy" Julius, as she persisted in considering him, though he was exactly her own age. So the two couples strolled back again to the palace, and then across the grass to the little gate which led to Kensington High Street.

"Here we really must take our leave," said William Stedman, decisively. "I have an appointment; and besides, Julius—" he added half a dozen inaudible words, which his brother did not answer, but turned sharply away.

Then Edna came forward, very dignified. This little woman could be dignified when she chose, in spite of her few inches.

"Indeed, Mr. Stedman, we will not trouble you to accompany us any farther. We have a call to make in Kensington. Good-bye."

She held out her hand—first to Julius, and then to his brother.

"Well, that is the coolest dismissal," said the former. "Must it be? Do you really agree to it, Miss Letty?"

But Miss Letty was making elaborate adieux to Dr. Stedman, and did not hear. Besides, she very rarely contradicted Edna. Her easy nature always yielded to the stronger will; it was least trouble. But when they had really parted from their cavaliers she was a little cross.

"Why on earth were you so peremptory, Edna? They wanted to see us home."

"Did they?"

"At least Julius did. And why not? It would have been rather amusing. If we ever meet them again, and perhaps we may, for Mr. Stedman says they always take their constitutional in Kensington Gardens—we ought to treat them a little more civilly, and let them see us home if they desire it."

Edna replied not, but the small mouth set itself closely together. No. Letty might say what she liked—fancy what she chose, but this should not be. Dr. Stedman should never think that either she or her sister were girls ready to meet the first advances of any idle youth. Love was no disgrace; it did nobody any harm; but the feeble pretense of it—flirtation or philandering—was a thing which this woman, pure and true, yet passionate-hearted, utterly scorned. If the Stedmans wanted to marry Letty—either of them—they must come and ask for her as a man should ask—and is a coward if he dare not ask under any circumstances.

Letty—always Letty. That the object of their admiration could be any other when Letty was by did not occur to Edna. And when Letty took her bonnet off, and shook back her bright fair hair, and looked into the glass with her eyes glittering with the novel excitement of the day, Edna thought the universal admiration her sister excited was not wonderful. If Dr. Stedman shared it—if that was the cause of his silence and evident preoccupation—well!

Edna stood a minute to face this thought. She was alone. Letty had gone down stairs, all smiles and excitement; at least, as much excitement as she was capable of—quite another woman after the afternoon's adventure, which was such a pleasant break in their dull life. Was it only that, or did she really care for one or other of the

Stedmans? And if one of them really asked her, would Letty marry him?

Such a possibility might occur. The man Edna loved might marry another, and that other her own sister: a supposition maddening enough to many—nay, most women. Even to this gentle little woman it gave the same sudden "stound"—which had come to her several times lately. She closed her eyes, drew a long hard breath, tried to stifle the choking in her throat, and to view her position calmly.

Jealousy, in any of its ordinary forms, did not affect her; her nature was too single, too entirely free from both vanity and self-consciousness. No wound could come to her through either of these points—nothing except simple sorrow, the agony of lost love. Besides, she was accustomed to view things in the plain daylight, without any of those distorted refractions to which egotistic people are subject. She saw that in such a case as hers there are but two ways open to any woman. If she loves a man and he does not love her, to give him up may be a horrible pang and loss, but it can not be termed a sacrifice—she resigns what she never had. But if he does love her and she knows it, she is bound to marry him, though twenty other women loved him, and broke their hearts in losing him. He is not theirs, but hers; and to have her for his wife is his right and her duty. And in this world are so many contradictory views of duty and exaggerated notions of rights, so many false sacrifices and renunciations weak even to wickedness, that it is but fair sometimes to uphold the *right* of love—love sole, absolute, and paramount, firmly holding its own, and submitting to nothing and no one—except the laws of God and righteousness.

"Yes," Edna whispered to herself as she sat down, feeling strangely weak and yet strong, and looked through the open window across the market-gardens, and down Love Lane, where in the August evening more than one pair of figures—lovers, of course—might be seen slowly strolling. "Yes, it is all clear enough, plain enough. Possibly we shall never meet him again—I hope not. But if we do, if he loves Letty, marries Letty—" she paused—"of course, I never say one word. He only does right, and she does right too—what I should have done myself. If he loved me, and I knew it, I would hold to him in spite of Letty, in spite of the whole world—hold to him till death!"

Involuntarily, her right hand closed over the other hand. Ay, small and fragile as it was, it was a hand that any one could see would hold, faithfully and firm, till death.

Oh that among us poor, wavering women, driven about by every wind of fancy, prejudice, weakness, or folly, there were more such hands! They would keep back many a man from sinking into the gulf of perdition.

CHAPTER XI.

"I've done it! I've tracked them as cleverly as if I were a bee-hunter on the American prairies. I've found their house—such a little one, in such a shabby neighborhood. No wonder they didn't like us to know it. I say, Will, don't you hear?"

"Yes," growled Will, who had just come in from a severe day's work, as his brother had done from a severe day's play. They were eating conjointly their final meal, half tea, half supper, roughly laid out and roughly served, in the dining-room, which was the one well-furnished apartment of the doctor's large, empty house—a good house in a good street, which as a doctor he was obliged to have, and had contrived to make externally comfortable for his patients—when they should come. But beyond this consulting-room all was dreariness—the dreariness of raw newness, which is much worse than that of ancient dilapidation.

William Stedman was wearied and dull, but Julius seemed in high spirits, insisting on talking and being listened to.

"I tell you I have found out where they live, though they were so confoundedly secret about it. It's a tiny house in one of the lanes beyond Kensington. They must be poor enough—poorer even than they seemed. But there they certainly live, and I vow I'll go and pay them a call to-morrow."

"Pshaw! don't make a fool of yourself."

"Make a fool of myself! You're uncommonly civil to-day! Pray, may I ask in what way would it be making a fool of myself? I like women's society, and these two are the very jolliest young women I ever—"

Will jumped up as if he had been shot. "Hold your tongue! you'd better!" cried he, violently; and then, catching his brother's look of utter amazement, he suddenly reined himself in, and, with a sort of laugh, begged Julius's pardon.

"Well you may! Why, what has come over you, Will? What on earth have I said or done amiss?"

"Nothing—decidedly nothing. Except that you might speak a little more respectfully of these friends of yours. And I do think, as I told you before you went, that it was hardly right, hardly gentlemanly, to hunt them out, when they so evidently wished to conceal from us where they lived. Just consider, we know nothing at all, in reality, concerning them, except their names."

"And themselves, which is a good deal. I flatter myself I know one of them, at least, pretty well. Miss Edna and I were capital friends, though I wasn't sweet upon her, as you thought I was. She's a very nice girl, but she's not to my taste exactly."

Will poured himself out his last cup of weak tea and answered nothing.

"Come now, be reasonable, old fellow. You're my elder brother, and I don't like to go against you. Why are you so fierce at me for wishing to keep up our acquaintance—a perfectly harmless, indifferent acquaintance—with the two Misses Kenderdine?"

"*They* evidently do not wish it."

"Oh, trust me for that," said Julius, with a laugh. "I know women's ways rather better than you. They only wanted to be followed—tracked down, like bee-hunting, as I said; and very amusing work it is, and rather cleverly I've done it. To-morrow I mean to knock boldly at their door—such a little door, only fit for a little fellow like me, so you needn't try it—send in my card, and request permission to pay my respects."

"And what is to come of it?"

"Nothing; at least nothing in particular. Just a little bit of harmless amusement."

"Amusement!"

"Why should I not have amusement. Nay, don't look as if you'd eat me up. Only consider what a dull life we lead, especially at this time of year. We're not bad enough, or rich enough, to do things jollily. I'd really like to be a good boy, if I could find out a house to visit at, a family house with nice girls in it, where I could go to tea sometimes. I'd do it, I assure you, as soberly and respectably as if I were my own great-grandmother."

"And that is your intention with regard to these ladies?"

"What other intention could I have? You may think of marrying, old boy, if you like. You have a profession, a house, and a settled income of two hundred a year; but as for me—bah!"

"We can neither of us think of marrying just yet," said the elder brother, gravely. "It would be an act of insanity—or worse—scoundrelism, to take a young girl and plunge her into a life of grinding poverty. But even that, I think, would be lesser scoundrelism than to intrude on the privacy of two young ladies who have neither parents nor brothers; to cultivate their acquaintance or friendship, as you choose to call it—but we couldn't be friends, it isn't in human nature. It would end in making them think, and other people say, we were their lovers; and then we must sheer off and leave them."

"Well, and if so? It would have been jolly fun while it lasted."

Dr. Stedman turned upon his brother with blazing eyes. "You're joking—you know you are. For me, I may be a very bad fellow—I don't think much of myself, anyhow; but I'm not such a scamp as that. And as long as I am your elder brother, and have the slightest influence over you, I'll hinder you from being one. You will seriously offend me, Julius, if you carry out your plan of visiting these two young ladies."

Will spoke quietly, the almost unnatural quietness of some smothered feeling or passion: with him a feeling was a passion, or it was nothing. He was not a merely intellectual man, or a sentimental man: it needed but to look at him to perceive that in him the full human tide of life ran strongly and deeply — the more deeply because so completely held in restraint. His measured words, his steady step—for he had risen, and was walking up and down the room—indicated faintly what lay concealed below.

But Julius did not notice it. Either he was too preoccupied by his own concerns, or else this was a novel development of his brother which he did not understand. He only said, lightly:

"You are very kind, but I don't consider myself a scamp, not just yet; even though, in spite of my elder brother, I do certainly intend to call upon the Misses Kenderdine to-morrow."

It would have been a pity had Edna seen what Dr. Stedman next did—Dr. Stedman, her calm, gentle, wise hero—exalted by her foolish love into all that a man should be. Nothing could excuse it, though it might be accounted for by the long under-current of mental struggle that must have gone on within him, before that last touch caused it to burst its boundaries, and forced him completely beyond his self-control. It was a wrong thing, and a ridiculous thing to do, but he did it: he seized his brother by the collar and shook him, as a furious big dog shakes a little one, which he must punish, but will not injure; then let him go, and leaned breathless against the wall.

Julius rose up, not furious, but smouldering in the white heat of passion which he so seldom showed.

"You shall repent this," he said. "I don't know whether you're mad or drunk, or what, but you shall repent it. I'll leave you now: you're not fit for civil men's company; but to-morrow— Good-night."

Julius had the best of it, and knew he had. Sometimes, though not many times, during their lives, the two brothers had quarrelled—most brothers do: and then generally the stronger and better-governed nature had won. But now they seemed to have changed characters, and the lighter and more superficial one carried the day.

"I have been a fool," muttered Will, as his brother deliberately lit a chamber candle, and passed him by, unobservant, or else regardless, of the hand which was half extended—the old affectionate, brotherly hand. Will drew it back immediately.

"Good-night," said Julius again, very stiffly, and walked out of the room.

Bitterly humbled and shamed, with the bitterest, perhaps the only shame an honest man can ever feel—the reproaches of his own conscience—Will sat down, wrapping his arms on the table, and laying his head upon them in an attitude of complete dejection. There he remained nearly motionless, for a long time. The last faint glimmering of an August sunset crept into the room and crept out again, leaving behind a dull twilight, almost darkness. Then the lamp-lighter's quick step was heard through the open window, as he went down the dreary emptiness of a London evening street, and flashed upon it gleam after gleam of lighted gas-lamps, till at last he reached the one opposite Dr. Stedman's window; it suddenly brightened up the room, throwing fantastic patterns through the window-curtains on the opposite wall.

Will Stedman sprung up as if he had been asleep and the light had suddenly wakened him.

"What a fool I have been!" he said aloud. "What a—" Forgive him, gentle souls of gentle women, if he used stronger language than I care to record. He was only a man, and he was hard bestead. "I wonder what Julius thought of me! what any one would think! Who would believe I could have done such a contemptible thing? How she would despise me!"

She? So the man had succumbed at last. Passion had taken hold of him: that passion which, seizing one like

William Stedman, completely masters him — turns his whole nature either to sweetness or bitterness. How had this come about, and for what woman? For that is the great test, the one fearful risk of a man's life. A woman will sometimes idealize a very inferior man, until her love for him, and her patience with him, exalt him into something better than he originally was, and her into little short of an angel; but a man almost invariably drops to the level of the woman he is in love with. He can not raise her, but she can almost unlimitedly deteriorate him. Why this should be, Heaven knows, but so it constantly is. We have but to look around us with ordinary observation in order to see that a man's destiny, more than even a woman's, depends far less upon the good or ill fortune of his wooing, than upon the sort of woman with whom he falls in love.

That William Stedman was a man to choose strongly, firmly, and irrevocably, no one who knew him, if ever so little, could doubt. That, having chosen, his character would be modified to a momentous extent by the object of his love, and that, once gaining him, she would have almost unlimited influence over him—was a fact also patent, for it belonged to common human nature. Not that he was a weak man, or a sensualist, to be led by an iron chain hid under passion's roses—his thirty years of brave and virtuous life furnished a sufficient denial to both suppositions. But his affections were very strong, and hitherto had been wholly undivided. He had no intimate friend, and not one relative living, except the brother whom he had guarded and guided all his days, in a way less brotherly than fatherly. Still, Julius had often been a great anxiety to him—more anxiety than pleasure; and besides, there comes a time in a man's life—in all lives—when ties, not only of instinct and duty, but of personal election, are necessary for happiness; when, in short, no tie satisfies, except *the* one which God himself made to be the root of all.

Was it so with William Stedman—this good brother; this eager, active worker in the world, who, as yet, did more for it than it had ever done for him, though he lived in hopes that if he fought on steadily there was a good time coming? Had fate suddenly met him in his busy life, caught him round a corner, grappled with him and bound him, throwing him into the reckless bitterness, the angry, dissatisfied craving of a man who feels the key-note wanting in his existence—who misses the soft, sweet harmony that would resolve all its discords into peace—the quiet blessedness which nothing ever gives to a man's life except a woman's love?

William Stedman's good angel standing behind him that night might well have wept over him, so unlovely and unlovable he seemed. But angelic wisdom would have known also that it was only the upboiling of the chaos out of which was soon to arise a perfect world.

He paced his dining-room—his well-furnished but ugly and dreary dining-room—till he was thoroughly wearied; and he had had a long day of hospital work besides; yet still the restless spirit was not half taken out of him. Then he went and listened on the staircase, but from Julius's room came no sound.

"What do I want with him, or he with me? Probably he is fast asleep, and has forgotten it all. Nothing ever makes much impression on him for long. Why should I sacrifice myself? He will be just as happy in any other house as in mine; and, besides, he might come here often. He would, if this house were made pretty and pleasant—as a woman could make it. They are as poor as we are—thank God for that! Yet what a difference there used to be between their parlor and ours! How neat her work-basket was! and how she used to stick little bits of flowers here and there about the room!"

While he thought, the man's hard features softened.

"*She* wouldn't let me be savage with Julius. She always had a kind word to say for him, poor fellow! She would be a good sister to him, I know. He liked her, too, and I was such a fool as to think that— Almost as great a fool as I was for a day or two over the beauty of the other one. Pshaw! mere flesh and blood—bones and epidermis. But *my* darling; my little bright, active, loving darling! she is all spiritual: makes me believe in spirit without the flesh. No death could kill *her*, or the love that lives in her. Oh, my God, if I had it for mine!"

A great convulsion came over his face, and his thoughts (which were altogether silent—he was not a person to stamp about and soliloquize) came to an abrupt stop—then ran rampant in a wild riot. At last he gathered them up together, and formed them into a resolution—strong and clear.

"I *will* have her; at least I'll try my best to get her. I am driven to it, whether or no. As for prudence—hang prudence! And with regard to honor—well, perhaps it's as honorable to speak out at once as to hold my tongue for another year or two, and let Julius go philandering after them, vexing and fretting her, and setting people talking besides; while if she were engaged to me—openly and fairly mine—nobody could say one word. Only let any one dare, that's all!"

He clenched his fist and struck it with such force against the table that he actually hurt himself, and then laughed at his own exceeding silliness.

"I'll take a walk and think the matter over. I shall get quiet then. But I must send the household to bed. How late it is! She would not have been so forgetful of other people." And after shouting down the stairs to the old man and woman who formed his sole establishment—one to attend upon patients, and the other to see to the comfortless comforts of the two young bachelors—Dr. Stedman closed his hall-door with a bang, and set off at a quick pace—anywhere.

His feet carried him to a place where he had very often walked this summer, but never in daylight; mostly, as now, taking it on his way home from night visits in that poor neighborhood which lay close by, whence, no doubt, the scarlet-fever came. Not a wholesome spot, especially in late summer and autumn, when the air was heavy with decaying vegetation. Yet to the end of his days William Stedman thought there was something pleasant in the faint moist odor, half perfume, of jasmine, clematis, and the like, and half composed of scents much less sweet, which came through the brilliant harvest moonlight, as he walked along under black shadowing trees and stirless hedges, past the Misses Kenderdine's door.

He knew it well enough—had discovered it long ago—though he had allowed his brother to take such a world of pains to find it; but he walked rapidly past it, and not till he was some distance off did he turn round to watch it, as men in love will stand and watch the casket that holds their jewel, to the end of time.

For he was in love—deeply, desperately—as rarely happens to a man twice in a lifetime. Perhaps all the deeper because, like Romeo with his Rosaline, there had previously appeared and vanished the phantom of a mock sun. It sometimes flashed upon him, this deep-hearted, high-minded, and somewhat exacting man, who in midst of all his passion never let his reason go—what a different kind of love his would have been had it been placed on mere outside beauty—like Letty Kenderdine's!

"My little darling! my bright, active, unselfish little darling! you are not plain to me. You are all sweet, all lovely!" and he opened his arms and closed them again over his breast as if he still felt her there, as on the stormy night when he carried her home insensible—that night when he vowed in his heart that no other woman but herself would he ever marry.

Let us look at him tenderly—this man who had no mother or sister, none of those holy influences which are often almost as blessed as that of a wife, if rightly and wisely and unselfishly used. But he had, as he said, nothing; and he felt his nature hardening and corrupting, and a kind of hopeless cynicism stealing over him.

"Oh, save me!" he cried, almost aloud, for the corner where he stood was as desolate as if he had been in a wilderness. "Save me from myself! Make a man of me! You could if you only knew it—if you only knew how bad I am, and how I want you to make me good, my little darling!"

And then and there he took his resolve, leaning on a

railing where many a lover must have leaned before, for it was all engraved with rough letters in twos and twos, encircled in rings or true-lovers' knots. Ah, to think what has become of the owners of those initials now! How many broken troth-plights, and death-partings, and marriages more fatal than deaths! Yet still then and there William Stedman resigned himself to the common lot, and made up his mind that he would risk his all on a brief yes or no from a woman's lips.

The poor old railing has long been broken down, and there is a range of handsome houses, in which you can pay morning calls and go to evening parties on the quiet spot where the lovers used to linger. But I think more than one person still living remembers it tenderly, and thanks God that William Stedman had strength and courage to take his destiny, and another's also, into his own hands, after the fashion of those four lines which every honest man would do well to repeat to himself when he goes a-wooing:

"He either fears his fate too much,
Or his deserts are small,
Who dares not put it to the touch,
And win or lose it all."

After that decision the doctor walked home with steadier feet and a bolder heart. He let himself in at his own door with a feeling that, come what would, he was master there —master of himself, and, in measure, of his fortunes; as a man always is who has courage to look his difficulties in the face, and push his way through them with a firm, steadfast hand.

To that singleness of purpose — to the consciousness that, in acting as he had determined to act, there was in his heart no mean intent, no thought which a good man need wish to hide, or a good woman blush to look at—he trusted the success of his suit. And if it failed—why, he was not the first man to whom such a thing had happened.

Though when he imagined the possibility—nay, probability, for his humility made him think it very probable—

of his love being rejected, he felt as a man would not willingly feel twice in a lifetime.

Dr. Stedman was no coward; and yet when he lit his lamp, took out his desk, and fairly sat down to it, his hand shook like a leaf.

The letter consisted only of a few lines—he *could* not write more. Some men take refuge in pen and paper, and revel therein; their thoughts and feelings flow out—and generally evaporate also—in the most charming sentences, which, even under the deepest emotion, it is a relief to them to write, and a pride in having written. But William Stedman was of another sort. To express his feelings at all was very difficult to him—to write them, and see them written, staring back at him in terrible black and white, was impossible. Therefore this letter, the first love-letter he ever wrote, was of the very briefest and most formal kind:

"Dear Madam,—Will you do me the honor to read this in private and alone?

"My brother has just told me he has discovered where you live, and means to call upon you. May I be allowed to do so first? I have but one reason for this, and one apology for the presumption of proposing it; that I consider neither my brother nor myself have any right to intrude upon you as mere acquaintances. And besides, a mere acquaintance I could never willingly be to you.

"You and I know one another pretty well: we shall never know one another any better unless I dare to ask you one question—Could you, after any amount of patient waiting on my part, and for the sake of a love of which I can not speak—consent to be my wife?

"To-morrow is Saturday. If, during the day, only one line comes to me by post, I will be with you on Sunday. If I may not come—but then I know you will answer me quickly; you would not keep in needless torture any creature living. Yours faithfully,

"William Stedman.

"Miss Edna Kenderdine."

Yes, that was the name—her name. He wrote it firmly enough. The die was cast, and now he must meet either fortune; and he thought he could. He did not even re-read his letter, or speculate upon whether or not it was a good letter, or the sort of letter to effect its end; for, even in the midst of his delirium of passion, he had sense enough to see that a woman who, in so momentous a crisis, could lay weight upon accidental forms of phrase or mistakes of expression, was not a woman to be much desired. One doubt alone he had—would she show her sister the letter? and if so, what would Letty say, and how might she influence Edna with regard to him?

But shortly he cast this perplexity also aside. A woman who, in such a case, could be influenced by sister or friend —or even parent—who could not ask herself the simple question, "Do I love him, or do I not love him?" and answer it herself, without referring the decision to any human being—such a woman might be good enough in her way, but she was not Edna Kenderdine—not the woman whom a man like William Stedman would ever care to marry.

Saying this to himself, and staying himself therewith a little—ay, even in the full tide and torrent of his passion —he closed and sealed his letter; then, with a vague dread of trusting himself with it till the morning, he went out again into the dark streets, and posted it with his own hand.

CHAPTER XII.

The postman was by no means a daily visitor at the Misses Kenderdine's door. It is a fact—amusing or melancholy, according as one takes it—that society in the aggregate does not very much run after resident governesses or poor school-mistresses; that they are not likely to be inundated with correspondence or haunted with invitations. Of course, under no circumstances are young, good, and lady-like women quite without friends or acquaintances; such loneliness would argue a degree of un-lovingness, or unlovableness, of which certainly no one could accuse the Misses Kenderdine. But this is a busy and a self-engrossed world; it has quite enough to do with its own affairs; and it likes to get the full value for all it bestows. The sisters, who had so little to give it, had not been troubled with any overplus of its affection. Still there were, in different parts of the country, a few households who liked and remembered the Kenderdines; and even at Kensington there were some houses where they occasionally visited, or went to one of those evening parties which in London middle-class society take the place of the countrified, old-fashioned "going out to tea."

They were expecting one of these invitations; so the postman's red coat gleaming against the green hedge of Love Lane attracted Letty's attention, and his knock roused her to jump up and take in the letter. Edna allowed her to go. She herself had not felt well all the day; the morning school had been an unusual burden to her, and, now it was over, she took refuge in her favorite American rocking-chair—a present from an old pupil—and rocked and rocked, as if in that soothing motion the uneasy feeling in mind and body—half-weariness, half-restlessness—would pass away. Though she knew all the while it would not; that there it was, and she must bear it, as many another woman had borne it before her—the dull heart-ache, the hopeless want. These sorrows do come, and they conquer even the bravest sometimes. May He who ordained love to be the crown of life have pity on all those to whom it comes only as a crown of thorns, or who have to endure the blankness of its absence—the agony of its loss! Both can be endured, and comfort will come at length, but the torture is terrible while it lasts. Edna endured it but in a small measure, and for a short time; yet the pang was sharp enough to make her, till the end of her days, feel unutterable pity and tenderness over those whom the world smiles over as "disappointed in love"—those from whose lives God has seen fit to omit life's first and best blessing; or else, though this is a lesser grief, to give it and take it away.

She was sitting listlessly rocking, not thinking much about any thing, when Letty re-entered with the letter.

"It is for you, dear. What a funny hand!—a lawyer's hand, I should say. Who can be writing to you, Edna?"

"I don't know," said Edna, indifferently, and then, catching a glimpse of the letter, checked herself, with a startled consciousness that she did know, or at any rate guess; that locked up in her desk in a hidden corner she had a small fragment of the very same handwriting—a most unimportant fragment—memoranda about trains, etc., for their railway journey; but still there it was, kept like a treasure, secreted like a sin.

"Miss Edna Kenderdine," read Letty, detaining the letter and examining it. "Then it must be from a stranger. A friend would know, of course, that you were Miss Kenderdine. Shall I open it for you, dear?"

"No," said Edna, and an unaccountable impulse made her snatch it and turn away with it—turn away from her sister, her dear sister, from whom she had not a secret in the world. At the first sentence she started, glanced at the signature, and then put the letter in her pocket, flushing scarlet.

Letty looked amazed. "What is the matter with you? Is it a love-letter? Do say!"

"It begins like a business letter, and the writer wishes me to read it in private and alone," said Edna, forcing her white lips—she felt, with a terrified consciousness, how very white she must be turning now—to utter the exact, formal truth.

"Oh, very well," replied Letty, a little vexed, but too sweet-tempered to retain vexation long.

She sat down composedly and finished her dinner—lingering a good while over the pudding—Letty liked puddings and all good things; while Edna sat, with the letter in her pocket, as quiet and almost as silent as if she were made of marble, for a quarter of an hour. Then Letty rose.

"Now I'll go into the kitchen, for I want to iron out my muslin dress. In the mean time you can read in peace your wonderful letter. You'll tell me about it afterwards, Edna, dear."

Touched by her sister's gentleness Edna returned a smiling "Thank you," and tried to look as usual while the dinner was being cleared away. But her head was whirling and her pulse beating fast—so fast that when she at last took the letter out and opened it the lines swam before her eyes. She had only strength enough to creep noiselessly up to her room at the top of the house, shut herself in, and lock the door.

There let her be. We will not look at her, nor inquire into what she felt or did. Women, at least, can understand.

Letty's muslin dress had, happily, a good many frills and flounces, and took a long time in ironing. Not that Letty grumbled at that: she had great pleasure in her clothes, and was the last person to treat them lightly or disrespectfully, or to complain of any trouble they cost her. This dress especially always engrossed so much of her attention and affection, that it is doubtful whether she once let her mind stray from it to such commonplace facts as business letters. And when it was done, she was good-natured enough to recollect that while she had the things about she might as well iron Edna's dress. She went up stairs to fetch it, when, to her surprise, she found the door locked.

"I will come presently," answered a very low voice from within.

"But your dress, Edna. I want to iron out your new muslin dress."

"Thank you, dear. Never mind. I will be down presently."

"It *was* a love-letter, then!" pondered Letty to herself as she descended. "I am sure it was. But who in the wide world can have fallen in love with Edna? Poor Edna!"

"Poor Edna!" Rich Edna! rich in the utmost wealth that Heaven can give to mortal woman! Oh, when there is so much sadness in this world—so much despised love

—unrequited love—unworthy love—surely the one bliss of love deserved and love returned ought to outweigh all else, and stand firm and sure, whatever outside cares may lay siege to it. They can not touch the citadel where the two hearts—the one double heart—has intrenched itself, safe and at rest—forever.

Edna's "love"—hopelessly and dearly beloved—had become her lover. He wished to make her his wife. Her solitary days were done: she stood on the threshold of a new life—in a new world. Never, until through the gate of death she should enter on the world everlasting, would there come to her such another hour as that first hour after she read William Stedman's letter.

Half an hour after—to so long a space extended her "presently"—Edna Kenderdine crept down stairs, and then crept on, still quietly, into her sister's arms.

"Kiss me, Letty! There are only we two."

In a few words—strangely few it seemed, and as if the whole thing were quite natural and known beforehand—Edna told her happy secret, and the sisters embraced one another and wept together, the harmless tears that women are sure to shed, and are not women at all if they do not shed, on these occasions.

At first Letty was considerably surprised—perhaps a little more than surprised—but she had the good taste and good feeling not to say overmuch on this head, and not to refer, even in the most passing way, to certain remarks of her own during the last two days, which must have been, to say the least, rather annoying to remember. But if Letty was a little disappointed and humiliated—and it was scarcely in human nature that she should not be—after having so confidently placed herself and Dr. Stedman in the position of the Irish ballad couplet:

> "Did ye ever hear of Captain Baxter,
> Whom Miss Biddy refused afore he axed her?"

her vanity was too innocent, and her nature too easy, to bear offense long. After the first surprise was over, her congratulations were given with sufficient warmth and sincerity.

"Well, Edna dear, you know I always liked him, and I dare say I shall find him a very good brother-in-law; and really it will be rather convenient to have a man in the family. But to think that after all the offers I have had, you should be the first to get married, or, anyhow, engaged. Who would ever have expected such a thing!"

"Who would, indeed!" said Edna, in all simplicity, and with a sense almost of contrition for the fact.

"Well, never mind!" answered Letty, consolingly; "I am sure I hope you will be very happy; and as for me" —she paused and sighed—"I should not wonder if I were left an old maid after all, in spite of my appearance."

Which catastrophe, so dolefully prognosticated, would have awakened a smile yesterday; but to-day Edna could not smile. Though her joy was only an hour old, it was so intense, so perfect, that it seemed to absorb the whole of life, as if she knew not how she had ever lived without it. Thinking of her sister who had it not—who did not even comprehend what it was—she felt so sorry that she could have wept over her.

But Letty's next words dispelled this tender regret.

"Still, Edna, if I were you, I would not be in any hurry to give the young man his answer. And in the mean time we will make some inquiries as to what sort of a practice he has—whether he is likely to be in a position to marry soon—and so on. Certainly it is by no means so good a match as I myself should have expected to make; but then you are different—I mean your ideas of things are much humbler than mine. Didn't somebody once say you had quite a genius for poverty?"

"*He* said it," and Edna hung her head, blushing; then lifted it up with a bright, proud, peaceful smile—"yes, he said it one day on the shore. He knew me even then, and understood me, thank God."

And there came before her a vision of her life to come —not an easy one; not that of a woman who slips into marriage to "better herself," as servants say—to attain ease, and luxury, and position, and all the benefits which "a good marriage" is supposed to confer. Hers would be a life in which every energy would be tested, every power put to use—which would exact unlimited patience, self-denial, courage, strength; the life, in short, of a woman who does not care to be a man's toy and ornament, but desires rather to be his helpmeet—supplying all he needs, as he supplies all she needs, teaching her through the necessities of every day how to fulfill the perfect law of love —self-sacrifice.

Edna knew she should have a hard life. Though Dr. Stedman was still tolerably ignorant about their circumstances, he had taken good care to inform her every thing about his own. She was well aware that he was poor—proud also—perhaps on account of the poverty. She guessed, with her quick-sighted love, that his temper was not the sweetest in the world—though she could find excuses for that. But she believed in him—she honored him, for she had never seen any thing in him that was not worthy of honor; and, last little fact of all, which included all the rest, she loved him.

Letty watched her a minute—with that happy smile on her face. "Well, Edna dear, if you are satisfied, so am I. It is, of course, your own affair entirely. I would only advise you to take time."

"Certainly I shall. It is sure to be a long engagement."

Letty shook her head pathetically. "Ah! if there is one thing more than another which I should object to, it is a long engagement. It wears a girl to death, and cuts off all her chances elsewhere. And suppose, in the mean time, she should receive a better offer?"

Edna dropped her sister's hand. "Letty, we had better talk no more. If we talked to everlasting I could never make you understand."

She spoke sharply, almost angrily; and then, seeing no anger, only mild amazement on Letty's beautiful face, she repented. With the yearning that every woman must have at this crisis in her life to fall on some other woman's neck and ask for a little love—a little sympathy on the new strange path she had just entered—she turned back again to her sister, who kissed her once more.

"Really now, I did not mean to vex you, Edna. Of course you know your own mind—you always did; and had your own way, too, in every thing—I'll tell him so, and frighten him."

Edna smiled.

"And what does he say to you? Do show me your love-letter—I always showed you all mine!"

But this was a different thing quite. Edna closed her little hand fiercely over it—her one possession, foretaste of her infinite wealth to come. It was hers—all her own, and the whole world should neither pry into it, nor steal it, nor share it.

"Well, never mind. You always were a queer girl," said Letty, patiently. "But at least you'll tell me when he is coming here. This is Saturday—I suppose he will want to come to tea on Sunday?"

And so the misty, beautiful, wondrous dream condensed itself into a living commonplace reality. There was a note written, which consisted of the brief word "come," naming the day and hour. This was sent by their servant, who looked much astonished, and hoped nobody was ill and wanting the doctor; and then the two sisters sat down side by side, for even Letty was silent a while.

At last, however, she could hold her tongue no longer, but began talking in her smoothly-flowing inconsequent way.

"I wonder what sort of a house he lives in, and whether it is well furnished. Of course we can't go and see—it would not be proper; but I will try and find out. And this house of ours—I suppose it will have to be given up. No man would like his wife to go on keeping school. He would never let her work if he could help it: in such a common way too. Ah, Edna, you are the lucky woman, after all! I wish I had somebody to work for me."

"Do you?" said Edna, absently.

"Oh, how nice it must be! To have nothing to do all day long, and every thing pretty about one, and perhaps a carriage to ride in, and no trouble at all. Heigh-ho! I wish I were married too, though it shouldn't be to any

HALF JOY, HALF SORROW.

body like Dr. Stedman. But, my dear, since it is to be, and you are fond of him, and, as I have said, you are your own mistress, and must please yourself, do just tell me what you think about things. In the first place, what ought your wedding-dress to be?"

"Hush," Edna whispered. "Please don't talk any more. I can't bear it." And then she threw herself into her sister's arms, and cried passionately—half for joy, half for sorrow. So the day ended—the day of days which closed up forever one portion of the sisters' lives: a day, to Letty, scarcely different from any other, but to Edna like that first day which marked the creation of a new world.

She scarcely slept all night; still, she rose and went to church as usual. She was neither afraid nor ashamed. She knew the Great Searcher of hearts would not punish her because in every thanksgiving was a thought of *him*, and every prayer was a prayer for two. She walked home with her sister through the green lane—Letty vaguely wondering what church Dr. Stedman attended—she hoped he did go to church regularly somewhere, for nothing made a man look so respectable, especially if he were a doctor. Edna had a sweet composure of mien—a gentle dignity such as had never been seen in her before; inasmuch as more than one stray acquaintance told her "how well she was looking." At which she felt so glad.

But during the afternoon—the long still Sunday afternoon—with the warm jasmine-scented air creeping in through the half-closed Venetian blinds, some of her nervousness returned, her quick restless movements, her little abruptnesses of speech. She went about from room to room, but could not sit long anywhere.

Letty watched her with a condescending interest, rather trying to bear. "It's natural, dear, quite natural. I used to feel the same myself when one of them was coming. Dear me! what a long time ago it seems since any body came to see me! But even one's sister's lover is better than none. I hope you will settle with Dr. Stedman to come every Sunday. And he might sometimes bring his brother with him, for it will be desperately dull for me, you know. Well, I declare! Punctuality's very self! For it is just five minutes to six, and I am sure I see a gentleman striding down Love Lane. I'll run down stairs and open the door; shall I, Edna?"

Edna assented, but she could not utter a word more. She stood at her window—the window where she was fond of sitting, and had sat so many an hour, and dreamed

COMING.

so many a maiden-dream. She watched him coming, a tall figure, strong and active, walking firmly, without pauses or hesitation, and though sometimes turning the head round to glance — Edna guessed whither! There he was, the ruler of her life, her friend, her lover, some day to be her husband. He was coming to assume his rights, to assert his sovereignty. A momentary vague terror smote her, a fear as to the unknown future, a tender regret for the peaceful, maidenly, solitary days left behind, and then her heart recognized its master and went forth to meet him; not gleefully, with timbrels and dances, but veiled and gentle, grave and meek; contented and ready to obey him, "Even as Sarah obeyed Abraham, calling him lord."

Edna long remembered, in years when it was a comfort to have it to remember, how exceedingly good Letty was that day; how she went down herself to welcome Dr. Stedman, and behaved to him—as he told Edna afterwards—in a way so womanly, friendly, and sisterly that it took away all his awkwardness; and by the time another little light footstep was heard on the stairs he was found sitting—as quietly as if he had sat there every Sunday for years — in the great arm-chair by the window, with his face pale indeed, but radiant with the light of happiness, the one only happiness which ever gives that look, turned towards the opening door.

It opened, and Edna came in.

I have said this little woman was not beautiful, not even pretty; but there was a lovesomeness about her — her neat, small, airy figure, her harmonious movements, and her dainty hands—which often grew into absolute loveliness—at least would, in the eyes of any man who had the sense to love her, and prize her at her worth. Woman as she was—all woman—she was

"Yet a spirit too, and bright,
And something of an angel light."

And as this man—this big, tall, and, it might once have been, rather rough man—looked at her, standing in the door-way in her lilac muslin dress, his whole soul came into his eyes. Though there was in him a mingled expression of dread, as if expecting that while he gazed her wings would grow, and she would fly away from him.

He rose, and advanced a step forward; then he and the lilac angel shook hands — humanly — in a most commonplace fashion. After which Letty, with astonishing tact, discovered the immediate necessity of "seeing about tea," and disappeared.

There are those who despise small rooms and homely furniture — to whom Love is nothing except he comes dressed in fine clothes, and inhabiting splendid drawing-rooms. Of course, under such circumstances, when Poverty enters in at the door, the said Love will surely fly out at the window. He has been far too much accustomed to think of himself and his own ease. Undeniably it is very pleasant to be rich, to inhabit handsome houses, and be dressed in elegant clothes; and there is a kind of love so purely external, selfish, and self-seeking, that it can not exist unless it has also these things. But the true love is something far, far beyond. And Edna, when William Stedman took her in his arms—just herself and nothing more —in her common muslin gown, with no attractive surroundings, for the parlor was small and humble as well could be—asking her if she could love him, and if she were afraid to be a poor man's wife — Edna knew what that true love was.

They sat long talking, and he told her every thing, including a little confession which perhaps every man would not have made; but this man was so conscientiously honest that he could not have been happy without making it—that his first passing fancy had been for her beautiful sister.

"And I like her still—I shall always like her," added he with an earnest simplicity that made Edna smile, and assured her more than ever of the love that was far deeper than all telling. "And—before you get anxious about it, I wish to say one thing—Letty shall never leave you, if you do not wish it, and I will always be good to her. Who could help it? She is so charming to look at—so sweet-tempered—so kindly. I like her exceedingly; but as for loving—"

Edna gave one shy inquiring glance into the passionate face; then, in the strange familiarity—sacred as sweet—which one little hour had brought about between them, she laid her head upon his shoulder, saying, gently,

"I am not afraid. I know you will never love any body but me."

And when at last Letty came in, after a most lengthy and benevolent rattling of the door-handle, William Stedman went up to her and kissed her like a brother.

"It is all settled, and you are to live with us. We never mean to part with you—except to somebody better than ourselves."

Thus quietly, in his brief, masculine way, he cleared off the only weight on Edna's mind—in the only way in which it could be done. And as she looked up to him with grateful eyes, loving him all the dearer because of the tenderness he showed to her own flesh and blood, he inly vowed that he would never let her know how, in resigning his first great happiness of a married home all to themselves, he had made a very great sacrifice.

Letty thanked him, not with overmuch emotion, for she was so used to be first considered, that she took it quite naturally. Then, with a little commonplace quizzing—not ill-meant but rather inappropriate—she sat down in Edna's place to pour out tea and enjoy the distinction of entertaining "the man of the family."

When the meal was ended, Dr. Stedman, in the aforesaid capacity, which he accepted in a cheery and contented manner, proposed that they should at once enter upon the question of ways and means.

"Which means being married, I suppose?" laughed Letty.

"Yes," he answered, with a deep blush, and then dashed at the subject abruptly and desperately. "I do not wish to wait—not a day after I get a hospital appointment which I have been long trying for, and have now a good chance of. With that and my profession we could live. And Julius, he will have enough to live upon too."

"Will he live with you? Then how can I?" asked Letty, bridling up with a sudden fit of propriety.

"No, not with us," was the answer, strong, decisive, almost angry. "As *she* knows," glancing at Edna, "there is two hundred a year which, if necessary, he can have—part or whole; but I will not have him living with me. Two men in one house would never do;" and then he told, cursorily, the "slight difference"—so he called it—which he had had with his brother, and how he had not seen him since, Julius having gone next morning on a painting expedition.

Edna looked grave, but Letty listened with considerable amusement. "And so Julius—I may say 'Julius,' as he will be my half-brother-in-law, you know—wanted to come and see us, and you prevented him? And if this quarrel had not happened you would not have written? Perhaps you would never have made up your mind to ask Edna at all?"

The silly woman had hit upon something like a truth, or near enough thereto to vex the man a little.

"I assure you, Miss Letty—but excuse my explaining. Your sister knows all."

Yes, Edna did know—all the pride—all the pain—the struggle between duty and passion—the difficulty of determining right from wrong—honor from cowardliness—

rashness from fearless faith. Many a man has gone through the like before his marriage—the woman neither understanding it nor pitying it; but Edna did both. She laid her little hand on his—

"No need to explain, I am quite satisfied."

"And Julius?" persisted Letty, who was beginning to find second-hand felicity a little uninteresting. "Does he know of all this between Edna and you?"

"No; but when he returns on Monday I shall tell him."

"And what will he say?"

"I think he will say, as a brother should—'It's all right. Be happy in your own way.'"

"But if he does not?" said Edna, tremulously.

William Stedman looked vexed. Perhaps he knew his brother better than she did, or was less accustomed than she was to think of others.

"I do not contemplate any such impertinent interference on his part. But if so, it can make no difference to me. When a man of my age chooses his wife, no other man, not even his own brother, has a right to say a word. Julius had better not; I would not stand it."

He spoke loudly, like a man not used to talk with or to listen to women; a man who, right or wrong, liked to have his own way. Truly he was far from perfect, this chosen of Edna's heart. Yet he had a heart too, and a conscience, and both these would have understood her momentary start—the slight shadow which troubled her happy face. But though the happiness lessened the peace remained, and the love which had created both.

"I think," she said, very gently, "that Julius is too generous to make us unhappy. He may be vexed at first, having had you all his life—and only you—like Letty and me here. But perhaps he is not quite so good as my Letty."

And thinking of her gentle sister, and contrasting their ways with the fierce ways of these two men—lover and brother, with whom her lot was to be bound up for life—Edna trembled a little; but the next minute she despised herself for her cowardice. What was love worth if it could not bear a little pain? In the darkening twilight she loosened not, but rather strengthened, her clasp of William Stedman's hand; and as he went on talking, principally to Letty, and about common things, the size and arrangements of his house, and his means of furnishing it, his good angel might have heard that the man's voice grew softer and sweeter every minute. Already there was stealing into him that influence, mysterious as holy, which, without any assertion on their part—any parade of rights or complaints of wrong—makes all women—Christian women—if they so choose it, the queens of the world. Already the future queen had entered into her kingdom.

He was still talking, being left respectfully by these inexperienced maidens to take the man's part of explaining and deciding every thing, when there came a knock to the door, so sudden and startling, in that quiet Sunday evening, that the little house seemed actually to reel.

"Probably some one for me," said Dr. Stedman. "I left word at home where I might be found if wanted; a doctor is always liable to be summoned, you know. It is not an easy life for him or for his household," added he, with a slightly shy and yet happy smile.

"Oh," cried Letty, "I wouldn't marry a doctor upon any account, as I always said to Edna"—whose conscious blush showed how completely the good advice had been thrown away.

But just this minute the front-door was opened, and the voice of a man, hurried and eager, was heard inquiring for the Misses Kenderdine; also, in not too gentle tones, whether Dr. Stedman was here?

"It is Julius," said Letty. But what happened next is serious enough to require another chapter.

CHAPTER XIII.

Julius Stedman entered the parlor in a rather excited state. Not with wine—that was a temptation impossible to the pure-living, refined young artist; but his excitement was of a kind peculiar to the artistic and nervous temperament, and might easily have been mistaken for that of drink. His face was flushed, his motions abrupt, his speech unnaturally loud and fast, and as he stood shading his eyes from the sudden dazzle of the lamp-light, even his appearance spoke against him; for his dress was dusty, his long hair disorderly, and his whole exterior very far below that standard of personal elegance—nay, dandyism—which was a strong characteristic of Julius Stedman.

He bowed to Letty, who was the first to advance towards him.

"I am ashamed, Miss Kenderdine, of intruding at this unseemly hour; but my brother—ah, there you are! I have found you out at last;" and he darted over to the doctor's chair. "You're a pretty fellow, Will; a nice elder brother!—a proper person to lecture a younger one, and teach him the way he should go—a good, honest, generous, candid—"

"Julius!" cried Will, catching him by the arm, and speaking almost in a whisper, "command yourself. You forget these ladies."

"Not at all!" And there was no abatement in the shrill, furious voice. "I have the highest respect for these ladies. And out of my respect, as soon as I came home (unexpectedly of course, like a fool that I was, to make it up with you), and found where you were gone, I came after you—I came, just to tell them the plain truth. Miss Kenderdine, this brother of mine, who comes sneaking here on the sly—"

"Julius!" Not a whisper now, but thundered out in violent passion; then controlling himself, Will added, "Julius, you are under an entire and ridiculous mistake. Either leave this house with me instantly, or sit down and listen to my explanation."

"Listen!—explanation!" repeated Julius, and looked bewildered from one to the other of the three whom he had found sitting together so familiarly and happily in the pleasant little parlor.

"Yes," said Will, laying his hand firmly and kindly on his brother's shoulder, "I will explain every thing: there is no reason now why I should not. I objected to your visiting here, because you had no right to come; and your coming was an injury to these ladies, and would have exposed them to all kinds of unpleasant remarks. But with me it is different. I came here to-day—and it is my first visit, I assure you—with a distinct right, and in a recognized character. Julius, I am going to give you a sister."

"A sister!" The young man turned frightfully pale, and his eyes sought—which face was it?—Letty's. Then, as with the strength of despair, he forced himself to speak.

"Tell me—tell me quick! This is so sudden!"

"Not sudden in reality—it only seems so," said William, smiling; "and you like her very much—you know she will make you a good sister. Shake hands with him, Edna."

"Edna—is it Edna?" And then, either out of his own natural impulsiveness, or in the reaction from a still stronger excitement, Julius darted forward, and instead of shaking hands, kissed her warmly. "I beg your pardon; but I can't help it. Oh, you dear little woman—so it's you, is it?—you that have all but brought about a quarrel between Will and me—the first we ever had in our lives."

"And the last, I trust," said Will, cheerily, submitting to have his hand almost shaken off.

"Never mind—never mind, now, old fellow. All's well that ends well. I give you joy. I'm quite content. She will be the best little sister in all the world. Shake hands again, Edna—let's shake hands all round."

But when he came to Letty, he stopped point-blank.

Letty extended her long fingers in a dignified manner, and smiled her benign smile—alike to all—upon the flushed, passionate young face.

"I suppose, Mr. Stedman, this makes you and me a sort of half-brother-and-sister-in-law. I am quite willing. I hope we shall always be very good friends—just like brother and sister, indeed."

"Thank you," was the answer, and the young man's excited mood sank into quietness, nay, into more than quietness—sadness. But this was nothing uncommon with Julius Stedman, who, after one of his fits of high spirits, generally fell into a corresponding fit of gravity and melancholy.

This, or perhaps his mere presence as an extraneous element in what had been such a peaceful trio—for, in these early days of betrothal, sometimes an easy negative third rather adds to than takes away from the new-found and still unfamiliar happiness—made the evening not quite so pleasant as before. In vain Will, with most creditable persistency, maintained conversation, and Edna by a great effort shook off her shyness, and, taking her place as hostess, presided at supper—endeavoring to be especially attentive to Julius, and give him a foretaste of the good sister she intended to be. For in the midst of all her own joy her heart warmed to him—this moody, variable, affectionate, lovable fellow, who seemed, as so many young men do, like a goodly ship with little ballast, the success of whose whole voyage depended upon what kind of hand should take the helm. Besides, though she knew it was womanish and ridiculous, she could not help having a sort of pity for any body who had lived with William Stedman for so long, and would not now live with him much longer. She could afford to be exceedingly kind and forgiving to poor Julius.

Still the cloud did not pass away, and in spite of every body's faint efforts to disperse it—except Letty's, who was not acute enough to see any thing, and went talking on in the most charmingly unconscious and inappropriate way—the awkwardness so spread itself, that it was quite a relief when the little quartette broke up. Dr. Stedman proposed leaving, and then stood with Edna at the window, talking for ever so long between themselves; while Letty, with a nod and a wink, went into the passage, beckoning Julius to follow her.

"We're terribly in the way—we two," said she, laughing. "I am afraid, on future Sundays, we shall have to retire to the kitchen—that is, if you persist in coming to take care of your brother when he goes a-courting. But it will be very dull for you with only stupid me."

"Only you!" said Julius, gazing at her as she stood

leaning against the lobby wall, seeming to illumine the whole place, poor and small as it was, with her wonderful beauty. "Only you!"

And Letty looked down, not unconscious of his admiration, and perhaps feeling just sufficiently ill-used by fate as to think herself justified in appropriating and enjoying it — that is, if she ever thought at all; or thought ten minutes in advance of the present moment.

"I suppose those two are very happy," said Julius, at length, with a glance in the direction of the silent parlor.

"Oh, of course. Every body is very happy at first—that is—I suppose so. Not that I know from experience."

Julius regarded her with piercing eyes, and then laughed, half carelessly, half cynically.

"Oh, you and I are old stagers, I suppose. We will not reveal the secrets of the prison-house. Probably, being in love is like being in prison."

"Eh?" said Letty, puzzled, and then added, confidentially: "I don't like to hear you mention prisons. I hope your brother is not in debt—so many young men are nowadays. Is he in sufficiently good circumstances to warrant his marriage? Not that I would say a word against it. Of course my sister knows her own mind, and acts as she thinks right; she always did. But will they not be very poor? And it is such a dreadful thing to be poor."

"A cursed thing!" And there was a gleam, almost a glare, in those wild, bright eyes of Julius Stedman, as he fixed them on the beautiful creature before him. A creature whom some fortunate man—say an Eastern sultan, or a Western duke—might have eagerly bought, the one with a ring, the other with a given number of piastres, and carried off to be robed in silks and hung with diamonds—laden with every gift possible, except that which, perhaps, after all, she might not care for, or only as it was accompanied by these other things—his heart. "Yes, poverty is a dreadful thing. There I quite agree with you, Miss Kenderdine."

"You might as well call me Letty, and so get our relations clear at once," said Letty, coquettishly.

"Thank you, thank you, Letty," and he seized her hand.

"I mean—our brother and sisterly relations," said Letty, drawing back, upon which Julius apologized, and also drew back immediately.

"As you were saying," observed he, after a pause, during which the low murmur of talking within came maddeningly to his ears, "those two, our brother and sister, regarded by our wiser eyes, are—simply a pair of fools. My brother's certain income, since you so prudently ask it, is only two hundred a year. Besides that he may make another two hundred by his profession, which comes to four hundred altogether. And four hundred a year is, of course, to a woman, downright poverty. I myself think Will is insane to dream of marrying."

"What did you say, my boy?" cried Will, coming behind him, with a radiant light on his face, though it looked thin and worn still, "insane, am I? Why, it's Julius, and not I that deserves a lunatic asylum. He has been in love, off and on, ever since he was fifteen, and never found any body good enough to please him for a month together. Wait, man! Wait till you have found the right woman, and have won her, too!"

"Ah, wait," said Edna, softly, as in a pretty demure sisterly fashion she put both her hands into those of her future brother, and then took them away to remove some stray dust that disfigured his coat-sleeve; "wait till that good time comes. And she will be so happy, and so very fond of you."

"Bless you, my little sister," said Julius, in a choked voice, as he suddenly bent down and put his lips to Edna's hand. "No, he's not mad, he's a lucky fellow, that scamp there. And he has had a comfortless life of late, I know that; and I have not helped to make it more comfortable. Perhaps we shall both be the better, we jolly young bachelors, for having a woman to keep us in order. Though you'll find me a tough customer, I warn you of that, Miss Edna."

"Never mind. I'll take you just as you are, and make the best of you."

With which light jest the two sisters sent the two brothers out under the narrow jasmine-scented door-way—out into the brilliant harvest moonlight, so dazzling white that it smote one almost with a sense of chill.

Will put his arm through his brother's, and they walked on a considerable way before either spoke. At last Julius took the initiative.

"Well, old fellow, this is a pretty go! Catch a weasel asleep! I certainly have been that unfortunate animal. I had no more idea that any game of this sort was afoot than—than the man in the moon, who perhaps has more to do with such things than we suspect. Of course, love is only a fit of temporary or permanent insanity. By-the-by, what a precious fool I was near making of myself to-night!"

"How?"

"Oh, in several ways; but it doesn't matter now. I've come out safe and scot-free. And pray, how long is it since you made up your mind to marry that little thing?"

Will winced.

"I beg your pardon, but she is such a little thing; though, I own, the best little woman imaginable; and has such neat pretty ways about a house—even such a shabby house as theirs looks cozy with her in it. How jolly comfortable she'll make us—I mean you; for, of course, I shall have to turn out."

Will said nothing—neither yes nor no. He felt upon him that cowardice, purely masculine, which always shrinks from doing any thing unpleasant. He wished he had had Edna beside him, to put, as plainly as his own common sense put it, the fact that a man has no right to lay upon his wife more burdens than she can bear; and that with his changeful, moody ways, his erratic habits, and his general Bohemian tendencies, Julius was, with all his lovableness, about the last inmate likely either to be happy himself, or to make others happy, in a married home. That is, unless the home were his very own, and the mistress of it had over him the influence which was the only influence that would keep Julius safe—that of a passionately-loved and loving wife.

All this Will thought, but could not explain. Therefore his only refuge was silence.

"Yes, it's all right," said Julius, somewhat coldly; "and quite natural too. I don't blame you. You have done a deal for me, Will: more than any brother, or many a father, would have done. I'll never forget it. And I dare say I shall be able to shift for myself somehow."

"There will be plenty of time, my dear fellow," answered Will, in rather a husky voice. "I shall not be married until I get something quite certain to start with —probably that appointment which you know I have been after so long. And then I shall be able to pay over to you, in whole or part, for as long as you require it, the other half of grandfather's money."

"Will, you don't mean that?"

"Yes, I do. In truth, she was so sore about you, and especially your being 'turned out,' as she called it, that she would not have had me without my promising that arrangement, which will make our marriage, whenever it does take place, none the worse for any body."

"But—"

"It's no use arguing with a woman, especially one who won't talk—only act. Edna is quite determined. Indeed I may say I have purchased her at the alarming sacrifice of two hundred a year, payable quarterly—"

"Will!" cried Julius, stopping suddenly, and looking his brother full in the face. The moonlight showed his own, which was full of emotion. "You're a pretty pair, you and she—six of one and half a dozen of the other. I see it all now. Give her my love. No; I'll take it to her myself. For me, I've been a selfish, luxurious rascal all my life; but I'll turn over a new leaf, hang me if I won't! I'll take an oath against light kid gloves, and rings, and operas. I'll dress like an old-clothesman, and feed like a day-laborer. And I'll work—by George, won't I work!"

"That's right, lad," said the elder brother, cheerily. "And you'll find it all the better when, some day, you have to work for two. Meantime, instead of the 'family house' you wanted to visit at, you'll have a brother's home always to come to. And she will make it so bright, as you say. Besides, Letty will be there," continued Will, dashing at this fact with a desperate haste, uncertain how it might be taken.

Julius did start, very uneasily. "Is she to live with you?"

"Yes; there was no other way. As must be obvious enough, Letty is not the person to be left to live alone."

"No," said Julius, concisely.

"I doubt whether she will like living with us, for we shall have a hard struggle to make ends meet, at any rate for the first few years; and she is not well fitted for poverty—Letty, I mean."

Julius was silent.

"But in that case, if she got tired of us, she could easily return to her old life as a resident governess, which she often regrets still—unless, in the mean time, some young fellow snaps her up, which is far from improbable. Her sister says she has had lovers without end, as was to be expected; but none of them were good enough for her. Edna hopes, when she does marry, it will be some nice, good fellow, with plenty of patience and heaps of money. Letty would never be happy unless she lived in clover and cotton-wool. Poor Letty! It's well for me that my Edna is different."

William Stedman must have been strangely blind—perhaps that little word "my" produced the blindness, and carried his thoughts involuntarily away—not to have noticed how dumb grew his talkative brother; how he walked on fiercely and fast, swinging his cane, and slashing at the hedges in a nervous, excitable way, as they threaded the narrow lanes, which were so pretty twenty years ago, but are now vanishing fast, in the streets, and squares, and "gardens" of Campden Hill. At last Julius said, with that sudden change from earnestness to frivolity which was too common in him to cause Will any surprise—

"Nevertheless, it's odd that you, and not I, should be the fool or the madman—for you certainly are both—to commit matrimony. Catch me giving up my freedom, my jolly, idle life, to tie myself to any woman's apron-strings! You'd better think twice of it: eh, old fellow? Edna's a good girl—I don't deny that; and likes you—I suppose; she'd be an ass if she didn't. But is there a girl alive who would go on caring for a man unless he had lots of money—could give her all she wanted? and they're always wanting something. All alike, all alike; and a precious lot they are, too. So—

'I'd be a bachelor born in a bower,'"

carolled the young fellow, startling the green lanes and a solitary policeman with the then popular tune of "I'd be a butterfly," and inventing a doggerel parody to it, which was, to say the least, rather inappropriate that quiet Sunday night.

"You are not yourself, Ju," said William. "You have got overtired. Didn't you say you had walked fifteen miles to-day? That was far too much. I shall have to keep a sharp look-out after you, even when we have a separate establishment."

And the elder brother, out of his deep heaven of peace, looked tenderly upon the foolish fellow who did not understand what peace was, who was making a mock of it, and trying, like so many other skeptics, driven into skepticism less by nature than circumstances, to believe that to be non-existent which was only non-beheld.

Then the two Stedmans, with their bachelor latch-key, entered their dull, dark, close house, which breathed the very atmosphere of dreariness and disorder. Julius went up to bed almost immediately; but William sat long in his empty dining-room, peopling it with wondrous visions, brightening it with hearth-light and lamp-light, and, above all, the perpetual light of a woman's smile — the smile which happy love brings to a woman's lips, never to be wholly lost from them until they are set in that last, loveliest peace upon which the coffin-lid closes—which seems to say even to mourning husband or children, "Be content—I am loving you still—with God."

William Stedman had to-day seen, beyond a doubt, this love in his betrothed's face; and he felt by that in his own heart that it would be his until death.

He knew, as well as his brother did, that he should be poor enough, probably for years; that, with most men, to marry upon his prospects would be the height of madness. But then they were men who had not learned, like himself, the calm self-denial which disarms poverty of half its dangers, half its dread, because holding as its best things the things which money can neither give nor take away; being far too proud for the ordinary petty pride of being afraid to seem what one is, if that happens to be a little inferior to one's neighbors. True, he had never starved, never been in debt; for neither alternative often happens to an unmarried man who has ordinary health, honesty, and brains—at least, if it does, he has usually only himself to blame. But William Stedman had been poor, very poor; he had known how hard it is to go on wearing a threadbare coat because you have not five pounds to spare for a new one; how harder still to crave for many an accidental luxury which you know you have no right to indulge in. And perhaps, hardest of all, to associate with people who, in all but money, are fairly your equals; and who never suspect, or never pause to think, how your every penny is as momentous as their pounds. In short, he had learned, in the many wholesome but painful ways that early poverty teaches, the best lesson that any young man can learn—to control and deny himself.

Therefore, fitter than most men was he to enter upon that "holy estate," which, perhaps, derives its very holiness from the fact that it requires from both man and woman infinite and never-ending self-denial—teaching, as nothing else can teach, that complete absorption of self into another, which is the key-stone and summit of true happiness.

Possibly William Stedman did not say all these things to himself, for he was not much given to preaching or to self-examination—in truth, he never had time for it; but he felt them in a dim, nebulous way; he "took stock of himself," so to speak, as to whether he was fit for the life which lay before him—fit to be trusted with the happiness of a sweet, fond, ignorant, innocent woman; whether he had strength for her sake to go on with hard work and little pleasure, to place his enjoyments in inward rather than outward things, and to renounce very much that to most young men—Julius, for instance—would be what he to himself had jestingly termed, like the linen-drapers' advertisements, an "alarming sacrifice."

He was not afraid, for he knew Edna was not. He knew that whatever he had to give up in the world without would be made up by the world within. That this little woman would come in on his cheerless, untidy hearth like a good fairy, reducing chaos to order, and charming away gloom and dullness by her bright, sweet ways. Besides that, he felt that with her direct simplicity, her unworldly tone of thought, her divine instinct for right and truth, she would come and sit in his heart like a conscience —a blessing as well as a delight, making him better as well as happier, and happier just because he was better.

"God has been very kind to me—far kinder than I deserved," said the young man to himself, thinking, in his happiness, more than he often found time to think, of the Source whence all happiness flows. And his heart melted within him; and the long pent-up storm of headlong passion, and frantic pride, and bitter self-distrust which had raged within him for weeks and months, and had come to a climax two days ago, when he felt himself driven mad by the sound of a voice and the touch of a little ignorant hand—all this calmed itself down into a most blessed quiet, like a summer evening after a thunder-shower, when every thing is so perfumy, fresh, and green, and the flowers are lifting up their heads, and the birds sing doubly loud and clear, even though the large-leaved trees are still dropping—as more than one great, heavy drop fell, in this sacred solitude, from William Stedman's eyes.

They came from a sudden thought which darted across him—the thought, not of Edna, but of his mother. He scarcely remembered her—he was only seven years old when she died; but he knew she was a very good woman; and he had kept up all his life this faint, shadowy remembrance with a sort of silent idolatry which had begun then in his childish yet tenaciously faithful heart.

He wondered whether she had any knowledge of what had happened to him to-day, and whether she would have been satisfied with the wife he had chosen; and he thought, the next time he saw Edna, he would tell her all these his childish recollections, and take her instead of pearls and diamonds, which she altogether refused to accept from him, the simple guard-ring which had belonged to his mother.

CHAPTER XIV.

It was now fully ten months since William Stedman and Edna Kenderdine had plighted that promise which, when made deliberately, wisely, and justifiably on both sides, should be held as inviolable as the subsequent vow before the altar — that is, if the love, which is its only righteous foundation, lasts. Otherwise, the best wisdom is that which Edna sometimes gave in answer to Letty's murmurings of the misery of long engagements, and the advantage of keeping "free." "When he wishes to be free, he is free. The moment he ceases to love me, let him go!"

But this contingency did not seem likely to happen. Though the promise had been made conditionally—that is, he had told her, in his deep humility, that when she found out all the bad things in him, she might break it at any time, and he should not blame her—still she found out all the bad things, and she did not break it. Perhaps he too discovered certain little earthly specks in his angel's white wings, just enough to keep her from flying away from him, and survived the discovery. For two people, who expect to find one another all perfection, must be taught such wholesome lessons; and doubtless these lovers had to learn them. But they had the sense to keep both their experience and their mode of acquiring it strictly to themselves.

"You two never quarrel," Letty would say sometimes, half puzzled, half vexed. "I thought lovers always quarrelled. I am sure I squabbled continually with all mine."

At which Edna smiled, and only smiled. Her sister's unconscious plurals precluded all argument. As well reason with the Grand Turk on the Christian law of marriage as talk to poor Letty of the mysterious law of love.

And yet she was most kind, most good-natured—an ever welcome and convenient third in the various week-day walks, and meetings for "sight-seeing," which Dr. Stedman contrived to steal out of his busy life, and add to those blessed Sundays which he spent with his betrothed, healing thereby all the cares and worries of the seven days past. And he was so good to Letty; he took such pains that she should never be forgotten in any pleasure which could be given her, that she liked Will very much. But still she moaned sometimes—Letty rather enjoyed moaning—over the probable length of Edna's engagement, and the misfortune of her marrying a poor man.

"For talk as you like, my dear," she sometimes oracularly said, "I am certain you would be a deal happier in an elegant house, with a carriage to drive in, and plenty of good society. And—don't look so indignant—I dare say he would love you better—men always do, you know—if you were a little better dressed."

But Edna only smiled, and smoothed out her pretty cottons and muslins as carefully as if they were silks and satins. Perhaps Heaven had mercifully given her a temperament that did not much care for luxuries, except those of Heaven's providing, common and free as air and sunshine—such as cleanliness, order, simplicity, and harmony. And then she was so happy, for God had sent her heart's desire. She sang over her daily work like an April thrush in a thorn-tree, building its nest through rain and shine. Letty complained bitterly of the delay which made school-keeping still necessary; Dr. Stedman openly grumbled at the school and all belonging to it; and often behaved exceedingly badly, and very like a man; but Edna was as gay as a lark, and never swerved from her firm determination not to be married till a small certainty made the marriage prudent as regarded them all. She declared she would work steadily on, like a brave independent little woman as she was, till the very day of her marriage.

"For," she said once, with her sweet, earnest face lifted up to the clouded one of her lover, "I see no pleasure, and no dignity either, in idleness. If you had not loved me I should have been a working-woman to the end of my days, and have worked cheerily too. When you can work for me, I'll work no more. But if you ever needed it, and I could do it, I would fall to work again, and you should not hinder me! I'd begin once more to teach my little butchers and bakers and candlestick-makers, and think myself honored in the duty."

And then the strong man would catch her in his arms, and thank God he had chosen a woman who, in the countless troubles that man's lot is heir to, would neither be selfish nor cowardly, a burden nor a snare; but, under her soft meekness, would carry about with her a spirit fearless as his own.

After much delay the long-hoped-for hospital appointment was given—and given to some one else. William told this news to Edna one dark night coming through the green lanes home from church—told it briefly, almost sharply; which showed how deep was his disappointment. She only pressed his arm, and said:

"Never mind. We are young still. It is said to be good to bear the yoke in one's youth."

"Yes, if it is not so heavy as to make one humpbacked for life," answered Dr. Stedman, with a laugh, tuneless and hard; then, stopping under the next gas-lamp, he saw Edna was crying—his poor Edna, whose life was no easier than his own! In the next dark place they came to, he turned and clasped her to his heart, with all the bitterness melted out of it, but with a passion of yearning that even she could not understand. After that they spoke of the lost hospital appointment no more.

Then, too, Julius fell into a very unsatisfactory state, physical and moral, which, even if Will had not confided it to her, Edna was too sharp-eyed not to see. He looked wretchedly ill, was often moody and out of temper; took vehement fits of work, and corresponding fits of despondent idleness. Whether it was that the home he was soon to quit lost even its small attractions for him, or from some other nameless fancy, but Julius became more erratic than ever: in his comings and goings entirely unreliable, save on those Sundays when, whether invited or not, he always presented himself with his brother at the Misses Kenderdine's door.

There might have been a pleasanter guest; for sometimes he sat whole evenings, like a cloud of gloom, by the cheerful fireside; or else startled the whole party by his unnatural flow of spirits. They bore with him — every body always did bear with Julius. And these lovers had a quality not universal among people in their circumstances — their own happiness made them very patient with those who had none. Besides, Julius was not always a dead weight upon Edna and Will; with astonishing tact he always contrived, early or late, to escape to the kitchen-fire, which, the servant being absent at church, was faithfully presided over by Letty's favorite cat, large and lovely as herself—and by Letty. There he and Letty shared each other's companionship for hours.

What resulted was sure to result, even if the two elders, for once in their lives sufficiently so self-engrossed as to be oblivious of others, had seen what they did not see until too late to prevent—that is, supposing they had any right to prevent it.

Letty too—she should not, at this point, be blamed too severely. She was like many another woman, not wicked, only weak. It was very pleasant to her to be adored, and it would be to nine out of ten of the women who read about her in these pages—girls who are taught from earliest maidenhood that the grand aim of life is to be loved rather than to love. She did not at all dislike — who would? — after her dull week's work, to have, for some hours every Sunday, those passionate eyes following her about wherever she moved, that eager breath hanging on every word she uttered, whether silly or wise; those looks, which said as plainly as words could say — sometimes joking, sometimes earnestly, when he glanced at the lovers —"Never mind them, *I* live only for you." Only looks. Julius never committed himself — never said a syllable which, to use Letty's phrase afterwards, could be "taken hold of." As for flirting, of course she was well used to "that sort of thing;" but this was admiration of a novel kind—persistent, permanent, and yet kept so safely within limits, and under the shadow of their approaching relationship, or connection, or whatever they chose to call it—that if at any time during the winter and spring Letty had been asked the direct question, which she never was asked — "Is Julius Stedman making love to you?" she would have answered, without any falsehood—that is, not in *her* notion of falsehood—"Oh dear, no! not the least in the world."

And yet all the while she was maddening him with her beauty, bewildering him with her caprices — sometimes warm, sometimes cold; having little quarrels, and making it up again; assuming the tenderest "sisterly" confidence, and then sliding off again into perfect coldness and unapproachable civility. Doing it all half consciously, half unconsciously; aware of her power, and liking to exercise it up to a certain extent—an extent that gave herself no inconvenience. But once, when the thrushes were singing on the budding trees of Kensington Gardens, as they walked there of evenings—and again, on the first day of the Royal Academy, when Julius took them all in great pride to see his first well-hung picture, and Letty looked so beaming and beautiful that every body turned to stare at her—then, seeing certain alarming symptoms in Julius, she drew in her horns, and was exceedingly cold and cautious for a day or two. "For," she reasoned to herself, and long afterwards repeated the reasons to Edna, "what was I to do with the young man? He hadn't a halfpenny."

Quite right, Letty Kenderdine—not a half-penny!—only a man's heart, or worse, a man's soul, to be lost or won, according as a woman chooses. But that, in these days, and with many people, is quite immaterial.

It was a day rather momentous—that first Monday in May—when Julius learned his picture was hung. Will had decided with Edna that they must all go to see it, and the sisters had a wild struggle after sudden spring bonnets, to be assumed at a few hours' notice; "for," said Letty, "we can't go at all unless we go respectable." And possibly William Stedman thought a little beyond respectability the happy face circled with white daisies under a round-brimmed straw bonnet — such as was the fashion then—which smiled beside him, so delighted in the brief holiday with him. For Letty—Letty always looked beautiful. She was a picture in herself. But, as fate so often balances things, she did not care half so much about the pictures as Edna did; nor, handsome as it was, did her face look half so beaming as that one from whence William Stedman learned to see mysteries of loveliness which had never come upon his darkened mind before. There was in him just enough of the poetic nature to wish he had more of it, and to be tenderly reverential towards the beloved woman who had it, and whom he thought so infinitely superior to himself. While she, who knew herself to have so many faults, to be at times so fierce and hasty, passionate and unwise, held a different opinion.

They examined the pictures, none of which Edna liked better than Julius's own—the landscape about which she had heard so much—painted as Julius dared to paint, and, in that anti-Pre-Raphaelite time, was greatly despised for painting—from absolute nature, instead of nature diluted through faded Old Masters—Claudes, Poussins, and Salvator Rosas—each a degree farther off from reality than the last.

"Yes," said Julius, a gleam of hope lighting up his melancholy eyes, as they followed a stray sunbeam which kindled in deeper beauty his beautiful work; "this year I think I have not wasted my time. Perhaps I may end in being an artist, after all."

"Were you thinking of being any thing else?" asked Edna, surprised.

Julius blushed slightly. "Oh, I think of so many things. A painter never makes money, and I want money—terribly. But let us look at the pictures, Letty." She was hanging on his arm, piloted carefully through the crowd. "You were admiring that portrait's velvet gown—here is another well-painted bit of velvet for you, and a bit of sentiment too—a girl taking a thorn out of a boy's finger. What a mildly determined air she has! she won't let him go, though he winces at the pain—just like a man, and just like a woman. The old story. She is beginning to hurt him even at seven years old."

"She ought to hurt him, nor be afraid of hurting him, if she can take the thorn away," said Edna, gently.

"Listen, Will! Now you see what lies before you! Bravo! Who wouldn't rather be a bachelor, if all men's wives are to be ready with needle and penknife to wound their spouses—of course, entirely for their good. Heigh-ho! What say you, Letty?"

"I beg your pardon; what were you talking about?" replied Letty, whose attention had been wholly distracted by a charming bonnet which she was most anxious Edna should see and imitate. But Edna was absorbed in a picture which she never saw after that day, and never even knew whose it was; but it fastened itself upon her memory, to be revived, even after many years, like invisible color, which some magic touch makes fresh as ever.

It was called "In another Man's Garden," and was simply a suburban cottage-door, painted with the intense realism then altogether pooh-poohed and despised. Thereat—also modern and real, down to coat, hat, and stick—stood a young man, bidding the cheery morning adieu to his wife and child before going to business—a happy, intensely happy little group, safely shut inside the rose-trellised walls. While outside, leaning against the gate, was a solitary figure—a broken-down, dust-stained, shabby man—gazing with mournful yearning into "another man's garden."

Edna looked at her betrothed, then at the picture; and her eyes filled with tears. She could not help it. She understood it all so well. So—out of his deep content—did he.

"Poor fellow!" said William, as if he were speaking of a real person.

"Oh, that's me!" cried Julius, with a short laugh. "I thought you would recognize the likeness. The painter is a friend of mine. He asked me to sit, and thought I looked the character to perfection. Do I, Letty?"

"What, the gentlemanly young man in the garden?"

"No; the blackguard outside. That was the character I personated. I got quite used to my battered old hat, and stockingless shoes, and coat all rags and tatters."

"Did you really put on these things? Oh, how nasty of you!" said Letty, turning away in great disgust.

The artist laughed again, more bitterly than before. "Then if I ever appear as a returned convict, or a repentant prodigal, it's of no use my coming to you, Letty?"

"Julius! how can you talk of things so very shocking? It makes me quite miserable."

Here Letty gave—and Edna caught, startling her into uneasy suspicion—one of those sidelong, downcast looks, which might well delude a man into that mad passion which, for the rest of the afternoon, gleamed in every feature of Julius Stedman's face, as he followed her like her shadow, and seemed only to live upon her smile.

"Something will surely happen; and oh, I wonder—I wonder what—" thought Edna, very anxiously; longing for the next Sunday, when she would have a quiet hour to lay all her anxieties upon the wise, tender, manly heart which was her comfort in all her troubles now.

But as yet there was no chance of a quiet word with William, for the four came home to Kensington ignominiously in an omnibus, to Letty's unconcealed dismay.

"Ah," sighed she, "how nice it would be if Dr. Stedman kept his brougham, like so many London doctors—I do so like a carriage!" At which Will laughed, but Julius looked dark and sad for the whole journey.

It was a recognized rule that the Stedmans should only be received on a Sunday, so the four young people parted at the Misses Kenderdine's gate, and Edna and Letty sat down to their late tea, very tired both of them—one a little cross, and the other just a little weary-hearted.

Edna could bear her own burdens—their own burdens, she and William together; but she thought, if an added weight were to come, and such a serious anxiety as a love-affair or marriage engagement between Letty and Julius must inevitably be, however it might end, her cares would be heavy indeed; for neither of these two were the sort of people capable of bearing their own troubles, to say nothing of lightening other people's.

As she looked at Letty, so handsome and so helpless, and thought of Julius, who had turned from the door in one of his sad, sullen fits, painful and yet pathetic as those of a naughty child, Edna felt her courage give way, and her heart sink with that strange foreboding of evil which comes sometimes, we know not how or why. Without saying a word to Letty—it would have been neither delicate nor wise—she pondered over the whole question, till at last, utterly bewildered, it settled itself into her one grand refuge for all distresses—"I will tell it to William next Sunday." And, comforting as this thought was, it brought also a vague longing for the time when their life would be all Sundays, when they would be continually together. With it came a fear—the fear that will come with deep love — lest something should come between them. Only, to their faith and constancy, nothing *could* come but death; and that she did not fear, for it would only be falling, as David wished to fall, into the hands of God—the same God who had already made them so happy.

"Yes, we have been happy—very happy, and I am very, very thankful!" thought poor Edna, and her serenity returned — the unchangeable peace of those who have the blessedness of being able to recognize their blessings.

Tired as she was, she took out her work and was sitting —let us boldly confess it—mending a large basketful of stockings, when there came a knock at the front door.

Letty started up from the sofa.

"That's William's knock—I know it is. Oh, what can have happened!"

"Nothing to be frightened at," said William, who was in the room almost as soon as she spoke. Good news, not ill, were written on his face. "I beg your pardon. I could not help coming." He shut the door behind him, and then, regardless of her sister's presence, clasped Edna tight in his arms. "It has come at last — come at last, thank God!" And in an ecstasy of joy which betrayed how sharp had been the unacknowledged suffering, he kissed again and again his betrothed wife — then went over and kissed Letty, and bade her wish him joy.

Presently, when he was sufficiently calm for a consecutive statement to be got out of him, Dr. Stedman told the great news—strangely little it would seem to some people, yet to these two was enough to uplift them into perfect felicity.

It was one of those bits of "good luck"—he called it nothing more, and always protested he had done nothing to win it — which occasionally turn the tide of a man's fortune by giving him, at the outset of his career, that slight impetus of help without which a fair start is nearly impracticable. A great lady, and good as great, who had been interested in Dr. Stedman's incessant labors among the poor, had offered him a permanent appointment as physician to a charitable institution which she had founded and principally supported. His salary was to be £300, and, by-and-by, £400 a year—a solid foundation of annual income; while the work could not interfere with his practice, but would rather give him opportunities for that continual study of his profession which a doctor so much needs, and which, at the begining of his career, he finds so difficult to obtain. Thus the lady, a far-sighted and generous woman, in securing his services, benefited both sides, and in doing a prudent did also a kindly deed.

"I wish she knew all the happiness she has given us!" said Edna, trembling and agitated; while Letty, as was her wont under all novel and exciting circumstances, began to cry. In fact, they all shed an honest tear or two, and then they sat down together—Edna close by William, holding Letty's hand on the other side—to try and realize the sudden bliss—this unexpected change in all their affairs.

"Does Julius know?" asked Edna, anxiously.

"No—the letter came after he had gone out. You know he almost always does go out of evenings. But it will be a brighter home for him to come to when you are there—and Letty."

William said this in all simplicity, as Edna at once perceived; and his evident unconsciousness of the idea which had lately entered her mind shook Edna's faith in her own quickness of perception. If William were quite at ease concerning his brother, why should she perplex herself or perplex him by speaking of this matter of Julius and Letty? So, for the present, she let it slip by; and when Letty benevolently quitted the room, and left her alone with her lover, she forgot every thing, as lovers do.

Forgive them, if so be there is any need of forgiveness. Life is so short, so changeful, so full of infinite chances of grief and loss, who would grudge to any body a little love, a little happiness? These two were ready to take both the sweet and the bitter, the evil and the good, believing that both come alike by the Father's will. Yet who can wonder that, as they sat together, knowing they were going to be married—not exactly "to-morrow," as Dr. Stedman had ingeniously suggested, but within a few weeks—and that, come weal or woe, they would never more be parted, it was surely pardonable if, for a while, they forgot every body but themselves.

"And you are not afraid to begin life with me—to be a poor man's wife? for it will be that, Edna. I can't dress you any better than this"—touching tenderly her gray merino gown; "and the carriage Letty wants, it may be years before I can give it you, if ever. Oh, my love, am I harming you? In marrying you now at once, while I have still only just enough for us to live upon, am I doing you any wrong?"

"Wrong!" she cried, as she clung round his neck for a minute, and then drew back, looking at him with the brightest face—the most radiant, and yet half-indignant eyes. "Wrong! you are showing me the utmost love, and paying me the chiefest honor that a man can give to a woman. You are taking me at your life's beginning, that we may begin it together. That is the right thing. Don't be afraid, William. I'll help you—I know I can, for I am not a coward, and I have *you*. Oh! if men were more like you, had your courage, your faith, there would not be so many broken-hearted women in the world."

"And there would not be so many bad, ruined men, I think, if women were more like my Edna."

So talked these two—foolishly, no doubt, and with a vicarious self-laudation which is very much the habit of lovers. And yet there was truth at the bottom of it—a truth which, day by day, as she and Letty busied themselves every spare hour in those innocent wedding preparations which every honest heart, either of friend or stranger, can not help taking pleasure in, forced itself deeper and deeper upon Edna's heart. No worldly show was there—no hiding with splendid outside formalities the hollowness within: she was going to be, as William said, a poor man's wife; and expensive clothes and extravagant outlay of any sort would be merely ridiculous; but Edna prepared herself for her great change with all the happy-heartedness that a bride should have, a bride who knows that down to the lowest depth of her soul is not a feeling that need be hidden, not a thought that God and her husband may not see.

One little thing made her sorry. Julius did not come to see her; indeed, he had taken himself off on an artistic tour in Wales, to be "out of the way," he alleged; but he wrote, after a few days' delay, an affectionate congratulatory letter, and asked her to seek out for him bachelor lodgings as close as possible to their own house, where he meant to be exceedingly jolly, and inflict himself upon them several times a week. And he sent her, as a wedding present, a lovely portrait of Letty, composed out of the many studies he had made of her face, which he said, briefly, "he knew by heart." At which remark Letty blushed a little, and pouted a little, saying it was "impertinent;" but was exceedingly gratified to look at her own exquisite portrait, and hear every body admire it and say how very like it was.

So fled the time, long, and yet how short—dwindling first into weeks and then into days, until the last breaking-up day came, and the two young school-mistresses, not without a few sincere tears, sent away their little pupils forever. After that there was only one more Sunday left for the Stedmans to come to tea in the old way, which for nearly a year had gone on now, and brought with it so much of peace and pleasure. No more now of those "courting days," which are said by some to be the happiest, by others the most miserable of their lives. Probably the real truth lies between both these facts, and that the happiness or misery is according as the lovers create it for themselves. Life is not all joy—neither God nor man can make it so; but it may be made all love. And love, that infinite and endless blessing, had been held out from heaven to these two, Edna and William; they had had eyes to see it, strength to grasp it, faith to cling to it. They had cause to be glad and thankful, and so they were.

CHAPTER XV.

Dr. Stedman came alone to spend his last Sunday with his bride and her sister. Julius had returned home and promised to come, but changed his mind and disappeared for the day.

"He is so constantly changing his mind and plans, that I hardly know what to make of him. I do wish he had a wife of his own," said the elder brother, with a sigh. "But a sister will be better than nothing: you must be very good to him, Edna."

"I will," said Edna, in her quiet way. And then they all spent together—contentedly, yet half solemnly—the last Sunday of so many Sundays, the last which would ever see them as they were. It hardly seemed real—this great change—and it had come about so naturally that they felt none of the agitation and excitement which a marriage brings. No one made any unnecessary fuss; and even when Letty took Dr. Stedman up stairs to see the bridal finery—the white muslin dresses and white bonnets gloriously displayed—he only said, "Very pretty," and came down looking happy, indeed, but rather grave.

Indeed they were all three a little subdued, and, arrangements being now completed—for the wedding was fixed for Tuesday—they had little or nothing to talk about. Tea over, they were sinking into a rather sombre silence, when, to their amazement, Julius appeared.

The sisters had never seen him since the day of the Exhibition, and the welcome they gave him was hearty and warm. He received it with eager happiness.

"Yes; I thought I would come, if only to have a last look at Edna Kenderdine. Though I know I am frightfully in the way: not wanted—never shall be wanted—anywhere—by any body!"

"Oh, Julius!" said Edna, reproachfully; then, without more words, she busied herself in getting him tea, and all those creature comforts which a man sorely needs, especially when he comes in worn and worried—as Julius did. After the first flush of excitement had faded, she saw, and was shocked to see, how great was the change in him during these few weeks. He had grown exceedingly thin, and had at times a restless, hunted look, as of a man pursued by one relentless idea which he vainly tries to master, but which conquers him against his will. He was quieted a little, however, during the tea and talk, and recovered his old self—so charming, brotherly, and kind.

William Stedman looked on, pleased and smiling, but he said nothing. Nor did Letty, which was a still more remarkable fact; and when Julius, having accomplished his usual aim by asserting volubly, to every body's great amusement, that he must retire to the kitchen, as his sole purpose in paying this final visit was to take a farewell sketch of it and the cat, disappeared, Letty drew herself up with dignity, and, instead of accompanying him, went up stairs. Whence, however, she was soon heard to descend, Letty being one of those people who prefer any body's company to their own.

"I hope she will be kind to him, even though he has neglected you and her a little of late," said William, innocently. "I do trust they will get on well together—our brother and sister. They ought, for there is such a deal of good in poor Julius. He shows it, by being so very fond of you. He told me last night, when I was urging him to end his nonsensical flirtations and get honestly engaged to some nice girl, that he would, if only I could find him such a girl as my Edna."

Edna laughed.

"Do you know he once made me half jealous—I mean when I began to want you myself, and fancied he did the same. Now, little Conscience, if it had been so, what ought I to have done? Given you up to my brother, eh?"

Edna's light laugh ceased. She thought a minute, and then said, seriously, "No; if you loved me, and I loved you, you ought to have married me in spite of all the world."

So talked they—half merry, half grave—recalling their past, or planning their future, and then scarcely talking at all—content with the simple fact of being together.

Meantime, in the kitchen there was also comparative silence. Not the talking and laughing which generally went on between Letty and Julius, who always ridiculed the extreme soberness of "the folks in love." Just a low murmur of conversation sometimes, and then long pauses—so long that even the betrothed pair in the next room noticed it at last.

"I wonder if the sketch is finished. Shall we go and see, William?"

"Not yet—please not just yet. I must leave early this evening, and you will not let me come to-morrow. But after to-morrow you will never get rid of me."

"Never, all my life! I am so" — sorry, a coquette would have said; but Edna, wholly true, had not a spark of coquetry in her, first or last. She said "glad."

"Thank you, my blessing of blessings!" And then they talked no more.

But when at length Edna, with a certain uneasy feeling that she could not get rid of, though she kept it strictly to herself, wondering at the long stillness, went to see, she found Julius sitting all by himself over the fire, which, out of its dull, burnt-out hollow, threw occasional sparks of flame, giving a ghostly look to the neat kitchen, as neat and pretty almost as a parlor, which Julius used to say was "the finest room in the house." He was so absorbed that, till Edna touched him on the shoulder, he did not notice her entrance.

"Where is the sketch, Julius?" asked Will.

"And where is my sister?"

"Gone up stairs. Hey, Will! is that you, man? I'm going home."

"Not this minute; not before supper," pleaded Edna.

"Supper! I've had mine. I've 'supped full of horrors,' like Macbeth. Now, 'to bed—to bed—to bed!' Edna, couldn't you give a poor fellow something to make him sleep—forever?"

"Ju," said Will, "what is the matter with you? You're half asleep now, I think; wake up, man!"

"I will," cried Julius, springing to his feet with a violent gesture. "I have been asleep; but I'm awake now. Give me my hat; I'll take a walk and come back to my senses, and to supper likewise, if you please, Miss Edna."

But he never appeared. Letty came down stairs flushed and uncomfortable-looking, and to William's jesting question if she and Julius had been quarrelling, gave an answer so sharp that Dr. Stedman said no more. Silently, uneasily, ended the last evening of so many merry evenings which they had spent in that little house, every corner of which Edna felt she should love to the end of her days.

Yet, as she stood at the door on the solemn dark night —for it had been raining heavily, and there was not a star visible — even though her hand was clasped in her lover's, and his safe arm round her, a weight of foreboding sadness gathered over her.

FOREBODINGS.

"Oh, William, if trouble should come!"

"We will bear it, whatever it is, together."

And when he said that, and drew her closer, and she felt the beating of his warm, living, loving heart, so tender and so true, she knew that she could bear it.

After Dr. Stedman was gone, Letty called Edna into the kitchen—Letty still flushed, and full of the excitement of a secret.

"Don't be running off the very minute you have sent your lover away. You might have some little sympathy with other people's love-affairs—mine, for instance."

"Oh, Letty!"

"Yes, you need not look so shocked. It has just come to that. I knew it would. I have been afraid of it for ever so long. Very provoking. A wretched business altogether. How could the poor fellow be such a goose! though I suppose he couldn't help it."

And Letty tried to look grave, while a furtive, gratified smile twinkled round the corners of her mouth.

"But you could have helped it, if it is as I suspect,"

cried Edna, greatly distressed. "How could you let him do it? For of course it is Julius—poor Julius!"

Letty nodded. "I promised not to tell any body, and of course I won't. You will notice, I have never mentioned his name, and I never told you of it, though I have suspected it for months. Poor fellow, he is desperately fond of me."

"Oh, Letty!"

Edna could not say another word. She saw, as in an ominous vision, Julius's face, as he snatched up his hat and rushed from the house—a wild, fierce, maddened face—full of that overwhelming passion, a compound of the senses and the imagination, which sometimes seizes upon a young man: whom, having played at love throughout his first fantastic youth, it takes hold of at last in terrible earnest, either making or marring him for the rest of his life. For Julius was one of those weak, loving natures who must cling to somebody, be in love with somebody. And he had fallen in love with Letty, the very last person, any third party would say, whom he ought to choose. But third parties are not infallible, and Edna snatched at a fragment of comfort and hope.

"Surely, Letty, you like Julius?"

"Like him? Oh yes; very much—in a sisterly way. I told him so. I promised to be the best sister possible to him, as I always have been, I am sure. But as to marrying him, that is quite another thing. Why he has not a halfpenny but what he earns, and he will never earn much—geniuses never do. He will be poor all his life. And, oh dear me, Edna," shrugging her shoulders with a trick she had learned at her Paris *pension*, "you know I have had quite enough of poverty."

"But you might wait."

"Wait—till my appearance was all gone. He is an artist, and has an eye for that, I know," said Letty, with the pathetic intuition which sometimes dawned through all her silliness, of favor being deceitful, and beauty vain—"Wait till I got old and ugly, and couldn't enjoy good-fortune when it came? Oh no, Edna! that would never do. Better even for the young man himself that I won't marry him. And yet he is frantically in love with me—he is, indeed. I had no idea there was so much earnestness in him about any thing till now. Would you believe, he almost frightened me."

And Letty, sitting at the kitchen-fire, meditatively warmed her lovely foot, glancing round half triumphantly, half pensively at her sister, whose heart slowly, slowly sank, heavy as lead. For vainly she sought in those beautiful eyes some trace of the feeling—call it love, nay, passion, if you will—which, however sad, however unfortunate, when earnestly and honestly felt, ennobles any woman; while that other side of it—the weak pleasure of conquest, the petty egotistical vanity of being loved—only deteriorates and degrades.

THE TWO WOMEN.

"Oh, how blind, how careless I have been!" cried Edna, almost in a sob. "And you, Letty, you have been playing with edged tools—you know you have. That poor fellow! And you guessed it all, yet you let it go on. How could you! But it is not quite too late. Perhaps you don't know your own mind—perhaps you really love him?"

Letty laughed. "How should I know? Certainly not in your sort of love. I'm very fond of him, and I told him so, as a sister. For any thing else—but it's no use thinking of that, as you must see; for us to be engaged, Julius and me, would, in our circumstances, be ridiculous—perfectly ridiculous."

Edna answered, with a strange harshness, which she repented afterwards, or would have done but that Letty did not seem to perceive it at all, "I think you are right. It would be even worse than ridiculous. When Julius is my brother, I shall warn him that the most fatal thing he could do would be to marry my sister Letty."

"Yes," said Letty, composedly misapprehending, "I considered that point also. Two brothers marrying two sisters rarely get on together. And then there would be the difficulty of the money-matters; for Julius said he only wished me to be engaged to him; he would never think of marrying me till he had an income of his own, and was quite independent of his brother. And I couldn't wait—I really couldn't, you know. So it is a great deal better as it is. Of course he will get over it; men always do," added Letty, looking as if she were comfortably persuaded to the contrary. "After all, it has been a little excitement. One isn't quite an old woman yet, I see."

And then, scarcely observing Edna's dead silence, Letty unbound her great golden sheaves of hair, and, while she brushed and combed them, chattered unceasingly of Julius—all he had said, all he had done; his frantic pleadings, his bitter despair; till Edna—thinking of the heart that would bleed for every wound of Julius's, the heart whose every emotion she kept sacredly to herself, and always would have done, whether she had loved him or not—Edna started up in a passion of wrath, and grief, and shame.

"Letty, hold your tongue! I won't hear you! the last time you talked like this I was a girl, and I did not understand it—did not mind it. Now I do. I say you have done a wicked thing. Every woman who thinks a man loves her, and lets him go on loving her till he asks her to marry him, and then gives him No—a cold, prudent, heartless No — does a wicked thing. I am ashamed of you, though you are my own sister. I am bitterly ashamed of you."

Letty opened her eyes in the utmost astonishment. She did not get angry; it would have been almost a comfort if she had done so; but she sulked a little, and then melted into tears.

"I couldn't help it, and you have no right to scold me. It was partly your fault; you should not have left us so much together, or you should have spoken to me beforehand. I always listen to what you say, Edna. You are very, very unkind; but now you are happy and going to be married, it does not matter what becomes of me."

And so, with that strange tyranny of weakness to which the strongest often mournfully succumb, she softened her sister's heart towards her, and, despite her common sense, her conscience, her bitter, bitter grief for Julius and Julius's brother, Edna kissed Letty, and scolded her, as she called it, no more.

Instead she talked to her, seriously and tenderly, of things concerning which she had often talked before, till she gave it up as hopeless. But now her reasoning was not, as then, out of theories which Letty had always set aside as "romantic," "impossible." She spoke of what she knew—out of her own blessed experience—of the sacredness of love, given or received; the wickedness of trifling with it; the awful responsibility it was—things once dimly dreamed of by Edna Kenderdine, but now seen by William Stedman's bride, with a fatal vividness and a passionate intensity of belief that made her fearless either of ridicule or contradiction: determined to speak out, whether listened to or not.

Letty did listen—as she said, she generally listened to

Edna—at the time; and this time, either through the excitement of the evening or because she was really touched by Julius's devotion, she listened with an expression of earnestness which made Edna almost believe she understood it all.

"What you say may be very true, Edna—I am sure I hope it is—only you seem to fancy love is the only thing in life. Now I think there are many other things."

"So there are; but love is the first, the best, the root and crown of all the rest. And more for men even than women. If that goes wrong with them every thing goes wrong. Oh, Letty, take care!"

"Nonsense! what must I take care of? It isn't my fault that men fall in love with me."

"No; but it is your fault if you treat them in such a way that they never believe in love again—that they despise it and despise you."

"Will Julius despise me, do you suppose? I hope not!"

"Then behave to him so that, whatever you make him suffer, he may still respect you. I don't know what has been—how far you have gone on with him; but oh, Letty, from this time be very careful how you treat him!"

"Bless us!" said Letty, half crossly, half laughing, "how seriously you do take it! I might be going to murder the young man."

"You do murder him, in reality, when you trifle with him—play fast and loose, warm and cold, as I have seen you do with some people. Don't do it with him—it will be the ruin of him. Oh, Letty!"—and she grasped her sister's hand in an agony of entreaty—"for my sake, for William's sake, take care!"

"What on earth am I to take care of? As if Julius were the first man that ever was crossed in love. He must just get over it."

"Yes; but how? We women don't understand. We can but break our hearts; but they—they turn wicked. If Julius does, I shall blame you."

Letty looked uneasy.

"I am very sorry. I am sure I did not mean any harm,

and I hope none will come, for it would be extremely unpleasant. But what am I to do? It is the most uncomfortable thing. Oh! I wish I had never been brought into it. I wish you were not going to marry William Stedman, or that somebody was going to marry me—some suitable man, with plenty of money, who would take me quite away out of all these troubles."

"Then you do not care—not one atom—for Julius."

"Oh yes, I do—I like him very much. I dare say I shall never get any one to be so fond of me again. I would take him to-morrow if he had a tolerable income, or a chance of getting on in the world. But he has none; and, as I told you, I can't wait—so he must go."

"Clearly," said Edna, setting her firm little mouth together, not without a curl of contempt in it, and rising to light her candle and go to bed.

"Oh, stop a minute—do help me! Tell me how I am to manage it all. What do you mean by my treating Julius so as to do him no harm, and to make him respect me?"

Edna paused to think. Unto her, in her brimming happiness of contented love, Julius's lot seemed bitter to an almost exaggerated degree. She mourned for him from the very depth of her heart, yet she could not, she dared not, urge Letty to accept him. She knew that "love bidden is love forbidden;" and that far safer for Julius would be a short, sharp blow, and over, than the torturing suspense of uncertainty and indecision.

"I hardly know what to advise, except that you must meet him as seldom as possible. I will manage that. But when you do meet, though you need not be unkind to him—still you must never let him doubt your mind. You must not waver; you must keep firm, Letty—as firm as a rock."

And then the impossibility of firmness to that weak, vain, pleasure-loving nature, which always did the easiest thing at the time, without much regard to consequences, forced itself upon Edna with a mounful foreboding. Yet, for a little while, Letty's evident sincerity gave her hope.

"I will do every thing you tell me; I will, indeed," said

she, her ever-ready tears flowing down apace. "Poor Julius! I am so sorry for him—so sorry if this makes you and William unhappy. For, of course, you will tell William, though I wish you wouldn't."

Nevertheless, Letty's looks betrayed a sort of satisfaction that William was obliged to be told.

"Yes, I shall tell William. Oh, my poor William!" sighed Edna to herself, knowing how keen would be the pain to that tender heart, in whom the best love of all only made all other affections the stronger. "Letty, we can't help what is past, but you *must* do what is right now; you must make William respect you, ay, and Julius too, even though you refuse him. I don't know it of myself—thank God! nobody ever loved me but William—still, I am sure it is quite possible for a good woman to turn her rejected lover into her truest friend—that is, if he had nothing to blame her for except rejecting him. But we will talk no more now. Let us go to bed, sister. Oh, my sister! my only sister!"

Worn out with all the emotion of the day, Edna threw her arms round Letty's neck, and they clung together—like sisters, in whom no difference of character could break the tie of blood—at least not yet. And then they went to sleep in peace together.

All next day—the day before the wedding—Letty went about the house with a very sad and serious face, though it brightened up occasionally—especially at sight of any thing in the shape of clothes. And when she tried on her own dress—a costume so tasteful and becoming, that she looked fit to be brides-maid to a queen instead of to that dainty, white-robed, yet plain little woman, who was to William Stedman all his heart's desire—Letty's spirits rose amazingly.

"I wonder if there will be any body to look at us; it is a shame to waste all these pretty things upon the parson and the clerk, and old Mr. Marchmont"—a city merchant, whose house had been Edna's only situation as resident governess, and who, in default of nearer friends, had claimed the pleasure of giving her away.

"Except Julius—if Julius comes," said Edna, gravely.

Letty looked a little conscience-smitten. "He is sure to come—he told me he should. He did not wish William to find out any thing, and, besides, it would be his last look of me. He means to go abroad—to Switzerland, I think. Poor fellow! I am really very sorry for him," added Letty, as she glanced in the glass, and could not—who could?—help smiling complacently at the charming image reflected there.

But Edna said nothing, and shortly afterwards went out of the room.

Strange! she could not have believed it of any body else, yet any one who knew her unselfish nature might have believed it of her; but Edna, even on her marriage-eve, thought less of herself and her own feelings than of poor Julius. Do what she would, she could not get him out of her mind. The contrast between him and the rest—William and she going off together on a marriage-tour to their old haunts in the Isle of Wight; Letty taken to a cheerful visit in the Marchmonts' luxurious home, where, among those wealthy, but rather dull city people, she, with her beauty and her familiarity with "high families," was very popular; and forlorn Julius left alone to bear his grief how he might—all this smote Edna with exceeding pain. She was one of those who find it hard to be happy when others are not; who would have leaned over the edge of paradise itself to drop bitter tears upon the poor souls in purgatory. And when, towards evening—the last day of her maiden life—she left Letty, still busy about some trifling adornment, and started on a quiet, solitary stroll, to consider what was to be done, and how and when she should tell the sad secret to William, she felt so unhappy that she could hardly believe to-morrow was her wedding-day.

Nevertheless, she walked on, trying to compose herself by walking, when she heard footsteps behind her, light, quick, and hurried, and, turning round, saw Julius.

She looked in his face, and he in hers, and both understood that each knew all. She put out her hand to him,

JULIUS AND EDNA.

he grasped it hard, and then turned away. They walked along side by side for some distance before either spoke. When Julius did, his voice was hollow and unnatural.

"I have been hanging about here all day. You know why; she would be sure to tell you. She promised not, but of course she did. Women always do."

"Yes, she told me."

"Well, I don't blame her. Perhaps, if I had told you

myself before now, I might have been saved all this. You knew her mind?"

"No," said Edna, firmly, afraid lest his eager questioning might betray her into any admission that might lead him astray, "I could have told you nothing, for I had not a suspicion of such a thing till last night—I mean, till just lately."

"You did suspect, then? *You* thought she cared for me?" said Julius, eagerly. "You must have seen I cared for her? More fool I! But it's over now. Women are all alike—all alike."

"Julius," said Edna, appealingly, and her soft eyes brimmed over. For he was so changed, even in those few hours—so haggard and wild-looking, with neglected dress and excited manner.

"I beg your pardon; no, you are different. I know Will has found his good angel, as he deserved. I deserved nothing—and got it. Edna, you once told me to wait till my time came. It has come, from the minute I first saw her beautiful face through the lodging-house window. It was a madness—quite a madness. If ever the devil comes to a man as an angel of light—as the Bible says he does come, you know—he came to me in the shape of your sister Letty."

"Hush!" said Edna, putting her arm through his, and drawing him on, for his loud voice and violent manner had caught the notice of a stray passer-by. "Come with me: I am going a walk, and you can tell me every thing."

"Every thing?"

"Yes, every thing," said Edna, with firmness, for he was so past all self-control that it became necessary. "You need not mind speaking to me—I never chatter to any body. Besides, to-morrow I shall be your own sister—William's wife."

"William's wife! Oh, happy, happy Will! But you'll promise not to tell him, not till after to-morrow? And you'll see how I'll behave. He shall guess nothing, for it would vex him so. Dear old Will! I'm right glad he is happy. Lucky, lucky Will!"

Edna could not speak for crying. Her tears seemed to calm her companion in some degree. He pressed her hand.

"Are you so very sorry for me, you good little woman? Then you think there is no hope?"

Edna shook her head in a silent negative. She dared not do otherwise. For, knowing her sister as she did—and seeing Julius now in the new light in which his passion had shown him—the expression she had used last night of "playing with edged tools" but faintly expressed the danger of any trifling. Foolish Letty!—she might as safely emulate the juggler's tricks of swallowing fire, or tossing up and catching gleaming daggers, as attempt, with her weak, womanish, uncomprehending nature, her small caprices and coquettish arts, to deal with such a man as Julius Stedman. Well might she say she was "frightened of him." Edna almost was. Never before had she witnessed the desperate agony of thwarted love, as shown in one who was capable, by fits, of self-repression —but of self-government had none. What passed between her and Julius for the next three minutes Edna hid in the deepest, darkest recesses of her pitying heart; she never betrayed it, not even to William.

At length she said, softly, "Tell me how it happened. How came you to care for Letty, or to fancy Letty cared for you?"

"Fancy! It was no fancy. You know better than that. She must have told you? No? Then I'll not tell. I'll not be such an ungentlemanly wretch as to tell. I was mistaken—that's all. But, Edna—I'm not a conceited ass, I hope. And when a girl lets you talk to her, sit by her, hold her hand, kiss her—"

Edna started, and then Julius also drew back in bitter shame.

"I was a coward to say it; but no matter. It was no harm: only 'sisterly.' She told me so. No blame to her, of course. Only, Edna, mind this, if a girl wants to send a young fellow to hell, body and soul, bid her treat him 'as a sister.'"

Edna walked on, sadly silent. Mad as his words were, there was truth at the bottom of them, though much might be said on the other side. For Julius implied, though he did not actually own, how this passion had come upon him—fierce as retributive justice—when he was first amusing himself, as he had often done before, with that tender philandering, half love, half friendship, saying nothing, yet implying every thing, by which so many a young man has broken the heart, and blighted the life of a young, foolish, innocent girl, who would only have laid to his charge the pathetic lament of Ophelia—when Hamlet says, "*I did love you dearly once;*" and she answers, "*Indeed, my lord, you made me believe so.*"

Yet two wrongs can never make a right: Letty was inexcusable. And the worst of it was, she would never be conscious that she needed excusing. But the mischief was done. Here was this young man, to whom a strong, real passion for a good woman, however hopeless, would have been salutary—might have shaken him out of his frivolities and follies, and awakened him to that new and holier life which elevates a man, less by possession than by striving after the nobleness which deserves to possess—but, trifled with by such a girl as Letty, he would sink lower and lower—whither? For there are no depths of depravity to which a man may not fall, from whose heart and lips come the bitter cry which startled Edna many a time during their miserable walk—"They are all alike—all alike. I will never believe in any woman more."

"But," she said at last, "you will believe in men. By-and-by you will come and talk to William. He will help you. Why," she said, trying at last playfulness, when all serious arguments failed, "you are not the first man who was refused and got over it, married somebody else, and lived happy ever afterwards. Even Shakspeare says, 'Men have died, and worms have eaten them, but not for love.'"

Julius laughed angrily. "No; I shall not die. You may tell Will that, if he cares about it."

"You know he does. It would break his heart—both our hearts—if you broke yours. But you will not. You will yet find a far sweeter woman, a far more suitable wife, than my sister Letty."

"Suitable? Yes, that was the word she used. It was not a 'suitable' marriage—that is, I could not give her a carriage and pair, and a house in Belgravia. Nor, indeed, could I marry her at all just yet. I could only love her, and she did not care for that. Edna"—and he turned fiercely round—"Edna, I'd honor the meanest milliner-girl to whom I came with only a wedding-ring, or perhaps with no ring at all, and said, 'Love me' (if she did love, and some of them do, poor things!), more than your fine lady who will accept any body, no matter who, so that she is well married. But it isn't marriage at all; it's—"

"Be silent," interrupted Edna, in her clear, firm voice, severely sweet as Milton makes that of his angels. "You are speaking of what you do not understand. You only see half a truth. Because one side of a thing is wicked, does it make the other good? There are people like what you say—who marry in unholiness, or who love, omitting marriage, in equal unholiness; but there are others who love with all their hearts, and marry because they love, like William and me. Come to us; we will take care of you. We will not let you 'go wrong.'"

"You can't help it."

"No; but *you* can. Julius, a man may be grievously injured by a woman; but if he lets himself be ruined by her, he is one of two things—either a coward or a fool. You are neither; you are a man. Be a man, and bear it."

He turned towards her, the sweet woman, so loved, so happy; who out of all her happiness could spare thought and sympathy for others—for his miserable self. She stood, looking up at him with her pale, tear-stained, eager face, through which, in midst of all her grief, gleamed that hopeful courage which women often possess so much more than men, given to them, perhaps, that they may the better help men. The strong spiritual attraction mastered Julius in spite of himself.

"You are an angel!" he said, in a broken voice. "I think, if any thing could save *me* from going to the devil, it would be my sister Edna. Tell Letty—no, tell her nothing. Tell William—"

"What?" asked Edna, seeing he hesitated.

"Every thing; I had rather he knew it. Tell him"—with a feeble smile—"tell him to-morrow afternoon. And then say, he need not vex himself, for I shall go to Switzerland to-morrow night—to work hard and trouble nobody. And, mind you, nobody need trouble themselves about me, since I shall come to no harm for three months—I promise you that."

"And afterwards?"

"God knows!"

"Yes," Edna answered, reverently. "God does know. And He never tries any one of us more than we can bear. Now, walk with me to the end of the lane. Then go straight home."

Julius obeyed, without the slightest resistance, and with the gentleness of a child.

Next morning, quite early—for they were to start at once, there being no wedding breakfast—with Letty looking charming as brides-maid, though a little nervous and agitated, but not unbecomingly so; with Julius as best man, very handsome, well dressed, and agreeable, but, on the whole, more absorbed in attention to the bride than to the brides-maid, which fact much surprised Letty's warm admirer, old Mr. Marchmont—next morning, William and Edna were married.

CHAPTER XVI.

A DARK wet November night—or evening; but it looked like night, for the houses were all shuttered up, and there was no light except the gas-lamps, and the one red doctor's lamp, to break the dreariness of the long, monotonous, shopless street, where every house was so exactly like another—outside at least. Within—what an immeasurable difference!

What is it makes a house bright? pleasant to go to—to

stay in—even to think about, so that even if fate totally annihilates it we recall tenderly for years its atmosphere of peace, cheerfulness, loving-kindness—nay, its outside features—down to the very pictures on the walls, the pattern of the papering, the position of the furniture? While other houses—we shiver at the remembrance of them, and the dreary days we spent in them—days of dullness, misery, or strife—these houses we would not revisit for the world!

Why? If a house with fair possibilities of home comfort is thoroughly comfortless—if there is within it a reckless impossibility of getting things done in the right way or at the right time—or if, on the contrary, it is conducted with a terrible regularity, so that an uninvited guest or an extempore meal sends a shock throughout the whole abode—if the servants never keep their places long—and the gentlemen of the family are prone to be "out of evenings"—who is to blame?

Almost invariably the women of the family. The men make or mar its outside fortunes; but its internal comfort lies in the women's hands alone. And until women feel this—recognize at once their power and their duties—it is idle for them to chatter about their rights. Men may be bad enough out-of-doors; but their influence is limited and external. It is women who are in reality either the salvation or the destruction of a household.

Dr. Stedman's household had done with its bachelor freedom, and passed into feminine sway — a sway more complete than in most; and yet there are many professional men who, like a doctor, are so engrossed by outside toil that they are obliged to leave every thing else to their wives. Well for them if, like William Stedman, they have married a woman who is fit not only to obey, but to rule. Especially so when, as in this case, there are few appliances of wealth to aid her—no skilled servants, no well-appointed and well-furnished establishment; but one which requires, in every point, not only the mistress's head, but her eye, and often her hand.

Thus, in the drawing-room, where Edna sat sewing, always sewing, and, for a wonder, Letty was sewing too,

MRS. WILLIAM STEDMAN.

there was a combination of old things and new; the furnishing being accomplished by means of devices which would have shocked a respectable — and expensive — upholsterer. Yet the general effect was neat and pretty; an ordinary eye would have discovered no deficiencies, and a good heart, even if discovering them, would have been touched by, rather than have laughed at, these pathetic incongruities.

The mistress was not unlike her house; carefully, though any thing but richly, dressed; still she was dressed for dinner, with her soft hair all smooth, and her laces dropping daintily over the little busy hands. Some people said—and not untruly—that Edna had grown a deal prettier since her marriage. Yet she was worn and thin, as if she had a rather anxious life; but there was no anxiety in her eyes at this moment—nothing but perfect content—perfect rest.

She listened—patiently, though with a far-away look, as if she only heard half of it—to Letty's incessant stream of rather fretful talk about the inconveniences of the establishment.

"I am sure I am quite glad to do all I can, and be of use in the house; but there seems no end to all we have to do, Edna. It's much harder work than keeping school, I think."

"Perhaps," said Edna, smiling; for there was some truth in Letty's complainings. Dr. Stedman, in his bachelor helplessness, had been compelled to marry first and "settle" afterwards; and the settling cost more trouble—and money also—than they had calculated on. Happily, there was Edna's share in the good-will of the school—Letty's being conscientiously invested for herself; still, as William, like the sisters, held strongly to the only safe rule for poor people—of never buying what he could not at once pay for — the difficulties of furnishing were not small; and it required all Edna's cleverness to reduce extraneous expenses, and make sixpence go as far as sixpence honestly would. Thus the first few months of their married life were not easy.

None the more so because Letty shared them. All people make mistakes sometimes; and Edna and William soon discovered that for a young couple to have the constant presence of even the least obnoxious "third party" is not to be desired. Poor Letty! they tried to keep her from suspecting this, and to make the best of it, till the change which she already began to talk about and long for—namely, going out again as a governess — should arrive; but still she helped to make the first six months of her brother and sister's marriage the most difficult portion of their lives.

Nevertheless they were happy—blessed as two people must be who love with all their hearts, and trust each other from the inmost depths of their souls. That their life was all smooth I do not aver; but it was like what learned men tell us of the great ocean—the storms only troubled its surface, and came from extraneous agencies, such as no life is free from; in its deepest depths was a perpetual calm.

Calmness, perhaps, was the strongest characteristic of Edna's face now. She had been a restless little woman heretofore — easily moved, ready to catch each flitting shade of pleasure or of pain; now she had learned the self-control which every human being must learn who has another human being to care for—bound by the only tie which entirely takes away the solitude of individuality. This fact alone made a difference wider than had before existed between her and Letty, and it made her also very patient with Letty.

She heard all the grumblings — giving an occasional gentle reply—till a loud knock thrilled through the silent house—the master's knock.

"There he is!"

And Edna ran down stairs to open the door to William —a foolish custom which Letty always condemned—declaring she wouldn't do it to her husband; it spoiled one's collar and one's hair, and gave far too much trouble! Uncomprehending Letty!

So William's first greeting at his own door was always his wife's face—bright and gay, with all the worry smoothed out of it and the anxiety banished—he had enough of both outside.

"All right, my darling?"

"Yes; quite right."

"I'll go up and change my clothes. I have just come from the hospital. Then we'll have dinner."

A doctor's wife has a hard life, as Edna found. Yet there was something grand in it, even in its dangers; something heroic enough to touch her sense of the ideal, which in this little woman was very strong. Continually there was much to be done, and as much more to be suffered — silently and without appeal. When Edna first married, and realized all that her husband went through daily and hourly, she found it very hard to bear. It was an agony to her every time he entered a fever-ward, and was sent for to those dens of misery and crime where a doctor is often the only messenger of good that ever comes. But now she bore all quietly. She knew his life was in God's hands—that he must do his duty, and she hers, which was to help rather than to hinder him. Yet often when she saw other wives whose husbands went into no danger, were exhausted by no hard work, and William came home, as to-day, utterly worn out, so that the smile with which he always met her only lasted a moment—the sinking at her heart returned, the deadly fear or wild outcry of prayer that all who love can understand.

But she said nothing; and when she took the foot of her husband's dinner-table, it was with the cheerful face that a wife ought to wear, and which does more good than food or warmth to a weary man.

"Oh, this is such a pleasant room!" said Dr. Stedman, looking round it with a sense of infinite rest, and comfort, and relief. "I am glad I have not to go out again. It is such a wretched night outside. I hope Julius will wait in Paris, and not be thinking of crossing till the weather alters. There is his letter, Edna, which came to-day. He speaks of being in London soon."

This was said looking at his wife, but not overlooking her sister, who maintained a demure silence.

To Letty William had never spoken one word on the subject of Julius, nor indeed very many to Edna. He had heard all, of course, and been deeply moved; but afterwards, with a man's sharp cutting of many Gordian knots which women wear their lives out in untying, he had disposed of that painful domestic complication by simply saying:

"What is done can not be undone. We shall not mend it by talking about it, and we may make it much worse. Let us say no more, and it will all gradually slip by."

Nor was he cold or hard to Letty; perhaps, man-like, he was ready to find excuses for a woman—and a woman so beautiful. Whatever he felt on the subject, he had only shown his feelings by writing long, and unfailingly punctual, letters to Julius, with a persistency rather rare in a man and a brother. And now—with that good common sense of his, which never made unnecessary fuss about any thing—he just mentioned, in an off-hand way, the fact of Julius's coming home.

"He comes home rather prosperous too. He has just

sold a large picture to your friend Mr. Marchmont, Letty."

"I am sure I am very glad to hear it," answered Letty, looking down.

"And he sends me back—honest fellow!—his quarter's allowance, saying he can well do without it, better than we; which is partly true, Edna, my dear."

"We'll keep it for him, in case he wants it," said Edna, kindly. "What has he been doing lately?"

"Read, and you will see. He and the Marchmonts seem to get on capitally. He has shown them Paris, and speaks a good deal of them; thinking of them much as you do—worthy, kindly people, with heaps of money and not too much of brains—except, perhaps, your pupil, Miss Lily, who he says is so pretty."

"Lily Marchmont pretty?" cried Letty. "I never heard such nonsense! Why, she is a mere roly-poly dot; as red as a cherry, and as round as a ball. What can Julius be thinking of? Is he falling in love with her? But, indeed, I should be very glad to hear of any thing of the kind," added Letty, with a sudden accession of demureness.

"So should I," replied her brother-in-law, gravely. "Nothing in this world would make me more glad than to see Julius married—happily married. He is the best fellow I know, and would be better still if he had a wife—just such a wife as mine."

And, with eyes overflowing with love, William glanced across the table to the sweet face that was all his sunshine, all his delight. Yet, just as in her case towards him, the joy was not without its attendant pain.

"You are looking pale, my wife; you have been overtiring yourself."

"A little. I was in town to-day. I was obliged to go."

"Those horrid omnibuses! Oh, I wish I could give you a carriage! Do you know, sister Letty, I am seriously thinking of following your constant advice, and starting a brougham, which people say is a *sine qua non* in the success of a doctor commencing practice; it makes such an excellent impression. Suppose I try it? Only you must be sure not to tell the mistress. She would be so exceedingly displeased."

He laughed while he spoke, and gave a glance over to Edna—half joking, half anxious—as if feeling his way, and seeing how the land lay. Was "the mistress" grown such an alarming little person, after all?

She smiled, but said not a word. Letty dashed eagerly into the question.

"I am sure Edna would never be so foolish as to object to any thing that was for your advantage. Besides, a carriage would be such a great convenience to us. You might have it all the day, and we could use it of evenings instead of a nasty cab, which always spoils one's dresses. And how grand it would sound—'Dr. Stedman's carriage stops the way'—at theatres and evening parties!"

"That implies you have both to go to. But I dare say you would. If I started a brougham, people would think I had no end of practice, which would create more. The world always worships the rising sun. Yes, perhaps it might be an advisable investment," added William, changing from his satirical tone to that of prudent worldliness, which agreed ill with his honest voice and mien.

"Not so much an investment as a speculation, since at present we have no money to pay for it," said Edna, gently.

"No more have half the world that rides in carriages. Yet how content it looks, and how comfortable its carriages are!"

"Very comfortable," said Letty, "and, if carefully lined, always so clean and nice for one's clothes."

"And consciences," added William, with a light laugh; "which I see, by her looks, is what Edna is thinking of— What! another message? Have I got to go out again to-night?"

And he rose, not looking particularly glad; but when he opened the letter he showed uncontrollable surprise and delight.

"Who would have thought it? While I was speaking about him, Julius was close at hand. Bid the messenger wait; he shall have an answer in a few minutes. Yes, Edna, you had better show it to Letty."

For Letty, not wholly unmoved, had come to look over her sister's shoulder at the few words which explained how Julius had just come in from Paris, and was at a coffee-house close by, where he said he would be glad to see his brother.

"Of course you will go to him at once, dear?"

"Certainly. Poor fellow, how very glad I am!"

And William's eyes were shining, and his fatigue all vanished. Then, suddenly, his countenance changed.

"I forgot—I really quite forgot for the minute; but, Edna?—no, I suppose *that* is not to be thought of. Yet it's hard that I can not fetch my own brother at once to my house. Of course nobody is to blame. Yet it is very sad—very annoying."

Dr. Stedman did not often speak so irritably, as well as sorrowfully. Edna knew not what to say. Letty drew herself up with a dignified air.

"I assure you, William, if out of consideration for me—"

"No; I'm not considering you at all," was the blunt answer. "I am considering my brother, Letty. I have never named this matter to you before, and do not suppose I am blaming you now; you had a right to give Julius any answer you pleased. Moreover, I have every reason to believe that he has quite 'got over it,' as you women say, and would no more mind meeting you than any other lady of his acquaintance."

"I am sure I am delighted to hear it."

"Only, if you do meet," continued William, pointedly, "it must be clearly understood that you meet only as acquaintances."

"Certainly," replied Letty, tossing her head, and retiring to the other end of the room, while the husband and wife consulted together in an undertone. At last Edna came up to her sister.

"Letty, should you object to Julius coming here for a day or two—that is, if he will come—if William can bring him back with him? It would make William so happy."

Then for goodness' sake do it! Really nobody hinders you. I don't. I am sure it is very hard for me to be the cause of family dissension. I will set you all free by-and-by. I will go away and be a governess as soon as ever I can." And Letty began to weep.

William was touched. "Come," he said, laying his hand affectionately on her shoulder, "don't be foolish, Letty. Don't let us be making miseries where none exist, or exaggerating any little difficulties that we have. Rather let us try to get through them. If you never cared for Julius, and Julius has ceased to care for you, there can be no possible objection to your meeting, or to his coming here. Shall I say so, and ask him to come?"

Letty brightened up at once. "Do, for I am sure it would be the very best plan. There is plenty of room in the house, you know. Besides, we are rather dull—Edna and I—with you away so much. And Julius used to be so very amusing."

So William departed; and after half an hour of rather anxious expectation, the two sisters welcomed the two brothers, in changed relations certainly, but with all the warmth and cordiality of yore. And then William and Julius stood on the hearth together, the elder with his arm on the younger's shoulder, and regarding him with eyes out of which beamed the old affection—the old admiration.

The brothers had always been strikingly dissimilar, but now the dissimilarity was particularly plain—not so much in face as in the difference which character and circumstances make in outward appearance, which increases rapidly as people grow older. Nothing could be a greater contrast to the hard-working doctor than the fashionable young artist—who laughed and talked so fast, with more than his former brilliancy; greeted every body, complimented every body; admired the house, and paid the tenderest attentions to its mistress.

"You have grown quite a foreigner. I should hardly have known you, Julius," said Edna. "There is scarcely a bit of your own old self left in you."

"Perhaps not, and all the better," answered he; then added, gayly, "but I don't see the least change—indeed, I should not like any change—in my little sister. I hope she means to be as good as ever to me?"

"No fear of that," said William, looking from one to the other in great content, and really almost forgetting Letty, who, on her part, took very little notice of the rest, but remained aloof in stately dignity.

Nor did Julius take any special notice of her, or manifest any agitation at meeting her; in fact, the whole thing passed over so very quickly and quietly that Edna almost smiled to think of what an anxiety it had been to her and William. Glad as she was, it gave her a certain sad feeling of the mutability of all things, and especially of men's love in general—lightly won, lightly lost. Was every man's love so, except her own William's?

"No," she said to herself, as she watched the brilliant Julius, the beautiful Letty—both equally self-controlled and self-satisfied. "No, we need not be in the least afraid. Nothing will happen."

Undoubtedly it was a relief and a great pleasure to spend such a merry evening. Julius gave endless accounts of his continental life, where he seemed to have made good use of his time—in bringing back sketches innumerable, and in making acquaintance with foreign artists of note—of whom he talked a great deal. He spoke also kindly, though with an undertone of sarcasm, of his rich and stupid patron, Mr. Marchmont.

"You saw a good deal of the Marchmonts?" observed Edna.

"Yes, they needed me, and I needed them; so we made it mutually convenient."

"And you call Lily Marchmont pretty?" here broke in Letty, irresistibly. "I never heard of such a thing! Lily Marchmont pretty!"

"Are not all young ladies pretty—just as all young men are estimable—when they are rich?" said Julius, laughing.

Letty drew back and spoke no more.

But as, in the course of conversation, Julius made as much fun of the young lady as he did of her respectable papa, Edna thought there was not much to be hoped for in his praise of Miss Lily Marchmont.

In truth, glad as she was to see him—gladder still to see her husband's happiness in his return—there was something about Julius which inexpressibly pained Edna. No human creature ever stands still; we all either advance or deteriorate, and Julius had not advanced—either in earnestness, or simplicity, or manliness. Externally, his refinement had degenerated into the air of the *petit maître*—the man who placed the happiness of his existence on the set of a collar or the wave of a curl; while his conversation, lively and amusing as it was, flitted from subject to subject with the lightness of a mind which had come to the bitter conclusion that there is nothing in life worth seriously thinking of. He was not unaffectionate, and yet his very affectionateness saddened her; it showed how much there was in him that had never had fair play, and how his best self had been stunted and blighted till it had shot out, by force of circumstances, into a far smaller and more ignoble self than Nature had intended. Of course, a strong character would have controlled circumstances; but who is always strong? Clever and charming as he was, Edna felt something very like actual pity for Julius.

He refused to stay in his brother's house, alleging that his ways were not their ways—they were married, and he was a gay young bachelor—he should scandalize them all; but he commissioned Edna to procure him lodgings close by.

"Such lodgings as I troubled you about once before, only the trouble was all wasted, like other things," said he. And this was the only reference he made, even in the remotest degree, to any thing of the past. Of the future he talked as little. Indeed, he seemed to live wholly the life of the present.—"Let us eat and drink, for to-morrow we die." As for his passionate love for Letty, he seemed to have quite forgotten it. But there is an oblivion which is worse for a man than the sharpest remembrance.

"Yes," said William's wife, as, Julius having left, and

Letty having gone to bed immediately, her husband came and sat beside her at their fireside—"yes, we might have spared ourselves all anxiety about Julius. Oh, William, how seldom does love last long with any body!"

"You did not surely wish this to last, you most unreasonable and contradictory little woman? You must feel it is far better ended?"

"I suppose so. And yet—" Edna was half ashamed to own it, but she was conscious that in the depth of her foolish, faithful heart she should have respected Julius much more if he had not in six little months—ay, it was this very day six months that he had poured out to her compassionate ear all the agony of his passion—so completely "got over" it.

She sat down by her husband's side for the one quiet half hour when the master and mistress of the household were left to themselves, to discuss the affairs of to-day, and arrange for those of to-morrow. Although so short a time married, Edna and William had already dropped into the practical ways of "old married people," whose love demonstrates itself more often by deeds than words—by giving one another pleasure, and saving one another pain; which latter, in their busy and hard life, was not the lightest portion of the duty. Neither ever dwelt much upon any thing that must needs be a sore subject to the other, and so a few more words ended the matter of Julius. It was William's decided opinion that their brother and sister should be left as much as possible to themselves—not thrown together more than could be helped, but still neither watched nor controlled.

"For," said he, "we really have no right to control them, or to interfere with them in the smallest degree. If there is one decision in life which ought to be left exclusively to the two concerned, it is the question of marriage. If I had a dozen sons and daughters"—Edna half smiled, faintly coloring—"I would give them all liberty to choose any body they liked; only taking care to bring them up so that they would choose rightly—in a manner worthy of themselves and of me."

"What an admirable sentiment, and so oracular, it ought to be printed in a book," answered Edna, laughing. William laughed too at his own energetic preaching.

"But now," said he, "I am going to preachify in earnest; and, my darling, it is about a very serious thing, which you must give all your wise little mind to, and tell me what you really think about it. I want to set up a carriage."

He said it a little hesitatingly, between jest and earnest. Edna looked up.

"You don't mean it, William? You are only jesting with me?"

"Not in the least. I mean what I say, as I am rather in the habit of doing," and the dominant hardness which was in his nature, as it is in the nature of every strong man, betrayed itself a little. "I have been thinking of the matter ever so long, and it is an experiment I feel strongly inclined to try."

Edna was silent.

"Something must be done, for my practice is no better than it was two years ago, except for my fixed salary, which, of course, we have need to be thankful for. Still, I want to get on; to make a handsome income; to give you every thing you need."

"That is not very much," said Edna, softly.

"I know it. You are a careful wife, my love. But our lot is somewhat hard."

"We knew it would be hard."

"Yes, but I want to alter things—to make a desperate effort to get on. This is a plan which many young doctors try. Some, indeed, say that nothing can be done without it. It is like setting a tub to catch a whale—baiting with one's last trout for a big salmon, as we used to do in my glorious fishing days of old. Ah, I never go a fishing now. Never shall again, I suppose."

"I wish it was different," said Edna, sadly. "You get no holidays, and I don't know when you will. They are among the pleasant things you have lost through marrying."

"My darling!" But there is no need to particularize William's answer, or what he thought of the loss and the gain. "And now," said he, at last, "let us go back to practical things. This carriage—"

He met somewhat uneasily his wife's fond, grave, questioning eyes.

"Yes, this carriage. Do you really require it? For the sake of your health, I mean? You are often very much worn out, William?"

"But not with walking; I wish I were! I wish I had enough of patients to wear me out. No, Edna, I can not conscientiously say I require a carriage, but I want it, just for the look of the thing. We must meet the world with its own weapons; if it insists upon being a humbug, why, I suppose we must be humbugs too. Don't you see?"

"I am afraid I don't."

Dr. Stedman laughed, not his own joyous, frank laugh, but one more like Julius's. "Oh, you are such an innocent, my darling. Why, many a fashionable doctor, now earning thousands, has started upon nothing, and lived upon credit for the first two or three years. Just make people believe you have a large practice, and you get it. Patients flock to you one after the other, like sheep. That 'sawbones'—in the funny tale by some young fellow named Dickens, which you read last night—who sent his boy about delivering unordered medicines, and had himself fetched out of church every Sunday on imaginary messages, had not a bad notion of the right way of getting on in the world."

"The right way, William?"

"Well, the best way—the cleverest way."

"But—the honest way?"

"I was not talking of honesty."

Edna regarded her husband keenly. Like every married woman, she had to learn that there is much in masculine nature difficult to understand; not necessarily bad, only incomprehensible. As, no doubt, William Stedman had before now found out that his angel was a very woman, full of many little womanish faults that his larger nature required to be patient with. It was good for both so to be taught humility.

"Don't let us discuss this matter to-night," said Edna, rather sadly. "Do let it rest."

"No, it can not rest. You do not see—women never can—that a man, if he has any pluck in him, will not sit quiet under ill-fortune. He must get on in the world, by fair means or foul. But this is no 'foul' means. It is only doing, for the sake of expediency, a thing which, perhaps, one does not quite like. Yet—"

"But how can you do it at all? Keeping a carriage, you say, will cost two hundred a year, and we have, altogether, only five hundred a year to live upon."

"Yes, but—in plain English, Edna, we must strain a point, and do it upon credit."

"Upon credit!"

"I see you don't like that, neither do I; but there is no other way."

"No way to get on in the world without making people believe we are better off than we really are, in the chance of becoming what we pretend to be?"

"You put the matter with an ugly plainness, considering how many people do it, and think nothing of it. Why, half London lives beyond its income—peers, ministers of the crown, professional and business men—why not a poor, struggling doctor?"

"Why not? if he can bend his pride, and reconcile his conscience to such a life," said Edna, with—ah, let us confess it—a slight thrill of scorn in her clear voice. "Only I should despise him so much that I should not like his name to be Doctor William Stedman!"

Will sprung up. He was more than annoyed—angry; with that sudden wrath which has its origin in sundry inward twinges, that sometimes hint to a man he is not quite so much in the right as he tries to believe himself to be. He walked up and down his dining-room, much displeased.

Let us give him his due. He was a very good man, and a truly good man is, in some things, better than any woman, because he has so much more temptation to be otherwise. But the best man alive, who is compelled to knock about in the world, receiving and giving many a hard thump sometimes, finds it not easy to preserve quite unstained that instinctive, ideal sense of right and wrong which seems to be set in every good woman's breast, like a deep, still pool in a virgin forest. Happy the man who can always come to its pure, safe brink, and find heaven, and nothing but heaven, reflected there!

It was not in William Stedman's nature long to bear anger against any one, least of all against his wife. They differed occasionally, as any two human beings must differ, but they never quarrelled; for the bitterness which turns mere diversity of opinion into personal disputes was to them absolutely unknown. After a time Dr. Stedman stopped in his rapid walk.

"William," said Edna, "come over here and explain what you mean, and I will try to understand it better. You must not be vexed with me for saying what I think."

"Certainly not. I told you, when I married you, that I wanted a thinking, feeling, rational, companionable wife, not a Circassian slave. A man must be either a fool or a tyrant who likes a woman to be his slave."

"And I am afraid I could never have been a slave, even to you," replied Edna, laughing, with her old gayety; "because I should first have despised you, then rebelled against you, and finally I believe I should have run away from you. But I won't do that, William—not just yet!"

She put her arms round his neck, and looked at him with eyes loving enough to have melted a heart of stone. She might be a very fierce little woman still: undoubtedly she was impulsive and irrational sometimes; but she loved him.

Dr. Stedman sat down again, and began to explain, repeating, though not quite so forcibly as at first, the many advantages of meeting the world on its own ground, and of guiding one's conduct by that intermediate rule between right and wrong — the law of expediency. No doubt all he said was very wise; but he did not seem to say it with his heart in it, and there was an undertone of sarcasm which pained Edna much.

"I wonder," said she, "whether all the world is a sham and the encourager of shams?"

"Or the dupe of them? It's a melancholy truth, Edna; but I do believe my only chance of getting a good practice is by pretending to have it already. Then, no doubt, I should soon become a successful physician."

"And if so, would you really enjoy it? Would you not rather despise the success that had been obtained by a lie?"

William started.

"You are awfully severe. Who spoke of telling lies?"

"An acted lie is just the same as a spoken one. And to spend money when you have it not, and do not know when you may have it, is nearly as bad as theft. Oh, William, I can't do it! I can't reconcile my conscience to it. You must act as you choose—I have no right to prevent you. Don't ask me ever to put my foot into your grand carriage, or to enjoy the prosperity that was purchased by a deception—a cheat!"

She spoke vehemently—the tears gushing from her eyes, and then she clung to her husband and begged his pardon.

"I have said it wrongly—violently; I know I have; but still I have said the truth. Oh, please listen to it! I want to be proud of you, William. I am so proud of you—the one man in the world that I am thankful to have for my husband and my—"

Edna stopped. Moved by some strong emotion, she hid her face, and began to tremble exceedingly.

William took her closer to him.

"What is the matter with you? My darling, what is wrong?"

"Nothing is wrong. Oh no! Only, will you listen to me?"

"Yes; say your say."

She repeated it—in quiet words this time, and Dr. Stedman listened also quietly; for he was too wise a man to be unreasonable.

"There, now, you speak like a rational woman," said he, smiling, "and you don't use bad language to your husband, for it was very bad, Edna, my dear. 'Liar' and 'thief' I think you called me, or nearly so."

"Oh, William!"

"Well, I'm not quite that — at present. And, my darling, I own there is some little truth in what you say. I am afraid I should not care for any success that was not fairly earned—without need of resorting to a single sham. And if it did not come—if I failed to make a practice after all, and found myself fathoms deep in debt, like some poor wretches I know—"

"Still, that is not the question. I was not arguing as to consequences. Dearest husband, don't do this, I beseech you, but only because it is *not right* to do it."

William paused a little—half thoughtful, half amused; then he said, with a smile—

"Well, then, I won't. But, my little woman, if you have to trudge on your two poor feet all your life-long, remember it's not my fault. Now kiss and be friends."

Ay, they were "friends." Neither goddess and worshipper—tyrant and slave—simply and equally friends.

"And now tell me, Edna, what you were going to say just now when you broke off so abruptly, and got into such a state of agitation as I never saw before? You foolish little woman! Why were you so fierce with me?"

"Because I did not want you to do any thing not quite right, or that you might afterwards be ashamed of, since you will have to think not only of ourselves, but"—her voice fell and her hand drooped—"of more than ourselves. Because next summer, please God, if He keeps me safe and alive—"

She threw herself on her husband's bosom in a passion of tears, and he guessed all.

"I was afraid to tell you," Edna said, after a long silence, "you had so much anxiety, and this will add to it. I know it must. Are *you* afraid? Are you sorry?"

"Sorry!" the young man cried, with all his soul in his eyes, as he clasped his wife to his heart. "I sorry? Let us thank God!"

CHAPTER XVII.

It was in sunshiny summer weather—like those days in the Isle of Wight when she was first married, that Edna's little baby came to her. The same evening there came to the tall elm-tree in their little bit of garden a blackbird, who, like Southey's thrush, took up his abode there, and sung—morning, noon, and night—his rich, loud, contented song to the mother, as she lay, a "happy prisoner," with her first-born by her side. In after-days, Edna never heard a blackbird's note without remembering that time, and its ecstasy of restful joy.

What need to write about it? a joy common as daylight—yet ever fresh: to the queen who gives an heir to millions, or the poor toiler in field or mill who brings only a new claimant for the inheritance of labor and poverty. But upon neither does the unknown future look with angry eye—the present is all in all. So it was with Edna. Her eldest son was born amidst considerable straitness of means and many anxieties; his mother made him no costly baby-clothes, nor welcomed him in a grand nursery, with every device of fantastic love: she only took him in her arms and rejoiced over him—as the Hebrew women rejoiced of old—her man-child, her gift from the Lord.

And William Stedman—the young man thrown ignorantly and unthinkingly, as most young men are, into the mystery and responsibility of fatherhood—how did he feel?

Whatever he felt, he said little: he was not in the habit of saying much—except to his wife. Nor, at first, did he take very much notice of the small creature in whom his own face was so funnily reproduced. But he never forgot something repeated to him by his sister-in-law during a certain fearful half hour when his wife lay, half conscious, her life hanging on a thread—"Tell William to be a *real* father to my poor baby."

Many a time, when nobody saw him, Dr. Stedman would creep in and look at his boy, a grave tender look, as if he were pondering on the future—his son's and his own—with infinite humility, yet without dread. More sadly wise than Edna in worldly things, and not having —no man has—that natural instinct for children which makes them a pure joy, and, at first, nothing else: yet it was clear that he too was striving to take up the conjoint burden of parenthood—accepting both its pleasantness and its pain; and so was likely to become worthy—oh, how few men are!—of being a father.

Letty did not understand her sister's felicity at all. She thought the baby would be a great trouble and a great expense, when they had cares enough already. She wondered how people could be so foolish as to marry unless they had every thing nice and comfortable about them—as was far from the case here, especially of late, when double work had fallen upon poor Letty's elegant shoulders. She had more than once declared that if ever a baby was born she would look out for a situation, and relieve her brother-in-law from the burden of her maintenance, and herself from the alarming duties of a maiden aunt. But Letty always talked of things much oftener than she did them; and besides— But it is useless attempting to analyze her motives; probably for the simple reason that she had no motives at all. As she said one day to Julius, who all this winter and spring had kept coming and going, sometimes absenting himself for weeks, then again appearing every evening at his brother's house, to sit with Edna and Letty, though he paid the latter no particular attention — "What did it matter where she went or what she did? nobody cared about her—she was a solitary creature, and therefore quite free."

The evening she gave utterance to this pathetic sentiment Aunt Letty was a very lovely object to behold. She had taken the baby; for, though not enthusiastic over it, she was a woman still, and liked to nurse it and "cuddle" it sometimes. As it lay asleep on her shoulder, with one of its tiny hands clutching her finger, and her other hand supporting it, she looked not unlike one of Raffaelle's Madonnas.

"Stop a minute—just as you are; I want to sketch you," said Julius, rousing himself from a long gaze—*not* at the baby, for whom, though it was his namesake, Uncle Julius had testified no exuberant admiration. But still, it being safely asleep, he continued sitting with Letty in the drawing-room, as he had got into a habit of doing of evenings, since Edna's disappearance up stairs.

"Dear me, Julius, I should think you were quite tired of taking my likeness; but Edna will be in raptures if you draw the baby."

Julius curled his satirical lip—more satirical and less sweet than it once was, and then said, with a certain compunction, "Oh, very well; I'd do much to please Edna, the dearest little woman that ever was born. How she puts up with a fellow like me is more than I can tell. I think—that night I walked our street with Will, and we did not know but that she might slip away from us before the morning, I would almost have given my life for poor Edna's."

The voice was so full of feeling, that Aunt Letty opened her eyes wide to stare at Uncle Julius—only to stare; the penetrating, yet loving gleam of sympathy was not in those large beautiful orbs of hers.

UNCLE AND AUNT.

"Not that my life would have been much of a gift," added Julius. "It is of little value now to me or to any body. Once, perhaps, and under different circumstances, it might have been."

Letty dropped her eyes. It was the first time her rejected lover had made any reference to those "circumstances," though she had sometimes tried, a little coquettishly, to find out whether he remembered them or not. For it was provoking, to say the least of it, that he should so quickly have overcome a passion which he had vowed would be eternal—that he could see her—Letty—in all her fascinations, weekly, daily, if he so wished, and yet be as apparently indifferent to her as he was to the many other young ladies of his acquaintance, whom he was always talking about and criticising, as probably he criticised her to them in return. The idea rather vexed Letty.

She, and even his own brother, knew little of Julius's life beyond what they saw when he made his erratic appearances and disappearances. Now, as of old, all his brother's friends were his, but only a small proportion of his friends were also his brother's. Julius cultivated a class of intimacies which William had never cared much for, and now cared less—the floating spin-drift of literary, artistic, and semi-theatrical society—clever men, and not bad men, at least nobody much knew whether they were bad or good, and certainly nobody much cared, brains being of far greater use and at a far higher premium than morals. With this set, lounging about during the day, and meeting of nights at various well-known symposia of men—only men, and not their wives, even if they had any — Julius spent much of his time. But he never brought these friends to his brother's house, or, indeed, said much about them, except that they were "such jolly clever fellows—so excessively amusing."

Amusement was, however, not his whole pursuit. He sometimes took vehement fits of work, which lasted a day or two, perhaps a week or two; then he would throw up his picture, in whatever stage it was, and devote himself to every form of ingenious idling. In short, he was slowly drifting into that desultory, useless existence, grasping at every thing and taking a firm hold of nothing, which, without any actual vice, is the very opposite of that calm, pure life—laborious and full of labor's reward—which is the making of a real man.

And its effects were already beginning to be painfully apparent. Sallow cheeks, restless eyes, hand shaking and nervous; brightening up towards night, but of mornings, as he confessed, utterly good for nothing except to lounge and smoke, or lie and sleep in thankful torpor—all these signs foreboded fatally for poor Julius. His brother began to doctor him for "dyspepsia;" but Edna, less learned, yet clearer-eyed, detected a something more—a sickness of the soul, far sadder, and more difficult of cure.

He who had no one to think of but himself, who earned a tolerable livelihood which he spent wholly upon himself, was beginning to look older and more anxious than his brother, with all his burdens.

Now, while Letty and Julius were talking lightly down stairs, in Edna's room overhead was a grave silence. William, coming in to spend a quiet hour beside his wife's sofa, had fallen dead asleep through sheer weariness. And Edna was watching him as Letty watched his brother, but with, oh! what a sort of different gaze! The difference which always had been, and would be to the last—eyes that said honestly, "I love you;" and the coquettish, down-dropped glance that inquired selfishly, "I wonder how much you love me?"

Women are often attracted by their opposites in men, and perhaps some woman, bright and wise, with large patience, and courage enough to sustain both herself and him, might have loved deeply and understood thoroughly this Julius Stedman. But Letty—beautiful Letty—was not that sort of woman. Therefore, while he made his last remark about his life being of no value to any body, she only sat and looked at him.

"Yes, mine is a wasted life, Letty. I shall end like that stranded ship on the Isle of Wight shore; you remember it?"

"Nonsense!" said Letty, blushing a little. "Or if it is so, it will be your own fault. You artists are always so miserably poor."

"Some of us do pretty well, though, if we run after titled patrons and high society. Or, if we happen to be especially fascinating, we marry rich wives, and—"

"Perhaps that is what you are thinking of doing?" interrupted Letty, with some acrimony. "Indeed it struck me there was more than met the eye in a hint Mrs. Marchmont gave me to-day, as I dare say Mr. Marchmont has given to you."

"What?" asked Julius, eagerly.

"That, if you liked to change your career, he thought so well of you, and of your extreme cleverness for every thing—business included—that he would take you into their house at once; first as a clerk, and then as a partner."

"'Marchmont and Stedman, indigo-planters!' How grand it would sound! What an enviable position!" said Julius, satirically; though not confessing whether or not the news had come upon him for the first time.

"Very enviable indeed," said Letty, gravely; "and especially with Miss Lily Marchmont to share it."

Julius winced, but turned it off with a laugh.

"Lily Marchmont—poor Lily! A nice creature! if she were only a little taller, and not quite so fat."

"She is getting as thin as a shadow now, at any rate," said Letty, in much annoyance. "But it is no use speaking to you, or trying to get any thing out of you, Julius. Indeed you're not worth thinking about."

"I was not aware you ever did me the honor to think about me at all."

"Oh yes," returned Letty, with an air of sweet simplicity. "Who could help it, when you are always here, and every body is so fond of you, and makes such a fuss over you? Edna told me that if any thing had happened to her, you were to come back and live here again. I was to tell you that she depended upon you to take care of and comfort William."

"Poor Edna—dear Edna—to fancy I could comfort any body! But this is ridiculous!" added he, abruptly. "Here are Edna and Will, both as jolly as possible, and that young rascal besides, to carry down the ugly name of Stedman to remotest ages. Every body is all right—except me—and as to what becomes of me, who cares? Not a soul in this mortal world. But I beg your pardon, and I am wasting your time. Just move your right hand,

Letty, please. No, fingers closer together. May I place them?"

"Yes, only don't wake the baby."

"That would be a catastrophe."

Julius knelt down, and with hot cheeks and hands that trembled visibly, tried to arrange his group to his satisfaction. Letty bade him "take care," and leaned her other hand on his shoulder, carelessly enough; she thought nothing of it. Besides, was he not, as she sometimes called him, her "half-brother-in-law?"

At her touch the young man looked up — a look no woman can mistake: it is madness, or deliberate badness, if she does mistake it; and then, turning, pressed his lips on her arm—not tenderly, not reverently, but with a passionate fierceness that was less a kiss than a wound.

So the barrier was broken down between them, and Letty knew—as any girl of common perception must have known—that the indifference was all a sham, that her discarded lover was just as desperately in love with her as ever.

Was she glad or sorry? She really could not tell; but she was considerably agitated. She started up, regardless of the baby, and shook down angrily her lace sleeve.

"Julius, you ought to be ashamed of yourself!"

"I am not. You used to let me kiss you once. Give me the right to do it again."

And he came nearer, and was on the point of carrying out what he threatened, when some instinct of gentlemanhood made him pause. But he grasped both her hands, and looked in her face, half mad with the passion that was consuming him. No sentimental philandering — no child's play, or silly flirtation—but a violent passion, the first he ever had, and—would it be the last?

Some women might have hated him for it, and the manner he showed it—strong, proud, reticent women, whose love must be given as a free gift, or else is wholly unattainable—but Letty did not hate him. Indeed she rather liked being taken by storm in this way.

"Let me go!" she cried. "See, you are waking the

baby!" Which remorseless infant now set up a howl loud enough to fright away all the lovers in Christendom.

Julius stopped his ears. "Take it away—horrid little thing! But Letty," and he seized her hands again, "you must come back to me at once, for I want to speak to you. I shall wait here till you come back, if it is till midnight, or next morning. So you had better come. Promise you will."

She promised, though with a very dim intention of keeping her word. In truth, all she wanted at that moment was to get rid of him—anyhow, in any way; for she felt rather afraid of him. "He looked," she afterwards confessed to Edna, "as if he could have kissed me, or killed me; it was all one, and didn't much matter which."

It was true. Men—no worse men than Julius—have sometimes killed the women they were in love with, on scarcely more provocation.

But when, having resigned her charge to nurse, Letty ran up into her own room, she began to recover herself. There was a pleasurable excitement in being once more made love to, when she had half feared such a thing would never happen again; that she should have to sink into a drudge and a maiden aunt, obliged to help in other people's work, and contemplate from a distance other people's joys—a picture not too attractive in the eyes of Miss Letty Kenderdine. Now, at least, she could be married if she chose—it was entirely her own fault if she were not. After her dull life in her brother-in-law's house, perhaps unconsciously, the spirit of the old song ran in her head—

"Come deaf, or come blind, or come cripple,
O come, ony ane o' ye a'!
Better be married to something,
Than no to be married ava."

And Julius Stedman was not a despisable "something." He had youth, good looks, good manners, good brains. Every body admired him—so did Letty too, in her way. And then he was so frantically in love with her.

"Poor fellow!" she thought, as she stood arranging her

hair at the glass, which gave back by no means a disagreeable reflection—"poor fellow! I'm sure I could have liked him very much, if he had but had a little more money."

She was here summoned for some inevitable house business, which she got through absently — there was little pleasure in keeping other people's houses. If she had one of her own, now—really pretty and comfortable—it would be quite different. And she caught herself reckoning, with arithmetical precision, how much it would be possible for Julius Stedman to earn per annum, supposing he painted a picture regularly every three months, as of course he might easily do, and sold it, which was a little more difficult.

So serious a calculation made Letty look a little grave —at any rate, quiet—when she entered her sister's room, and stood watching the group there. William, shaken from his sleepiness by the energetic howling of his little son, had resigned himself to circumstances, and now sat looking very tired indeed, but exceedingly amused and contented, watching that young hero take his supper. While the mother—the pale, bright-eyed, smiling mother —but God only knows what is in the hearts of mothers. It was but a poor room, plainly furnished too; but in its narrow compass it rounded the whole circle of this world's best joys.

"Come here, Letty," said William, kindly; "just look at that young gentleman. Isn't he enjoying himself? He will be taking a walk in the park, and giving his arm to his Aunt Letty, in no time."

Letty laughed. Perhaps she was a little touched by the happiness before her; perhaps there came also a little of the sad feeling which must come to the best and most unselfish of unmarried women at times, to see the rest of the world running its busy race, enjoying daily its natural joys, and she shut out. She, Letty Kenderdine, handsome and admired as she was, or had been, was now first object to no one—except that poor fellow down stairs.

"Letty looks as grave as a judge," said Edna, turning a

moment from her sucking child, her little blossom of Paradise, to the common world. "Is any thing the matter?"

"Oh no!" answered Letty, with a novel reticence, and blushing extremely. "Only— When is William coming down to supper?"

"I don't know," said William, stretching himself out in lazy content, and regarding tenderly his wife and son. "Tell Julius— By-the-bye, is he here still?"

"I think so."

"Tell him I wish he would get his supper without minding me. If he had been up nearly every night for a week, and had a wife and baby on his mind besides, I am sure he would excuse me. You'll take care of him, won't you, Letty? See that he is comfortable, and be kind to him. He has been so very kind and good lately—poor Julius!"

Letty felt that fate was against her. To explain to William—then and there—William, whom she was always a little afraid of—the reason why she could not go down and entertain his brother was simply impossible. At least, she said to herself that it was. Besides, would it not be better in every way, would save trouble and prevent future misunderstandings, that she should just hear what Julius had to say, give him his answer, and put a stop to this nonsense at once? For it must be put a stop to—of course it must. And then she would again go out as a governess; and who knew what might happen? Some wealthy, sedate, respectable widower — about whose circumstances and position there could not be the least doubt —who would not expect too much, and would make her very happy and comfortable. And then she thought of Julius — how handsome he was, and how wildly in love with her; and Letty sighed.

She took as long a time as possible to order supper, and again went up into her room while it was being laid, to give to her dress a few last touches, so as to make herself look as well as possible.

Yet it would be unfair to human nature to declare that Letty was quite composed, quite cold-blooded. As she looked in the glass at the fair face which was already beginning to fade, she thought of Edna, who never was pretty, who had not cared whether she was pretty or not, to whom growing old had no terrors; for was she not wife and mother, loved with a love that was at once strong and tender, protecting and adoring? Letty's heart beat a pulse or two faster. Yes, such a love would be "nice" to have. Neither solemn nor satisfying, delicious nor desperate—merely "nice." But of course it could not be. A year's experience of what marriage is—upon a limited income—had given Letty a deeper dread than ever of poverty.

"Oh, dear me!" thought she, "why are some people so very fortunate and others so very unfortunate—and all for no fault of their own?" And then she gave the final brush to her shining hair, and went down to "that poor fellow."

He was a poor fellow. He was mad—literally mad—with a passion against which he had struggled as much as was in his nature to struggle, but in vain. This insanity—shall we anatomize it? I think not. God knows what an awful thing it is; and some women know it too, and have witnessed it, as Letty did now. But seldom the best or highest kind of women; for the lover is very much what the loved one makes him to be; and no passion, however hopeless, which has not been needlessly tortured by its object, stung with coldness one day and lulled by tenderness the next, is ever likely to degrade itself by grovelling in the dust—as, his first burst of impetuous tyranny over, Julius grovelled this night.

"Oh, have pity on me, Letty!" he cried, throwing himself before her, kissing her hands, her feet, the very hem of her gown. "I have tried all these months to forget you, to live without you, and I can not do it. If you will not marry me I shall go to utter ruin. For I can understand now how men drink themselves to death, or take to gambling, or buy a pistol and—"

"Oh, stop!" exclaimed Letty, shuddering. "Please do not talk about such dreadful things. You are very cruel to frighten me so."

And she began to sob—real honest sobs and tears. They drove Julius quite beside himself for the time being.

"I frighten you? Then you do care for me? I'll make you care for me!"

He sprang from his knees and clutched her—a clutch rather than a clasp—tight in his embrace, and kissed her innumerable times.

"Julius, for shame!" was all she said, still sobbing angrily, like a child.

He released her at once.

"You are right. I am ashamed of myself. I have acted more like a brute than a gentleman. Shall I go away, and never enter your presence more?"

"I—I don't quite see the necessity of that," said Letty, half smiling.

And then the poor frantic fellow snatched her to his arms once more, and vowed that if she would only say to him one loving word, neither heaven nor hell should prevent his marrying her.

"But," said Letty, when she had suffered him to calm down a little, and had taken a brief opportunity to arrange her hair, and seat herself in her proper place at table, in case any body should come in, "what in the wide world are we to marry upon?"

"Never mind—I'll see to that. I shall be as strong as a lion, as bold as Hercules, as patient and hard-working as —well, as my brother Will himself, if you only love me, Letty—only love me. Oh, say it!—say it over and over again!" and his dry and thirsting eyes seemed ready to drink in, like water in the desert, every look of this beautiful, beloved woman. "Tell me, my sweetest, that you really love me?"

Letty hardly knew what had come over her. As she afterwards confessed to Edna, it was the greatest piece of folly she ever committed in her life—she could scarcely tell even if it were speaking the truth or not—but what could she do? She was obliged to say something just to quiet him. So she looked in her lover's face, and answered, smilingly, "Yes."

It is not the first time that a man's undoing has been the woman's doing.

CHAPTER XVIII.

Dr. Stedman did not get the quiet evening he had promised himself—a comfort in his busy life only too rare. He might easily have indorsed, out of his own experience, the brief question and answer recorded of two companions—"My dear friend, when shall you take a little rest?" "In my grave!" But if any such thought came across him, this brave Christian man would have smothered down the weak complaining, knowing that life is meant for labor, and the grave is our only place of righteous rest—or, perhaps, not even there.

Still, for the time being, the hard-worked doctor felt excessively tired—too tired to talk much. He laid his head on his wife's shoulder, and watched the baby, who was fast asleep across her lap, until his face gradually softened, so that it was difficult to say whether child or father looked most peaceful and content. Very like they were too—with that strange inherited likeness which is seen strongest immediately after birth—often then vanishing, to reappear years after in the coffin; but it made the young mother's heart leap when she looked at her child.

"I am so glad he is like you, dear," she said. "I hope he will grow up your very image. I could not wish him a better blessing."

"I could—ay, and I'll help him to get it as soon as ever he can."

"What is that?"

"A wife!—and just such a wife as his mother!"

"Oh, Will!—oh, papa, I mean—for you must learn to be called that now," said Edna, with her own merry laugh, though all the while in each eye was a bright, glittering tear. And then she held up her face to be kissed, and the two overfull hearts met silently together over the little creature that owed its being to their love—whose future was to them utterly, awfully unknown—except as far as it lay, humanly speaking, in their hands and in their love —to guide or misguide—to ruin or to save.

"And now I must go down and bid good-night to Julius—Uncle Julius. I wonder whether his nephew and namesake will at all take after him."

Edna shrank involuntarily, and then said, with the infinite yearning pity that happy people feel towards those who have missed happiness,

"Yes, you should go down to him for a little—poor Julius!—and bring me up my work-basket out of the little room behind the dining-room, for I have his gloves there, which I promised to mend three weeks ago. Oh, what an age seems to have gone by since then!"

"Yes, thank God!" muttered Will, as he went away quietly—all the house seemed in dread of that great enormity, waking the baby—and hunted for several minutes in the little room—his wife's special room, with all her household relics sattered about, Letty's regency not being remarkable for neatness. But the right mistress would soon be back again to resume her place, and put every thing in order. And oh, to think what might have been! —of the households of which he happened to have known several lately—where the mistress had vanished thus, and never come back again—alas! never more.

The young husband shuddered, and then, with a thrill of thankful joy, put the sickening thought away from him, and went back into his ordinary life and ordinary cares, of which not the lightest was his brother Julius.

In early youth people find it hard enough to bear their own burdens; later on, they learn to be thankful when these are only their own; for each day brings with it, in a manner that none but the wholly selfish can escape from, only too heavy a share of the burdens of other people. As Will fulfilled his wife's small mission, he pondered with an anxiety, sometimes dormant, but never quite subdued, over his brother Julius.

The dining-room was so silent that at first he thought Julius was gone, and so came suddenly in there—to see, what made him for the moment instinctively draw back, feeling himself exceedingly *de trop*.

The supper-table, laid an hour before, remained just as it was; while, sitting on a sofa together, very close together, with his hands clasping both hers, and his eyes fixed on her face—the intense, passionate gaze which told but one possible tale—were Letty and Julius.

Both started up, and sprang apart; but Letty recovered herself much the sooner, saying, in quite a careless voice, though her cheeks were hot and her manner slightly nervous,

"Come in, William. We have been waiting for you."

William stood, quite confounded, doubting the evidence of eyes and ears. Then he said, rather sharply, "You need not have waited, for I told you I was not coming;" and paused for some explanation.

But none came. Letty, with great composure—she was used to these sort of things—took her seat at the table, and, officiating there, managed not only to eat a good supper, but to keep up an easy conversation. True, she had it all to herself. Will was too honest to say more than half a dozen commonplace words and shrink into silence; and Julius, after meeting a warning glance from Letty, did the same.

But the young lover was, like a lover, painfully nervous, trembling with smothered excitement. He could not look his brother in the eyes; yet William was struck by the mixture of sadness and rapture that came and went in lights and shadows over his sensitive face. His was not the calm of assured happiness, but the fitful, desperate joy of a child who has hunted down a butterfly, and caught it under his cap, yet scarcely dares to believe it is safe there, or to look for it, lest he should find it flown away, after all.

Supper over, Letty, with a brief good-night to Julius, coquettish rather, but careless and indifferent as any other good-night, vanished up stairs, and the two brothers were left alone. Julius took up his hat to go.

"Ju!" said Will, laying his hand on his shoulder, and

looking him hard in the face, "have you got nothing to say to me?"

"No, nothing!" The words came out hurriedly, and then he repeated them in an altogether changed and suppressed tone—the sudden and causeless depression which was one of his characteristics. "No, nothing!"

Will, of course, said no more.

But when he had shut the hall-door upon his brother, he went up to his wife with a countenance on which it was hard to say whether anger or grief predominated.

"Oh, husband, what is the matter?—what has vexed you?"

"Vexed is hardly the word; but I am sorely grieved and perplexed. Where is Letty?"

"Gone up stairs. She looked in here a minute, and went away."

"Did she say nothing—tell you nothing?"

"No."

And then, seeing how pale his wife grew, he told her in a few words all he had seen.

"If I had not seen it, I could not have believed. I don't know how you women feel in such matters—that is, ordinary women: not my wife—I know her mind!—but if Letty is not engaged to Julius, I might say a few sharp words concerning her, even though she is your sister."

Edna was silent. The strong tie of blood, which in tender and faithful hearts will bear such long straining, kept her silent; but she looked exceedingly sad.

"The girl can not know what she is doing," said Dr. Stedman, rising and pacing the room in exceeding annoyance. "It is like the fable of the boys and the frogs—sport to her, and death to him; for he is just as mad after her as ever. I saw it in his eyes. And she will never marry him; she would marry nobody that is not well off; I heard her say so only yesterday."

"Are you sure of that?"

"Quite sure; and I entirely agree with her. It would be madness in any poor man to think of marrying *her*. She wants, not an honest man to love, which some people

I could name were silly enough to care for and think worth having, but an establishment and a few thousands a year."

Edna would not answer. She knew it was true.

"Not that I blame her; and I hope she'll get her wish," said Will, waxing hotter every moment. "But in the mean time she shall not make a fool of my brother Julius. And it's not merely making a fool of him, she is making him despise her, and, through her, all women. Edna, when once a man gets that into his head—that you are not better than we are; that there is nothing worshipful about you; nothing for a poor fellow to look up to and hold fast by in this wicked, contemptible world—it's all over with him. If he does not respect women, he respects nothing. He goes down, down, to the bottomless pit. Oh, I wish I had been wiser, and had never taken her into my house, or never let my brother set foot within it; for I know what he is, and what she is. She will be the ruin of him."

William spoke with a passion that even his wife could hardly understand; and yet she felt he had right on his side.

"But," she pleaded, "perhaps we entirely mistake. She may have accepted him."

"Then why not say so? Why should he not say so? I gave him the chance. Of course a man holds his tongue till he is really engaged. Ju and I have never once named Letty's name between us. But depend upon it, there's something wrong, something bad, or weak, or cowardly, when a man dare not tell his own brother that he is going to be married. And as for her—Edna, I am sorry, sorry to my heart, to think ill of your sister; but I can not help it."

"No, you can not; I see that. Still she is my sister; and, as you said, she does not know what she is doing."

Will stopped in his angry walk, and contemplated the little figure sitting on the sofa corner, in white dressing-gown and cap, so matronly, calm, and sweet.

"You are right, my darling; she does not know. Women never do. I was not such a very bad fellow as a bachelor, not in the worst sense, only selfish, rough, worldly; but oh! how I have learned to hate my old self now! How thankful I am that a certain little woman I know came and laid her fairy hands on me, and led me right, as only women and wives can! Strong, pure, loving hands they must be; if they are not, if they lead not the right way, but the wrong—Edna, if Julius goes to the bad, it will be Letty's doing."

"What is Letty's doing? and why is William in such a passion? Have I got into disgrace about the dinner again? I'm always getting into disgrace, I think. Nobody can please him but you, Edna."

Letty stood at the door with a pretty air of innocent sulkiness, her candle in her hand, which, while in the dusky twilight it hid from her the faces of her brother and sister, vividly displayed her own. Such a lovely face—more dazzling than ever in its expression of mischievous triumph—a face that, whether or not it could soothe or comfort a man, had assuredly in it the power to drive him wild.

"So you have nothing to say to me, after all? And you both look exceedingly comfortable, and don't want me, I'm sure. Good-night, then, for I'm going to bed."

"I have something to say to you, Sister Letty," replied William's grave voice. "Stay; for I had better say it at once."

Now, in her secret heart, Letty had a great respect for William. He was the only young man of her acquaintance who had come within fair reach of her charms and not succumbed to them—who had been to her the kindest of friends, but never a lover; over whom, well as he liked her and showed it, her fascinations had not the slightest influence. She knew it, and stood in awe of him accordingly.

She set down her candle, and answered rather meekly than otherwise:

"Well, if you are going to scold me, I had better take a chair, for I am rather tired—your brother kept me talking so very long. But, then, you told me to make him comfortable. And, really, Julius is so clever—so exceedingly amusing."

She spoke flippantly, and yet not unobservantly; she

seemed wishful either to throw dust in her brother-in-law's eyes, or to find out how much he really knew of the state of things. But her finesse was all lost upon William. He said, bluntly and angrily,

"I wonder, Letty, you dare look me in the face and mention my brother's name."

"Dare! Why should I not?"

"You know why."

There was an awkward pause, and then Letty said, carelessly,

"Oh, if you mean because he once made me an offer and I refused him, as I have refused a dozen more. I couldn't help that, you know."

"No, and I never blamed you for it. But it ought to have been a plain, decisive 'No,' as I understood it was, and an end to the matter. Now—"

"Well, Dr. Stedman, and now?" mimicked Letty, half mischievously, and yet for some reason or other unwilling to betray herself until the very last.

"It isn't an easy thing to say to a lady; but I have eyes in my head," said William, much annoyed, "and, from what I saw this evening, I can only conclude—"

Letty began to laugh. "Oh, pray don't conclude any thing! You are so very particular!"

William Stedman turned away in anger—in something worse than anger—contempt, and was quitting the room abruptly, when his wife caught his hand.

"Oh, stop! Letty, do explain things to him. Will, perhaps she meant nothing; or she may not quite know her own mind."

"Then she ought to know it; it is mere weakness if she does not. And in such cases weakness is wickedness. You women dance with lucifer matches over powder magazines. I beg your pardon, Miss Kenderdine. Your love affairs are no business of mine; nor should I take the liberty even of naming them, were it not that Julius happens to be my brother. I know him, and you do not. As I have just been saying to my wife, if you do not take care you will be the ruin of him."

"Shall I?" said Letty, a little frightened, and a little touched, also, for there is something in an honest man's righteous wrath which carries conviction to even the shallowest natures. "Perhaps I may be. I told him so; but it won't be in the way you imagine. I didn't mean to tell you—not just yet, for there's many a slip between the cup and the lip—and I know I am doing a very silly thing, which I didn't mean to do, only somehow he persuaded me; but— Well, brother Will," and she laughed and cast down her eyes, "instead of abusing me, you had better kiss and forgive me, for I'm not going to harm Julius. I promised I would marry him—that is, as soon as he can afford it."

She held out her hands in a pretty, beseeching way, and her eyes glistened with something not unlike tears; in truth, the beautiful Letty had not often looked so womanly and so sweet.

William was melted. He embraced her warmly, and said he was glad to have her as a double sister. As for Edna, she sprang to Letty's neck—almost forgetting the baby—and did—as women always do on these occasions; women who, judging others' hearts by their own, believe true love and happy marriage to be the utmost blessedness of life.

Then they all three settled down, as people will settle down from the highest tide of emotion to corresponding ebb, a little dull, perhaps, seeing that, after the first warm impulse, each of them had necessarily some reserve. Besides, they were not very romantic—at least, Will and Letty were not. As for Edna? Mercifully Heaven puts into some natures, especially those destined for a not easy life, a certain celestial leaven—a sense of the heroic, lovely, and divine—which the world calls romance, but which they themselves know to be that which sustains them in trial, braces them for bitter duties, comforts them when outside comforts are faint and few. Edna was a "romantic" woman. You saw it in her eyes. Whether she was the better or the worse for this her life showed.

"My darling, you look as pleased as if you were going to be married yourself."

"Do I, Will?" and she took a hand of her husband and sister—her two dearest on earth—and cast a fond look on a third small creature, still so much a piece of herself that she hardly regarded it as a separate existence at all. "Yes, never was a happier woman than I am this night, with you and baby, and Letty and Julius all right. Oh, how glad I am!—how very glad I am!" and the wife's and mother's heart danced within her at all the joy that was coming to her sister.

"I know Julius will be a good husband, not so good as William—nobody could be that—but very, very kind and good. And, Letty, you will be his lady and his queen. Don't laugh. We are queens, we women—queens and handmaids too, and as royal when we serve as when we rule. It is only when we step down from our throne and turn into nautch-girls and harem slaves that we degrade ourselves and our husbands too."

"You are talking poetry, my love," said Will, with a tender patronizing; "and so I must turn the tables, and talk a little prose. Sister Letty, may I ask, when shall you and Julius be married?"

Letty didn't know. She hoped rather soon, as she had a great objection to long engagements.

"And what are you going to marry upon?"

"Ay, that is the difficulty which your brother and I were talking over just when you came in."

"What, already?" said Edna.

"Yes, why not? It was the most important point of the matter; for, as I told him, I have been poor all my life, and very uncomfortable I have found it, so I am determined when I marry it shall not be to poverty. I told Julius he must contrive to make an income—a good settled income—within a reasonable time, or our engagement must necessarily fall through. Though I should be sorry for that, for I do like Julius; he is handsomer than any body I ever knew—and so exceedingly amusing."

The husband and wife met each other's eyes with an anxious, mournful meaning, and then hopelessly turned the matter off with a jest.

"Edna, my wife, I am afraid you are by no means the handsomest person of my acquaintance."

"Nor you the most amusing of mine."

"Yet, you see, Letty, we contrive to jog on together, but shall be delighted to be outdone by you and Julius. Let us reckon. Since the whole question apparently resolves itself into pounds, shillings, and pence—how much does he make a year—not counting—"

"Not counting your allowance to him, if you mean to refer to that. He told me of it to-night, but says he will not accept it any more."

"I did *not* mean it, but am very glad to hear it," returned William, gravely. "No man ought to marry upon another person's money. But how does he intend to manage without it."

"That is the thing; and I wish you would try to persuade him," cried Letty, anxiously. "There is a matter on which I have been persuading him with all my might; in fact, I have told him I don't think I can marry him unless he does it."

"Does what?"

"Gives up art and takes to business."

"Takes to business—which he so dislikes!"

"Gives up art—which he loves so much!"

"You may say what you like, both of you," Letty replied to these exclamations, "but I know it would be the most prudent. I have said my say, and I mean to stick to it. He has grand ideas, poor fellow, about how well he should get on when we were married, and he had me for his model—his inspiration—his muse, I think he said, but I told him that was all nonsense; he had much better have me as the mistress of a good house, with every thing nice and comfortable about me. I should be happier, and he too. Now, William, don't you think so?"

"My dear sister, I have given up thinking much about these matters of you and Julius. I have no call to interfere or do any thing but offer my best wishes."

"And your advice—pray give him your advice," cried Letty, with more anxiety and eagerness than she had yet shown. "Make him understand how foolish he would be to reject Mr. Marchmont's offer—of entering his house of business, first as a salaried clerk, then becoming a junior partner."

"Did Mr. Marchmont really offer that? I wonder Julius never told me."

"He only told me to-night, or rather I told him; I heard it this morning. It was the first thing which made me think seriously of marrying him."

The excessive candor of Letty's worldliness often disarmed indignation. Dr. Stedman could hardly help smiling.

"Letty, you are the oddest girl I ever knew! Whatever else you may be, you are no hypocrite. And so you want me to help you in turning my brother's life clean upside down. Is he mad enough to do it, I wonder, for you or any woman alive?"

"I don't consider it mad; and I am almost sure he will do it for me. He had nearly promised me when you came into the room."

"Well, that is some consolation. It was not a kiss I intruded upon—only a bargain."

"William, do be serious!" cried Letty, really annoyed. "Can't you see what a good chance it is? Here is old Mr. Marchmont with no son—only Lily—"

"Perhaps he does it with an eye to Lily, as you hinted once she liked our Julius."

"Oh no, that was all a mistake;" and Letty tossed her head. "At least Julius won't marry Lily—she is never likely to marry any body. For all her red cheeks, she is dying of consumption, and they know it."

"Poor thing — poor father and mother!" said Edna, stopping in her busy hushing of the baby to listen. "But perhaps she really liked Julius, and for her sake, even though she is dying, they wish to do him good."

"That is your romantic version of the affair, but the plain sense of it is that Julius has received such an offer: if he accepts it, I'll marry him; if not, I won't. So there is an end of the matter. And now I'll go to bed."

But still she lingered, watching her brother and sister. Edna sat leaning against her husband; and he had his arm round both her and the child, his rugged, yet tender face looking down protectingly upon both. A pretty picture, unconsciously made, yet full of meaning, which even Letty saw. Something of nature—sweet, true, human nature—tugged at her heart-strings.

"Don't be vexed with me, I know I am not so good as you two. I can not, for my life, see things as you do; but I'll try my best, indeed I will. Please don't be angry with me."

And sliding to her knees, she laid her cheek on Edna's lap — or, rather, on the baby — and kissed the sleeping hands which lay there curled like tiny rose-leaves. God knows what was in the woman's mind; perhaps a momentary gleam—all womanly—of that maternal instinct which in some women is stronger even than conjugal love—exists before it, and long survives it; or, possibly, only a sudden thought of how far removed she was both from her sister and from that innocent babyhood, fresh from heaven, which none of us can look at without wonder and awe. But there she knelt, and shed on the tiny hand and pretty white frock — her own working — more than one tear; maybe the purest, honestest tears that Letty Kenderdine ever shed.

"Go away, William, please," whispered Edna; and when the door closed upon him she took her sister in her arms, wished her happiness anew, and, moreover, told her how to earn it and keep it—as women well-beloved always can. The listener, if she did not understand much, at least listened with a tender, touched expression; and when the two sisters parted for the night they felt more thoroughly sisters, more near together, than they had ever done in their lives.

For William, he followed his first natural impulse, snatched up his hat, and, late as it was, went off straight to his brother's lodgings.

It was still dusk, not dark; and through the balmy summer night the nightingales were singing shrill and clear—as they used to sing twenty years ago from the tall trees of Holland Park. But Kensington High Street shone all a-glare with gas-light still, for it was Saturday night; and filing through it and its wretched-looking crowds came a string of grand carriages from some entertainment at the Palace. Dr. Stedman looked carelessly in at the lovely faces and flashing diamonds, and thought of the little figure in the sofa-corner, and the other one, as yet scarcely to him an entity at all, asleep on her lap. His heart leaped—the husband's and father's heart. He had tasted the life of life: he could afford to let its empty shows go by.

With a blithe step Will entered his brother's room—half-parlor, half-studio—which, though a good room in a handsome house, was always strewn with what the doctor called artistic rubbish. Still Julius's keen sense of beauty and fitness had hitherto kept it in some sort of order. Now it had none. Utter neglect, all but squalid untidiness, were its sole characteristics; and the owner sat alone, not even smoking, though the room was redolent of stale tobacco, but lolling on the table, his head hidden upon his arms, so absorbed, or else half asleep, that he did not even notice the opening door.

"Hollo, old fellow, what's the matter with you? A pretty sight I find you, after turning out at this late hour just to wish you joy."

"Wish me joy!" Julius sprang to his feet, his flushed face gleaming wildly. "What do you mean?"

"What do *you* mean, you deceitful, shut-up, unbrotherly fellow, not to tell me what I should be so glad to hear? Of course she told."

"What did she say?"

William laughed, though a little vexed at this excessive reticence, till the agony of suspense in Julius's face startled him.

"Don't mock me, Will; tell me what she said—what she really thinks; for, before Heaven, I declare to you this minute I have no idea whether she will take me or not. I only know that if she does not—" He laughed hoarsely, and made a sharp, quick sound with his mouth, like the click of a pistol.

"Don't be a fool," said Will, angrily; then clapped him on the shoulder. "You are a fool, of course; we are all fools in our day about some woman or other. But cheer up; you'll get what you want. Letty said distinctly to her sister and to me that you and she were engaged to be married."

Evidently Julius had been strung up to such a pitch of excitement and despair, that, with this sudden reaction, his self-control entirely left him. He threw himself back in his chair, covered his face with his hand, and sobbed like a woman or a child. Alas! there was about him, and would be till the day of his death, much both of the woman and the child.

Will walked to the window. If the young man had been any one else— But all his life Julius had won from him an exceptional tenderness. The look of slight contempt faded from his face, leaving it only grave and sad; and it was a kind and cheery hand he laid on his brother's shoulder once more.

"Come, come, Ju! this is not exactly the way to begin life; for you are beginning it quite anew, as every man does when he is engaged to be married. I give you joy, my lad, and so does Edna."

"Thank you both."

The brothers shook hands, brotherly and friendly; and then, without more waste of emotion, Will plunged into the practical side of the affair, asked Julius what were his future plans, and especially what was that offer of Mr. Marchmont's to which Letty had alluded, and which seemed too extraordinary to be true.

"Yes, it is quite true. Sit down, and I'll tell you all about it."

And then, with some natural and not discreditable hesitation, he confided to his brother one of those romances in real life which, when we authors hear of and compare with those we invent, we smile to think that were we to make our fiction half as strange as truth nobody would read us.

The rich merchant's only child had fallen in love with the poor artist, frantically, desperately, and held to him with a persistent passion that, being concealed, came in time to sap the very springs of life. In fact, she was dying —merry, rosy-faced Lily Marchmont—dying literally of a broken heart. How far Julius was to blame nobody could say: he himself declared that he was not — that he had never made love to her, never intended such a thing. And when at last—Lily's secret being discovered—her miserable parents betrayed it to him, and made him this proposal for her sake, he declined it. Whatever he had done, he did the right thing now. He was too honorable to degrade a woman by marrying her for mere pity, when he felt not an atom of love.

"You did right," said Will, with energy. "And all this was going on, and we knew nothing—you kept it so close. What you must have suffered, my poor fellow!"

"Never mind me; there's another I think of much more. Poor little thing! God forgive me all the misery I have caused her!" And could she have seen Julius then, Lily might have felt herself half avenged.

"Does she know about Letty?"

"Yes; I told her — clear and plain. It was the only honest thing to do. But it signifies little now; she is dying; and before she dies she wants her parents to adopt me as a son—to take me into the house of business, either in London or Calcutta—only fancy my going out to Calcutta!—first as a clerk, with a rising salary, and then as a partner. She settled it all, poor girl, and her father came and implored me to accept. But I never thought of it, not for one minute, till they told Letty, and Letty urged me to agree. She has no scruples about poor little Lily."

"And Lily?"

"Lily only thinks of Letty—that is, of me through her. She wants me to be happy with Letty when she is gone. Oh, it's a queer world!"

Will thought so too, as he recalled the merry little girl, whose governess his wife had been, who had now and then come to his house, and whom he knew Edna was fond of

— rich, bright, prosperous Lily Marchmont — dying. He looked at the haggard face which even happiness could not brighten much: he remembered his talk with Letty that night—Letty, who considered it almost a misfortune to marry Julius—and the strange incongruities and inequalities of life forced themselves upon his mind. Yet perhaps things were less unequal than they seemed—perhaps in the awfully uncertain future there might come a time when Lily Marchmont in her grave would be more happy than either Letty or Julius.

However, to forecast thus mournfully was worse than useless—wrong. Will rose.

"I must go now. My wife will wonder where I am. Yes, lad, as you say, it is a queer world; but we must make the best of it. You'll come over to breakfast to-morrow?"

Julius hesitated.

"Of course you must. Letty will expect you."

Poor fellow—how his whole countenance glowed! Yes, that was the one thing certain in all this perplexity. Julius was deeply, devotedly in love; and out of a man in such a condition can be made any thing good or bad.

"You're very far gone — quite over head and ears, I see," said Will, smiling. "I wonder you never told me till now."

"How could I, while I had nothing to tell, except that I was perfectly mad? She kept me in a state something like Tantalus or Ixion, or some of those poor ghosts that I've been trying to paint here. I ought to be successful in painting hell; these six months I have assuredly been in it."

"You're out of it now, though, old fellow; so cheer up and forget it. You'll be all right soon. A man is not half a man till he is married; and when he is, he may face the whole world. That's my opinion and experience. Now I'm off. Good-night!"

CHAPTER XIX.

Julius accepted Mr. Marchmont's offer, and Letty Kenderdine accepted him — that is, conditionally, promising to marry him as soon as his income warranted what she called a "comfortable establishment." The exact sum, or the exact date, she declined to give, and she wished the engagement to be kept as private as possible. "For," said she, "who knows what might happen? and then it would be so very awkward."

So they were betrothed, to use the good old word—now almost as obsolete as the thing—and two days afterwards Lily Marchmont died, slipping away, quietly and happily, to a world which long sickness had made to her a far nearer world than this. Her former governess, Mrs. Stedman, was with her at her death-bed, and mourned her affectionately and long.

Julius also, let him not be too harshly judged. For many days after Lily's death, even amidst his own first flush of happiness, he looked pale and sad; and while playing the devoted lover sudden glooms would come over him, which Letty could not in the least understand, and which affronted her extremely. Doubtless she was very proud of him and his prospects; for in her secret heart she had always looked down upon the profession of an artist as not quite the thing—not exactly respectable. Besides, how could it ever have supplied the house in Phillimore Place, or some place like it, upon which she had set her heart, and which she furnished and refurnished, imaginarily, a dozen times a day? Likewise, her mind was greatly occupied by her future carriage, and the difficulty of deciding whether it should be a brougham or a britzska, Julius being gloriously indifferent to both. But all these splendors loomed in the distance; his present income was only £300 a year—a sum upon which Letty declared it was quite impossible to marry.

So she lived on in her brother-in-law's house, and her lover in his lodgings hard by, meeting every day, and enjoying, or they might have enjoyed, to their fullest content, the sweet May-time of courtship; when restless hearts gain strength and calm, and true hearts grow together, learning many a lesson of patience and forbearance, self-distrust and self-denial, from which they may benefit all their lives to come, if they so choose.

But these two were rather uncomfortable lovers. They did not "shake down together," as Will insisted they must be left to do, without any interference from the sympathetic Edna, to whom—luckless little sister!—they both came in their never-ending small "tiffs," forsaking her, of course, when the troubles were over. No doubt Julius was madly in love still, which, considering the silly things Letty often said and did, and how little of real companionship there was between them—affianced lovers though they were — sometimes roused Edna's surprise. But she comforted herself by the common excuse that tastes differ, and people who seem the most glaringly dissimilar to others, often between themselves find a similarity and suitability which makes them grow together, and in the end become perfectly united and happy.

"As, truly, I hope, Letty and Julius will be," repeated Edna for the twentieth time, concluding a talk on this subject with the only person to whom she ever confided it. "Dearest, what a mercy it is that each one thinks his or her choice best, and nobody ever wishes for anybody else's wife or husband!"

Will laughed; it was impossible to help it; but as he kissed her earnest, innocent eyes — as innocent as her baby's eyes—he thanked Heaven for the safe assuredness of his own lot, even though at the same time he half sighed over the uncertainty of his brother's.

Dr. Stedman was no poetical optimist, or purblind dreamer; just an honest, ordinary man, working hard among the world of men, with his eyes wide open—as a doctor's must be—to all its misery and sin, yet shrinking from neither; walking straight on, through foul ways and clean, with a steady, upright, pure heart, as an honest man can do. But being thus sadly wise, and seeing only too far into the depths of things, made him more than ever anxious over his brother Julius.

For the first few months of his engagement Julius seemed happy. He had gained, as he said, his heart's desire; and he was young enough to bear a little of hope deferred. His changed career he did not actually dislike. Either he had a little wearied of unsuccessful Art, and business, with its settledness and regularity, had a soothing and strengthening effect on his excitable temperament; but he vowed that his "erratic" days were done, dubbed himself a regular "city man," came home punctually; and daily, as the clock struck eight, his little, slender, lissome figure might be seen hurrying round the street corner, and his quick, impetuous knock was heard through the evening quiet of Dr. Stedman's house. Then he would just put in his smiling face to what was formerly a consulting-room, then the dining-room, and afterwards the domain of Edna and baby; would give a brotherly jest or two, and leap up stairs, three steps at a time, to the drawing-room, where sat, always sweetly smiling and prettily dressed, his expectant Letty.

They were pleasant days, these courtship days; and a pleasant sight were the two lovers—when in their good moods—both so handsome, light-hearted, and bright. Still dark days did come—they come soon enough in all loves, and all lives—and then Edna had a hard time of it. Yet still, in her fond romance, her earnest faith in the saving power of love, she put up with every thing, hoping for the best, and determined to do so till the end.

Which end, after six months of love-making, seemed as far off as ever, until an unexpected turn of affairs brought it to a crisis.

One January night Julius came in, "all in the sulks," as Letty called it—one of those moods to which he was so liable, and to escape which his betrothed always, as now, ensconced herself behind the safe shelter of the family circle, and sewed away, unconscious, or pretending unconsciousness, of the sad, passionate, beseeching looks which followed her every movement. She had grown used to his devotion—it was nothing new now; and the silly woman threw away as dross that which some other woman—poor Lily Marchmont, for instance—might have gathered up and stored as the wealth of two lives.

But Letty stitched and stitched, wholly occupied with the effect of her white tarlatan and pink ribbons.

"And, after all, I shall have to ruin it in a common street cab. How very provoking! Will, do you ever mean to set up your carriage?"

"You would not benefit much by it, Letty," returned Will, rather gruffly, since from behind his newspaper he often saw more than he was given credit for. "I suppose you will not live with us always."

"Heigh-ho! It looks very like it."

Julius winced. "That is not my fault, Letty, as well you know. May I tell William and Edna what I was telling you yesterday, and ask their opinion?"

"If you like; but I take nobody's opinion. I said, and I say it still, that five hundred a year is actual poverty. Look at Edna; she has not, to my certain knowledge, had a new dress these six months."

"Because she wanted none," said Edna, hastily. "But come, Julius, your news! Has Mr. Marchmont raised your salary? He told me he should; you were so clever—had taken to business so aptly—were sure to get on."

Julius shook his head despondently. "He thinks so, but Letty doesn't. She will not trust herself to me—not even with five hundred a year."

"No," said Letty, setting her lovely lips together in the hard line they would sometimes exhibit. "You may all preach as you like, but I don't approve of poverty; and any thing is poverty under a thousand a year."

"Then we may as well part at once!" cried Julius, violently.

Letty stopped her sewing, to turn round upon him a placid smile.

"Indeed, my dear Julius, I sometimes think that would be by far our best course."

Julius answered nothing. His very lips grew white; his anger ceased; he was ready to humble himself in the dust at Letty's feet.

"Letty, how can you?" whispered Edna in passing. "You speak as if you did not love him at all."

"Oh yes, I do," returned Letty, carelessly, as she devoted all her energies to her last pink bow. "But he might wait a little longer for me without grumbling. He is not near so wretched as he makes himself out to be—has comfortable lodgings—heaps of friends."

"Take care! Better not drive me back to my 'friends.'"

"Why, Julius? Were they so very—"

"Never mind what they were—I have done with them now. Only keep me from going back to them. Dearest, if you wish to save me, keep me beside you. Take me, and make the best of me, my Letty—my only love!"

The latter words were in a whisper of passionate appeal, such as a man sometimes makes to a woman—a cry for help, strength, salvation, such as she, and she only, can bring. But this woman heard it with deaf, ignorant ears, neither understanding nor heeding.

"Oh, my dress—my beautiful new dress—you are trampling over it, ruining it! Julius, do get away!"

He moved aside at once.

"I beg your pardon," and the old satirical manner returned. "I ought to have remembered that woman's first object in life is—clothes."

But the next instant, when Letty rose to quit the room, he threw himself between her and the door.

"Have I vexed you? Oh, say you are not displeased with me. It will kill me if you quit me in anger. Oh, Letty, I will work like a horse in a mill to get you all you want."

"I am sure I want nothing, except not to be married just yet—until you can make me comfortable," said Letty, in an injured tone. "And you do worry me so" (which perhaps was true enough). "It's very hard for me."

"It is hard." Then suddenly and impetuously, "Would you like to get rid of me? Because—there is a way. No, not that way," seeing Letty looked really frightened. "I am not such a fool, though I have sometimes said it. And the other way would be almost as sure. Mr. Marchmont could secure me a thousand a year — your great ambition—if I would at once go out to India for—let us say twenty years."

"Go out to India — for twenty years!" cried Edna. "Oh, Julius, surely you would never think of such a dreadful thing!"

"Is it so dreadful, my kind little sister?" replied Julius, tenderly. "But Letty, my own Letty, what does she say?"

Letty had turned eagerly round, on the point of speaking, but when her sister spoke she drew back, a little ashamed.

"Of course, as Edna says, it would be a very dreadful thing in some ways—especially at first; but you might get used to it. And consider, if you were to make your fortune, as Mr. Marchmont did—as people who go out to India always do—"

"And you would share it? Or"—a new idea seemed to strike the desperate lover—"you might help me to win it. Tell me, if I went out to India, would you go too?"

Letty looked down demurely. "Perhaps I might. I don't know. I always had a fancy for India, where one could ride in a palanquin, and have plenty of diamonds and beautiful shawls. Yes, perhaps I might be persuaded to go—sometime."

Julius covered her hand with grateful kisses, and Letty allowed herself to be led back to the fireside, where the project was entered into seriously in family conclave.

But, in truth, Letty, assuming for the first time in her life a will of her own, decided the question. In one of those rare fits of resolution which the weak and irresolute take, she had convinced herself that going to India was the best thing possible for herself and Julius. "Herself and Julius." Her unconscious wording of the matter was the key to it all.

"For Julius, all places were alike to him, so that he had Letty beside him—Letty wholly his own. He betrayed even a wild delight at the idea of having her all to himself —away from all her kith and kin, in the mysterious depths of India. He was in that condition when the one passion, less a passion than a monomania, swallows up every lesser feeling — overwhelms and determines all. So, after discussing the point inconclusively until past midnight, he went away, and came back next evening at his usual hour with the brief words, "I have done it."

"Done what?" asked Letty.

"Exactly what you wished me to do. I have arranged with Mr. Marchmont to go out to Calcutta. And now, my dearest, you can set about your preparations at once."

"Preparations for what?" said Letty, innocently.

"Our marriage. We must be married and go out in three weeks — only three weeks. Oh, my Letty! my Letty!"

He clasped her in his arms, almost beside himself with joy.

But Letty drew back, primly protesting, "She had had no idea of such a thing. She did not like being married in such a hurry. How could she possibly get her things ready? Besides, she had never promised—she was quite certain she had never promised. No, if he went, he must go by himself."

Julius stood literally aghast.

"What have I done? Oh, Edna!" for, seeing him turn deadly white, Edna had sprung up from her work and caught him by the arm. "Edna, this is what comes of trusting a woman."

And then ensued one of those scenes—only too common now—of anguish, bitterness, protestation, appeals, ending by Letty's being moved to tears, and Julius to contrite despair accordingly. Edna said nothing; they had both grown quite careless of her presence at such times; and how could she, or any third person, interfere between them? She was only thankful William was not by—William, who had not so much patience as she. But she trembled as she thought of the future of these two lovers, who made love not a blessing, but a torment—a burden, almost a curse. If it were thus before marriage, what would it be afterwards?

Presently the storm lulled. For once Letty had overstrained her power. Even in this Armida's garden where she held him bound, the poor Rinaldo began to feel blindly for his old armor, and to struggle under his flowery chains.

"It is of no use talking, I must go, and by the next mail. I promised Mr. Marchmont, and I will keep my promise. Am I not right, Edna?" And he walked across the room to her.

She held out her hand to him. "Yes, I think you are."

Then Letty, seeing her sceptre slipping from her, gave way a little, and said, in a complaining tone,

"You are all very unkind to me. How can I go out in three weeks? And to be married and left behind a 'widow bewitched,' as Julius proposes, would be dreadful. If he would go first, and make all comfortable for me, and I could follow in six months or a year—young ladies often do it under proper escort."

"And would you—oh, my darling—would you come out to me all alone?"

And Julius, again in the seventh heaven of rapturous devotion, was ready to consent to any thing, if only he might win her, even thus.

The matter was settled, and Letty having got every thing her own way, made herself sweet as summer to her lover, who hung upon her every look and word; so that the brief intervening time before his departure was the smoothest and happiest of his whole courtship. This, without any hypocrisy on Letty's part; for she was really touched with his devotedness. And besides, in great crises, people rise to their best selves; and many a love, which would soon wax meagre and threadbare in the daily wear and tear of life, drapes itself heroically and beautifully enough at the supreme hour of parting.

So Julius sat, in his last evening at an English fireside

—his brother's, of course; for he declared that beyond it was not a single soul whom he cared to say good-bye to; sat, not broken-hearted by any means; for the excitement of this sudden step, and his eager anticipations in his new career, seemed to deaden pain. Still, he kept desperate hold of Letty's hand, and gazed continually in her face with that eager passionate gaze, half of artist, half of lover, neither of which seemed ever to tire of its beauty. And now it wore a softness and tenderness which made parting grow into a delirious ecstasy, less of grief than joy.

Edna and William were not sad neither. Their long suspense over these two was apparently ended; the future looked bright and clear; nor did they blame the lovers for a somewhat selfish enjoyment therein. For they knew, none better, this happy husband and wife, that those who mean to become such have a right to be all in all to each other, to go out cheerfully together into the wide world, and feel all lesser separations but as a comparatively little thing.

"Yes," Will said to his brother; "I'm glad you're going—thoroughly glad. You may have your health better in India than here, if you take care. And you will have a wife to take care of you. You will do well, no doubt—perhaps come back a nabob before your twenty years are out. And though I may be old and gray-headed before I see you again, still, my lad, I say, I'm glad you're going."

Thus talked he, to keep his own and every body else's spirits up, while quick as lightning the final minutes flew by. Edna sat behind the tea-urn in her customary place, and was waited upon by Julius in the long-familiar way. He tried so hard to be good and sweet to her, and to pay attention to her baby, who, not to detain the mother, had been brought down unlawfully, cradle and all, to a corner of the drawing-room, where he contributed his best to the hilarity of the evening by sleeping soundly all through it.

"Poor little man! he will actually be a man, or nearly so, before I set eyes on him again. I only hope, Edna dear, that he will grow up a better man than his namesake. And yet not so—" Julius turned round, his countenance all glowing. "Not a better man than I mean to grow—than *she* will help to make me."

Letty smiled—her sweet, unmeaning, contented smile—and that was all.

She sat by her lover's side—sat and looked pretty; did not talk much, except to give a few earnest advices about practical things; the sort of house—or bungalow, she believed they called it—which she should like him to take; the number of servants and horses which they should keep—all which facts she was found to have informed herself upon very accurately. She promised, faithfully and affectionately, to get her "things"—which seemed her chief care—ready without delay, so as to follow by the first feasible opportunity; and she begged Julius to write her every particular about Calcutta, and every information necessary for her own voyage thither.

But she never once said, as some fond, foolish women might have said, "Take care of yourself—the dear self which is all the world to me."

Thus passed, in the strange unreality of all parting hours, this last evening, as if every succeeding evening would be just like it, and its cheerful chat, its quiet fireside pleasure, would come all over again next night, instead of never coming again in all this mortal life; as by no human possibility could it come—just as now—to these four.

At last Dr. Stedman looked at his watch. There was only time to catch the train to Southampton, whence Julius was to embark the following morning.

"I'll close up your portmanteau for you, Julius, my lad; you never could do it for yourself, even when we were at school. Come, Edna, come and help me."

Edna, shutting the door close behind her, followed her husband; and as she stooped over him while he was fastening the valise, she kissed him softly on the shoulder. He turned and kissed her also, both feeling, as in moments of sharp pain like this all such married lovers must feel, the one intense, unspeakable thankfulness that "naught but death parts thee and me."

"Julius, ready?" Will called outside the drawing-room door; and shortly afterwards his brother appeared—Letty likewise. She looked pale, and was crying a little. For him—never as long as they lived did Edna and William forget the look in Julius's face.

"Now, not a minute to spare," Edna said, as she threw her arms round her brother-in-law's neck and kissed him fondly, forgetting all his little faults, remembering only that, to her at least, he had never been aught but brotherly and good. "Take care of yourself! oh, do take care of yourself!"

"Take care of *her!*" he answered, hoarsely. Then staggering blindly forward, indifferent to all beholders, he snatched frantically to his bosom the woman whom he so madly loved.

"Oh, be true to me!" he gasped. "For God's sake be true to me! Edna, don't let her forget me! Letty, remember your promise—your faithful promise!"

"I will!" said Letty, with a sob, and offered her lips for the last kiss. It was given in a frenzy of passion and grief; then Will took his brother by the arm, and lifted rather than led him to the cab at the door—and they were gone.

* * * * * * *

About nine months after this night a group of three persons found themselves all in the gloom of a muggy, disagreeable November evening at the entrance-gate of one of the docks of East London, whence trading vessels start for the Indies. It was William Stedman, his wife, and her sister. They groped and stumbled through the dirty devious ways, guided by a man with a lantern, which showed dimly the great black hulls of ships laid up in dry-dock, or the ghostly outline of masts and rigging. Strange, queer noises came through the dark—of men shouting and swearing, the lading of cargo, the tramp of horses and carts.

"What a horrid place! Oh, I wish I had never come here! I wish I were not going away at all!"

"Never despair, Letty! Take my arm! We are safe now. This is certainly the 'Lily Marchmont.'"

For by the "Lily Marchmont"—strange, pathetic coincidence—Letty Kenderdine was going out to India to be married to her lover.

Julius had waited—been compelled to wait—until some good opportunity offered for the safe-conduct of his bride; for Letty was not the person to do any thing without a due regard to both comfort and propriety. Indeed she delayed as long as she could, until all possible excuse for hesitation was removed by the offer of a passage in this ship, which belonged to the firm, and was taking out to Calcutta Mr. Marchmont's nephew and his young wife. With them Letty could reside until she was married, and the wedding could take place from their house with all *éclat*, for they were well-to-do and very kindly people.

So the matter was settled; though Letty might have lingered yet longer, had not the strain of narrow means and an increasing family rendered her brother-in-law's house a less desirable home for her than even the comparatively small establishment which awaited her in India. New clothes were now scarcer than ever to poor Mrs. Stedman; they were all wanted for little Julius, and for another little child that was to come by-and-by, not long after Aunt Letty was gone. In Edna's face was increasing, day by day, the anxious, worn look which all mothers have at times, and never wholly lose—never can lose—until their sons and daughters close the coffin-lid upon the heart that can suffer no more. Still, when Letty said to her sister, as often she did, "Oh, Edna, I wonder you ever married!" there would come such a light into the thin face—such a holy patience and thankful content—as none but wives and mothers ever know.

But the cares of Dr. Stedman's household were numerous enough to lessen his sister-in-law's regret at leaving it. She did regret a little, clinging to them both with a curious, fitful tenderness as the time went by; but still she made up her mind — and her trousseau, absorbing therein all her own money, which William had carefully kept for her, declaring that her help in his house was a full equivalent to him for her residence there—and departed. Not, however, without many complainings and self-pityings, even to the final moment; when after a visible hesitation, as if at the very last she were half inclined to draw back, poor Letty climbed up from the gloomy dry-dock side to the still gloomier deck of the "Lily Marchmont."

But when they descended to the bright, cheerful, handsomely fitted-up cabin, where every thing had been arranged for the comfort of the young married couple and her own, her spirits revived. Her fair looks made her at once popular with strangers, and as she stood talking to the young Marchmonts—after being briefly introduced to the only two other passengers, a little fat elderly Dutchman and a lady, his sister, who were to be landed at the Cape of Good Hope—Letty Kenderdine was herself again. Well dressed—for she had made the utmost of her small means, and even contrived a little present or two from Aunt Letty to the baby that she would not see; well-preserved, and, though past her first youth, much younger-looking than Edna, Miss Kenderdine shed quite a sunshine of feminine beauty abroad in the little cabin. Her sister, forgetting all parting pain, smiled to think what a sunshine she would also bring to poor Julius, yearning for her so terribly in his busy, lonely, anxious life of amassing wealth—wealth that perhaps he, with his careless artist temperament, might never have cared for, certainly never would have struggled for, excepting for her sake.

But Letty herself seemed less absorbed in the future than in the present. When her four fellow-passengers quitted the cabin, to allow her in quiet a few farewell words with her own friends, she glanced after them depreciatingly.

"Good people, I dare say, but dull, very dull. I am afraid I shall have a dreary voyage. I wish I had taken the overland route—if only I could have afforded it. Oh, Edna, the misery of poverty!"

And then, struck with a sudden compunction—a sudden impulse of tenderness for these two, so contentedly bearing theirs, and sharing with her, for these last two years and more, every little comfort they had, Letty flung herself into her sister's arms.

"Oh forgive me! You have been so good to me, both of you. I'll never forget you—never! Do not forget me."

"No, no!" said William, as he hurried his wife away, for he saw that the trial of parting was more than she could bear. "Kiss her, Letty, and bid her good-bye."

But — the sharp, final wrench over — he himself came back again, to say a last kind word to his sister-in-law, on whom depended his brother's whole future in this world.

"Letty," whispered he, very earnestly, "I trust you. Make Julius happy. Remember, his happiness all rests with you."

"I know that."

"Never forget it. Be to him all that my wife is to me. Good-bye! God bless you!"

Letty leaned over the ship's side, violently sobbing.

"Go back into the cabin, Letty dear," Dr. Stedman called out. "Is there nobody who will be kind enough to take charge of my sister?"

"May I assist you, Miss?" said a funny Dutch voice, and William thankfully consigned her to the care of the elderly merchant.

Next morning, spreading her white wings in the winter sunrise, and moving as gracefully as when a poor little hand, now mere dust, had given her her christening libation, the "Lily Marchmont" weighed anchor and sailed away to the under world.

Fifteen Years After.

CHAPTER XX.

It was a small junction station on one of the numerous lines of railway that diverge from London Bridge, and a dozen or so of passengers were walking up and down the narrow platform, in the early dark of a winter afternoon, waiting patiently or impatiently, as their natures allowed, for the never-punctual train. They consisted chiefly of homely people—Kentish farmers, laborers going home, and London youths starting for their Saturday-to-Monday holiday. The only first-class passengers—in outward appearance at least—were a lady and a little girl, who sat in the small waiting-room, absorbing the whole of the welcome fire. She was a tall and remarkably handsome woman—handsome still, though she must have been quite five-and-forty. So fair was her skin, so regular her features, that, but for an expression of rooted discontent which never left her, she would have been almost as comely as a young lady in her teens.

The child—her own—for she addressed her as "mamma," was not like herself at all; being a short, round-faced, button-nosed little maid of about twelve years old; far from pretty, but with a sweet, sensible look, which we sometimes see in little girls, and prognosticate tenderly what sort of women they will grow up to be—what comforts at home, and helps abroad—what unspeakable blessings to all about them as daughters, sisters, and— Well! men are sometimes so blind that these good angels of maidenhood never turn into wives or mothers. But they are not left forlorn; Providence always finds them work enough—ay, and love enough, too, to the end.

This little plain child hovered about her handsome mother with a tender protectingness rather amusing, if it had not been so touching, to see; feeling if her feet were warm, collecting her parcels for her — they had evidently been shopping—and then beginning a careful search for a missing railway-ticket, about which the lady worried herself considerably.

"We shall have to pay it over again, Gertrude, I suppose," said she, appealingly, to her little daughter, as if she were already accustomed to lean upon her. "Your papa will be cross, and call me stupid, as usual. However, we'll not mind. Don't look for the ticket any more. Papa can pay when he meets us at the station."

She spoke languidly—she seemed rather a languid lady —and shaking out her voluminous silk dress, and gathering up her ermine muff and boa, rose and stood at the waiting-room door. Her little daughter, who had no incumbrances except a pet dog—a small Skye terrier, which she carried fondly in her arms, and vainly tried to keep from barking at every body and every thing—stood silently beside her, noticing all that was passing, with a pair of bright, acute, and yet most innocent childish eyes.

"Mamma," at last she said, "do you see those three soldiers with their knapsacks? I am so sorry for them, they look so shivering and wretched this cold day. They seem as if they were just come home from India or somewhere. For how shabby their uniforms are, and how brown their faces, nearly as brown as the Caffres that used to—"

"Oh stop, child, don't talk about Caffres; don't put me in mind of our dreadful life at the Cape. Now we are safe in England, do let us forget it all."

"Very well, mamma; only please, would you look at those soldiers? I am sure they have been in a great many battles, and gone through a deal of hardship. That one, the shortest of them, with his face half covered in a long, gray beard, has the very saddest eyes I ever saw."

The mother directed a careless glance to where her compassionate little girl indicated.

"Yes, he does look ill, poor fellow. Perhaps he has had fever, or cholera, or something; don't go near him. It is so cold standing here, I think I will return to the fire, while you wait and watch for the train. It can not be very long now."

She took out a watch all studded with brilliants, but it had stopped; and with a discontented exclamation about her watches being "always wrong," she settled herself in her old position, her feet on the fender, staring vacantly into the blazing coals.

Hers was a face so remarkably handsome that it could not pass unnoticed, and noticing, you would not only admire, but pity it—in perhaps a deeper degree than the little girl pitied the three broken-down soldiers. For therein any experienced eye could read too plainly the tale of a disappointed life; ay, in spite of all the fine clothes and evident associations of wealthy ease, the lady's look, fretful, weary, inane, reminded one of the sigh of the young beauty exhibiting to her late brides-maid her marriage jewels.—"Ah, my dear, I thought I should have been perfectly happy when I had a diamond necklace. And yet—"

That mysterious "and yet," the one hidden hitch in the wheels of existence: most of us know what it is, but some contrive to get over it, and make the wheels run on smoothly enough to the end. This woman apparently had not done so. There was no badness in her face; none of the sharp maliciousness visible in too many faded beauties; but her mouth, that feature which time and developed character alter most, indicated incurable weakness, unconquerable discontent.

She sat, paying little heed to any thing that passed, warming her feet over the fire, and leaving every thing to her young daughter, until an unpleasant episode roused her from her lazy ease.

The dog, accustomed to genteel and well-dressed company, took offense at a little innocent admiration which had been shown him by one of the shabby soldiers, the youngest and strongest-looking; and showed it indiscriminately, as his betters often do, by barking furiously at another of them, the gray-bearded man, who came shivering to catch a distant glimpse of the waiting-room fire; at which presumption Bran began to growl furiously, and at last, springing out of Gertrude's arms, flew at him, bit his heels, tore his already ragged trowsers, and even set his teeth in the flesh. The soldier, uttering an execration, shook him off, and then giving the creature an angry kick, sent him howling across the platform on the rails, where a train was just gliding up.

"Oh, my doggie, my doggie, he'll be killed!" screamed Gertrude in despair, and instinctively darted after Bran. Nobody saw her, or else nobody had the sense to stop her. In half a minute the train would have been upon her, and the bright, kindly little life quenched forever, had not the gray-bearded soldier, with a spring as light as that of a hunting leopard, leaped on the rails, caught her, and leaped back again—the train advancing slowly, but so close that it almost touched the little girl's frock as it passed. Of course every body thought the dog was killed, until the poor brute came yelping out from under the carriages, terribly frightened, but quite unharmed.

"Oh my doggie, my doggie!" cried Gertrude again, in an ecstasy of joy, snatching him up in her arms, and neither thinking of her own danger, nor how she had been rescued. Nor, in the confusion, did any body else notice it; so the soldier got no thanks, which did not seem greatly to astonish him. He retired, sullen and angry, rubbing his hurt leg, while a sympathetic crowd—porters, passengers, station-master and all—gathered round the lady and child, who seemed perfectly well known at the junction, and far too respectable for any body to suggest, as, had Gertrude been a poor woman's child, would assuredly have been done, that she should be taken up and brought before a magistrate for attempting to cross the line.

They passed on, respectfully escorted by porters and guard, to their first-class carriage, the lady's long dress sweeping across the very feet of the poor soldier, who still hung aloof, rubbing his leg and growling to himself. Now, however, he just looked up, and caught her profile as she went by.

A violent start, a sudden step forward, and then the poor fellow recovered himself and his manners.

"Who is that lady?" asked he of a porter.

"Her there? Oh, she's Mrs. Vanderdecken, of Holywell Hall. Her husband's the richest old cove in all these parts; and that little 'un is their only child. Whew! if miss had been killed, there'd have been a precious row."

"Mrs. Vanderdecken, of Holywell Hall," repeated the soldier, as if to fix the words on his memory, and clenching his thin yellow fingers tightly over his stick, for he was shivering like a person in an ague. "Holywell Hall. Where is that? how far from here?"

"Eight miles. Second station after this is the one you stop at. I'd go there, gov'nor, if I was you. For I seed you catch hold o' the little miss; and depend upon it, if you tell him, her father 'll come down with something 'andsome. If he don't believe you—for old Van's a bit of a screw over his money—call me for a witness. Eh! the fellow's off already. He's a sharp 'un, that."

"Stone! Hollo, Jack Stone!" shouted the other two soldiers. "Stop, that's the wrong train!"

But wrong or right, their comrade had leaped into it, already moving as it was, and, leaving all his baggage—not much to leave—behind him, was carried off rapidly and irrecoverably in the opposite direction from London, whither the rest were apparently bound.

They made a few grumbling remarks to the station-master, telling him the name of their companion—John Stone, late of —— regiment, discharged invalided; and leaving his box to be claimed if he called for it, went on their way.

Meanwhile Stone had jumped into the carriage—a third-class—next to the one occupied by the lady and child. They were alone, in all the dignity of wealth, but he had plenty of company, cheery, conversational; and especially well-disposed, as the humble British public almost always is, towards a red coat, and one that has apparently seen foreign service. Besides, it was just after the Indian mutiny, and the British heart was at once fierce and tender, and burning with curiosity. But frank and talkative as third-class passengers generally are, there was something in this soldier which made them hesitate to speak to him, and look at him several times before interrupting the brown study into which he fell, as he curled himself up in his corner. The last bright western glow showed his sallow and sickly face, sickly enough to touch any heart, at least any woman's, with keen compassion; and at last one old woman, a decent lady with a market-basket in her hand, did venture to address him.

"You be just home from furrin' parts, I reckon, soldier?"

"Yes."

"From India, likely? I had a son as was killed at Delhi. Maybe you've heerd of Delhi, sir?" For the good soul seemed to feel, instinctively, the minute he opened his eyes and looked at her, that she was speaking not exactly to a common soldier, or at least to one who might have dropped to that from something higher.

"Delhi? Yes, I have been at Delhi."

"Was it there you was shot?" touching his arm, which was in a sling. "Shot, like my poor Tom; only not killed."

"No, worse luck!" growled the man, as he turned roughly away; but the old woman would not be beaten.

"Yes, it's bad luck either way for poor soldiers. Either they get killed—as my Tom was—or they come home fit for nothing, with a pension as won't half keep them, and too old to turn to any thing like a trade, as you'll find, my man. You'll be over fifty, I take it? Got a missis, or any little 'uns?"

"No."

"Eh, that's a blessing," sighed the old woman. "I've had to look after poor Tom's five. Well, they're not bad children," continued she, addressing herself to the company at large, "and they'll take care of me some o' these days—so it's all right. Good-night, for I'm stopping here, to tea with Tom's wife—and there's little Tom a-waiting for me. He's very fond of his granny. Good-night, soldier; maybe you're going to see your own folk. A good journey, and a happy coming home."

"Thank you," said the man, with a sharp laugh, then curled himself into his corner so repellantly that none of his fellow-travellers had the courage to address him more.

Meanwhile Mrs. Vanderdecken and her daughter composed themselves, after their great fright and agitation, in the solitude of their comfortable carriage. The former made considerable use of her smelling-bottle, which she really needed, and Gertrude caressed and comforted her doggie until stopped by her mother's sharp voice.

"Do let that stupid dog alone, and tell me how all this happened. You were within an inch of being killed, child. How could you frighten me so?"

"I couldn't help it, mamma. The soldier kicked Bran."

"Kicked Bran!"

"Oh, but I don't wonder at that," said the child, hastily; "for Bran bit him, and I am sure hurt him very much. Still, he was the man that jumped on to the rails after me. I didn't remember at the time, but I'm sure of it now."

"Why didn't you say so, child, and I would have given him some money; he would be sure to expect it—those sort of people always do. Now he may be finding out who we are, and coming and bothering papa for a reward, and that will make papa so angry. Oh, Gertrude, my dear, how very stupid it was of you!"

"I know it was, mamma," replied Gertrude, half humbly, half indifferently, as one well used to complaints and scoldings.

"Perhaps after all we had better say nothing to papa about the matter. You are quite safe, my child," and the mother's eyes had a touch of sincere affection in them, "and so it does not signify."

"Only I should have liked just to have said 'Thank you' to the poor soldier, and asked if Bran had hurt him very much. Naughty, naughty Bran! You ought not to bite people just because they are shabby-looking. I wouldn't. I'm ashamed of you."

And the little loving hand, pretending to beat him, was licked by the loving dog, who perhaps, after all, had a moral nature not much inferior to his neighbors. For rags are rags—ugly and unpleasant things—which seldom a man sinks to unless, in some way or other, by his own fault. True, there may be what the French law courts call "extenuating circumstances;" but how is a dog to judge of these? Rags are rags, and he treats them accordingly.

Most bipeds would have treated similarly the poor soldier, for he could not have been a good man—scarcely even a respectable man—since when, on putting his head out to ask, "Is this Holywell station?" he was answered roughly, as porters usually answer third-class passengers, he returned evil for evil in language equally rough—nay, worse, after the manner of soldiers. It contrasted ill with the delicate appearance, small hands, refined features, and so on—which had made the old woman call him "sir;" or else it showed that, in whatever rank of life he had been born, he had dropped from it down and down, acquiring gradually the habits and manners of the class to which he fell. If he had been born a gentleman—which was possible, remembering the many foolish youths who run away and "list," to repent it all their lives afterwards—no one could accuse John Stone of being a gentleman now. The terrible law of deterioration, as certain as that of growth and amendment, had worked in him, equally as in the unhappy-looking lady in the next carriage, who was probably a lovely, merry girl once. For the soldier, whatever he might once have been, was now neither interesting nor attractive. Even his gray hairs, if they indicated old age—which is not the case always—failed to indicate also that

"Honor, love, obedience, troops of friends,"

which, as Shakspeare says, ought to "accompany" it. They only affected one with a sense of pity. Wrinkles were there—not few; weary crow's-feet were gathering round the dark deep-set eyes; but of the quiet, the dignity, the blessedness of old age, this man had none.

The train stopped at a small station hidden between two gravelly, furze-crowned banks; and a porter, passing from carriage to carriage, shouted the name of the place. It startled the soldier out of a sleep, or a dream—it might be either: he leaped hastily on to the platform, where half a dozen other passengers were also getting out—among the rest, Mrs. and Miss Vanderdecken.

"There's papa!" cried the little girl, and ran towards a figure, short and round, and made rounder still by a large fur great-coat.

The old man—he looked not far from seventy—greeted and kissed her with evidently a fatherly heart, and then stood waiting by the open door of an extremely elegant carriage, which—what with its size and its handsomeness, its spirited pair of horses, its burly coachman and two footmen, much taller and grander-looking than their master—shed quite a lustre upon the little road-side station, and was evidently regarded with no small respect by the other passengers, who crept humbly out—passing behind it, or ducking under the horses' heads—all save the soldier.

But he, too, stared with the rest at this dazzle of wealth, which formed such a contrast to his own lonely and forlorn poverty. He watched Mr. and Mrs. Vanderdecken get into their carriage, followed by their little daughter, who—sweet soul!—had sharper eyes and a longer memory than they had; for just before driving away she whispered in her mother's ear,

"Mamma, I do believe there is that poor soldier."

"Nonsense—impossible!" answered the lady. "And, Gertrude, do learn to speak more softly, or, deaf as he is, papa will hear many things we don't want him to hear. Hush, now!"

"Very well, mamma;" and Gertrude relapsed into her corner; but too late, for Mr. Vanderdecken, in the shrill, suspicious tones of deaf persons, asked "what the child was talking about?"

"Only about some people who amused her on the journey to-day," said the mother. "She is always taking such fancies—little goose! But what are we waiting for? Mr. Vanderdecken, will you bid the coachman drive on? You know we are going out to dinner to-night. I wonder, is it raining?"

She put her head out of the carriage window, and the station lamp fell full on her face, which must once have been so beautiful, and had a certain kind of beauty still.

The soldier, detained by the porter at the gate, leaned forward to stare at her. No—not stare—glare is rather the word: an expression that might be in the eye of a hunted animal coming at last face to face with its enemy—its destroyer—the Nemesis which had pursued it everywhere, as the spectral hounds pursued Actæon, even to the deeps of hell.

But this is poetic phraseology, which may appear simply ridiculous in describing a poor, broken-down, invalided soldier gazing at a rich and handsome lady: so let us content ourselves with merely saying that—in common with the rest of the world—John Stone took a good look at Mrs. Vanderdecken, as he was certainly justified in doing, and then moved away, walking rather staggeringly, as if his feet were weary or numb, to the farther end of the station.

Ere long he reappeared and presented himself before the station-master.

"I could easily have cheated you, and got away without paying; but I'm an honest man, you see," he laughed. "I came from ——," naming the junction: "being in a hurry, I jumped in without a ticket. What's to pay?"

His red coat, and perhaps his gray hair and weather-beaten, sickly looks, stood him in good stead, for after some demur his word was taken, and he was allowed to pay the few pence of fare required.

"I assure you it's all right," said he, taking off his knapsack, and showing hidden there a purse full of sovereigns. "I'm a capitalist, you see—there was plenty of 'loot' for all of us at Delhi. Telegraph for my baggage, which I left on the platform at ——. Name, John Stone,—th Regiment; and you may keep my traps here till you see me again, which you may pretty often, for I mean to stop in these parts."

"Very good, sir"—the "sir" being due partly to the sight of the sovereigns, and partly to an impression made apparently on others besides the old woman, mother of defunct "Tom"—that this man was a little above an ordinary private soldier—better born—better educated. If better in any other way, who could tell? Alas, the higher the height, the deeper the fall!

He fastened up his knapsack again, undid from it his gray soldier's overcoat, and wrapped himself in it, with a shivering look-out, for the brief bright sunset had closed in a drizzle of rain. With a careless nod to the station-master, he shouldered his property and passed out; then stopped.

"Hallo, porter! you'll be civil now, I dare say. Which is the road to Holywell?"

"Holywell village, or Holywell Hall?"

"Not the hall, this time. Is there a village too? How far off?"

"Three miles."

"Straight road? No missing of one's way, as fools do sometimes, and I always was a fool. Come, look sharp, man, for it's turning out a wet night, and I haven't a carriage to go home in, like your big Mr. Vanderdecken."

"Do you know him, sir? Then maybe you belong to these parts, and are going home?"

"Yes, I'm going home some day. But not just yet. I don't look very fit for work, do I now? but I've got a precious deal of work on my hands to do before I go home."

"I'm glad to hear it," returned the porter, a little frightened at his excited manner; he had heard of such things as sun-strokes in India; this poor soldier might have had one, and got his brain a little turned. So, putting up compassionately with his oddness and roughness, the man, who was a good specimen of the thoroughly respectable British peasant, as railway porters often are, let him civilly out of the station gate, and took a good deal of pains to direct him in the right road, and start him off therein—not sorry to be safely rid of him.

"That's a queer fish," said he, confidentially, to the station-master. "He's seen some rough usage in his life, I reckon. A little cracked here," tapping his honest forehead. "Hope the poor fellow 'll do no harm to hisself or his neighbors."

Meanwhile John Stone pursued his road innocuously enough. Whether "cracked" or not, he seemed to meditate no evil to any body. He walked quickly on, more quickly than his delicate appearance would have made probable, until he came to a place where there were a few small houses and a church, when his speed suddenly flagged. He leaned against the church-yard wall, behind which a few scattered grave-stones glimmered in the rainy dark, and coughed convulsively and painfully, so that a woman, standing at her open door, crossed over to look at him, saying,

"You seem rather-bad like."

"Not I; only I've walked fast, and my breath's short."

"I'll get you a drink, if you like."

"Thank you;" and accepting the literal "cup of cold water"—for he would take nothing else, though she offered him beer—John Stone leaned a few minutes longer against the low wall, with the church-yard on one side of him and on the other the open cottage door, casting into the darkness a flood of cheerful light.

The soldier cast his eyes from one to the other of these two houses—of the living and the dead—neither of which opened for him. Perhaps he thought thus, for he sighed, then thanked the civil woman, in a softer tone than he had yet used to any body, adding, in answer to her question,

"No, I can get on quite well. I'm not in a consumption, though it looks like it. I'm used to this cough—it's only that my heart is rather queer: I once had rheumatic fever."

"Eh, rheumatic fever leaves folks' hearts queer as long as they live. I know that by my master. He had it terrible bad ten years ago, and I've got to look pretty close after him still. Have you got a missis to look after you?"

"No. Good-night!"

It was said sharply, fiercely almost, as the soldier suddenly started off at his old quick pace, and disappeared into the gloom.

Another long mile did he tramp through muddy country roads, guiltless of gas or pavement, or even raised footpath, to guide the traveller from their miry abysses. Sometimes he came upon a few cottages, but they were all closed and dark. It was growing into one of those dreary November nights when every body is glad to shut even the humblest door. At last he passed them all by, and came out upon a high common, across whose blank gloom nothing was visible except a huge windmill, which stretched its ghostly arms skyward, and interposed its still blacker bulk against the level darkness; for not a star had appeared, the rain came driving and pelting, the wind had arisen, and now on the exposed ground blew fiercely enough. It seemed, in travelling over the miles of invisible country below, to have carried with it, like an overtaking fate, all the damps and fogs of the unknown or forgotten region it had passed over. It pierced to the bone the Indian soldier, and then blew him about at its mercy, helpless as a withered leaf.

He tried to draw his cap over his eyes, and pulled his coat closer about him, so as to meet it like a man—a Briton—this wholesome British wind; but he had just come from a foreign climate, and the time of youth and strength was with him gone by. After struggling on a little, he cowered and quailed before the blast, and sank down, vainly trying to shelter himself under a furzy bank, muttering something between an oath and a moan. At this moment two glow-worm-like lights came glimmering across the pitch-dark common, travelling nearer and nearer till he distinguished the sound of horses' feet; and there passed him a close carriage, satin-lined, and with a lamp inside, so as to show plainly the two occupants. They were an old man, and a lady, still only middle-aged, or she looked so, in the becoming splendors of her dinner-dress, her white fur, and her velvet and her diamonds. She sat in her corner, and her companion in his—neither paying any heed to the other, as wealthy married couples going out to dinner could scarcely be expected to do. They looked comfortable, indeed, but not happy—it is a curious fact that "carriage-people" seldom do look happy; and as they drove slowly past, the soldier had no difficulty in recognizing the magnates of the neighborhood, Mr. and Mrs. Vanderdecken.

Of course they no more saw him than if he had been a bush at the road-side. But he saw them, and as soon as they had passed he leaped up and shook his fist at them, in a manner that almost justified the railway porter's suspicion as to his sanity.

"Curse you! curse you! by day and by night, by bed and board, eating and drinking, sleeping and waking—curse you!"

Was it the frantic howl of poverty against wealth—of failure against success—of misery against happiness? Or was it something deeper still—some old link of the past which these fine folks stirred in the breast of the poor soldier, so as to turn him, for the time being, into a veritable madman?

Yet he was neither mad nor sun-struck, and when his sudden fit of fury had subsided, he gathered himself up to try and battle with the wind a little farther. He seemed to have been long used to "rough it," as soldiers must.

Presently he came to the verge of the common, and saw, through the misty, rainy gloom, a line of houses, implying some sort of a village; and coming nearer, the wet and weary man caught the welcome glow and sound of a blacksmith's forge. He entered it.

"Is this Holywell?"

"No—Holt. Holywell's nigh half a mile farther."

Stone leaned against the door-way, utterly worn out.

"Can I get a night's lodging here?"

"I reckon not. There's no public near, except Mother Fox's over the way, where there's 'good entertainment for man and beast.' If one don't suit 'ee, tother may. Ho, ho!"

"Ho, ho! I wish I was a beast," laughed the soldier, with

"CURSE YOU!"

a careless air, as if he were accustomed to put up with all sorts of jokes, and every kind of company. "Then, at least, I'd get a dry stable to put my head into, this horrible night. But come, show me the way to Mother Fox's."

It was a small, old-fashioned, village public-house, and as he looked in at the door, which opened at once upon the bar, he was stared at hard by the little knot of Saturday-night customers, whom the landlady was serving as fast as she could.

"Can you give me a night's lodging here?" said he.

Either his voice sounded unlike what might have been expected from his appearance, or some other cause made the busy landlady stop and notice him, and at once he recognized in her the inquisitive old lady who had addressed him in the railway-carriage.

"Bless us, is that you? Who'd ha' thought it? But come in, my good man, and I'll make you very welcome. I've a warm heart to soldiers. Deary me, how wet you are!" feeling his coat-sleeve; "and you're just as thin as a skeleton, besides. Come in to my kitchen fire and warm yourself."

"Thank you," said Stone, gentler. Under all his surly ways lurked a vague, pathetic gentleness, or as if he had been gentle once. "You are very good to me, Mrs.—"

"Fox, my name is—Dorothy Fox; and this is the Goat and Compasses, a very respectable house, though I say it as keeps it, and uncommon comfortable."

"And you can take me in?"

"Well, sir," said she, after eying him over again pretty sharply, "we don't usually take in travellers as we knows nothing of; indeed the place is too small. But my daughter's away; and if you likes to take her room till Monday, you can."

"How do you know I shall not take myself off without paying my bill on Monday? We're a bad lot, we soldiers."

"So poor Tom said. But you can't harm me much, and I'll trust you. Come along."

He followed her, and was soon basking in the blaze of the huge fire with an air of comfort that seemed to afford his hostess real pleasure. She looked at him inquisitively, especially when he took off his forage-cap and showed his bare bald crown, though the fringe of curly locks under it, unlike his beard, was still black, or only slightly touched with gray.

"You're not so old as I took you for, my young man—for you're young compared to me. How many years might you have been in the service?"

"A dozen or more, perhaps. I don't remember."

"Then you didn't 'list as a lad? Volunteered, maybe?"

"Ay."

"And you're only just back to Old England, did you say? You must find every thing very strange?"

"Very strange. Get me my supper, will you? I'm starving."

He spoke in a sharp, irritable tone, which even a woman and a landlady could not well submit to; so she brought him his bread and cheese in offended silence, and troubled him no more till he had moved from the table to the old-fashioned settle near the fire-place, where, overcome by weariness and warmth, he soon fell fast asleep.

PRIVATE JOHN STONE.

Then Mrs. Fox's heart relented. He must have been so excessively tired, poor fellow! and, besides, heavy slumber is such a softener of most faces. Not of all—some people look all the uglier or the wickeder; but others seem to slip back through the gates of sleep—as of death—into the land of their pristine innocence, and wear a look so helpless and appealing that one could not hate even one's direst enemy if one came upon him fast asleep.

John Stone slept, in his great exhaustion, as soundly and softly as a baby—slept, sitting as he was, for no doubt his military life had accustomed him to go to sleep anyhow, anywhere. He scarcely moved from his original posture, but just let his head fall against the high back of the settle; while his hands, thin and yellow, dropped upon each knee, and then curled up drowsily, like a baby's hand. His forehead lost its knotted wrinkles, and if one could have seen his mouth through that long, rough grizzly beard, doubtless it would almost have smiled.

For he seemed, under the influence of the pleasant warmth and the strange contradictory vagaries of slumber, to be carried entirely out of the present into some golden dream-land. He gave vent to a little low sound—almost like a laugh—and then began to talk in his sleep—at first quite unintelligibly, and then uttering a name: "*Betty*," Mrs. Fox thought it, and concluded it was his wife's or his sweetheart's — probably long dead and gone.

"Poor fellow! maybe that's what he 'listed for. Likely he's seen a peck o' troubles," said she to herself, looking at him, and uncertain whether she should wake him or not, for it was time to shut up, only she grudged rousing him out of what seemed such a happy slumber.

But Fate broke it, as she does many a deeper dream. There was a sudden clatter of pewter pots and glasses in the bar, creating such a stir that the soldier started up with the frightened look of one who did not know where he was.

"Never mind—there's nothing the matter. You dropped asleep and was a-dreaming, my dear," said Mrs. Fox, patting him on the shoulder with a motherly air. "You're at the Goat and Compasses, the best public in all these parts, and Dolly Fox 'll make you very comfortable. Your bed's ready—hadn't you better be a-taking yourself off now?"

"Thank you," said the soldier, shaking himself wide awake, though he still stared about him somewhat wildly. "Yes, I remember all now. Give me a light. I'll go to bed—I'll go to bed."

He disappeared, and was not seen or heard of again till far into the Sunday morning.

CHAPTER XXI.

SUNDAY was a quiet and respectable day in Holt village. No Cockney Sabbath-breakers or Sabbath holiday-makers, according as people choose to term them, had as yet found out its prettiness, or, if they had, its distance from the nearest railway station saved it from being a place of easy resort. Consequently, its Sunday was still a rest-day. No swarms of destructive feet trod down its green fresh common, where fern, thyme, and heather flourished, and the bright yellow furze blossomed all the year round. No tea-garden, or bedizened public-house, or even a solitary refreshment-stall, destroyed the delicious peacefulness and thorough rurality of the spot—the windmill, the forge, Mrs. Fox's small, whitewashed, old-fashioned inn, and a few cottages of similar date, being the only harm it had as yet received from bricks and mortar.

And on this Sunday morning, when, after a wild rainy night, the weather brightened up, as it does sometimes in November, and the whole earth and sky became transfigured into a wonderful blueness and clearness that showed the landscape, distinct and exquisitely-colored, for many, many miles—this upland common, so fresh and breezy, quiet and fair, was a sight to do a man's heart good in spite of himself. That is, a man whom nature had made sensitive to external influences—as not every man is; but to those who are, life's delights are doubled. Also, perhaps, its pains.

John Stone crawled down, late and lazy, to his long-waiting breakfast in Mrs. Fox's parlor.

"Pull down the blind—I hate sunshine," was all he said to her, as he fell languidly to his solitary meal.

When she came to remove it, she was dressed all in her Sunday's best, and hinted that Holt church "went in" at eleven o'clock, and it was a good mile's walk across the common.

"I never go to church," said the soldier, abruptly. Then, as with a second thought—"But don't let me hinder you from going. I shall want nothing more."

"Thank'ee. Only what shall you do when I'm out?—for I always lock up the house o' Sundays. I'm a lone widow as can run no risks."

Stone laughed. "Do you think I look like a swindler or a burglar—that I shall break open your cupboards and carry off your plate? No, no. I'm a bad fellow enough, but I'm not in that line of business. Make your mind easy, old lady. Lock up your house, and I'll turn out and wander about somewhere till you come back."

"You're very obliging," said Mrs. Fox, looking somewhat compunctious. "I'll be back in two hours, and you might amuse yourself that while seeing the Park. It's a pretty park—the Vanderdeckens'."

John Stone jumped up from his chair, savagely pushed it from him, and began walking up and down the room.

"Big people, are they? and have a fine place, no doubt? I'll go. Where is it?"

"Just across the next common. You turn along the park palings till you come to a stile, where there's a board put up with 'Please to keep the footpath.' That's old Vanderdecken's doing. He couldn't stop the right of way, but he narrowed it down as much as he could, and made the place as private as possible. That's the trick of your stuck-up new-comers, as never knew their own grandfather. Not like the good old families that are quite sure o' themselves, and so they're never frightened to let us poor folk come a-nigh them, lest we should find out that the only thing as makes the difference between us and them is clothes."

Either John Stone, who looked a clever fellow himself, was struck by the old woman's sharpness—or in his loneliness he rather liked a little conversation—but he did not discourage her gossip. He even asked a question or two about these Vanderdeckens, and when they had come to the neighborhood.

"Three years ago. He bought the Hall, which was just

dropping to ruin, and built it into a big house—far too big for him, poor silly old man, for he has got no son to come after him — only one little daughter. But he's mighty fond of her, they say — fonder than he is of any thing, except his money."

"He's a miser, then?" said the soldier, eagerly.

"Not exactly—or else, like most of your miserly folks, he'll spend pretty well where he fancies it, or where the money shows. Though I'm not saying aught agin the Vanderdeckens; she's a kind lady enough, and wonderful good-looking, and sees after the schools, and has her finger in all the charity doings. And he has restored Holt church—they're very regular church-goers, both on 'em——and put in it a big painted window in memory of Anne, only sister of Jacob Vanderdecken, who died at the Cape of Good Hope some'at about fourteen years ago. You sees I knows it all off by heart, sir, for I sits opposite to it every Sunday; and sometimes when I'm inclined to be sharp upon 'Old Van,' as we calls him hereabouts, I've thought folks' memories are so short in this world, that there must be some'at not bad in a man who remembers his sister for more than a dozen years. But I beg your pardon for going on like this."

"No, no," said Stone, absently. "As you say, folks' memories are short, very short. There's a proverb about a man's name outliving him half a year, if he builds churches; and about funeral baked meats that did coldly furnish forth marriage tables."

"Be that in the Proverbs—the Bible, I mean?"

"No, in a much better book." Then, seeing how shocked and scandalized the good soul looked, he half apologized. "You think me a heathen, or an infidel?"

"Not a bit of it, sir. I hope you're a good Christian."

"There you mistake," said the soldier, looking up with gleaming eyes. "I'm no thief. You needn't be afraid of my robbing your house and murdering you. But I am no Christian. I don't believe in any thing or any body."

"I'm sorry for it. But you're young still, I reckon, and

perhaps before you die the Lord will bring you to a better mind."

"Will He? Then why hasn't He done it already? Why didn't He do it years ago?"

"I can't tell, sir," and the old lady laid down the table-cloth she was folding, and clasped together her withered hands. "That's just what I said to myself when poor Tom was shot, while Jim Brady beside him, as was nobody's son and nobody's husband, and all the village was glad to get rid of—Jim hadn't a scratch. Why doesn't the Lord do a many things that He doesn't do, and leave undone a lot more that one thinks He ought to do? I can't tell, sir, and I suppose nobody can. However, there's the bells beginning, so I'll go to church and say my prayers; that can't come amiss, anyhow."

The soldier was silent till just as she had cleared every thing away, when he said, suddenly,

"I'll go to church with you, Mrs. Fox, if you are not ashamed of my company."

"Oh, sir."

"But, mind you, I'm not like you. I don't go to say my prayers: I go for my own—amusement. Yes, we'll call it amusement," and he laughed.

"Never mind, if only you'll go. Them as isn't against Him is for Him, says the Bible. And you'll see our church; and as for our parson, whether or not you like his sermon, it'll do you good only to look at his face."

So in a few minutes more that strangely-matched pair of church-goers—they could not be called worshippers—the stout landlady in her best black, permanent widow's weeds, and the thin, spare, sickly soldier, took their way across the common, guided by one of those fine peals of bells such as are heard nowhere but in England. It poured through the windless, sunshiny air in the familiar chime—ting, ting, ting, ting, ting, ting, ting, ting—and then a clash, as if the whole eight bells had rushed upon one another and fell crushed into one solid mass of music. The soldier stopped to listen; his hollow face grew still more wan, and his lips began to tremble.

"You like our bells? we reckon 'em very fine," said Mrs. Fox, gratified. "I suppose it's pretty long since you've heard a good chime of English bells?"

He nodded. "What's that?" pointing to something in the view, perhaps to make a diversion in the conversation.

"What do you mean—them steeples?"

"No, that queer sort of building, which seems crawling along the horizon like a big caterpillar, with two towers, like horns, one at its head and the other at its tail?"

"You're very funny, sir," answered Mrs. Fox, excessively amused. "I dare say you must have been rather a droll chap altogether when you was young. A caterpillar! Well, it is like it; and to think that you didn't know what it was! To be sure, you've been a good bit away from England. But did your folk never send you any newspapers, and never tell you about the Crystal Palace?"

"No," replied the soldier, in such a sharp, trenchant tone, that Mrs. Fox determined never to mention his "folk" to him again. She was convinced there was "some'at wrong" concerning them, and though by no means deficient in feminine curiosity, still there had been quite enough of household tragedy in her life of seventy years to make her comprehend that every heart has its own burden of grief, and that it is often kindest and best to notice nothing, but to "let sleeping dogs lie." So, without farther questioning, or indeed any conversation at all, she took her companion across the common and down a village street to the church, against the low wall of which he had leaned the night before.

It was an old building, but modernized into comfortable unpicturesqueness. Nothing about it was very noticeable, except a solitary yew-tree, which kept guard over a few ancient, nameless graves. Of the modern memorials one caught Stone's eye, as it would any body's, being a long, wooden board, planted lengthwise on a grave, with the name and dates very plain, and underneath, bigger and plainer still, the warning text "*Watch, therefore, for ye know not at what hour the Lord cometh.*"

The soldier turned and regarded it with some curiosity,

which slowly faded away into a contemptuous sneer. He might have been going to say something sneering, doubtless, but the old woman beside him was walking on so quietly with her grave Sunday face; and likewise he seemed to notice for the first time that she was in widow's weeds. So, infidel as he was, or called himself, Stone shut his lips together and followed Mrs. Fox in silence to the church-door.

"Take off your hat," she whispered—not too soon, for he was marching into the half-filled church like a man in a dream, regardless alike both of the place and the people.

Still, when warned, he recollected himself, and obeyed, blushing a little, like a reproved child.

"I beg your pardon, Mrs. Fox; I had forgotten my manners. I have not been inside a church-door these fifteen years."

"Oh, my dear soul, how shocking! Stop, stop!" again restraining him. "The church is free; but somehow we always leaves them foremost seats for the gentry. Sit you down here."

For he was going right up to the chancel, where, close in front of the white-spread communion-table, which some old-fashioned folk still call, and believe to be, "the Table of the Lord," was a handsome pew, oak-carved, crimson-cushioned, and well furnished with Bibles, prayer-books, and hymn-books of the hugest size.

"You mustn't go in there, it's the Vanderdeckens' seat; but you can see their window just as well from here, and the clergyman, too. Do sit down, sir."

For she still kept putting in the instinctive "sir," as with a suspicion that the man was, or once had been, what people term a gentleman. And he both interested and fidgeted her so much that the poor old woman hurried over as fast as possible her customary prayer, and then turned, uneasy as a hen over a young duckling, to see what her *protégé* was doing.

Nothing dreadful, certainly. Whatever he himself might be—Jew, Turk, infidel, or heretic (Mrs. Fox classed them all together, as the Prayer-book does, and knew no more)

—he had sat down decorously and harmlessly beside her, staring about him a little too much, perhaps, but still not more than many well-bred people stare, at "the gentry" who came filing in—the good old families who lived in the good old red-brick houses, solid and square, of the Georgian era, which Mrs. Fox had pointed out on their way to church.

"None o' them's the Vanderdeckens, though; they always comes in by the chancel-door; and she's worth looking at, being a fine woman still, and dresses mighty grand. I sees her in a new bonnet every second Sunday at least."

John Stone bent his head assentingly to this whispered feminine communication, and then sat quietly and decently enough, his hands clasped on his knees, and his eyes steadily fixed at the opening door, too much in shadow to be very noticeable, else he too might have been worth looking at. He had been decidedly handsome, and, had he had a smooth life, might have been handsome to extreme old age; but it was one of those artistically moulded faces, dark yet delicate, and all alive with what our grandmothers used to call "sensibility;" in which a hard or troubled career soon wears out all the beauty, and, indeed, alters the whole appearance; so that after some years a mother would hardly recognize her own son. And his bald head and full gray beard gave him, at first sight, the look of a man not far off sixty, though, examining him closer, he was not nearly so old.

He sat staring about him; for, as he had averred, he came to church not to pray, but merely to amuse himself, until, last of all the congregation, appeared the Vanderdeckens.

They were a group of three—father, mother, and little girl. A big footman preceded them to their pew, showed them in, placed an additional book there, and left them. Then this wealthy family dropped their heads on their hands for a minute's space of prayer like other "miserable sinners."

Yet undoubtedly they looked exceedingly comfortable. Mrs. Vanderdecken's violet silk dress was rich in hue as the painted window, and her ermine furs were dazzling as the purest snow. Certainly she knew the art of dressing well, and had every opportunity for exercising it. Her little girl, too, was clad as a rich man's daughter should be, though no splendor of clothes could make her any thing but an ordinary child, in whom one vainly sought the smallest trace of the mother's beauty. Another thing, also, one did not find, happily—the mother's peevish, unsatisfied expression, which dulled all her loveliness, like a sweet landscape overspread with mist and rain.

Gertrude's quick eyes roamed round the church, and soon met John Stone's. She whispered something to her mother, and then Mrs. Vanderdecken also turned, and fixed her eyes—her large, blue, soulless, uncomprehending eyes—upon the poor soldier. Fixed them leisurely, looked him all over from head to foot, apparently seeing nothing in him but a very shabby, broken-down fellow, and then turned back again to her daughter, whispering something back. Something kindly, no doubt; for the little girl blushed and looked pleased, and continued her investigation of the soldier in shy glances, which she hardly restrained from breaking out into positive and most undecorous smiles.

But the mother did not look again. She had done her duty—all that could be expected of her; and then the poor man evidently passed from her memory. He did not belong to her and her circle of thought at all; she put him aside, and settled herself to her comfortable devotions.

Mrs. Vanderdecken was, as Mrs. Fox had said, decidedly worth looking at; and John Stone did look at her all church-time. Just a glance or two did he expend upon the little fat old man beside her, one of those men who are only remarked in society as their wives' husbands; yet there was an obstinate protrusion of his under-lip, and a glitter in his small, keen eyes, which accounted for Mrs. Vanderdecken's hesitation at "telling papa," and implied at least a possibility that the large handsome lady married to the ugly little man was not so much "the gray mare" as appeared probable.

John Stone apparently was a student of human nature, for he seemed to take in all this, and more. From his post of observation he let not a movement in the Vanderdecken pew escape him. No avenging ghost could fix upon it and its occupants steadier or stonier eyes. He paid attention neither to the prayers nor to the sermon; merely got up and sat down when Mrs. Fox urged him to do so, but otherwise made no pretense of worship. Whatever he was, he was at least honest. And when, escaping from his hard, fierce stare, which harmed them not, for they never saw it, the Vanderdecken family, with the humbler portion of the congregation, bent their heads to receive the final benediction, "the peace of God which passeth all understanding," this man, in whose countenance was no peace, held it up, as if at once hating them and accusing them to the silent heaven, which had beheld all, and prevented nothing.

"Come," said Mrs. Fox, touching him as he stood erect and motionless, "the likes of us always goes out first, the gentry afterwards. Though it's being sacrament Sunday, the most of 'em stops behind; the Vanderdeckens always do, except the little miss. Come along," she added, sharply.

She led him, walking more like an automaton than a man, down the church aisle, and out into the air, which blew sharply across the church-yard, and made him shiver with Indian sensitiveness all over.

"Let's make haste," said the old woman. "It's coming on to rain, and I've my Sunday clothes on; besides, I want to get home and cook a bit o' some'at hot for your dinner—you'll want it this sharp day."

"Thank you; you're very kind to think of me," said—with a sudden change of voice—the poor soldier.

It did rain, and rained, soppily and soddeningly, the whole remainder of the day, as these bright winter mornings have a trick of doing; so neither Mrs. Fox nor her charge, as she now seemed fairly to consider him, crossed the threshold again. Stone spent half the afternoon in sleeping, with his head against the settle, dropping off as if from sheer weakness, on the intervals of smoking his pipe, which he did to an unconscionable extent. Beyond it, indeed, he seemed to care for nothing, neither amusement nor occupation; asked for no books, though Mrs. Fox brought him several; good Sunday books — "Pilgrim's Progress" and "Hervey's Meditations among the Tombs." At last, pitying his utter indifference to every thing, she risked her Christianity enough to fetch him a newspaper. But the world seemed to have completely slipped from him, or he from it, so that he took no more notice of the "Times" itself than if it had been a sheet of blank paper. Never was there a sadder spectacle of a man with nothing to do, and no strength to do it—a sick soul in a worn-out body. And yet, whenever he fell asleep, the boyish, innocent look came back, till the old woman stood and watched him with an expression of pity that she could not suppress.

"I doubt if you're long for this world, and maybe you'll not be sorry to get out of it," said she to herself, looking at him from over the big Bible, which she always scrupulously read of Sunday evenings. "Poor fellow! I shouldn't like to be your mother, I reckon. My Tom's happier where he is, and so am I, than if he'd come back to me like you."

Yet the remembrance of poor Tom was so strong, that when, just before bed-time, Stone asked her abruptly if she would take him in for a few more days—a week or two, perhaps—Mrs. Fox, though she had never seen the color of his money, assented.

"You can stop if you like, for I've a weak side to soldiers. Maybe you're a long way from your home?"

"Yes—a long way."

"Then you're right to try and get a bit stronger before you go there. Holt is a healthy place, they say, and then there's Holywell. You may spend half your time in wandering about Holywell Park."

"I mean to."

"If you'd like me to name you to the butler there—he's a friend of mine—you could come and go about the place as you fancy, with nobody to hinder you."

"Nobody will hinder me."

It might have been said either as fact merely, or else a threat, for the tone of it caught Mrs. Fox's attention. She shook her head.

"Ah, my man, I'm afeared you're one of them radicals as hates all rich folk, for nothing on earth *but* being rich folk, while we belongs to what they calls 'the lower classes.' But I never troubles my head about such things; and when you're as old as I am, and have gone through all I have gone through, mayhap neither will you."

The soldier was silent.

After a while he said, "I've been thinking, Mrs. Fox, that I ought to tell you my name, or give you some warrant for my respectability."

"Just as you like, sir. Of course it's better and more satisfactory to all parties, and, besides, our rector, he always calls when he sees a new face in church, for he's as good as a father to the whole parish, and I'd like to be able to tell him I'd got a decent man in my house. Who shall I say, sir?"

"John Stone, private, —th Regiment; discharged invalided, with a pension. Besides, in case I should starve upon that — your British nation is not too generous to broken-down soldiers—look here!"

He showed her, as he had done to the railway-porter, the bag of sovereigns.

"It's loot—honest loot, I assure you; at least, so far as loot ever is honest. And perhaps your millionnaires — your Vanderdeckens, for instance—make their money in no more creditable way."

"Oh, sir, I never heard any thing to Mr. Vanderdecken's discredit. He's a very respectable gentleman."

"Well, so am I; that's all. Will you trust me now?"

The old woman looked at him hard. "I think I'd have trusted you anyhow. But I can't tell. I've been took in a good many times. I often think the world's made up o' two sorts o' folks—them as puts upon others, and them that is put upon theirselves; and it's pretty hard for the last, only maybe the Lord loves 'em best, after all."

"Does He?"

"Don't you sneer, sir; you may live to think different from what you do now. Young folks fancy they've found out every thing, but old folks know they've never done learning."

"You're a wise woman, Mrs. Fox."

"I wish I was, sir; I wish I was! But good-night to you. You've had a dull Sunday, if this is your first Sunday in England."

An innocent trap which caught nothing. Stone neither answered yes nor no.

"Anyhow, you'd better go to bed now, and perhaps you'll feel not so bad on Monday morning. Good-night. As the young ladies used to say where I was nurse-maid forty years ago (I was brought up among my betters, sir, and I'm used to their ways), 'Sound sleep, pleasant dreams, and a blithe waking.'"

"Never in this world, and there may be no other—I hope not, for I could not stand it. I am so tired—so tired!"

It was not said bitterly or blasphemingly, only in utter weariness; and Stone left his thin, wasted hand for a minute in the old woman's palm, which had grasped his own in rough cordiality. But she was so shocked at what he had said that she dropped it at once; whereupon he slowly turned away, took his candle, and went up stairs, to meet that long, lonely night which is either the utmost fear or the only comfort of such as he—till God prepares for them that bed which may be sweeter than they know.

CHAPTER XXII.

Holywell Hall, whatever it had originally been, was now transformed into one of those splendid modern mansions peculiar to England and to the taste of English merchant-princes. Exclusively modern—for, like Mr. Vanderdecken, these commercial magnates have seldom known a grandfather; and most of them see the wisdom of escaping entirely from the sombre glory of unattainable ancestral dignity into the tangible magnificence of present wealth.

Every thing at Holywell was solely of to-day, except a wall or two left standing for picturesqueness, and the gigantic trees of the park, which could not well be regrown, and made trim and new, or very likely Mr. Vanderdecken would have done it. In the house he did as he chose. The upholstery was of the latest style; the tables, chairs, mirrors, and pictures—all being equally regarded as furniture—had not one antique flaw. In fact, the whole contents of the mansion might have come—half of it did come—bran-new and specklessly perfect, from the Great Exhibition of All Nations, then just closed. It was altogether a very splendid abode, complete in all its arrangements, and lacking nothing that money—which can purchase taste, among other trifles—could supply.

The only thing it wanted—if, indeed, such a want is worth mentioning—was that intangible something which may be called the soul of a house, in contradistinction from its body; which makes you conscious of the presence and influence of somebody who loves the dwelling and takes pleasure in it, either for its own sake—we can get attached to dead bricks and mortar, for want of any thing better—or for the sake of some human being belonging to it. This soul, which can inhabit and inform with its own beauty and brightness a very poor abode, does not always dwell in a rich one, and certainly did not dwell at Holywell Hall.

Nevertheless, it was a fine place, and perfect of its kind; quite above criticism, indeed, except that a captious observer might say, if it had a fault, it was that, like its mistress, its handsomeness verged on too much of splendid solidity. You found in it none of the play of variety, the sweet little untidinesses, such as a book out of its place, a bit of work left in a chair, or a child's toy on the floor, which make a house look inhabited and home-like. From end to end you might traverse Holywell Hall and not discover aught amiss, not even in Mrs. Vanderdecken's boudoir, where she sat every morning—scarcely for business, domestic or otherwise; she had nothing to do; but merely because most ladies in the neighborhood had such a room, and were always found sitting there before luncheon. They also — as she found on coming home from abroad—had the good old English habit of needle-work; so Mrs. Vanderdecken likewise adopted it, and was generally seen with a beautiful embroidery-frame before her, where she was making a fender-stool for a charity bazar. At least, she put in a stitch or two when she felt inclined, and her own or Gertrude's maid continued and completed the task.

The effect of the elegant work, and the diamond-ringed fingers moving over it, was very good; while as for the room, it was perfect, and arranged with an especial view to those rosy half-lights which set off to the best advantage a lady whose complexion may naturally be supposed beginning to fade a little — very little in this case; and all that art could do to sustain waning nature was undoubtedly done for wealthy Mrs. Vanderdecken.

Yet she looked dull, as she almost invariably did of a morning, for visitors rarely came so early, and she never saw Gertrude till lunch. The child was always up and at work by eight, with her daily governess; while the mother never rose till after ten, leaving her husband and daughter to breakfast alone together, as they had done ever since the little girl was two years old.

Gertrude was an only child. Mrs. Vanderdecken would have liked a son best—a son and heir to all this property. Still, she was very fond of her little daughter. Women, who seem otherwise to have no heart to speak of, have very often the mother's heart—at least, that natural instinct which belongs equally to brutes and human beings, yet it is a sacred instinct in its way. Mrs. Vanderdecken had it. She had petted Gertrude extremely during infancy, and now, as she was growing up into a companion, clung to her, as such silly women do cling to any body who will take a little of the burden of existence off their shoulders.

I have called her a "silly" woman; but perhaps that is

not quite fair. There was no absolute silliness in her, no more than there was absolute badness; she looked merely negative—made up of negatives: the kind of woman who, if left alone, will willfully do no harm to any one, but sleep through life like a Persian cat upon a velvet cushion—sleek, and a little uninteresting; but quite harmless—or looking so, at least.

She herself seemed interested in nothing to any great degree. She had no favorite pursuits. Her sitting-room was in perfect order; the book-case untouched; the piano unopened. She idled wearily over her embroidery, yawned two or three times, and pulled out her jewelled watch to see how the time went on—time, which to some gallops so fast, but which with her seemed perpetually to crawl. At last, unable to bear her weariness of it or of herself any longer, she rose and rung the bell.

"Tell Miss Vanderdecken to come up to me the minute she has finished lessons."

But when, shortly after, the child came bounding in with an exuberance of life that made her almost pretty for the time being, the mother's only welcome was a fretful reproach.

"How rough you are, Gertrude! and how very long you have been at lessons! What detained you?"

"My history, mamma. I was in Queen Elizabeth's reign, and I wanted to finish it."

"That is a trick you have; when you begin a thing you never rest till you have finished it. You are just like your aunt—"

Mrs. Vanderdecken stopped suddenly.

"Not like my aunt Anna, surely; though papa fancies it sometimes. But I hope not; for nurse says she was quite an elderly person—and so fat. I would rather be like my other aunt—Aunt Edna; isn't that her name?"

"Yes."

"Didn't I bring you this morning a letter from my aunt Edna?—that is, I thought so; for the post-mark was Brook Street," said the child, hesitatingly, as if treading on a forbidden subject.

"It was from your aunt Edna. She remembered my birthday, which nobody else has done for many a year."

"Oh, mamma, why didn't you tell me your birthday? and I would have given you something pretty, and wished you 'many happy returns.' Isn't that what they say in England?"

"I don't know; I have almost forgotten."

"Dear old mammy—darling mammy!" cried the child, fondling her. "Now, won't you show me the letter from Aunt Edna? I should so much like to see it! I wonder if she writes as nicely as she talks? Where is it? in your pocket? Do give it me."

"Little girls should not expect to see their mamma's correspondence," Mrs. Vanderdecken answered, coldly; "and you know so little of your aunt, that it is impossible her letter can interest you. She is well, and so are all the family. That is enough for you to know."

Gertrude looked disappointed, but urged no more.

"And, by-the-bye, child, you need not say any thing about the letter to your papa. He does not know the Stedmans, and they are in such a different sphere of life from ourselves that it is not likely we shall ever be very intimate with them. So the less we talk about them the better."

"Very well, mamma."

The child's answer was given with that careless acquiescence which neither implies assent nor obedience. Perhaps, unperceptive as she was, the mother had sense enough to discern this, for she said, after regarding her daughter uneasily—

"You must really mind what I say to you, Gertrude. You are always taking fancies to people, and you are not old enough to choose acquaintances for yourself. Promise that you will make none without telling me. You ought to tell me every thing. I mean your papa and me, of course."

"But, mamma, you don't always tell papa every thing?"

Mrs. Vanderdecken looked extremely annoyed, and her vexation took refuge in displeasure.

"You naughty, impertinent child, how dare you say such rude things to your mother—your poor mother, who has no comfort in the world but you!"

Neither the anger nor the pathos seemed to affect the child very deeply; probably she was well used to both. She only stroked her mother's hand with a sort of patronizing affection.

"Dear old darling, I didn't mean to vex you. I'll never do so no more—till the next time—and I'll be the goodest girl that ever was, if you will only let me go once again to see my aunt Edna."

Mrs. Vanderdecken turned away very bitterly.

"You ungrateful girl, you don't care two pins for your mother now. It is all your aunt Edna."

"No, it isn't; how could it be?" returned Gertrude, practically. "Because my mother is my mother, and my aunt Enna I have only set eyes on twice, an hour each time, counting the hour last week when I met her at the Crystal Palace with Cousin Julius."

"Julius; is that their eldest boy's name? Oh yes; I remember now. You seem to have caught it up very readily."

"Because I thought it such a funny name; and when we were walking together by the fountains, I asked him who they had called him after—was it Julius Cæsar? and he said no, it was after an uncle he had, who had been dead a great many years."

"Yes; a great many years."

There was something in Mrs. Vanderdecken's manner which struck the child—who was as quick to observe as her mother was slow—for she said at once,

"Did you know him, mamma? What was he like? Was he my uncle also? Did you ever see him?"

No! the lady was just going to reply, but the contemptible lie—the lie of fear—died upon her lips. Falsehood was so difficult, so impossible, with her young daughter looking right in her face with the honest gaze of a child.

"Yes," she said, "I did know him once a little. But he was no relation of yours—only Dr. Stedman's brother. He went out to India, and died there."

"How did he die?"

"He was drowned, I believe."

"Where? in the sea?"

"In the River Hoogly, I think; but I never heard much about it. And now, my dear, you need not catechise me in this way, for I really can tell you nothing more. And you must not ask any more about—about Mr. Stedman."

"Why not? Oh, I understand," and the little maid's face suddenly became tender and grave. "We ought to be careful in speaking about people that are dead. And perhaps they were very fond of him—his own relations, I mean—and very sorry when he died."

"Perhaps they were," said Mrs. Vanderdecken.

She rose from her chair and stood, her full height, opposite the full-length mirror. Her lips were a shade paler than their usual rich color, and she evinced a slight uneasiness and gravity of manner, such as most people show in speaking of any unpleasant subject, a shocking accident, or discreditable history, just enough to convince the quick-witted Gertrude that something mysterious lay behind, and make her resolve, poor little unconscientious girl as she was—alas! she had had no example of conscientiousness—that, in spite of her mother's prohibition, she would question Cousin Julius closely about his uncle the very next time she got a chance of seeing him.

"There is the bell; let us go down to luncheon," said Mrs. Vanderdecken, with an air of relief, and, taking her little daughter's hand with an appealing sort of fondness, which sat touchingly on the large, splendid woman, she passed slowly down the marble staircase, crossed the hall, and entered the dining-room; where, in somewhat cheerless state, she, Gertrude, and the governess, were accustomed to take their midday meal together.

She was very silent throughout it; but then who could expect her to talk much to a mere governess? She never interfered in the teaching, but always showed the utmost distaste for, and ignorance of, the proceedings of the school-room. And, whenever she addressed the little elderly lady who taught Gertrude, and had been a teacher of

MRS. VANDERDECKEN AND DAUGHTER.

children all her days, it was with a reserved dignity that showed plainly the great difference between poor Miss Smith and Mrs. Vanderdecken, of Holywell Hall.

Yet she was not unkind, or uncivil, or unlady-like: here, too, the extreme negativeness of her character prevented her from doing any thing decidedly amiss, and no doubt Miss Smith would quite agree with Mrs. Fox, and with most other people, in finding no fault with, nay, even praising, the great lady of the parish. It takes so little to gain popularity when one has an indefinite number of thousands a year.

Meantime, Gertrude chattered incessantly to her mamma or her governess, with the wondrous merry heart of twelve years old, so that gradually the vexed look—it was only vexation, not sorrow—passed from the mother's face, and she listened with a lazy smile, glad to catch the present pleasure—and such an innocent pleasure, too. If she ever looked really happy, this poor rich woman, whose life seemed so barren of every thing but riches, it was when in the company of her little girl.

"It is very odd," said she, half to herself, when the governess had retired, and the child still went chattering on; "but though, as papa says, you are like the Vanderdeckens, and not a bit like me—still there is about you sometimes a queer look of your aunt Edna."

"Are you sorry for that, mamma?" For while Mrs. Vanderdecken spoke she had slightly sighed.

"Sorry! what makes you fancy such a thing? Dear me, no; except that your aunt Edna isn't pretty—never was. Still, as I always tell you, good looks are of no importance. I'm sure I never got any benefit from mine!" (with another sigh)—"No, child; you are better as you are, and I dare say your aunt Edna would tell you the same thing."

"Would she?" and Gertrude indulged, for a wonder, in a few moments of silent meditation. "Please, mamma, when is Aunt Edna coming here?"

"I really don't know."

"Will she never come here?"

"How can I say? Your papa asks to his house whoever he pleases; and probably he doesn't want to ask my sister."

"But don't you want her, mamma? Did you ever really tell papa you wanted her? Shall I tell him?"

"Oh dear no; not upon any account," said the lady, hurriedly, caught, as she continually was, by her honest child, in the very ambush under which her weakness hid itself. "The fact is, the Stedmans are so different from us that we do not care to invite them; nor do we think they would enjoy themselves if they came. But, for all that, she is a good person, an exceedingly good sort of person—your aunt Edna."

So saying, Mrs. Vanderdecken rose and ordered the carriage, while Gertrude, who hated being shut up in a close brougham, begged to be allowed to take a run in the park with "old nurse," a colored woman, over whom she ruled supreme.

"Just as you like," the mother said, peevishly; "you are always glad to go out with any body but me, and to do any thing that I don't particularly want you to do. And what you can find to amuse you in the park these dull, damp winter afternoons is more than I can see."

"Oh, mamma, I can amuse myself anywhere if only I am let alone."

"Just like your aunt Edna—as like her as two peas!" muttered Mrs. Vanderdecken. Then, in her velvet, fur-trimmed cloak, with her filigree gold card-case in her hand, she stepped into her carriage, to pay the never-ending, still-beginning round of visits, which constituted the principal duty and solace of her life.

Then her little daughter trotted off: trotted is just the word for the round, compact little figure, pattering resolutely upon its small dots of feet, the merry face shining under a round cap of chinchilla fur, the hands tucked inside her muff, and gathering close about her a scarlet cloak, like little Red Riding Hood. She was not a pretty nor even a picturesque child; but she was a child, which is a great deal to say for her in the present generation. And, withal, she was a quaint, self-contained, self-dependent little soul, not taking much after either parent, but belonging to some far-back, long-forgotten Dutch type; while, ever and anon, there reappeared in her that curious likeness to her mother's English sister, which seemed at once to annoy and to touch Mrs. Vanderdecken.

She trotted through the park, this funny little maid, appearing and disappearing among the bushes, in her scarlet brightness, not unlike a cheery, plump, merry robin-red-breast.

It was one of those dull days when, foreigners say, Englishmen are all inclined to go and hang themselves. The mossy walks, once so soft and green, were now spongy and sodden; dead leaves lay everywhere in rotting masses, except the few left on the trees, which fluttered mournfully against the murky sky. Every thing was at the transition-time, when earth seems as if she could not reconcile herself to winter, but lies, abject and helpless, grieving over her own decay, with the grief of a man over a wasted life, or a woman over her love-life all done. Dark days, dreary days, whether in the year or in human existence; yet they must come to us all.

Ay, even to poor little Gertrude; though as yet she understood them not, nor seemed in the least affected by the gloominess of the day. She went gayly on, stamping on the wet moss, and leaving it in little ponds, shoe-shaped, behind her; or kicking the dead leaves about at every step, in exceeding fun. Soon she quite distanced the nurse, who, indeed, was only too glad to be let slip, and returned to the house, as was her custom, telling nobody —and well certain that Gertrude would tell nobody—of her absence; inconvenient candor being by no means the rule of the Vanderdecken household. So Gertrude came alone to her favorite play-place—an odd-shaped ornamental pond, possibly, in far-back centuries, the original "holy well." Several oaks, now huge and hollow with age, with quantities of ferns and even stray brambles growing in their hearts and on the crevices of their gnarled arms, had been planted round its brink. Also a yew-tree, whose enormous branches swept the water, and stretched over it almost to the island in the centre, which some later hand had made and adorned with rhododendrons and other flowering plants. A somewhat dreary spot, because it was not wholly Nature—Nature never is dreary—but had in it a forlorn mingling of art. But Gertrude made herself quite happy there; and after feeding her water-fowl, the only inhabitants of the spot, who swam towards her in a chilly appealingness, as if the black-looking pond were almost too much, even for ducks, she climbed to her favorite post—the arm of the largest oak-tree which overhung the water—and sat swinging there, Ophelia like—not singing, certainly, but indulging in castle-building, as this solitary rich man's child, so unlike both her parents, was rather prone to do.

Hers was, however, a very modest and matter-of-fact castle: nothing more than a pretty summer-house, which she would coax the gardener—Gertrude was hand-in-glove with all gardeners and humble folk on her father's property—to build for her, and to which she would invite, if possible, who? Casting her thoughts round about, she could find no better visitors, or more to her mind, than her aunt Edna's five boys, with Cousin Julius at their head, if only Cousin Julius—a big manly youth—would condescend to come. Perhaps there, under the influence of tea and cake and cousinly feeling, she might coax out of him what she was sure must be most romantic and mysterious—the whole history of his uncle and namesake, Julius Stedman.

In default of this, she began to invent it for herself, being in the habit of making up stories, heroic and pathetic, at will. By-and-by she grew so absorbed in her own imaginations that she let her muff drop off into the water, and was nearly following it herself, when a strong hand caught hold of her.

It was a man, who had crept near and been watching her intently for several minutes, only in her absorption she neither heard nor saw him. Probably he had not meant to be seen, since he had hidden himself behind the yew-tree, save for the instinct which made him stretch out a hand to save the child from falling into the water.

"Take care, little miss," said he, gruffly. "That's an unsafe seat for a child like you. Are you alone?"

Yes, she was alone. Not a creature to protect her from the grim man, who spoke so roughly, as if he hated her, and was ready to do her any sort of mischief. But Gertrude was not a cowardly child; if frightened at all, it was usually at supernatural things; and this was only a man. In fact, as she perceived the minute she took courage to look at him closer, a man already known to her by sight —the poor soldier who, she believed, had saved her life, and whom she thought a good deal of since. Surely he never meant to harm her.

She did not scream, but looked him composedly in the face.

"Yes, I am quite alone. Why did you ask me? What are you going to do to me?"

"Do to you, simpleton! what should I do? Eat you up, as the wolf ate Red Riding Hood? Do I look like it?"

And he laughed—a horrid kind of laugh, the poor little girl thought—and glared at her with the wildest eyes she had ever beheld, or ever imagined, in ogre or giant. Yet he was a small man, comparatively—thin and sickly-looking; and while considerably frightened, she also felt sorry for him. Perhaps he was a little crazy; and she had heard that madmen ought to be humored and treated as if one were not the least afraid of them. So she answered, though inwardly quaking, as gently as she could,

"You would be a very bad, cruel man to kill a poor little girl who never did you any harm."

"Indeed!"

"And if you did kill me," gathering courage as she spoke, "you would be punished for it. Papa would have you hanged."

The soldier laughed again. "And how would that benefit you? For instance, your father's hanging me would not bring you back to life again? It might comfort him, though; for revenge is sweet—very sweet—"

And he went on muttering to himself the rest of his sentence.

Gertrude now grew seriously alarmed. She would have run away home; but the man leaned against the oak-tree trunk, and so blocked up her passage. She was compelled to remain sitting on the branch, with her poor little legs dangling over the pond. Thus they kept their positions, these two; for her jailer seemed to have forgotten her pres-

LITTLE RED RIDING HOOD.

ence and dropped into a fit of musing, till at last Gertrude ventured to address him again.

"Please, kind man, let me go. It can't do you any good to be cruel to a little girl like me. I'm very sorry for you, you look so ill; and I would give you some money only I have none in my pocket. But I'll tell mamma about you when she comes home."

"Is she out, your mother?"

"Yes, out driving. You might wait for her at the lodge-gates, and she would be sure to give you something. She is very good, is my mamma."

"That's a lie!" answered the soldier, fiercely.

Then the little maid forgot her fear in a sudden blaze of indignation.

O 2

"How dare you say so? What do you know of my mamma? She is a lady, and you only a common man—not even a gentleman, or you wouldn't talk to me about 'lies.'"

"Shouldn't I?" returned the man, eying in a sort of curiosity the small, fearless face, all ablaze with wrath. Then he said, "You're not like her—not one bit. I won't harm you; you may step down. Allow me to assist you, Miss Vanderdecken."

He offered her his hand with such a courteous air—not like an ogre at all, she thought, but more resembling the politeness of the young prince in the "White Cat," or the Beast, after Beauty had turned him human by loving him—that Gertrude regarded the man with dumb surprise. Instead of taking to her heels, as she had meant to do, she turned and offered to shake hands with him.

"Good-bye. You seem to know my name. I am much obliged to you, and so will my mamma be; for she knows who you are"—(the soldier started)—"and so do I too."

"Indeed! Who am I?"

"I think you are the man who pulled me from under the train one Saturday night. I have not said much about it since; for mamma does not like talking about unpleasant things; and she is easily frightened. But I know quite well that but for you I should have been dead and buried, and gone to heaven by this time."

He smiled at the quaint wording; but he could not deny the fact. In truth, with the peculiarity of his nature, in which impressions that seemed slight at first, instead of wearing out deepened down with time, during these three days it had more than once occurred to him, with a strange, creepy feeling, how very near he had been, and the child too, to the "going to heaven" which she talked about—going *together*. How odd such an accident would have appeared! and what a queer coincidence it would have been if they two had been dragged out dead from under the train, and identified (as, though careless enough about himself living, he always took care his body should be identified)—himself and Mrs. Vanderdecken's little daughter!

Half in mockery, and yet drawn towards her by an attraction for which he could not account, and with not at all the sort of feeling which he expected to have had towards her, he intently examined the child.

"Would you have liked to 'go to heaven,' as you call it?"

Gertrude pondered a minute. "No; at least not just yet, I think."

"Why not?"

"Because I am quite happy as I am."

"Happy!" echoed the man, and looked half-contemptuously, half-pitifully at the child. "Is any body happy, do you think? Is your mother happy?"

"Of course she is. No, stop a minute;" and the honest little face took an expression which, in its flitting, shadowy sweetness, reminded the soldier of another—far back in ghostly ages; even as we sometimes see, with a start, the dead and the lost come back to us for a minute in the likeness of some little one of a new generation. "No, I am afraid mamma is not always happy, for she sometimes tells me I am the only comfort she has; and I am sure that is very little."

A gleam of satisfaction—wild satisfaction—lit up the countenance of the poverty-stricken soldier. "Really! she is not happy? All her riches can not make her happy—nor her husband neither? She and your father quarrel sometimes, don't they?"

The man seemed quite carried away out of himself, or he must have seen the astonishment, mixed with reproof, of the little girl's look.

"You must be a very odd sort of person to talk to me in this way about my papa and mamma. What can you know of them? I am very, very sorry for you, and very grateful to you for saving my life; and any amount of money that papa could pay—" Here the little girl stopped, confused, touched by an instinct stronger than all her education.

"I suppose you think—doubtless your mother has taught you—that money can do every thing; but it can not. I want nothing. I know I saved your life; and I prefer to hold you in my debt for doing so. You may say this to your papa, if you like."

Gertrude looked puzzled. "I wish I could tell him, and then he might thank you as I do. But papa knows nothing about this accident or about you; mamma would not let me tell him."

"Then she keeps secrets from him—from her own husband?" said the soldier, eagerly.

"I don't know what you mean about keeping secrets; and, indeed, if you will let me go away, I had rather not talk to you any more," answered the little girl, almost beginning to cry, with a vague fear which she could not quite get over; while, at the same time, her keen sense of the romantic—and under her funny little Dutch outside there was a deal of romance in Gertrude Vanderdecken—was interested and excited to the highest degree.

The soldier had apparently meant more conversation; indeed, he had taken the trouble to divest himself of his overcoat, and made of it a cushion for the little girl on the tree-arm beside him; but now he took it up again.

"Very well: you can go whenever you like. Good-bye."

"Good-bye." Gertrude began walking off as fast as she could, for twenty yards or so, then turned and looked behind her.

The man was sitting as she left him, with his elbows on his knees, gazing down into the black water. His appearance and attitude were so forlorn, so wretched—he seemed so utterly lonely, sitting there on the dreary December afternoon, with the damp, white mist beginning to crawl over every thing—that the little girl, who was going home to a good fire and a bright drawing-room, where she always shared her mamma's cozy five-o'clock tea, felt her heart melt towards him.

She returned, and touched him on the arm.

"I beg your pardon; I forgot one thing. Tell me who you are, and where you live? If it is in this parish, I am sure mamma will come and see you; for she has her district, and goes round regularly—unless when she sends nurse and me instead. And I should like to come and see you too. What is your name?"

A simple question—the simplest possible, and given with the most innocent, up-looking, kindly eyes; yet it made the soldier start, grow pale, and then blush violently all over his face. He turned sharply away.

"What does my name matter to you? Why do you question me? What right has your mother to come and see me?"

"Oh, she always goes to see poor people, or sick people; all the ladies in the parish do. But she shall not come if you do not wish it. Indeed, if you dislike it so much, I will tell her nothing at all about you."

"That's right," said the man. And then, with a sudden thought, he added, "if you will promise to tell your mother nothing at all about me, I will meet you here every afternoon, if you like; and I'll tell you all sorts of pretty stories, and queer tales about foreign countries. I have been half over the world, I think, and seen curious things without end."

"Have you, really?" said Gertrude, opening wide eyes of delight. Here was an opportunity such as she had often longed for—an adventure delicious as any fairy tale; and the small fact of its being a surreptitious enjoyment did not lessen, but rather increased, the charm of it to this poor little soul, who had never been brought up to that holy atmosphere of simple truth which makes want of candor as impossible to the child as it is to the parent. There is a rough and bitter proverb, "As the old cock crows, the young cock learns;" and those who sow in small shams not unfrequently reap in large deceptions. In this case Gertrude's better nature made her hesitate a little. "Mamma always bids me tell her every thing; but then to hear endless stories, as you say—oh! it would be so nice!"

"Very nice," sneered the soldier; "and all true, of course. Every body always tells the truth, your mamma included. Come, shall we make a bargain, and shake hands upon it?"

Yet, as the warm little hand dropped upon his, in the sudden foolish confidence of childhood, on his side too, the man's higher nature felt a slight upspringing of conscience, but he battened it down tight and close. To the little girl herself he knew he intended no harm—nay, he rather liked her than otherwise, and, for aught else, what did it matter?"

"Very well, my dear," said he kindly, trying to teach himself to speak to her as he supposed children were accustomed to be spoken to. "Then we have made what the Scotch call 'a paction' between us. Take care you don't break it. I shall not."

"Nor I. But," her curiosity getting the better of her, "I should so like to know your name."

"John Stone."

"Thank you—and good-bye again, for I hear the carriage coming."

She flew off like a bird—like the little winter robin that she so much resembled—and left him alone in the gloomy, darkening mist.

CHAPTER XXIII.

Almost daily, and for many days, John Stone the soldier and little Miss Vanderdecken met—accidentally it appeared, but nevertheless by design—in quiet nooks of the wintry, deserted park. Sometimes Gertrude's nurse was with them, sometimes not. At any rate, Stone contrived to secure the woman's fidelity, both by money and by talking to her in her native Hindostanee, she having been originally an *ayah*, brought from Calcutta to the Cape. This done, he had no other fear of premature discovery, for at Holywell Hall, as in most large establishments, the comings and goings of any individual item therein was scarcely noticed, not even though it were the young lady of the house. Besides, every body was accustomed to Miss Gertrude's independent proceedings, which formed such a contrast to her mother's graceful laziness;

consequently, the carrying out of this surreptitious adventure was easy enough.

The only trouble in the matter was the child's own conscience, which sometimes woke up, and she begged leave to tell every thing to her mamma; but Stone always quieted her with promises that she should do so very soon. Besides, he said, if she were ever found out, and asked any questions, she had nothing to do but to tell her mother the direct truth.

"But suppose mamma is angry with me, and forbids me to see you any more, what shall I do?"

She spoke in eager anxiety, for the fascination of this man's company, the charm of his talk, and the interest inspired by his looks and manner—so unlike a common soldier, and so very like, she thought, to a prince in disguise, as she every day expected he would turn out to be—had quite intoxicated the romantic child. She was not exactly fond of him—was almost afraid of him sometimes, for he had such queer ways—such sudden bursts of excitement; and yet day and night she never got him out of her mind, and was always thirsting to meet him again and hear something new.

"Your mamma angry?" repeated Stone, with a sneer. "I thought fine ladies were never angry. However, in that case, just send her to me—John Stone, lodging at Mrs. Fox's, of the 'Goat and Compasses,' and I'll make things straight for you directly."

"Will you, really? And will you explain to her that it was all because you made me make a promise, and I could not break it? People should never break their promises."

"Did she teach you that?"

"No, but papa did; papa is very particular. He says, true in small things, true in great; that if you deceive one person, you'll be sure to deceive another; and he sometimes talks about all this in such a way that he makes mamma cry."

"Why?" asked Stone, grasping at the family skeleton which the child had betrayed, and investigating it with the zest of a ghoul burrowing into a grave.

"Oh, because she is a little frightened of him, I think; and yet he does not mean half he says. He is never unkind to me. Only he dislikes mamma's asking him for money; and sometimes he gets into a passion, and calls her ugly names, and she begins to sob, and wishes she had never married; and it makes me so unhappy, you can't think. But I ought not to tell you all this."

"It's no matter. I'll not tell again. I can keep a secret. Besides, I have nobody to tell it to."

"Have you no relations—nobody at all belonging to you?"

Stone shook his head.

"I wish you had had a little girl of your own for me to play with. You were never married, I suppose?"

"No."

"But you had a father and mother—perhaps brothers and sisters, once?"

"No sisters."

"Oh, what a pity! It must be so nice to have a sister. I have no relations at all; at least, none that I shall ever see much of. But that is a secret too," added the child, looking graver. "I can't imagine why it is, but mamma can not bear my talking much about my aunt—the only one I have—Aunt Edna."

The soldier started. He had been sitting, with the child beside him, in the hollow of an old oak, telling his Munchausen-like stories, of which how much was fiction, how much fact, he alone knew; and afterwards he had fallen into a sort of dream, as he was prone to do, watching the sunset, and listening to a wren on a tree-top near, singing as loud and merrily as if it were the year's beginning, instead of its close. Now he seemed startled out of his meditation into exceeding agitation.

"I beg your pardon, say that name again. I was not listening. Your aunt who?"

"Aunt Edna, mamma's only sister; indeed, I never knew she had a sister till about a year ago, when, in driving through London, we saw the name on a door—Dr. Stedman. That is Aunt Edna's husband. He is a doctor, you must know."

"And he lives—where?"

"In Brook Street, Hanover Square," answered the little maid, delighted with the importance of giving information. "It is but a little house. When mamma called there she wondered how they could live in such a pokey hole, but she supposed it was because they were poor still."

"Poor?"

"That is, compared with us; but I don't think they can be really poor people; or if they are, they don't mind it. They all look so happy and merry—Aunt Edna and her five sons."

"Five sons, has she?" said Stone, who, after his first violent start, had settled down into an attitude which he was prone to fall into—stooping forward with his hand over his eyes. He said he had had moon-blindness, and sometimes wore green spectacles. "And—her husband—your uncle?"

"Oh, you mean Dr. Stedman. Of course, he is my uncle; but I have never seen him. We have only called once, and they never come here."

"Why not?"

"Nobody seems to want it, except me. But I want it very much. I should so like to have my cousins to play with, especially Cousin Julius."

Stone sprung up, and then suddenly sat down again, catching hold of a half-rotten branch, and breaking it in little pieces as he spoke.

"I beg your pardon. Go on, child. Tell me all about your aunt and uncle and cousins."

"Would you really like to hear?" cried Gertrude, highly delighted. "Not that there is much to tell; for I know so very little about them. But they live in Brook Street, as I said, and they are such a happy family, and seem so fond of one another. Two of the boys are bigger than Aunt Edna—she is a very little woman, you must know—and they pet her and play with her, and yet seem so proud of her. They tell her every thing, Julius says, just as mamma desires me to tell *her*," added the child, sighing — only, somehow, I can't. Don't you think there is something about a person which makes you tell them things? But you can't do it just because they desire you, any more than you could love people because they compelled you to love them."

The little girl had hit upon a great mystery—perhaps the greatest mystery in parental government; but no such ethical or moral question interested the soldier. Yet he did seem interested—keenly, painfully—in what she was saying.

"Go on. Tell me more."

"About Aunt Edna and her house? Oh, I am sure it must be the happiest house in the world. No wonder they don't care to come to ours."

"Is that so? Who says it?"

"Mamma."

"Oh, then, of course, it must be true."

"I wish you saw my aunt Edna. I do like her so!" cried Gertrude, enthusiastically. "She is not pretty, and is not a fine lady at all—dresses very plainly; but then she is so bright, and sweet, and kind. The first time I saw her she took me on her knee and kissed me, and cried a little, saying to mamma that she once had a dear little girl of her own, but it died when a baby. However, she seems very happy with her five boys. Oh, I could be so fond of Aunt Edna if they would let me! But—hark! I think I hear wheels. I must run in-doors before mamma comes home. Good-bye."

"Good-bye," said Stone. He had seemed to pay little attention to her latter words; but when she was quitting him he called her back. "Stop. Your uncle is a doctor, you say. I might want one. I am ill sometimes. Give me his address."

Gertrude gave it eagerly.

"Oh, do go to him! I am sure he would do you good. And then, perhaps, you would see Aunt Edna and my cousins, and would tell me all about them when you come back. Only you had better say nothing to them about me."

"Of course not."

"I wonder," said the little girl, lingering, as a sudden brilliant idea struck her, "whether you, having been at Calcutta, and actually sailed up the Hoogly River, might know any thing about—about—"

"What?"

"Oh, nothing particular. Yes, it is something particular, as I can guess from mamma's telling me never to speak about it. There is a secret which, if I could find it out, might be as interesting as any of the stories you have told to me. Listen:" and she placed her lips to his ear in the approved fashion of mystery-mongers. "Cousin Julius told me that he had, once upon a time, an uncle."

This communication made nothing like the impression she intended. Stone heard it, sitting, rigid as his name, with his eyes fixed on the ground. At last he said,

"Is he alive?"

"No—dead many years ago, mamma told me."

The soldier started a little.

"How did he die—how did she say he died?" asked he, after a pause.

"He was drowned in the Hoogly. But there's Nurse beckoning. I must run. Good-bye."

"Good-bye;" and Stone sat where she had left him, pondering.

"Dead—drowned!" he repeated to himself, and then laughed. "Dead, years ago! Well, it's all true—all true; and better so."

He rose, hearing the rumble of distant carriage-wheels, and hurried by a short cut to a corner of the park, where he generally lingered at this hour, behind a thick holly bush which was near the park gates. Thence he could watch Mrs. Vanderdecken drive slowly through in her phaeton, or brougham, or landaulet—she had an endless variety of carriages—but always alone, always dull, as if nothing ever had given or could give her pleasure in this world.

When she had passed, Stone started up from his hiding-place, and ranged wildly over bush and brake, like a man out of his senses, till he came out upon the common, where, seeing decent laborers walking decently homeward in twos and threes, he also did the same, and soon found himself at Mrs. Fox's door.

The good woman had been very kind to him, though, as she told confidentially to all her neighbors, she thought him a little "cracked." But as he was quite harmless, and paid his bill regularly—every morning, because, he said, no one knew what might happen before night—she did not object to have him staying with her. He had his meals in her parlor; gave hardly any trouble; went early to bed, and was late to rise; never complaining of either his food or his lodging. He took very little notice of any body, yet there was in him a pathetic gentleness, which won the heart of every creature—certainly every woman —who had any thing to do with him.

"I'll be bound he has seen better days, and had folk mighty fond of him some time," was Mrs. Fox's deliberate opinion. "What has brought him to this pass, goodness knows."

"Drink, perhaps," somebody suggested.

But Mrs. Fox indignantly repelled this accusation, though she owned he sometimes looked as if he had been drinking, and, besides his tobacco, there was now and then a queer smell in his room, like a druggist's shop. But it was not brandy, she was certain: nothing ever passed his lips but water in her sight, and, if out of it, she would soon have discovered the fact, for she was a great lover of temperance, even though she kept a public-house.

So, much as they talked him over, the little circle which revolved round the "Goat and Compasses" could come to no conclusion about John Stone, except that he was "rather queer," but certainly not sufficiently crazy to be treated as a lunatic. Still, they let him alone as much as possible—all, save the good landlady, who, partly from a love of patronizing, and partly through real kindness, took him in her charge entirely, and, it must be owned, very devotedly.

"Mrs. Fox, what is the earliest train to London to-morrow?"

She was so amazed at the question that she forgot her ordinary deference, which rather increased than diminished the more she had to do with "Mr." (as she now always called him) Stone.

"My dear soul, you don't mean to say you're going up to London?"

"Yes."

"Well, I'm glad of it. It'll amuse you, maybe. Is it for good, or only for a day or two?"

"Only for a day or two. 'For good,' as you say, I am not likely to go anywhere. I shall leave my traps with you, and return very soon. Come, come; I dare say, in your heart you're not sorry to be rid of me."

The old woman shook her head with one of her sententious remarks.

"Them as their friends is glad to get rid of, Mr. Stone, are generally those as have never tried to make 'em want 'em. You're no trouble here—quite a pleasure; and you'd better stop with me till you goes back direct to your own folks."

This latter was a thrust, deliberate and prudential; for she often felt her responsibility very great, and would have been really thankful to find out something definite respecting the lonely, sickly man, who might at any time fall ill, or even die upon her hands; but Stone took no notice of what she had said. Indeed, after the matter of the train was fixed, he scarcely spoke another word, but smoked incessantly till he went to bed.

He was very late up, so late that he nearly missed his breakfast and his chance of a lift to the station in the butcher's cart, which Mrs. Fox had kindly arranged for him. And as she started him off he looked so haggard, so feeble, that she shook her head more ominously than ever.

"He'll go off some day like the snuff of a candle. I wish I knew who his friends were, and I'd write to 'em, with his leave or without it, that's all."

But the busy and the poor have not too much time even for compassion, and before Stone was a mile away even his kindly hostess had forgotten him.

Not a thought from her, or any human being, followed the solitary soldier as he took his journey, and at length found himself dropped into the wild whirl of London streets, which he trod with an uncertain step, and dazed, bewildered air, as of a man who had never been there before, or so many years ago that his experience was no help to him now whatever.

Besides all this, he had at first a frightened look, as if he expected continually to be recognized or spoken to—a fancy which country people often have, till they understand London better. London — that mad Babel — so crowded, yet so intensely lonely, that among the myriads one jostles against, to meet a known face is almost an impossible chance. So he was drifted on—this atom, this nomad, this forlorn bit of humanity—in the great human tide that went surging right and left down either side the street. Gradually he let himself be swept on by it, as unimportant and unnoticed as a bubble down a stream.

He turned westward, more by instinct than design, apparently—for he walked like a man half blind and stunned. By slow degrees, however, he seemed to grow accustomed to the crowd; breasted it less awkwardly and timorously, and looked around him a little, as if trying to recollect the places he saw—above all, to recollect himself.

Thus he got on as far as the Cheapside corner leading to St. Paul's Church-yard, when the sudden boom of the great cathedral bell, striking eleven o'clock, sent such a shock through his frail, nervous frame, that he leaned staggering against a shop-window.

"Halloo, man! are you drunk, or what?" cried a passer-by, catching hold of him, but meeting no answer, no resistance, let him go again. "You're ill, sir. You'd better get into a cab and go home;" but there was no cab at hand, so the stranger hailed an omnibus which Stone silently indicated as it passed, and civilly helped him into it, perhaps feeling that he was safer among companions than alone.

The omnibus was full of the usual average of omnibus

passengers, all busy and self-absorbed, every one going his own way, and paying little heed to his neighbor. Nobody noticed Stone, who turned his face to the glass and watched the gliding by of the various familiar objects along the great western outlet from the city. They were scarcely changed. London looked precisely as he had left it, even after this long interval of twelve years. It seemed only yesterday that he had taken his last omnibus ride homeward on this very route, the day he left England, a young man, with life all before him and nothing behind. Now?

Well, we all of us must meet such crises; times when some sharp, sudden curve of the river of life brings us face to face with the lost past, and we stand and gaze on it for a moment or two—startled, saddened, or smitten with intolerable pain — then, knowing it irrecoverable, turn our backs upon it, and go on, like our neighbors, our inevitable way.

Most men, who have at all neared their half century of existence, can understand this feeling; but then few have such a past to look back upon as John Stone.

He rode on a good distance, and then got out and walked through the quietest and least frequented streets of the West-End, losing himself several times. The only place he stopped at was, oddly enough, an upholsterer's shop, in the window of which there happened to be for sale a large swing glass. Stone looked at himself in it, carefully, from head to foot.

His was a figure certainly peculiar, but not peculiar enough to attract notice among the many odd fishes who swim safely and unobserved through London streets. Spare and short—the shortest stature admissible by the regulation height of the army — the faded scarlet just glimmering under his gray coat, the foraging cap pulled closely over his brows, and the rest of his face almost hidden by his spectacles and long beard, any special personal appearance he had was so concealed that his own mother might have passed him in the street and not have known him.

Apparently, he satisfied himself as to the result of his self-examination, for shortly, paying no heed to the jeer of a small London boy that "P'raps he'd know that 'ere party agin when he met him," Stone turned away from the mirror and passed on — walking much more confidently than before.

He reached at last Brook Street, that favorite habitat of physicians and other strictly respectable but not ultra-fashionable people, and walked right down it till he came to Dr. Stedman's door.

A quiet, unpretending door it was, and belonging to one of those small houses, at least much smaller than the rest, which are sometimes to be found in this neighborhood. The brougham standing opposite to it was of the same character; a neat doctor's carriage, arranged with all appliances for books, etc. — evidently that of a man who works too hard not to economize time as well as money by every possible expedient. The coachman, a decent elderly man—one of those servants who are not only thoroughly respectable, but confer respectability on their employers—sat on his box, waiting patiently for his master.

He had not to wait long. Punctually at twelve o'clock Dr. Stedman came out, and stood on the door-step talking to a poor woman who had just run up to him: so that the soldier, if he wished it, had a full opportunity of observing the physician whom he had said he might consult some day.

Dr. William Stedman—as his door-plate had it—was a tall, strongly-built, middle-aged gentleman: fair-featured —a little florid, perhaps—but with the ruddiness of health only. He was muscular, but not stout, and very wholesome-looking, even though he was a doctor and lived in London. His mouth was placid, his eyes were kind. His whole appearance was that of a man who has fought his battle of life somewhat hardly, but has got through the worst of it, and begins now to put a cheerful sickle into the harvest of his youth—to reap what he has sown, and prepare to go forth rejoicing with his sheaves. A season, often the very best and brightest of existence to such a man; and the very bitterest to a man who has come to his harvest-time with no harvest ready, and finds out the awful inexorable truth, that whosoever has sown the wind must reap the whirlwind.

While Dr. Stedman stood, talking to his patient or applicant—a very poorly-clad and sad-faced woman—John Stone watched him intently. He even crept on a little farther, holding by area-railings as he went, that he might see him better; and so remained until the physician, having finished his talk with the woman, dismissed her, and then, as with a second thought, called her back, took her into his carriage, and drove away.

When he was gone Stone clung to the railings tight and fast. One of his violent fits of coughing seized him, and for a little he could hardly stand or speak.

No one took any notice of him—those things are too common in London. He came to himself soon, and then paused to consider what he should do. Bodily exhaustion guided him as much as any thing, and the horrible fear that he might drop in the street. He went into the nearest shop, a baker's, and asked for a penny loaf and a glass of water. But after he had munched a few mouthfuls he put the food aside, and taking out of his pocket a queer little Eastern-looking box, which emitted a still queerer smell—not tobacco—he extracted and ate a small fragment out of its contents.

"What's that?" asked the baker's wife, uneasily. "Not poison?"

"Oh no! It's my physic—my food—my drink—my chief comfort in life, I assure you!" said Stone, in an excited manner, as, laying down sixpence, and forgetting to take up the change, he hurried out of the shop, and was soon lost once more in the maze of London streets.

Lost—how sad a word it is—how sad, and yet how common! And who are the lost? Not the dead—God keeps them—safe and sure; though how and where we know not, until we go the way they all have gone. But the living lost—the sinners, who have been overtempted and have fallen—the sinned against, who have been hunted and tortured into crime—the weak ones, half good, half bad, with whom it seems the chance of a straw whether they shall take the right way or the wrong—who shall find them? He will one day, we trust; He who in His whole universe loses, finally, nothing.

Poor Stone had much of this "lost" look as he wandered about London—uncertainly, idly, like a man who has given up all stake in life and takes no particular interest in any thing. Sometimes he stopped at a shop-window, generally a print-shop, and vacantly gazed at its contents; but he never lingered long anywhere; and being in his exterior neither a beggar nor a rogue, but just up to the decent level which makes a man an object neither of fear nor compassion to his fellow-creatures, he was not much noticed by any body, but just allowed to go his own way—to work or be idle—feed or starve—live or die, as it pleased himself and Providence.

Wherever he wandered during that long day, Stone always came back to the little house in Brook Street, hovering about it as a ghost might haunt its body's grave; walking to and fro, sometimes on one side of the street and then on the other, and watching every one who went in and out.

There were many, for Dr. Stedman's seemed both a full and a busy house. People were perpetually coming and going, not a few with those eager, anxious countenances that are ever haunting a doctor's abode. He appeared to have a good practice, and to be not without friends, for several daintily-dressed lady visitors called; and one or two gentlemen in carriages, grave, professional, eminently respectable—the sort of connections which gather round a man when he begins to rise in the world, and the world discovers that it may be rather proud of him than otherwise.

John Stone the soldier saw all these things. Pacing the street, and sometimes, that he might awaken no suspicion, hanging about with other forlorn and shabby-looking loungers on area-steps and at shop-windows, he watched with hungry glances the continually opening door. Once, struck by a sudden impulse, he even went up to it and laid his hand upon it, but just that minute two young lads came springing up the steps behind him, all life and gayety.

"Halloo! here's an old soldier. Did you want my father, eh, my man?" looking into the stranger's face with a frank bright smile which carried with it such a ghostly likeness that, after a moment's eager glance at the lad, Stone, trembling like an aspen, shook his head in silent negative, and went shambling away.

"They must be his boys, of course," muttered he to himself. "Such big lads! *His* boys. It seems like dreaming. But I'm always dreaming." And he laughed, but the laugh was half a moan.

After a few minutes the two lads reappeared, bringing out with them in triumph a little lady, well furred and cloaked, and evidently prepared to meet the still damp day and enjoy it as much as either of her sons. For mother and sons they were, there was no mistaking that. The elder gave her his arm, patronizingly and tenderly, as if it were a new right which he was rather proud of claiming, while the younger walked beside her, seizing by force her umbrella and bag, and flourishing them about with great liveliness. Both lads were so full of themselves, and of her, guarding her on either side, and enjoying her company with undisguised delight, that they were rather regardless of passers-by, and the elder brushed past Stone somewhat roughly.

"Take care, Julius," said the lady, in a gentle, feminine voice, fit to win over any number of boys, and yet rule them too, for there was neither weakness nor indecision in it. Then, turning to the soldier, she added, "I beg your pardon, my son did not mean to be rude to you."

Stone made no reply, and after a passing glance at him she walked on. However, ere crossing the street, she looked back and said a word or two to her second son, who immediately came and spoke to him, civilly and kindly.

"Are you not well? Is there any thing I can do for you?"

"No, nothing. Let me alone!" said Stone, sharply, and hurried away.

A few minutes after, however, he was haunting the same street—the same door. Almost that instant the doctor drove up to it, when two little lads not long past babyhood, going out with their nurse, blocked his way.

"Papa! papa!" rose in unison, a perfect shriek of welcome.

Dr. Stedman stopped and tossed them up, one after another, in his strong arms.

"My Castor and Pollux, is it you?"

"We're not Castor and Pollux, we're David and Jonathan. Papa, give us another toss."

"Not to-day; I'm very busy. Run away, Gemini. Nurse, is mamma at home?"

And hearing she was not, a momentary cloud crossed his face.

"Ah, well, she'll be back by dinner-time, and so shall I. Tell her so." And he hurried in with the preoccupied look of a man who has no idle moments to lose. Very soon he came out again, and was hastening to his carriage, when his quick eye caught sight of the figure leaning against his area-railings.

"Did you want me, my good man? Any message? Are you a patient of mine?"

"No."

"I don't remember your face. But you look ill. I am unfortunately in haste," taking out his watch; "but still I could spare fully three minutes, if you wanted to consult me."

"No."

"Good-afternoon, then."

"Good-afternoon."

Preoccupied as he evidently was, the kind physician gave one half-compassionate glance behind him, then closed his carriage-door and drove away. John Stone stood in the street alone.

Yes, quite alone now—alone as few men ever are until their death. He had come hither with no definite intention beyond the natural impulse of most men, to see old places and familiar faces again. Afterwards, driven by some vague yearning, some last clinging to this world and all its tender ties, he had experimentalized thus on a mere chance, hardly knowing whether he wished to succeed or fail. He had failed.

It was neither improbable nor unnatural that he should have done so, and yet the certainty of it smote him hard.

"I am quite safe," he said, bitterly. "Nobody knows me. I may go among them all as harmless as a ghost."

And not unlike a ghost he felt—a poor, wandering ghost revisiting the upper world, where his place was now as completely filled up as, perchance, even the best-beloved, most honored dead would find theirs, could they return after a season to the hearths they sat at, the friends and kindred who once loved them so well; ay, and love them still, only with a different sort of love. It seems sad, and yet it is but a law of nature, most righteous, most merciful, if we look at it as we believe our dead do, grieving no more, either over themselves or us, but rejoicing in their new and perfect existence.

But Stone was a living man still, and he found his lot hard to bear; yet it was, in some sense, his own choosing. He had slipped away, first in madness, and then with a stunned indifference to life and all its duties; suffering himself to drop without a struggle into the great sea of sorrow, which at some crisis in our lives is ever ready to overwhelm each one of us. It had closed over him. He had gained his desire. Years of oblivion had rolled between, changing the terrible present into a harmless past; and now his own place and his own people knew him no more.

He turned into Hanover Square, and walked round and round it, in the gloom of the early dusk, avoiding the houses, and keeping to the inner circle, where a white frosty fog hung over the trees like a shroud.

"It's all right," he muttered, talking to himself, as was

his habit—the habit of most solitary people. "They are happy, perfectly happy, as they deserve to be. They have wholly forgotten me. Of course; they could not but forget. What was there to remember except pain? And yet—oh Will! Kind, loving, good old Will!"

A sharp sob broke his words. Ashamed, he turned to see if any chance passer-by was near him; but there was no one. The place was—as London squares are on a winter evening—lonely as a desert.

"Five sons the child said he had. Plenty to keep up the name—the honest, honorable name—which he used to say I should make famous some day. I? What a mockery it seems now! Five sons. Not a bad help for a man when he gets old. That eldest—the big fellow, so like his father—must be the one that was the baby. *She* used to pet him and play with him."

He ground his teeth as he spoke, and talking to himself no more, sped on round and round the circle, like a man possessed; sometimes stopping from sheer exhaustion, and then hurrying on again as if there were an evil spirit behind him. At length, quite worn out, he crawled back to the old spot—the bright little house in Brook Street.

It looked doubly bright in the now thickly gathering darkness of the street. The Venetian blinds had been drawn down, but not closed, so that any one looking through the interstices could see into the room quite plainly.

A cozy dining-room, warm and cheerful; gilt-framed prints shining on the crimson-papered walls; a large bookcase at one end; a mirror and sideboard, garnished with what looked like presentation-plate, goblets, a claret-jug, etc., on the other; between, the shining, white-spread family dinner-table, with chairs all round it, evidently meant to be filled as full as it could hold. Standing on the hearth-rug, apparently waiting and watching, but knitting still—for the fire-light flickered on the glancing needles, and made a star of light out of one fine diamond which glittered on the rapid little hands—was a figure that looked like the good fairy, the presiding genius, the guardian angel of the whole.

She was a little person, thin and fragile, more so perhaps than a matron should be, and her face was not without a look of care — or rather the faint reflex of care gone by. And when it fell into repose there was, as there is in almost all faces past their youth, a slight sadness, enough to make you feel that *she* had felt and understood sorrow. Her hair was already whitening under her little lace cap, and her black silk dress had not the slightest pretense of girlishness about it. Yet there was a youthfulness, light and gay, and an almost childish sweetness in both face and figure, that withstood all the wear and tear of time. It made folk say, even ordinary friends, but especially her boys and her husband, "Ah, mamma will never be an old woman!" No, never: for while her heart beat it would be a young heart still. When, more than once, at the sound of wheels she lifted up her face to listen, the brightness that came into her eyes was like that of a girl hearing the lover's footstep outside the door.

THROUGH THE WINDOW.

Stone watched her, clinging meanwhile to the railings, grasping them hard, as if the cold iron had been a warm, loving hand. Perhaps for a minute his heart misgave him—his bitter, cynical, unbelieving heart. One step, one word, and might he not pass out of the loneliness and cold into—what? Would it be a welcome? After all these years, all this change, would it be a welcome? He looked down on his rags—they were becoming such, for his money was dwindling away; he put his hand to his head, where the deadly food which he had been chewing at intervals since morning was slowly but surely confusing his faculties, making him more and more unfit for and averse to all society, or any thing that might snatch him out of the drugged nocturnal elysium which alone enabled him to bear the torments of the day.

"No—no; too late! To them I should only be a burden and a shame. Better as it is—better as it is."

And just as the doctor's carriage drove up, and the door, opening of itself, showed a dainty head leaning anxiously forward from the lighted hall, Stone slunk back hastily, and staggered away, round the street corner, into the misty square.

Half an hour afterwards, he crawled back again, but by that time the Venetian blind had been closed; the house was all dark. Only through an inch of the upper sash, which was left open for air—it was such a small house for a large family—the hungry, weary, shivering man fancied he could hear the clatter of knives and forks, the chatter of lively voices, of parents and children, around the cheerful dinner-table, where all met together after the labors and pleasures of the day.

"Will!—Edna!"—he called, but faintly, and as hopeless of reply as a bodiless spirit might feel, vainly trying to make itself known to the living flesh and blood unto whom it was once so near. "Will—Edna—you were fond of me once, and I was fond of you. I'll not harm you or trouble you. Be happy! It is quite true—I am dead, dead. Good-bye!"

He hurried away, and was soon lost in London streets—the glaring, splendid, wicked, miserable streets—once more. Lost!—lost!—lost!

CHAPTER XXIV.

"MAMMA, only listen."

"Please do, mammy, darling!"

"Lovey! we'll be so good."

"Children, will you hold your tongues, and not speak more than three at a time? The dear old mother is perfectly deafened with you."

Mrs. Stedman smiled at her eldest son — her "right hand," as she often called him—her grave, kind, helpful Julius; but it being, as he said, quite impossible for her to hear herself speak just then, she only shook her head with a Burleigh-like solemnity, and waited till the outburst subsided.

She had all her young flock at home for the holidays, which, especially in winter, most mothers will recognize as a position not the easiest in the world. Yet Edna was well fitted to be the mother of boys. Within her tiny feminine body lurked a spirit unconquerable even by the husband who adored her, and the sons who inherited their own from her. Bright, brave, active, decided, she had learned to hold her own in the midst of the most tumultuous state of things, as she did this day. And however gently she might utter it, all knew and recognized that her yea was yea, and her nay nay. No one ever attempted to gainsay or dispute either.

There are bad women—God have mercy on them! fallen angels, worse than any men — by whom lovers, husbands, sons, are led on to destruction: but almost worse than these are weak women, who have sufficient good in them to make them half loved, while they are wholly despised, by the men belonging to them. Now, whether Mrs. Stedman's sons loved her or not, it was at once seen that they respected her — respected her, as gentle, wise firmness is ever respected; and relied on her, as upon quiet strength, whether of man or woman, children always learn to rely.

Silence being restored, she said—

"No, boys; I am very sorry for you, but you can not go skating to-day. The ice is not thick enough."

"But, mamma, I saw ever so many on it when Bob and I took Cæsar down to the Serpentine after breakfast."

"You did not go on it yourselves?"

"Of course not. We promised, you know," said Will, with an injured air, at which his mother patted him on the shoulder tenderly.

"That's my good boy—my good boys, whom I can always rely on. It is hard for you, I allow that; and many harum-scarum fool-hardy lads may tell you your mother is a great coward—"

"No, no, no!" cried all the lads in chorus, and declared she was the "pluckiest" little mother that ever lived.

"Very well," she answered, laughing; "I am glad you think so." And then seriously, "No, boys, I hope I can bear inevitable risks, nor do I shrink from lawful dangers. Julius will have one of these days to take his turn at the fever hospital; Will may go in for a Civil Service examination, and be off to India; and Robert turn sheep-farmer in Australia, as soon as his schooling is done. I'll hinder none of you from risking life in doing your duty; but I will hinder you, so long as you are in my care, from throwing away your lives in any reckless manner. A pleasant thing for papa and me if you went out this forenoon, and were brought home at dinner-time—drowned!"

"Ju says I'm born to be hanged, and so I shall never be drowned," observed Bob, dryly.

"Drowned," repeated Will, meditatively. Will was the clever one of the family; always striking out new and brilliant ideas. "It would be a curious thing to try what drowning is like. People say it is the easiest death that any one can die—quite pleasant, indeed. Mamma, did you ever know any body who was drowned?"

"Hush!" said the eldest brother, quick to notice the

slightest shadow in his mother's face. "You forget Uncle Julius was drowned."

No more questions were asked. Though the children knew no particulars, they were well aware that over the life and death of this unknown uncle, their father's only brother, hung a tender, sad mystery, which made their mother grave whenever his name was mentioned; and their father sometimes looked at Will, who was thought to resemble him—looked, and turned away with a sigh. And when sometimes, being deluded, as fathers delight to be, into telling tales of his own boyhood to his boys, these adventures chanced to include Uncle Julius, he would break off abruptly, and his hearty merriment changed into the saddest silence. Also the elders noticed that, except concerning those boyish days, their father never spoke much of Uncle Julius. Whether the latter had done something "naughty," though nobody ever hinted at such a thing, or whether he had been very unhappy or very unfortunate, the lads could none of them satisfactorily decide, though they often held long arguments with one another on the subject. But one thing was quite clear—Uncle Julius must have been a remarkable person, and very deeply loved by both their parents.

So, being boys trained from babyhood in the sweet tact which springs from lovingness, they let Will's malapropos remark pass by without comment, and hung round their mother caressingly till they brought her back to her own bright self again.

"Yes," she said, laughing, "you are very good boys, I own, though you do worry mamma pretty well sometimes."

"Do we, darling? We'll never do so any more."

"Oh no, not till the next time. There, there, you babies!"

And she resigned her little fur-slippered foot for the twins to cuddle—the rosy, fat, good-tempered twins, rolling about like Newfoundland puppies on the hearth-rug—laid one hand on Bob's light curls, suffered Will to seize the other, and leaned her head against the tall shoulder

EDNA AND HER SONS.

of her eldest son, who petted his mother just as if she had been a beautiful young lady. Thus "subdivided," as she called it, Edna stood among her five sons; and any stranger observing her might have thought she had never had a care. But such a perfect life is impossible; and the long gap of years that there was between Robert and the twins, together with one little curl—that, wrapped in silver paper, lay always at the bottom of the mother's housekeeping purse—could have told a different tale.

However, this was her own secret, hidden in her heart. When with her children, she was as merry as any one of them all.

"Come now," said she, "since you are such good boys, and give up cheerfully your pleasures, not because mother wishes it, but because it is right—"

"And also because mother wishes it," lovingly remarked Julius.

"Well, well, I accept it as such; and in return I'll make you all a handsome present—of my whole afternoon."

Here uprose a shout of delight, for every one knew that the most valuable gift their mother could bestow on them was her time, always so well filled up, and her bright, blithe, pleasant company.

"It is settled then, boys. Now decide. Where will you take me to? Only it should be some nice warm place. Mother can not stand the cold quite as you boys do. You must remember she is not so young as she used to be."

"She is—she is!" cried the sons in indignant love; and the eldest pressed her to his warm young breast almost with the tears in his eyes. That deep affection—almost a passion—which sometimes exists between an eldest son and his mother was evidently very strong here.

"I know what place mamma would like best—next best to a run into the country, where, of course, we can't go now —I propose the National Gallery."

Which was rather good of Bob, who, of himself, did not care two-pence for pictures; and when the others seconded the motion, and it was carried unanimously, his mother smiled a special "Thank you" to him, which raised the lad's spirits exceedingly.

It was a lively walk through the Christmas streets, bright with holly and evergreens, and resplendent with every luxury that the shops could offer to Christmas purchasers. But Edna's boys bought nothing, and asked for nothing. They and she looked at all these treasures with delighted but unenvious eyes. They had been brought up as a poor man's children, even as she was a poor man's wife — educated from boyhood in that noble self-denial which scorns to crave for any thing which it can not justly have. There was less need for carefulness now, and every time the mother looked at them—the five jewels of her matron crown — she thanked God that they would never be dropped into the dust of poverty; that, humanly speaking, there would be enough forthcoming, both money and influence, all of their father's own righteous earning, to set them fairly afloat in the world—before William and she laid down their heads together in the quiet sleep after toil—of which she began to think, perhaps, a little more than she used to do, years ago.

Yet when the boys would stop her before tempting jewellers' or linen drapers' shops, making her say what she liked best, Edna would answer to each boy's questions as to what he should give her "when he got rich—"

"Nothing, my darling, nothing. I think your father and I are the richest people in all this world."

And when she got into the National Gallery, and more than one person turned to look after her—the little mother with such a lot of tall boys—Mrs. Stedman carried her head more erect than usual, and a Cornelia-like conceitedness dimpled round her mouth. Then, she being slightly fatigued—she was not the very strongest little woman in the world—Julius settled her carefully in the most comfortable seat he could find, and left her there in the midst of the pre-Raphaelite saints and martyrs, and mediæval Holy Families, to spend some quiet minutes in pleasures which throughout her busy life had been so rare. For many of Edna's special tastes, as well as her husband's, had been of necessity smothered down. In the long uphill struggle of their early married life luxuries had been impossible. During all the years when her little ones were young she had read few books, scarcely seen a picture, and confined her country pleasures to watching the leaves bud and grow green and fall, in Hyde Park or Kensington Gardens. It was rarely that the busy mother got even a few minutes' rest like this to go back to the day-dreams of her youth—now fading away in the realities, sad or sweet, of her maturer days.

She almost felt like a girl again as, after a brief rest, she rose and took leisurely the circuit of the room, where many an old familiar picture looked at her with ghostly eyes—pictures fixed on her memory during the days when Letty and Julius, she and William, used to haunt this place. The years between seemed to collapse into nothing, and for a moment or two she felt almost as she felt then—at the outset of her life, in the tender dawn of her love: her heart full of hope that colored every thing rose-hue, and faith in God and man that never knew a cloud.

Well, that time had gone by for them all four. She and William were middle-aged parents now; Letty and Julius—poor Letty! poor Julius!—she hardly knew which to grieve over most, the living or the dead.

So had passed all these passing shows of mortal life, fleet as a shadow that departeth; and still the fair Saint Catherine stood beside her wheel, smiling her martyr's smile, and Del Piombo's ghostly Lazarus arose out of the dark sepulchre, and the numberless Madonnas who used to thrill Edna's heart with an exquisite foreboding of what mother-bliss must be, sat, calm as ever, holding their Divine children in their arms—always children, who never grew up, never died. And Edna thought of her own little lost baby—her one girl-baby of three months old—and tried to fancy how she looked now, perhaps not unlike these. Continually, among all her living children—her perpetual daily blessings—came the memory of this one, a blessing too, as our dead should always be to us, more and more perhaps the older we grow, since they bridge over the gulf between us and the world unseen. Edna was not the less a happy and a cheerful mother, that besides all these breathing, laughing, loving children, she had still another child—a little silent angel, waiting for her in the celestial land.

While she was thinking of these things in her own peaceful way, and enjoying the old delicious atmosphere of beauty and grace, which had been the fairy-land of her youth, her boy Robert, after romping about, tormenting alternately his two elders and the twins, came back to her.

"Mamma," said he, in a loud whisper, "there's a very grand lady staring at you, and has been for ever so long. She looks as if she wanted to speak to you, but couldn't make up her mind. Do you know her?"

Edna looked round. No mistaking the stately figure, the sweeping satin robes.

"Yes, I know her," blushing while she spoke, and startled at the difficulty of explaining to her boy that it was her own flesh-and-blood sister, as near to her as Julius or Will to him, who thus met her, looked, and—would she pass by? "I know her, Robert, but do not let us turn that way. She has seen me; she can come and speak to me if she chooses. It is your aunt, Mrs. Vanderdecken."

"Oh!" said Bob, with difficulty repressing a whistle. "What a stunning woman she is! But why doesn't she come and speak to you, mamma—"

"Hush! she is coming."

She came, slow and stately, and held out her hand with a patronizing air.

"You here, Edna? I thought you never went anywhere."

"Oh yes, I do sometimes, when my children carry me off with them. And you—who would have expected to find you here?"

"I came with my little girl. She is learning drawing under a celebrated artist—a lady artist, of course, who brings her here once a week or so to study the old masters. I leave them to go round together while I sit still. I don't care for pictures."

Edna was silent.

"Besides, I am rather glad to give the child something to amuse her, for she has been rather mopy of late."

"Not ill, I hope?"

"Oh no, only cross. Do your children never take sullen or obstinate fits, Edna? and how do you contrive to

MRS. VANDERDECKEN AND SISTER.

manage them? I wish you could teach me how to manage mine," and Mrs. Vanderdecken sighed.

While speaking her distantly polite manner had changed into a sort of querulous appeal—Letty's old helplessness and habit of leaning upon every body, especially her sister. She made room for Mrs. Stedman beside her with something of a sisterly air.

Now Edna and her husband, without much speaking, had tacitly made up their minds on the subject of the Vanderdeckens. They both felt that ties of blood, so far as the duty of showing kindness goes, are never abrogated—but intimacy is a different thing. To keep up a show of respect where none exists—of love when it has been long killed dead—is the merest folly, or worse, falsehood. The doctor's wife had not an atom of pride in her, and the condescending airs of her magnificent sister fell upon her perfectly harmless, almost unperceived; but Letty's total ignoring of the past, and meeting her, both on the two former occasions and to-day, as indifferently as if she were a common acquaintance, was such a mockery of kinship, that she who had believed in flesh-and-blood ties with the passionate fervor of all loving hearts—until they are forced into disbelief—drew back within herself, utterly repelled and wounded—until she heard that sigh. Then she said, kindly,

"Letty, if I can help or advise you I would gladly do it—I have been a mother so many years now."

"Ah, yes. How many children have you? I quite forget. But they are all boys. Now, I do think one girl is more trouble than half a dozen boys; at least, if she is such a self-willed little puss as mine. I often tell Gertrude I wish when she was a baby I had broken that obstinate will of hers."

"Don't say so," replied Edna, earnestly. "I like my children to have a will of their own. I would never break it—only guide it."

"But do they obey you? Are they at all afraid of you? Gertrude is not one bit afraid of me."

"Children that obey from fear mostly turn out either hypocrites or cowards. We rule ours by the pure sense of right. God's will, which we try to teach them, is the real will to be obeyed, far beyond either their father's or mine."

"Ah, I can't understand you—I never could. But Edna"—falling into the confidential tone of old days—"what would you do if one of your children had formed an acquaintance which you objected to, though you could not absolutely forbid it, and, let you argue as you might with them, they wouldn't give it up?"

"Robert," whispered his mother, "run back and stay with your brothers for a little. I want to talk to your aunt."

And Robert, though dying with curiosity, obeyed.

"There! your boy obeys you in a minute, Edna. Now I might reason with my girl for an hour on the subject of that horrid old soldier. But I will just tell you the whole matter."

She drew closer to Mrs. Stedman, and in vexed and injured tones explained, in her own lengthy and contradictory fashion, how Gertrude had made acquaintance with some poor invalided soldier who lived in the village, had taken a great fancy to him, and, now that he was laid up ill at his lodgings, wanted to go and see him. When refused, she had sulked and fretted till she made herself quite ill.

"The child must have a tender heart," remarked Edna.

"Of course she has, and I'm sure I encourage it as much as possible. In her position she will have to be very charitable, so I always take her with me on district visiting, and put her name down below my own in subscription-lists. But this is quite another matter. I told her I would give the poor man money, or send him his dinner every day, but as to her going to see him, it was quite impossible. Why, he lodges at a small public-house."

"Is he a bad man, or a man of low character?"

"How can I say? soldiers often are. But to tell the plain truth" — the plain truth generally came out at the tail end of Mrs. Vanderdecken's confidences—"I don't like to say too much against him, for he certainly once saved the child's life — pulled her from under a railway train; and though I must own he has taken no advantage of this as yet, I mean in extorting money, still he might do so, and that would make Mr. Vanderdecken so angry."

"Indeed! but you, I should have thought—"

"Ah, Edna, one isn't always a rich woman because one is married to a rich man. I have every thing I want—can run up bills to any amount, but—would you believe it?—I rarely have a sovereign in my pocket to do what I like with. Not that I think Mr. Vanderdecken means to be unkind; it's just his way; the way of all men, I suppose."

"Not all," said Edna, and thought of her own open-handed Will, who trusted her with every thing; who, like herself, never wantonly wasted a penny, and therefore had always an honest pound to spare for those that needed. And she looked with actual pity at her sister — so wealthy, yet so helplessly poor. "Yes, I can see yours is not an easy position. But does the child still fret? What does her father say?"

"Oh, he knows nothing at all about it. We never tell papa any thing. At least," noticing Edna's intense surprise, "we are obliged to be very careful what we tell him. You see, Edna, my marriage is not exactly like yours. I being so very much younger than Mr. Vanderdecken, and perhaps—well, perhaps a little more taking in my appearance," she smiled complacently, "he is apt to be just a bit jealous. He can not bear the least reference to my old ties, which accounts for my not seeing as much of you, dear, as I might do."

"I understand," replied Edna, gravely.

"And to tell the whole truth" (it was dropping out bit by bit), "if I were to say to him that that poor soldier came from Calcutta, as Gertrude informs me he did, my husband, who has never forgotten the—the rather peculiar circumstances of my marriage, would be quite furious. It's natural, perhaps, but," with a martyr-like sigh, "of course it is a little awkward for me."

"A little awkward!" Edna Stedman turned upon her sister full, steady, indignant eyes. "A little awkward!" she repeated, and stopped.

And this was all that remained of the past; the terrible tragedy which even yet she and her husband could hardly bear to speak of; the agony of suspense which had darkened their life for months and years, until it was ended by receiving chance evidence which convinced them that Julius was not lost, but dead. His story was brief enough.

On coming down to meet his betrothed at the ship, and finding her gone — she having quitted it at the Cape of Good Hope to be married to Mr. Vanderdecken—he had suddenly disappeared.

Disappeared totally, leaving his lodgings just as they were—and lying on the table, in an envelope addressed to Messrs. Marchmont and Co., a brief holograph will, bequeathing every thing he had to his brother, adding, "that he would never be heard of more."

He never was. At first it was thought he might have committed suicide — gone voluntarily to face his Maker and ask Him the never-answered question of so many miserable lives; but when the news was communicated to Dr. Stedman, he refused to believe this. He thought rather that a fit of frantic despair had induced his brother to run away, so as to lose himself and his own identity for the time. So he instituted wide inquiries, and inserted advertisements in newspapers half over the world. But in vain.

At last Julius's Indian servant brought to the office of Marchmont and Co. an old coat of his master's, and a pocket-book, in which was written "Julius Stedman." Both these he said he had got from an English sailor, who took them from a drowned "body," quite unrecognizable, that had floated past his boat, down the Hoogly, three years before. How far the story was true could never be proved, but, in default of all other evidence, it was at last accepted and believed.

So that was the end. After another year's clinging to desperate hope, the will was proved, the family put on mourning; and now for more than twelve years Julius Stedman had been numbered among the dead.

How much of all this Letty knew, Edna could not say, she herself having told her only the final fact in a letter which was never answered. Yet when she looked at her sister and remembered Julius, whom she had so often watched sauntering about these very rooms with his beloved on his arm, Mrs. Stedman thought, had Letty forgotten? Was it possible she could forget?

"Gertrude, you stupid child! don't you see how you are trampling on my dress?"

The peevish tone, the entire absorption in this small annoyance of her little girl's rough but affectionate ways—yes, Letty had forgotten! All that fearful history of a ruined life — ruined, by whose doing? — was regarded by her as "a little awkward," nothing more.

But it was useless to speak, or to feel, in the matter; indeed, Edna was incapable of a word. She only drew her little niece to her side and caressed her, in that lingering loving way with which she always looked at little girls now. And then lifting up her eyes, she saw entering the room, and glancing eagerly round in search of her, her husband.

"I had actually a spare hour this afternoon, Edna, so I thought I would follow you. Nurse told me where you were gone. I found the boys at once. Now, lads, off with you home, for it is growing dark. Mamma and I will just idle about for a little, and drive home together."

And Dr. Stedman sat down beside his Edna with the air of a man who, after nearly a score of married years, still enjoys a stolen half hour of his wife's company, and thinks her society the pleasantest in the world. The lady sitting on her other side he never noticed at all.

Now Edna knew her husband well; his strong, faithful, tender heart, which yet, under all its tenderness, had a keen sense of right and wrong, honor and dishonor, that no warmth of friendship or nearness of blood could ever set aside. She was well aware how he felt regarding Letty, and dreaded, with a kind of sick dismay, any meeting between them. But there was no alternative; it must take place.

"William," she said, touching his hand, "this is my sister. You did not recognize her, I see."

The blood rushed all over Dr. Stedman's face, and he stepped back a moment with uncontrollable repugnance. Then he seemed to remember that at least they were a man and a woman—a gentleman and a lady. He bowed courteously, and when Letty offered him her hand he did not refuse it.

"I hope your husband is well? Is this your daughter?"

"Yes. Gertrude, shake hands with Dr. Stedman. She is a little like Edna, is she not?"

"Oh no," he replied, hastily; "oh no!"

And this was all that passed.

For a minute or two more the three stood together, as they had stood so often on this very floor;—with a fourth, who was now—where? They must have thought of him, they could not but have done so, yet none of them gave the least sign. Alas! if we were all to speak out loud concerning these ghostly memories that rise up at many a festive board, or walk beside us with soundless feet down many a noisy street, what good would it be? Better keep a decent silence, and go on patiently between the two awful companies which are ever surrounding us—the seen and the unseen—the living and the dead.

Though all preserved their composure, the position was so painful that even Mrs. Vanderdecken perceived she had better end it.

"I must go now," she said. "Dr. Stedman, would you allow one of your boys to call up my carriage?"

"I will see you myself to it, Mrs. Vanderdecken."

Coldly but courteously he offered her his arm, and they went descending the staircase together.

Edna, hardly knowing what she was about, so like a dream did it all seem, wandered mechanically on, looking at the mute pictures round her, chiefly portraits of dead men and women, on whose faces were strange histories—the equal histories of living men and women now.

Preoccupied as she was, she involuntarily stopped at one —Andrea Del Sarto's portrait of himself. Robert Browning must have had it in his mind when he painted that wonderful word-picture of Del Sarto and his wife, "his beautiful Lucrezia, whom he loved." All that sad story is plainly foreshadowed in the face—full of a man's passion and a woman's sensitiveness, perhaps also a woman's weakness, which looks out from the centuries-old canvas;

a face, typical of the artist-nature, in all ages: often, too, foreboding the artist's fate.

While looking, and moralizing over it, Edna suddenly recognized why the portrait had struck her with a strange familiarity. It was almost as like him as if it had been painted from him—poor lost Julius!

She stood absorbed, for it seemed to speak to her with its sad soft eyes, out of the depths of years, when she felt a hand on her shoulder, and turned round to her husband.

"Edna, what were you looking at?"

"That head. Don't you see the strong resemblance?"

Dr. Stedman, less imaginative than his wife, might have passed it by, but the emotion in her countenance guided him at once. He too saw, as if it had risen up out of the grave, not Del Sarto's face, but his dead brother's, full of genius, life, and hope, whereon was no possible foreboding of the fate to come—a fate from which neither brother nor sister could save him.

Cain's appeal, "Am I my brother's keeper?" though uttered by a murderer, is not wholly untrue or unjust. Beyond a certain point no human being can help or save another. We think we can; we are strong and fearless, till taught in many a bitter and humbling way that we are poor and blind, weak and miserable, and that in God's hands alone are the spirits of all flesh, their guidance and their destinies.

But this is a hard lesson to learn. Edna saw, as she had seen many a time before during those heavy years when her husband went mourning for his brother—ay, at times even amidst the happiness of his most happy home—the sharp pain amounting almost to self-reproach, as if surely something had been left undone, or done unwisely, by him, or Julius's career would never have ended thus, in a grief the mystery of which was ten times worse than that of ordinary death.

She answered, as she sometimes ventured to do, the unspoken thoughts which by long experience she had learned to trace in William's mind, almost as accurately as if they were in her own.

"Nay, dearest, you must not grieve. You could not help it—nor I. It was not our doing, and he is at rest now."

"Yes, he is at rest. But—she?"

Will spoke beneath his breath—fiercely too—so that his wife knew well enough how much, for her sake, he had suppressed during the last half hour. Nor could she deny the truth—which he felt, though he did not utter it—that if ever a man's life was wasted and destroyed it was that of poor Julius; and it had been Letty's doing. And yet—and yet—oh, if God reckoned up against us, not only the evil that we meant to do, but that which we have been either carelessly or foolishly instrumental in doing, where should any of us stand?

"Forgive her!" implored Edna, as some such thought as this passed through her mind—she, the mother of five children, who had all these young hearts in her hand, as it were, and knew not how in the unseen years to come they might be sinned against or sinning—needing from others the pity or pardon which their mother was not there to show. "Husband—forgive her! I think even Julius would do it, now."

"I'll try."

Dr. Stedman pressed his wife's arm close to him and abruptly turned away.

For a little while longer they wandered about the rooms, talking of indifferent topics, for Edna knew that there are some things too sore to be spoken much about, even between husband and wife: until the rare comfort of an idle hour together soothed them both, and made them feel, as married people do, that all trouble is bearable so long as each is left to the other. Perhaps even after then—for such love is not a mortal but an immortal possession.

Then they descended, arm in arm, to where, in the chilly dark of Trafalgar Square, the doctor's comfortable brougham was waiting.

"I am glad I have a warm cozy carriage to put my darling into now," said William, as he wrapped her well up, and, stepping in beside her, took her hand with lover-like tenderness.

Edna laughed—almost the laugh of her girlhood—to hide the fact of two big tears which came now as quickly to her eyes as they used to do then.

"Will, you are so conceited;" and then leaning against his shoulder—creeping as close to him as the propriety of Pall Mall allowed, she whispered, "Oh, how happy we are—what a blessed life has been given to us—God make us thankful for it all!"

CHAPTER XXV.

Gertrude missed and fretted after her friend the soldier for many days. He and his stories had taken firm hold of her imagination, and his feebleness and sickliness, together with the fact of his having saved her life, had made a strong impression upon her fond little heart.

Being questioned, she had told her mother, as she always did when catechised, every thing she was asked: so Mrs. Vanderdecken now knew all particulars regarding John Stone that were known to Gertrude herself. But this roused in her shallow and self-absorbed mind no suspicion beyond an uneasy feeling that her daughter's propensity for "low" society—gardeners, keepers, and the common people generally—must be stopped, and that this was a good opportunity for doing it. So, having ascertained, in a roundabout way, that Stone was still lying ill at the "Goat and Compasses"—though not dying, or likely immediately to die—she communicated these facts to Gertrude, and promised, in the half-and-half way in which the weak mother often pacified the strong-willed child, to send and inquire for him every day—in return exacting a promise that Gertrude would on no account demean herself by going personally to see him.

This precaution taken, the lady left the whole matter to chance, and troubled herself no more about it—Letitia Vanderdecken being, like Letty Kenderdine, one of the many people who never shut the stable-door until the steed is stolen.

But one luckless day, when she rolled away in her splendid carriage for a three hours' drive, her little daughter having contrived to get rid of nurse, went roaming the park in weary longing for something to do, somebody to play with—a permanent want with the rich man's daughter. At last, in a sort of despair, poor little Miss Vanderdecken was driven to perch herself, like any common child, on the stile which divided Holywell Park from the furzy moor, where she could watch, and envy not a little, the groups of common children who, just turned out of the school-house, were disporting themselves there.

It was one of those soft days, mild as spring, which had followed the breaking up of the frost, and the January sunshine, pale but sweet, slanted across the moorland like a sick man's smile. Crawling along like a fly upon a wall, and, like herself, idly watching the school children, Gertrude perceived her friend John Stone.

Now, her mother had forbidden her to go and see him, and Gertrude always literally kept to her promises; but she had never promised not to speak to him if she met him—Mrs. Vanderdecken, who had heard, not without a vague sense of relief, that the sick man was not likely soon to get better, having never thought of providing against such a possibility. Consequently, the first thing the little maid did was to jump down from her stile and greet him in an ecstasy of delight, at which Stone was much bewildered.

He must have been very ill, so ill as almost to confuse his mind, for he regarded the little red-cloaked elf as if he had never seen her before.

"I don't remember you. What do you want?"

Gertrude was a quick child, and possessed by instinct that precocious motherliness which some little girls show to all sick people whom they have to do with. She said, gently,

"Oh, I dare say you have forgotten me, you have been so ill. I am Gertrude Vanderdecken, the little girl you used to tell stories to, and I have missed you so much."

"Missed me? Is there any body in the world who would have missed me?"

"Oh yes, and I would have come and seen you had I been allowed, but mamma said—"

"Who is your mamma?" Then, as if memory came back in a sudden flash, overwhelming him and changing his dull apathy into that fierce, half insane look which always made the child shrink, though she was too ignorant to be much afraid. "Oh yes, I know, I remember. Go away; I want to get rid of you, of all belonging to you. Leave me; let me die quietly—quietly."

He stopped, and fell into such a paroxysm of coughing that it left him quite exhausted. He found himself sitting on the stile, with the little girl holding his hand.

"You have not left me, child? I told you to go."

"But I did not wish to go," said Gertrude, who had been slowly making up her mind to a proceeding daring, indeed, and worthy of the tender romance which lay deep in her nature. She determined, henceforward, to take this poor sick man under her immediate protection, though in what way she did not quite know; and the first step was to get over her mother's violent prejudice against him. She thought if they could once meet, if her mamma could but talk with him quietly, his poor worn, sickly face and shrunken figure, and above all the air of refinement, which made him so different from the "common people," as Mrs. Vanderdecken called them, would make her as much interested in him as Gertrude was herself.

So she concocted a plan for a sudden and unexpected interview between the two—her mother and the poor soldier—which did her little brain considerable credit, and was almost as romantic as the stories she read, or those she was in the habit of making "out of her own head."

"This is far too cold a place for you to sit in," said she, demurely. "Come with me, and I'll take you to our winter garden, where you'll find it so warm; almost like being in India."

"Oh!" said Stone, shivering, "if I could only get warm! I feel as if I should never be warm again!" and the impulse of physical suffering, which seemed uppermost in him now, added to that state of weakness in which a sick person can be persuaded by any body to any thing, made him submit to Gertrude's guidance, almost in spite of himself. She took him by the hand and led him across the park; but when they came in sight of the white, stone-fronted, handsome house, she stopped.

"Is your mother there?"

"I think not: she is out driving—at least she was out."

"No prevarication; no weak deceptions; you'll learn them soon enough. Where is your mother?"

"I don't know," said the child, boldly, "and if I did I wouldn't tell you, for you look as if you meant to be rude to her, and you ought not, for she has never done you any harm, and would be very kind to you if she knew you—I am sure she would. She is exceedingly charitable to"—poor people, Gertrude was going to say, but stopped.

"Exceedingly charitable! A most amiable, generous lady — quite a Lady Bountiful! And that is the house she lives in; whence she would kindly throw a crumb or two to a poor wretched fellow like me, or if I laid me down at her gate she would send her lap-dog out to lick my sores. Excellent—excellent!"

Gertrude was no coward, or she might have been frightened at the way the man talked and looked. But when she set her mind upon doing a thing, she rarely let it slip undone.

"Come," she said, taking firm hold of his hand again, "don't talk—talking is bad for you. Just come with me into the winter garden." And he came.

It was one of those floral palaces originated by Sir Joseph Paxton, and now often to be seen in the domains of our merchant princes, who, like Mr. Vanderdecken, seldom enjoy or appreciate, but only pay for them. Under a high circular glass dome grew fresh, as if in their native clime, all sorts of tropical bulbs—palms, bananas, and so on—while ranged round, in that exquisite art which knows its best skill is to imitate nature, were a mass of flowering plants, which burst upon the eye in such a glory of form and color as to transform January into June.

When, the instant Gertrude opened the door, the moist,

warm, perfumed atmosphere greeted Stone's delicate senses, he drank it in with a deep breath of delight.

"Truly this feels like what Mrs. Fox would call 'another and a better world,' which a week since I was supposed to be going to. I wish I were there now."

"Where?" asked Gertrude, innocently.

"In heaven, if there be such a place. Do you think there is, child?"

She looked puzzled, half shocked, and answered, a little primly, "Mamma says we ought not to talk about those sort of things except on Sundays."

"Ha! ha! Of course not. What should she know about heaven any more than I? But tell her, when she gets there, as no doubt she will, being such a very benevolent lady—tell her to look over the gates of it at me, frying slowly, down in the other place."

Here, catching Gertrude's horrified look, Stone paused, struck by the same vague compunction which makes the profligate hold his tongue before an innocent girl, or the drunkard snatch from the young boy's hand the accursed glass.

"Never mind me, I was talking nonsense. I often do. My head is not quite right. I wish somebody would put it right." And he sighed, in that sad helplessness which went to the very bottom of the little maiden's heart.

She planned, with the quickness of lightning, the rest of her scheme.

"I know somebody who would cure you at once. Did you ever go to see him, as you said you would—Aunt Edna's husband, Dr. Stedman?"

Stone sprang up from the easy garden-chair where the child had placed him, and glared round him with the eye of a hunted animal.

"Don't speak about him, don't remind me of him, or tell him of me. Let me go! I am a poor lost, miserable man, that only wants to lay him down and die, in any quiet corner, out of every body's reach. I have changed my mind now—I'll promise to harm nobody, punish nobody, only let me die."

"But I don't want you to die," said Gertrude, upon whose childish ignorance two-thirds of his wild talk fell quite harmlessly—considered, as he said, to be mere "nonsense." "If you went to Dr. Stedman he would make you well. I am certain he would, for I have seen him myself now, and he looks so clever and so kind. I would go and tell him or Aunt Edna all about you, only something happened last week."

"What happened? Any of them dead?"

"Oh no!"

"That's right. They must live and be happy. Nobody ought to die except me; and I can not. Oh that I could! I am so tired, so tired!"

He looked up at the child, as she stood over him, in her precocious womanly protectingness. Her little firm face trembled, but only with pity. She was not one bit irresolute or afraid.

"It is great nonsense talking about dying," said the little maid, imperatively. "You are not nearly so old as papa, and I won't let him die for many years yet, for I love him dearly, and he is very good to me, even though he was cross at that thing which happened."

"What was it?"

"Perhaps I ought not to tell you. Mamma said I had better not talk about it, it was not respectable to have coolness between relations; but one day when we were in London we met the Stedmans—Aunt Edna, and her husband, and all the boys—and when I told papa, for he asked me, as he always does, where I had been and who I had seen, and, of course, I was obliged to speak the truth—wasn't I now?—he was so excessively angry, and told mamma he would not let his little girl have any thing to do with them, for he hated the very name of Stedman."

"Why? Did he say why?"

"I think, because of that uncle I told you about, the poor man who was drowned. He must have known about him, and disliked him, for he began speaking of him to mamma, abusing him very much, calling him a penniless, worthless fellow, and that every body must have been glad when he died."

"Every body glad when he died!" repeated Stone beneath his breath.

"Papa said it, and mamma seemed to think so too; but then she never dares contradict papa when he is in one of his passions. Still, for all that," continued Gertrude, chattering, and as if glad to have out in words what she seemed to have been deeply thinking about, "I can't get the poor man out of my head. I feel sorry for him. He might not have been a very bad man, or would have grown better if he had had any body to be kind to him. But away from his brother and Aunt Edna, living out there in India quite alone, with nobody to take care of him or be fond of him, what could he do?"

"Children and fools speak truth," cried Stone, violently. "But I've heard enough. What does it matter? He is dead now—dead and forgotten. What's the use of prating about him?"

Gertrude turned upon the soldier the wondering reproach which nature—no, Heaven—often puts into the innocence of children's eyes: "Why do not you, too, feel sorry for the poor man?"

"Sorry? Not I. There is a saying, 'As you make your bed, you must lie upon it.' He did. But no! he did not make it: it was made for him—full of briers and thorns and stinging serpents. A wicked woman did it all!"

Gertrude opened her eyes in the utmost astonishment.

"Should you like to hear about her, child? It would be a pretty tale—a very pretty tale—as interesting as any you ever heard. And you could tell it to your mother afterwards. Ay, tell her—tell her. That is a grand idea! I wonder I never thought of it before."

Stone's whole frame quivered with excitement as he spoke; but Gertrude's own curiosity was too eager for her to notice his agitation much.

"Oh, do tell me—I should so like to know! But how did you come to know about him—this Julius Stedman—was not that his name?"

"Yes," answered Stone, slowly. "Julius Stedman—that was his name. He was the friend—of a friend of mine."

"And what was he like? Did you ever see him?—with your very own eyes?"

Stone paused again ere he answered, with a queer sort of smile, "No, I never met him."

Then, regaining forcibly his self-possession, he began, and in his old fashion—he had in a remarkable degree the artist faculty of graphic narration—he told, as vividly as any of his other stories, the story of the young painter and the beautiful lady with whom he was so passionately in love.

Nature stirs in a child's heart often sooner than we think: there are very few little maidens of twelve who can not understand and appreciate a love-story. Gertrude listened, intensely interested.

"And was she very beautiful? As beautiful as"—the child stopped for a comparison—"as mamma?"

Stone laughed.

"You may laugh!" said Gertrude, rather angrily, "but mamma was once very beautiful. Every body says so; and she has lots of portraits of herself, done when she was young—only she keeps them locked up in a drawer, for papa can not bear the sight of them. But they are so lovely, you don't know! Mamma must have been quite as handsome as that lady—what was her name?"

"What is your mamma's name?"

"Letitia; but I heard Aunt Edna call her Letty."

The soldier dropped his head within his hands. Some ghostly memory, sweet as the hyacinth-breaths beside him, which every spring comes freshly telling us of many a spring departed—dead, and yet for ever undying—must have swept over him, annihilating every thing but the delusive, never-to-be-forgotten dream of passionate love; for he said to the child—the child so utterly unlike her mother that her flesh-and-blood presence affected him less than this accidental word—

"Not Letty. No, we'll not call her Letty. It was such a pretty name—such a sweet, dear name! And she was a wicked woman, as I said. She murdered him!"

Gertrude drew back, horrified.

"I don't mean that she killed him bodily—with a pistol or dagger. But there are other ways of murdering a man besides these. I'll tell you how she did it. And you'll not forget, child?—you'll tell it, word for word, to your mother some day?"

"Oh yes," said Gertrude, and again bent all her mind to listen.

It was a touching story even to a child. How, far away in India, the young man had worked—at work he did not care for—to make a home for his betrothed bride: how he had strained his means to the utmost, that she should have therein every luxury she could care for ("she liked luxuries—pretty clothes, handsome jewelry," said Stone, in parenthesis); and how, almost beside himself with happiness, he had gone down to the ship to meet her—his all but wife—his very, very own.

"And she came?" cried Gertrude, breathless with emotion.

"The ship came," said Stone, in a cold, hard voice. "She was not there."

Gertrude almost sobbed. "Was she—was she dead?"

"Oh no! only married."

And then he related, in a few sharp, biting words—for his breath seemed almost gone—how, on the voyage, a rich man had fallen in love with her ("She was so very beautiful, you know!"), and she had landed at a port halfway, where his estate was, and married him.

"What a wicked, wicked woman! I hate her!" And as she said this Gertrude clenched her little hand. Tears—those holy childish tears which burst out irrepressibly at any story of cruelty or wrong—fell thick and fast; and her whole frame was trembling with more than sorrow—indignation. "I hate her!"

Stone had said revenge was sweet. He tasted it fully now. But the taste could not have been quite so sweet as he expected; for, instead of exulting over it, he drew rather back.

"Hush, child—don't say you hate her!"

"But she was wicked—you told me so."

"If I did, you need not say it. Children can not understand these things."

And a strange remorse came over him—the childless man—for having put into any daughter's hand a weapon that might pierce her mother to the heart. He had not thought of this at first: he had thought only of revenge—revenge, no matter how, or by what means—but now, when he heard the child's words, and saw her little face glowing with righteous wrath, he shrank back from the fire his own hands had kindled.

"Stop a minute," he said. "The world might not judge her so harshly. Many people would say she had only made a prudent marriage; and that the man—her lover—if he had any manhood in him, ought to have got over it, lived an honest life, and died beloved and respected."

"But he did die: he was drowned, I know. Where was it?—how?"

Stone could not answer. Even a hardened liar might have been staggered by the accusing earnestness of the child's eyes. And this man, once so gentle—who, however often sinning, never sinned without repenting—he knew not what to do; until, whether for good or ill, fate interposed.

Fate, sweeping along in the purple silken robes and white ermine mantle of Mrs. Vanderdecken herself.

"Gertrude! Bless me! My dear Gertrude!"

No wonder, perhaps, at the reproving sharpness of the lady's tone. It was a trial. To see—sitting in her beautiful conservatory, and beside her very own daughter—a man, not merely one of the "lower orders," as she termed them, but the very man for whom, from being indebted to him for an unpaid kindness (weak people so shrink from the burden of gratitude!) she had conceived as much repugnance as her easy nature was capable of feeling. The more, as he paid her none of the almost servile respect which Mrs. Vanderdecken was accustomed to receive from her inferiors; made no attempt to rise or bow, did not even take off his hat, but sat doggedly there, staring at

MRS. VANDERDECKEN AND THE SOLDIER.

her. Once, as her voice and the rustle of her dress reached his ears, he shivered. It might have been a blast of cold air from the opened door, or else—who knows?—some breath that the still beautiful woman had brought with her from the rose-gardens of his passionate youth—those lost love-roses, of which, though form and color have been obliterated in dusty death, the perfume never wholly dies.

As to Mrs. Vanderdecken, all she beheld was a shabby-looking, bearded man, with a pair of gleaming eyes, which looked as if they would burn her up—devouring all her grace and quiet grandeur, though without—and she felt this, dull as she was—without having the slightest awe of either.

"Gertrude," she said, uneasily, "who is this—this person?"

"Mamma, don't you remember him? Mr. Stone—whom Bran bit—who was so good to me. He has been very, very ill, and I brought him in here because it is so nice and warm. He likes warmth—he has just come from India, you know."

"Oh, indeed," said Mrs. Vanderdecken, carelessly.

Gertrude whispered in earnest entreaty, "Mamma, please speak to him—be a little kind to him."

"I am sure, my dear, I am always ready to show kindness to any poor people who need it, and especially to poor people in whom you are interested. But, really, you sometimes choose such extraordinary sort of folk to make such friends with, and show your charity in such an unsuitable way! In this instance"—and her cold eye wandered carelessly over the shabby soldier, and she spoke with the tone of dignified rebuke which she was in the habit of using to the drunkards and slatterns of her district—"you must perceive, my good man, that for you to meet Miss Vanderdecken in this way, and let her bring you into our own private domains, is quite unpardonable. In fact"—growing more angry under the absolute silence of her hearer—"I consider it a most impertinent intrusion, and desire that it may never occur again."

"Mamma—oh, mamma!" pleaded Gertrude, but Stone took no notice whatever. He sat, as if in a dream, staring blankly at Mrs. Vanderdecken.

The lady at last grew a little uncomfortable, so fixed was the gaze, so impassive the attitude of this strange fellow, who seemed to exercise over Gertrude a perfect fascination.

"Come in, child—tea has been waiting this half hour, and I have to dress. You forget we have a dinner-party to-night. For you," turning to Stone, "as my daughter says you are an invalid, I will overlook your rudeness—for once; and since she is kind enough to take an interest in you, I shall be glad to assist you—with soup-tickets, or out of my village clothing-fund, if you will give me your name and address, also—I always exact this—a certificate of character."

"No," thundered out the broken-down man, confronting the elegant rich woman. "I'll give you nothing—I'll accept nothing from you. Let me go!"

He rose, and staggered past her, then turned, and seeing her left hand hanging down—white, glittering with many rings—he seized it, regarded it a minute, crushed it in his own with a fierce pressure, and flung it away.

Mrs. Vanderdecken gave a little scream, but the conservatory door had closed, and he was gone. Then her indignation, not unmixed with fear, burst out.

"Gertrude, this *protégé* of yours is the rudest fellow I ever saw—a perfect boor. A thief, too! for I am certain he meant to rob me. Didn't you see him make a snatch at my rings? I wonder if they are safe—one, two, three—yes, all right. What a mercy! Only think, if he had stolen these beautiful diamonds!"

"Mamma!" cried Gertrude, half in reproach, half in entreaty, for she did not know what to say. Undoubtedly the poor soldier had been very rude, and yet she could not believe him to be a thief. But all her little plan had fallen to the ground. She saw her mother was seriously displeased, and her common sense told her it was not without cause. The poor child thought she would never try romantic schemes for doing people good again.

Perplexed and miserable, she walked by her mother's side into the house, where she received her cup of tea, and the severe scolding which accompanied it, with a sad humility, and then waited beside Mrs. Vanderdecken while she dressed for a dinner-party. The little plain child had an ardent admiration for her mamma's beauty, and while she was meditatively watching the maid comb out those masses of long light hair, in which there was scarcely a gray thread visible, Mrs. Vanderdecken, chancing to turn round, saw her little girl's earnest looks, and smiled, mollified.

"Come, my dear," said she, holding out her hand, "I'll not scold you any more. We will be the best of friends, if only you promise to have nothing more to do with that ruffianly soldier."

"But I can't promise; and he isn't a ruffian, indeed," said Gertrude, piteously, yet very decidedly. She was an obstinate little thing, and had a trick of always holding fastest to her friends when they happened to be down in the world. "You would not say so, mamma, if you once heard him talk as he talks to me—as he had been talking all this afternoon."

"All the afternoon!" cried the mother, in dismay; "a young lady like you to be talking a whole afternoon with a low fellow like him! It's dreadful to think of. I am perfectly ashamed of you. What on earth were you talking about? Tell me every word. I command you!"

Here Gertrude became much perplexed. Somehow or other, whenever she spoke of the Stedmans, she had always got into trouble with either father or mother, or both; and so she had resolved, in that strong, reserved little heart of hers, to shut them up tight there, and never refer to any of them again. She had kept this resolution so well that, in spite of the charming excitement of this afternoon's discovery concerning poor Uncle Julius, for the last half hour she had borne her mamma's reproaches in perfect silence, nor let herself be betrayed into the slightest allusion to the story which had interested her so much. Now, being plainly questioned, she was obliged to speak out.

"I'll tell you any thing you choose, mamma," said she, sullenly, "but I know it will only make you cross. I was hearing a long story about a person whom neither you nor papa like, and whom you told me never to speak about, and I wouldn't speak, if you didn't ask me."

"What nonsense, child! Who was it?"

"Uncle Stedman's brother—Julius."

Had a ghost risen up before her Mrs. Vanderdecken could not have been more startled. Her very lips whitened as she said,

"There must be some mistake. Gertrude, how could you possibly know—"

"Of course I know, mamma. Didn't I hear you and papa talking about him? and didn't you yourself tell me who he was, and that he was drowned? I know all about him now," added the child, with childish conceit. "Mr. Stone told me his whole story."

"His whole story?"

"Yes, mamma, about his being an artist when he was young, and his falling in love with a beautiful lady, and his giving up painting and going to India to make a fortune for her sake; how she promised to come out to him and marry him; how—"

"Stop, child," interrupted Mrs. Vanderdecken, with a subdued and even frightened air; "please don't go chattering on so fast. I can't attend to you. Wait till I am dressed. Take your book and be quiet for a little."

Gertrude obeyed, yet still cast furtive glances at her mother, who arranged her dress and clasped her ornaments in a hurried, absent manner, quite unusual for one who was generally so particular about these things.

"Mamma, what is the matter with you? Are you ill? You look so white."

"Nonsense, child."

No more passed until the maid was dismissed, and the lady sat down on the sofa by the fire, her toilet complete — and an especially resplendent toilet it was; but, for once, it proved no consolation to her.

Mrs. Vanderdecken was very nervous; nervous was the word — not startled, or shocked, or grieved, but merely frightened. A vague apprehension seized her of something going to happen. Was it because, after this long, safe blank of many years, somebody had turned up who knew something of her past life, or merely because of the surprise of hearing from her little daughter's lips that once familiar name? True, it was only a name. Julius Stedman was dead, and could not harm her. Living he might, or she fancied so, being a coward in her heart, and knowing well her husband's jealous temper, nurtured by that faint fear similar to the one which Brabantio first puts into the mind of Othello:

"Look to her, Moor: have a quick eye to see:
She has deceived her father, and may thee."

For—such is human nature, and so surely does fate take its revenge—it had been one of the troubles in Mrs. Vanderdecken's married life to be not seldom taunted for her broken pledge by the very man for whom she had broken it. Mr. Vanderdecken, of course, had known all about Julius Stedman at the time, but, being passionately in love, he had seen in her falseness to one man no obstacle to her marriage with another, since that other happened to be himself. Afterwards, when the desperation of love had cooled down into the indifference that was sure, at best, to be the outcome of such a marriage, he despised his wife, and took care to let her see that he did, for doing that which he himself had persuaded her to do. It was natural, perhaps, and still, poor woman! it was rather hard.

"Gertrude," she said, turning with a helpless appeal to her child, who, thinking still that she was not well, had stolen up to her and taken her hand—"Gertrude, you must not vex your poor mother, who has nobody to be a comfort to her but you. You must make her your chief companion, and tell her every thing, instead of taking queer fancies for old soldiers and such like."

"But, mamma, I never take any fancies that make me forget you," said the little girl, earnestly. "And that story, it was no secret. He said I might tell it you whenever I liked."

"Did he? Who is he? Oh, you mean the man John Stone? Didn't you tell me that was his name? Did he ever know that—that person?"

"Uncle Stedman's brother, whom you dislike so? No; he told me had never seen him in his life."

Mrs. Vanderdecken breathed freer. Struck with a vague apprehension, she had been beating about the bush, afraid, and yet most anxious to find out how much her daughter knew; but now she ventured to say, carelessly, taking out her watch,

"I have just ten minutes left. You may tell me the story if you like, and if it amuses you."

"It wasn't at all amusing, mamma. I think it was the saddest story I ever heard. Just listen."

And then, with the vividness with which Stone's words had impressed it on her mind, and with a childish simplicity that added to its touchingness, she repeated, almost literally, what she had just heard.

Her mother listened, too much startled—nay, terrified—to interrupt her by a word. The whole history was accurate down to the remotest particulars, facts so trifling that it seemed impossible for any stranger to have heard them—nay, they had escaped her own memory, till revived like invisible writing, by being thus brought to light in such an unforeseen and overwhelming manner. It seemed as if an accusing angel spoke to her from the lips of her own child; as if, after all this lapse of years and change of circumstances, the sins of her youth, which she had glossed over and palliated, and almost believed to be no sin at all, because no punishment had ever followed them, rose up and confronted her. Also, her condemnation came from the one creature in the world whom she loved dearly, purely, and unselfishly—her only child.

"Was she not a wicked woman, mamma?" said Gertrude, lifting up her glowing face and looking straight into her mother's. "After she had made him miserable so long, first pretending she liked him, then to change her mind and refuse him? When she had at last faithfully promised to marry him, and he was expecting her, and was so happy, to break her word and go and marry another man?"

"Who was the man?" asked the mother, in an agony of dread. "Did—did he tell you the name?"

"No; only that he was rich, and Mr. Stedman was poor. That was why she did it. Wasn't it a wicked, cruel thing? Oh, mamma," cried Gertrude, in a burst of indignation, "if ever, when I grow up, I were to meet that lady, I should hate her. I know I should. I couldn't help it."

Mrs. Vanderdecken shivered. All through her fineries—her silks, and laces, and jewels, she shivered; and clutched the hand of her little daughter as if she were drowning—

like that poor, drowned Julius — and her child's affection were the only plank to which she clung.

But soon every other feeling was absorbed in apprehension—the overpowering, irrational terror which seizes upon all weak natures when brought face to face with a difficulty the extent of which their cowardice momentarily exaggerates. Therefore, she did what such folks generally do, she adopted the line of pacification and deprecation.

"Gertrude, my dear, I am glad you have told me this story. It is exceedingly interesting, and it was kind of you to be so sorry for the poor man. Perhaps he never meant to rob me, only just to look at my diamonds. I wonder how he came to know these facts, if they are facts. Did he tell you any thing more?"

"No, mamma."

"I should almost like to speak to him myself. He might have heard particulars which the family would be glad to know."

"Oh, mamma, if only you would see him! May I go to him and tell him you will?"

"No, no!" said Mrs. Vanderdecken, hastily. "Not upon any account, my dear. Don't go near him; and if you meet him, promise me—hark! isn't that your father?"

And the sound of heavy boots coming up stairs made her not wince and look annoyed, as was her wont, but actually tremble.

"Gertrude," she cried, in an agony, "promise me that you will not breathe a word to your father of all this."

"Very well, mamma," said Gertrude, greatly puzzled, and a little vexed; but she was used to her mother's feebleness and inconsistencies, and had learned to regard them with a patience not wholly unallied to contempt.

Yet she was fond of her, and when, ere her dismissal, she got a warmer kiss than usual, Gertrude went away quite happy.

Not so Mrs. Vanderdecken. Out of the smooth surface of her dull, easy life had risen up a great fear. Avenging Fate, whipping her with the cruellest scourge by which wrong-doing is ever punished, had humiliated her before, and caused her to stand in actual dread of, her own child.

CHAPTER XXVI.

Mrs. Vanderdecken's alarm and uneasiness did not abate, as she hoped it would. In the pauses of her dinner party, while smiling upon every body and doing the honors of her splendid establishment to all the "best" people of her acquaintance, it stood behind her velvet chair, ghost-like, and would not be driven away. Not though the blessings surrounding her were real and tangible—plate, and furniture, and elegant dresses; polite neighbors treating her with the utmost consideration and attention, as was due to the wealthy and lady-like millionnaire's wife who had come into their circle; while the things she dreaded were faint and shadowy, belonging to a period in her life which she would fain have swept away into total oblivion.

She said to herself many times how ridiculous it was to be so afraid! As if nobody besides herself had once been a governess, or had had a poor lover whom she had given up for a rich one! Why, such things happened every day; and if this disreputable fellow, Stone, had known something of Julius Stedman, was that any reason that the mistress of Holywell Hall should trouble herself about him? A five-pound note, no doubt, would settle the matter and get him away from Mrs. Fox's, perhaps induce him to quit the neighborhood, where he could only have come for the purpose of extorting money. But five pounds to the elegant wife of the miserly Mr. Vanderdecken was as unattainable as if it had been five thousand.

As she pondered, smiling all the while sweetly on her right-hand neighbor, Sir Somebody Something, Stone's face, haggard, and wild, and sad—yet certainly not that of a mercenary impostor—rose up before her threateningly, and once or twice that evening, when a gentleman named casually the "Goat and Compasses," she felt herself grow hot with fear, lest some fatality should bring into the conversation the names she dreaded—John Stone or—Julius Stedman.

She woke next morning with the feeling of "something going to happen" stronger than ever; and, as was her nature, the more her fear pursued her the farther she tried to flee from it. All day she avoided being left alone with her daughter, and did not venture once to refer to the subject of the Indian soldier. For, when she came to consider it, her plan of seeing him herself became difficult. What was she to say to him? How question him about poor Julius without betraying that this story, which had so oddly come to his knowledge, was the last which she would have desired to have repeated to her daughter, or to any of her neighbors? In truth, to try and stop the man's mouth seemed more dangerous than letting him alone. It would be horrible if he should recognize in her—Mrs. Vanderdecken — the woman who had so acted that even Gertrude, her own little Gertrude, called her "a wicked woman," and declared she "hated" her.

Alas! there was the sting, or else it was Heaven's finger of light touching Letty's foolish, vain heart. More than her husband's anger, her neighbors' gossip, she dreaded the condemnation and contempt of her child. It seemed as if now for the first time the errors of her youth took their true aspect, merely from the dread she had lest her daughter should hear of them; and, looking back on her past, she knew what its blanks and misdoings must have been by the longing she had that Gertrude's life might not be like her own.

Two days afterwards came Sunday, and still nothing had occurred, and the mother had managed so that not a word had passed between her and Gertrude respecting John Stone. She had almost contrived to persuade herself that the man was got rid of entirely, when, coming into church, she saw him sitting in the free seats beside Mrs. Fox, as on the first day, and watching the Vanderdecken pew with those fierce eyes of his, which he never removed during the whole service. Mrs. Vanderdecken shivered under them, and looked another way. Church being over, she hurried out; but though he did not attempt to speak, or to interfere with them in any way, he followed them silently to their very carriage door.

From that time every Sunday the man was in his place, and many a week-day when she drove out she saw him hanging about on the common, or near the lodge gates, watching, she fancied, for her carriage to pass. But Sundays were the worst. Then, the church being free to all, she could not escape. Nobody could hinder his coming or order him to change his seat; so there he sat, staring at her, not with admiration, and still less with impertinence, but with a cold, blighting contempt that was almost a malediction. She felt as if he haunted her—that miserable man—whom she thought sometimes she must have seen before, yet could not remember when or where.

For Mrs. Vanderdecken was not a woman of imagination—an accepted fact she never thought of contradicting or disbelieving. To doubt that Julius Stedman was dead, or that John Stone, who knew so much about him, might possibly be himself, was a flight of fancy far beyond her. Besides, she never liked to face unpleasant things, and it was sufficiently difficult to have to put off from time to time Gertrude's earnest entreaties with the promise that "she would see about the poor fellow by-and-by."

This sort of life went on for several weeks, and Gertrude's tender heart being pacified by the sight of her friend every Sunday, she had almost ceased to worry her mother about him, when a small chance raised in Mrs. Vanderdecken's mind a new alarm.

Though she never looked towards the man, and tried hard not to see him, still one Sunday morning she did see him, drawing his thin hand wearily through his scanty gray hair and abundant beard. It was a remarkable hand, and hands often keep their individuality when time has changed all else. It startled Mrs. Vanderdecken by its likeness to one which in the days of her girlhood had so often clasped hers.

What if it were possible—if this wretched, disreputable

soldier could be her old lover, not dead after all? She had been sorry for his death, but had never had courage to ask particulars about it, and beyond Edna's brief communication by letter, that he had been "drowned," of the circumstances of his end she knew nothing. During their three short interviews the sisters had never once mentioned Julius's name.

Now, Letty thought, if she could only find out exactly when and where and how he died, it would be a comfort and protection to her. Protection against what? She could not tell. She only knew that with this continual dread upon her mind—with the figure of that shabby man, whoever he was, pursuing her constantly—her life was a daily burden to her. The trifling annoyance had grown into a perpetual and morbid fear.

To throw it off, she determined one morning, without telling Gertrude, to go to London, and find out as much as she could from her sister Edna.

It is a strange thing, and sad too, but sisters do sometimes come to meet as these sisters met; with mere courtesy—no more; to call one another, as these did, by their married names—"Mrs. Vanderdecken," "Mrs. Stedman," and to sit amiably conversing together on indifferent topics like any other ordinary acquaintances. Alas! their fates had drifted them apart, as brothers and sisters will drift, when there exists between them no real sympathy, no tie stronger than the mere natural instinct of flesh and blood. That may remain, and duty keeps it alive in a measure; still it is only the mummy of love that they dress up in decent clothes for the world to look at. The soul of love—deep, close, fraternal love—is not there.

So it is, and must always be. Better accept the fact as Edna accepted it, and received civilly her sister's civil call, though internally thankful that her husband was out, and that none of her children were at hand to see into what the fraternal bond can degenerate, under given circumstances and with certain characters.

And yet she was sorry for Letty, and when her grand, patronizing manner, and her air of extreme condescension, as she examined the "little poky house," having slightly worn off, Mrs. Vanderdecken betrayed unconsciously her inward troubles, though in a roundabout, irrelevant fashion, Edna felt more sorry still.

"Was that what you came to speak to me about?" said she, with her usual directness. "Yes, it must be a great grief, to have your child setting up for independent action, making disreputable acquaintances, and persisting in them after you have forbidden them entirely."

"But I have not done that, not exactly, for I doubt if I could make her obey me."

"There I think you are wrong," answered Edna, in her quick, decided way, which made the people who did not like her—no person is liked by every body—say she was too much given to preaching. "I would lay upon children as few restrictions and commands as possible; but those made must be rigidly enforced. And for that low fellow, who, from what you say, is probably no soldier at all, but an impertinent beggar, I would never allow Gertrude to exchange another word with him."

"Do you think so? I wish I could do it; I wish I dared."

"Dared! What! dare you not do an unpleasant thing for the good of your own child?"

"It isn't that, Edna, not quite; but I will explain the matter another time," said Letty, hurriedly, finding that it was impossible to get a true answer to the false impression which she had somehow contrived to give, and now felt difficult to remove. "I'm sick of the subject; let us talk about something else. What a fine young fellow is that eldest boy of yours! I met him at the door going out with his brother."

"Will and Julius are constant companions. I hope they will grow up the same, and be friends as well as brothers. It is so sometimes, though not always," said Edna, with a slight sigh. "Their father and I often look at them with a full heart, and wonder what their future will be. For Julius we have no fear. You remember how healthy he was—so good and sweet-tempered, even as a baby."

"Yes," said Letty, with a little return of her stiff manner.

"But Will—the boys ought to have changed names, I think—Will is so delicate, so sensitive, in many things so strangely, painfully like—"

Edna stopped.

Mrs. Vanderdecken felt that now or never was her chance, if she wanted to find out any thing about her old lover; and her desperate anxiety to be free from the doubt which had lately come made her bolder than usual.

"Yes, Will is likely to give you some uneasiness. He does not look strong, as if he had something of that family weakness—was it consumption, or what?—which showed itself so plainly in poor dear Julius."

"Poor dear Julius!" He had sunk to that, uttered in the half-pitying, half-indifferent tone in which dead people, whose death is felt to be rather a gain than a loss to their friends, come to be spoken of sometimes.

"And, by-the-bye," continued Mrs. Vanderdecken, seeing that Mrs. Stedman remained quite silent, "I have often wished to ask you, did you get that full information which you were in search of when you wrote me the fact—the mere fact—of his death in India?"

"Yes," replied Edna, in a grave, constrained tone. "We have, alas! no reason to doubt his death; though at first we had, and it was a long time before we could reconcile ourselves to believe it."

"What!" cried Letty, turning pale; "was he not dead, after all? I thought he was drowned in the Hoogly?"

"We supposed so, but his body was not found, and so we hoped he might be yet alive—had gone up the country, or sailed to Australia, or perhaps come direct home to England, and then shrunk from finding us out; but I will not trouble you with these matters."

"It's no trouble. Please tell me. I should like to hear."

And though Mrs. Vanderdecken testified no distressing emotion—indeed, the absolute fact that Julius was dead proved such a relief to her that she could speak about him without any hesitation—still she looked sad and grave, rather touched than not.

"Do tell me all about him, Edna. Poor fellow! I did not mean him any harm. I had no notion he would have taken it so much to heart. Please tell every thing."

And she listened, not without feeling, while Edna did tell her "every thing:" down to the miserable ending of that life, whose blessing she might have been, instead of its fatality and its curse.

"Poor fellow—poor fellow!" said Letty, sobbing a good deal. "And was he really not seen after that day when he went to the ship and found me gone?"

"Never. We advertised for him half over the world; the advertisements could not but have reached him somewhere, if alive. And he would have come home to us, I am sure he would. He knew how we loved him."

"It must have been very painful," said Mrs. Vanderdecken. "And so—"

"And so, after two years of suspense, we got the evidence I told you of. And some months later we received his pocket-book, with his name written inside it, which he always carried about with him, for it held"—she hesitated —"it held a lock of your hair. It is all we have left of him. Would you like to see it?"

"I think I should," said Letty, in a low tone.

"Then come up stairs."

Letty followed to her sister's bed-room—a sacred room, consecrated by both birth and death; a mother's room, where several toys strewn about showed that the children had still free admittance into its precincts. But there was no baby in the house now, and the little crib, which had been occupied successively so many years, was removed from its place beside the bed, and exiled into a far corner, to be used as a receptacle for spare blankets and other extraneous things. The room and all its appointments were comfortable enough, but well worn, and a little old-fashioned, as if long after the need for economy was gone her love for the familiar objects made Mrs. Stedman averse to any change in her apartment.

"That is your old dressing-table and the wardrobe too. I could almost fancy myself back in the small house—

where was it? I forget—that you lived in when first you were married."

"Could you?" said Edna, as she unlocked a drawer, and took therefrom a faded, water-stained book.

Letty held it gently, crying a little over it.

"Poor fellow! poor Julius! He was very fond of me."

Asking no more questions, she returned the pocket-book to her sister. The tribute to the dead was paid, and its painfulness got over. Her emotion had been sincere enough, but she was not sorry to end it and revert to other things. She began turning over the various contents of the drawer.

"What have you here? A pair of baby-shoes? I should have thought your stock of them had been worn out long ago."

"These belonged to my little girl that died." After a pause Edna added, "You never lost a child, Letty?"

"No."

And then the two sisters—mothers both—stood by the small treasure-drawer, where, besides the shoes, lay one or two other trifles: sleeve-ribbons, a sash, relics of the dead that we all are prone to keep somewhere or another, and learn in time to look at quietly, as one day others will look at relics of us. While gazing, their common womanhood and motherhood melted both hearts. Letty silently clasped Edna's hand.

"How old was she, poor little lamb?"

"Only four months. She was such a little delicate thing always, but the prettiest of all my babies. I was ill for nearly a year after she died, and gave a deal of trouble to my husband; but he was so good to me—so good!"

"Ah!" said Letty, sighing.

"However, I got well in time, and the year after that my twins were born—twins like you and me, you know," added she, affectionately. "They comfort me, and now I am quite happy again. Only sometimes I wake in the night, fancying I hear my little girl crying to me from her cot, and—it's hard, Letty, it's hard."

Edna leaned her head on her sister's shoulder and burst into tears.

Letty caressed her, kindly enough; but she was puzzled to know what to say, and so said nothing. Edna soon dried her eyes, and quietly locked up the drawer.

"That's right; you don't fret about baby now, I hope? It would be wrong, with all your five sons."

"I know that; I know all is right both for her and me, and I shall find my little angel again some day. Will you come down stairs, Letty dear? I hear the bell for the children's dinner."

At this meal "Aunt Letty," as she condescendingly announced herself, was an object of great curiosity and awe. The young Stedmans evidently viewed her with a slight distrust — all save Will, who, imaginative lad as he was, fell a captive at once to his beautiful aunt, sat beside her, paid her his pretty, boyish gentleman-like attentions, and watched her every movement with admiring eyes—the very eyes of his uncle Julius. Pleased and flattered, touched perhaps in spite of herself, by some of those ghostly memories which the new generation often so strangely brings back to us all, Mrs. Vanderdecken took especial notice of the boy, and said to his mother, half sighing, that she wished she had a son like Will.

And during the hour she staid Letty was almost the old Letty over again. She placed herself in the fireside circle, where, with the mother at its centre, the younger children soon made themselves merry, and the two elders, busy with book and pencil — strangely enough, Will was very fond of drawing—occupied themselves steadily and quietly, sometimes joining in the conversation just enough to prove that they were accustomed to be to their parents neither playthings nor slaves, but, so far as their years allowed, rational, intelligent companions. She talked kindly rather than patronizingly, and seemed anxious to make herself popular. Letty never could bear not to be popular —for the time being.

Also—let us give her her just due—there was something in the atmosphere of this warm, bright little house which touched the heart, such as it was, of the unsatisfied rich woman, who had a mansion to dwell in, but no home; a millionnaire to provide for her, but no husband; and who, let her try to compel it as she might, could never win from her only child any thing like the tender, mindful, reverential love that she saw in these five boys towards their mother.

"How fond your children are of you!" she said to her sister, as she stood arranging her purple ribbons round her still fair face, careful as ever to set it off to the best advantage. "And they seem to obey you too. Now Gertrude is fond of me, poor little thing, but she never minds me one bit. I wish I could take a leaf out of your book."

"Do you?"

"And then your boys all seem to get on so well together; never a cross look or a sharp word; but I suppose that is because you are never cross and vexed yourself."

"Oh yes I am," said Edna, smiling. "But we are so many people in such a small house, that we should never manage at all if we did not learn to keep our little tempers to ourselves. Isn't it so, Twinnies?" patting the round, curly heads which had intruded up stairs. "Come, jump up on a chair and kiss your aunt Letty—your great, tall auntie—and tell her she must be starting—Will and Julius shall take her to the railway station—and she must come and see us again as soon as she can."

Mrs. Vanderdecken distributed most affectionate adieus all round, and departed with her two nephews. But she took care to dismiss them at the earliest opportunity, to avoid any possible chance of meeting at the train either some of her grand acquaintances, or, worst of all, her husband.

At the journey's end her carriage was waiting for her, and she drove alone through the lovely Kentish country, beginning to wake up into all the freshness of early spring. Did it remind her—after her long absence from such scenes, for they had wintered in town last year—of many a long-ago spring? that in the Isle of Wight, for instance, when Edna nursed and petted her, and Dr. Stedman was kind to her, and Julius adored her. Or, perhaps, of later springs, when she and Julius sauntered about as affianced lovers, and watched the leaves come out and the thrushes sing in Kensington Gardens? Days when they were all poor together—poor and hard-working, but very happy, or, looking back, it seemed that they were. And as she smoothed down her silken gown, and leaned lazily back on the cushions of her carriage, Mrs. Vanderdecken gave more than one sigh to the memory — now a perfectly safe and comfortable memory to dwell upon — of poor, drowned Julius, lost in his prime, forsaken, dead, and forgotten.

Passing the school-house, she recollected that she had told Gertrude to wait for her there, thinking it a safe place of detention between the governess's hour of leaving and her own return. But, with fatal precaution, she had overshot her mark; for, the moment after having descended, she saw, sitting on the bench beside the school-house door, with Gertrude standing beside him and eagerly talking to him, the man John Stone!

Mrs. Vanderdecken's anger, not unmixed with fear, left her absolutely dumb. But Gertrude ran to meet her without the slightest hesitation—betraying no sense of having done wrong.

"Oh, mamma, I am so glad you are come! I have been waiting to tell you something — something so wonderful, which Mr. Stone has just told me. You will never be angry with him any more. And Aunt Edna will be so glad; every body will be so glad."

"At what, my dear?" asked Mrs. Vanderdecken, a faint, cold fear thrilling through her.

"Stoop down and I'll whisper it, for it is a secret still, and only you and I are to know," said the little maid, her eyes bright and her cheeks glowing. "But he says—Mr. Stone, I mean—that he is quite certain Uncle Julius is not dead at all."

Had a thunder-bolt dropped at her feet Mrs. Vanderdecken could not have been more startled. For a moment she was silent, then she took to the usual refuge of fear—incredulous anger.

"Don't tell me such ridiculous nonsense. I don't believe a word of it. And you, Gertrude, you ought to be ashamed of yourself. Did I not forbid you ever to speak to this—this fellow again?"

"No, mamma," replied Gertrude, boldly, "you forbade me to bring him into the park, but you never said I was not to speak to him. I met him quite by chance, and he walked on beside me. How could I help it? the common was as free to him as to me. Besides," added the little creature, roused to rebellion by what she considered injustice, "I would not have helped it if I could. Nothing should ever make me behave unkindly to a poor sick—"

"Folly! I tell you, child, he is nothing but a low impostor."

"I beg your pardon, madam! What were you pleased to call me?"

Stone had followed, walking feebly with the help of his stick, and now stood before the lady, taking off his hat to her with an air of mock deference.

Voices change, like faces, in course of years; or perhaps he intentionally altered his; or still more probable was the truth of the old adage, "None so deaf as those who will not hear." But even now Mrs. Vanderdecken showed no sign of having recognized who he really was. Her reply was given in unmitigated anger.

"I do not know who or what you may be, but I know you have no business with my daughter. I said, and I say again, that you are a low impostor. If you persist in following us about so impertinently I will tell my husband, and he shall give you in charge to the police."

The man stood a minute, face to face with her, apparently feeling neither insulted nor afraid. Then he said, in a very low voice,

"Mrs. Vanderdecken, you will neither tell your husband, nor will you give me in charge to the police; I am quite sure of that. Look here!" and he took from his waistcoat pocket a letter, an old, foreign-looking letter, on which was still visible, in a woman's hand, the address, "Julius Stedman, Esquire, Calcutta." "I have half a dozen more of these. They came into my possession—never mind how. They are not very interesting reading, but they might be useful. I was just going to show them to your little girl here."

"Oh no! for pity's sake, no!" gasped the mother, in an agony of terror; and, placing herself so that Gertrude could not see the letter, she hastily bade her run away and call the carriage, remaining in it till she herself came.

Then, half blind with dread, she turned back and forced herself to look at this man, to find out who he really was—whether only John Stone, a poor wandering wretch, who had somehow got hold of her story, and, still worse, of her letters—or some one more formidable still; *who*, she dared scarcely imagine.

There he stood, with the sun slanting on his bare, bald head and gray beard, leaning on his stick, his threadbare coat wrapped round him, the mere wreck of a man—as much a wreck as that poor broken ship which they had used to watch the waves beating on, off the Isle of Wight coast, and yet, like it, preserving a certain amount of dignity, even of grace, amidst all his downfall. A man deeply to be pitied—perhaps severely blamed—since every one has his lot in his own hands, more or less, to redeem or ruin himself—but a man who in his lowest plight could not be altogether despised.

"I see, madam, you do not remember me, though I have the fortune—or misfortune—accurately to remember you."

"How? Who are you? But no, it is quite impossible!" cried the frightened woman, shrinking back, yet knowing all the while how useless it was to shrink from a truth which every second forced itself more strongly upon her.

At that critical moment there came out of the schoolhouse two of her friends—the rector's wife and sister, who, having heard that she was expected, waited to consult with her about a school-feast—for the Vanderdecken purse and the Vanderdecken grounds were always their prime stronghold in all parish festivities.

They met her with much *empressement*—these kindly women, whom she liked, and who liked her—for Letty Kenderdine's old pleasant ways had not faded out in Letitia Vanderdecken. She would have gone forward eagerly to meet them, but there—just between her and them—watching her like her evil genius, haunting her like an impending fate—stood this shabby, disreputable man. The man who had been the betrothed of her youth—whose arms had clasped her—whose lips had kissed her; to whom she had written those silly letters that a *fiancée* was likely to write, and unto whom she had been false with the utmost falseness by which a woman can disgrace herself and destroy her lover—an infidelity than which there is none greater or crueller, short of the infidelity of a married wife. There he stood—she was certain of it now—not John Stone, but Julius Stedman.

How it came about that he was still alive, or what had brought him hither, she never paused to think. She only recognized that it was, without a doubt, her old lover, risen up as from the very grave to punish her: to bring upon her her husband's jealous anger, her daughter's contempt, her neighbors' gossip. No wonder that the poor, weak, cowardly woman was overpowered with an almost morbid terror—a terror so great that she did not even perceive the faint fragment of right that she still had on her side—namely, that for any man, let him be ever so ill-treated by a woman, to take upon her this mean revenge, was a cruelty that condemned himself quite as much as it did her.

But there he was, undoubtedly, Julius Stedman; and Mrs. Vanderdecken felt that if the earth would open and hide her from him she should be only too thankful.

Alas! the earth does not open and hide either sufferers or sinners when they desire it. They can not escape. They must stay and meet the consequences of the sin—learn to endure the suffering.

Mrs. Vanderdecken slipped a step or two aside, and

received her rectory friends with a nervous, apologetic smile.

"I beg your pardon, but I was just speaking to this poor man, a very honest and respectable person, in whom I have complete reliance, and for whom I am most anxious to do all I can. I wanted to hear his story, but I will hear it another time, if—if he will kindly excuse me now—"

"Certainly," said the man, with a formal and stately bow. "Certainly. I have no wish to intrude upon you, madam. I am quite at your disposal any day. Good-afternoon."

He took off his hat once more, first to her and then to the other ladies, and walked away slowly in an opposite direction.

"I know that man by sight," said the rector's wife, looking after him in some surprise. "He comes to church pretty regularly, I think."

"Yes."

"Poor fellow, he seems as if he had seen better days. My husband must call upon him. What is his name?"

"John Stone," replied Letty, faintly.

"And you have been kind to him, as you are to every body. You are a real blessing to our parish, my dear Mrs. Vanderdecken."

CHAPTER XXVII.

Mrs. Vanderdecken's intense fear—a fear which it was now impossible either to fly from or to set aside—made her cleverer than ordinary. She carried on the conversation with her friends till she had furtively watched this man—once her lover, now her bitterest enemy—safe out of sight. Then she stepped into her carriage, much agitated indeed, but still able by a violent effort to control herself before her daughter, and account for her nervousness by saying how very much worn-out she had been by her journey to London.

"But why did you go, mamma? Oh, I remember; it

was about a bonnet. Still, I would not have you so tired and looking so ill for all the new bonnets in the world."

"Don't talk to me till we get into the house and have had our tea. Then I shall be rested, and you can tell me all your story."

"Very well, mamma," replied Gertrude, with her customary acquiescence, and then sat looking out of the carriage-window, amusing herself with her own thoughts, which were generally quite as interesting as her mother's conversation.

Upon her new discovery the little girl's fancy dwelt with a tenderness indescribable. Stone had told her that for many months Julius Stedman had been "out of his mind"—though carefully tended by some natives who took pity upon him, but never even knew his name. That he came to his right senses in some up-country station—all but penniless; and had enlisted for a soldier—seen much service—and was finally sent home to England invalided—at which critical point in the story Mrs. Vanderdecken's carriage appeared.

But Gertrude had heard enough. Her imagination was vividly excited. That most divine doctrine of Christianity, which comes as a natural instinct to the young—the gospel of repentance and the forgiveness of sins, the joy in heaven over one sinner that repenteth—was deep in the inmost heart of this child. Her eyes filled with tears as she thought of poor Julius Stedman, looking not unlike the prodigal son in her pictorial Bible, coming home to his brother and sister; taken into the bright little house at Brook Street, and there made happy to the end of his days. She forgot one thing, which over-tender people also sometimes forget, though it is not forgotten in the parable—that the prodigal first said, "I have sinned," and that in no way had Stone ever hinted that Julius Stedman—wherever or whatever he might be—was in the least sorry for any thing.

But this was an ethical question about which the child did not trouble herself. She only waited with painfully restrained impatience till she had leave to tell her tale.

This was not for an hour or more. Mrs. Vanderdecken kept putting off, on any excuse, what she so much dreaded to hear. At last, getting one of the not unfrequent telegrams that her husband would dine in the city and not be home till next day, she took a little more courage, and stretching herself on the sofa in her morning-room, prepared to hear the worst, and to take things, hard as they were, at least as easy as she could.

"Now, Gertrude, while I have ten minutes to spare, tell me what was that silly story about Dr. Stedman's brother being still alive, which Mr. Stone told you."

For she had satisfactorily discovered that as Stone only did the child know him; he had, for some reason or other, been careful to preserve his incognito; nor, to Gertrude at any rate, had he identified himself with Julius Stedman —if, indeed, he was Julius. Sometimes a wild hope that he was not, that her own fears and some chance resemblance had deluded her, came to comfort Mrs. Vanderdecken. So, as carelessly as she could, she repeated the name of John Stone, and found that her daughter received it with equal indifference. So far she was safe.

But when she began to hear the story, so minute in all its details, she felt that, though a child might be deceived, no grown person could be, into believing it a tale told second-hand. Gertrude's accurate memory and vivid imagination reproduced, almost as graphically as it had been given to her, the history of the young man's passionate despair—how, having lost his bride, he determined to lose himself—at once, and completely as if he had been dead.

"He wished his friends to think him dead, mamma. He thought they would be happier if they did: if he could drop out of the world and be utterly forgotten. Was that right?"

"I can't tell. And where is he? How did Stone know him?" cried the mother, with eager deceit—or perhaps wishful even to deceive herself.

"You forget, mamma; but then you know you are not very good at remembering things," said Gertrude, patronizingly. "Have I not told you ever so often that Mr. Stone declares he never met Uncle Julius in all his life?"

Obvious as the quibble was, Mrs. Vanderdecken took it in for the moment and breathed freer.

"Oh yes, yes; go on, child."

"After he turned soldier he was knocked about the world in all directions. I'm afraid," Gertrude added, gravely, "that he was sometimes very naughty. Mr. Stone says so: but he wouldn't tell me what he had done. I told him I thought the naughtiest thing of all was his not writing to his brother, who loved him so dearly, and would have been so happy to get him back again."

"Did he ever come back?"

"Yes. That is the delight of it. Mr. Stone says he is certain he is in England—in fact, I almost think he knows where he is, though he did not say so. I fancy he—Uncle Julius, that is (oh, please, mamma, let me call him Uncle Julius, for I feel so fond of him)—must be very poor, or very miserable, or something; for when I asked why he had not gone at once to his brother, Mr. Stone said, 'No, he would never do that, for his misery would only disgrace him.' But, mamma, that can't be true, can it?" said the child, appealingly. "I am sure if I had a brother, and he were ever so miserable—nay, even if he had done wrong, and were to come to me and say he was sorry, and would never be bad again—I would take him in and be glad to see him, and feel it no disgrace, even if he were in rags and tatters, like poor Mr. Stone. Would not you?"

"Yes," said the mother, and knew she was telling a lie, and that one day God would surely condemn her out of her own lips, before the face of her own child. She turned paler and paler, and scarcely could utter the next question—apparently needless, and yet which she felt she must fully assure herself of before she ventured a step farther. "But the lady—she who went out to India—did not Mr. Stone tell you the name of the lady?"

Gertrude's lip curled with the supreme contempt of indignant youth.

"No, he told me nothing about her, and I did not care to ask—the false, mean, mercenary woman! Don't speak of her, mamma; she isn't worth it."

No, the mother did not attempt to speak. She only turned her face to the wall, with a half-audible groan, wishing she could lie silent forever—silent in the grave, where, at least, her child could not have the heart to say such cruel words, or she herself, hidden in the dust of death, would not be able to hear them. And yet she knew they were true words—true as the warm light in Gertrude's eyes when, feeling that she had somehow vexed her mother, though she could not in the least guess how, she crept closer to her, and began caressing her and amusing her with careless words, every one of which stung like wasps or pierced like arrows.

"You see, mamma, she must have been such a very heartless woman, as well as faithless, and such a coward too. She never sent one line to Uncle Julius, to tell him she had changed her mind—left him to be told by somebody else—any body who cared to tell him. It was the ship's captain who did it, when he came on board; and he fell down on the deck as if he had been shot. Mr. Stone says it felt like being shot—that he laughed—and it did not seem to hurt him at all for a minute, and he got up and staggered back to the boat and landed again. After that his mind went all astray. Poor man! Poor Uncle Julius!"

"There, that will do," said Mrs. Vanderdecken, faintly. "You have talked so much you have quite made my head ache. I think you had better go to bed now."

"Oh no; it is hardly eight o'clock; and, besides, you will want me to wait upon you, and get you your paper-case and things. You know you have a letter to write, mother dear," said Gertrude, coaxingly.

"What letter?"

"To Aunt Edna, of course, telling her that Dr. Stedman must come here at once."

"Why?"

"Can't you guess, mamma? To see Mr. Stone, and get

out of him every thing he knows about Uncle Julius. He would not tell me, but of course he must tell Dr. Stedman, who is Uncle Julius's very own brother. No time ought to be lost. You'll write, of course, mamma?"

"Of course," replied the mother, actually shivering with fear as this new difficulty in her position opened itself out before her. Vainly she turned it over in her troubled brain, wondering how she was to escape it. Escape, indeed, was what she most thought of; whether she could not, by continuing utterly to ignore him, and keeping still in dead silence the secret which he had so far kept, get rid, temporarily or permanently, of this man, who might be Julius Stedman, and yet might not. But in either case it could not signify much, nor for very long. He was apparently in bad health—he might not live. If he were Julius, he probably had his own good reasons for not wishing to be recognized by his brother; since, during all the weeks he had remained in England, he had made no effort to see him. And let the silly, romantic Gertrude have what notions she might, theirs could not be a pleasant meeting. Indeed, as a physician in good practice, it might seriously injure Dr. Stedman to have thrust upon him a brother so low in the world. Was it not advisable, perhaps, to keep them apart?

So reasoned this woman, long used to view all things by the light of custom and convenience, and half persuaded herself to take the easiest course, of letting things alone, when she was startled by the voice of her daughter—the funny, decided little voice, which often half coaxed, half governed her to do many things against her will.

"Mamma, shall I bring you your letter-case now? The post-bag will go in half an hour; and here is your favorite paper with the crest upon it. I'll get you an envelope immediately."

Mrs. Vanderdecken knew not what to do. This, which seemed to her child the most natural and simple course imaginable, was to her nearly an impossibility—a dread indescribable at the time, and the opening up of endless future troubles. For of the great enmity that the man

Stone—or Julius Stedman, whichever he was — bore her there could be no doubt. He would do her harm if he could. Instead of aiding, she would thankfully have annihilated him: not out of cruelty — poor Letty was not naturally cruel—but out of mere fear. Yet, are not half the wickednesses and barbarities of this world done out of simple fear? She did not mean to be wicked — she would have been horrified had any one suggested such a thing — yet more than once the dim thought crossed her mind—oh, if only that poor sickly man, whoever he was, had slipped away from the world, instead of coming here to be the torment and terror of her life!

Not daring to refuse her daughter—for what possible excuse could she give for so doing?—she sat with the pen in her hand — her irresolute, trembling, jewelled hand — until the stroke of nine, and then laid it down.

"I am so tired, Gertrude, so very tired, and I hate writing letters. It is too late now, for I ought to word it carefully, so as not to startle them. I'll write it the first thing to-morrow."

"Very well, mamma," said Gertrude, passively; she had had only too much experience of her mother's dilatory ways, her weak habit of putting off every thing till "to-morrow." Still, she would not complain, this good child which Heaven was teaching, as it has to teach the luckless children of some parents, by negatives. Though bitterly disappointed, she held her tongue, and indeed begun, as she often did, quietly to lay her own plans for doing what her mother would most likely leave undone—or do too late. But before she could settle any thing to her satisfaction, nurse came to carry her off to bed, where she laid her busy little head down, and slept off in multitudinous dreams, in which Uncle Julius, Aunt Edna, and all the rest figured by turns, the intense excitement of the day.

Not so her mother. Mrs. Vanderdecken not seldom had to pay the penalty of an idle, luxurious life: her sleep often fled from her. In the wakeful, silent hours every small grievance became a mountainous wrong. No wonder then that the same thing befell her now; and after a miserable night she arose sick, unrefreshed, driven by sheer desperation into what yesterday would have been the very last thing she had dared to do—a resolve to go and see for herself whether her fears were true or false; whether she really had at her very door Julius Stedman, returned alive, who, though he could have no actual scandal to bring against her—Letty Kenderdine, with all her folly, had ever kept her fair fame clear—was acquainted with the numerous love affairs of her youth: in her vanity she had often teased him with them, and laughed at his ridiculous jealousy. Now, even if he did no worse, he might repeat them all, and make her the by-word and the laughing-stock of her neighbors. The idea of this low fellow, who, whatever or whoever he had been, had now sunk to be a lodger in a village ale-house, giving out to all the drunken hangers-on there that he was once the lover—the plighted husband—of Mrs. Vanderdecken of Holywell Hall! It nearly drove her wild.

To prevent this, by almost any sacrifice, she was driven to the daring expedient of attempting an interview—a private interview—with the man who called himself John Stone.

At first she thought of sending for him to her own house—but Gertrude might wonder, the servants might gossip—besides, the man might refuse to come. In any sight she had had of him he had seemed more and more resolved to make her feel she had cause to be afraid of him, not he of her. Better seize him of a sudden, before he had time to settle what advantage he should take of her—whether he wanted revenge or only money. For still she clung feebly to her old delusion, that money could do any thing, atone for any thing.

Yet as she pondered over these things—considering how she might best protect herself from him—there came more than once to her a vision of her young lover, who would have given his existence to protect *her*, who worshipped the very ground she trod upon, who, though poor in worldly wealth, had been rich in every thing else—most rich in the only treasure which makes life really happy—

honest, hearty love. And though she had got all she wanted—nay, was in a far higher and more prosperous position than she had ever dreamed of as a girl—still she felt that something was missing out of her life—something that never would come into it again. She could understand dimly what that text meant—"To gain the whole world, and lose one's own soul."

This feeling did not last, of course. Letty's nature was too shallow for any emotion to last long; and she shortly turned away from it to consider how she could accomplish, with least observation, her meeting with Stone.

It happened to be her day of district visiting, when the village was accustomed to see her carriage waiting about while she went from cottage to cottage, splendid and condescending, though sometimes a little alarming to the inmates. But Mrs. Fox's house was not included in her list, partly because the good woman was not quite poor enough to warrant her dwelling being taken by storm by a rich neighbor, who had no other excuse than the superiority of wealth to give for so doing, and partly because Mrs. Vanderdecken did not consider a public-house exactly "respectable."

Great, therefore, was the landlady's surprise when the Holywell equipage stopped at her door, and its mistress, leaning out smiling, requested to know if there was not a person named Stone lodging there?

"Yes, sure, ma'am; has been here since before Christmas; a very decent man, or I wouldn't have had him in my house, I can assure you. A soldier, ma'am, just come from India."

"So I understand. I have had friends in India. I should like to see him—and—it would be a pleasure to me to do any thing I could for him. Will you tell him so?"

"That I will, Mrs. Vanderdecken, and I'm real glad too," added the old woman, confidentially; "for, to tell you the truth, he's sometimes a great weight upon my mind—poor Mr. Stone: not for fear he won't pay me—he does that reg'lar—but I can see he's poor enough, and very sickly, and has such queer ways. I was thinking of telling our rector about him, in case any thing did happen."

"Don't, don't!" said Mrs. Vanderdecken, eagerly. "The rector has only too much upon his hands. If you want things for your lodger—food or wine—just send to the Hall."

"You are only too good, ma'am; and I've said to Mr. Stone often and often what a kind lady you be. But here he comes to speak for himself. My dear soul," darting up to him and whispering in his ear, "do look alive for once. Here is somebody come to see you—a kind lady as says she has friends in India, and wishes you well."

Stone, who had been creeping lazily across the common in the sunshine of the lovely spring morning, looked about him in his wild, weary, confused fashion—he seemed sometimes half asleep, as if it was a long time before he could take any new idea into his bewildered brain.

"Don't bother me, Mrs. Fox, pray! Ask the lady who she is and what she comes about." And then, deaf and blind and stupid as he seemed, he perceived the face leaning out of the carriage window. The mutual recognition was instantaneous.

"What do you want with me?" asked he, hoarsely.

"I want to speak to you—just half a dozen words. Will you come into my carriage, or shall I get out?"

"You had better get out."

Driven desperate by her extreme fear, Letty obeyed. As she did so the mere force of habit made Stone come forward to assist her—as any gentleman would assist a lady—but by this time Mrs. Vanderdecken had recovered her prudence. Pretending not to see him, she rested as usual on her footman's arm, and descended leisurely from her carriage.

"Mrs. Fox," said she, carefully addressing herself to the landlady, "can I have a word or two with your lodger in your little parlor? And, coachman, walk the horses up and down the common; it is rather chilly this morning. Don't you find it so after India, Mr. Stone?"

Truly, Letty had rather gained than lost in the art of keeping up appearances.

"Mr. Stone, my dear," whispered the landlady, pulling him by the sleeve as he stood motionless. "You're forgetting your manners, quite. Do go in and speak to the lady—Mrs. Vanderdecken—she is such a kind lady, and might turn out a good friend to you."

And considering him woefully blind to his own interests, which were somehow or other in her charge, the old woman fairly pushed him into the parlor and shut the door.

So the two—once lovers—stood face to face together and alone; even as when they had parted fifteen years ago, expecting to meet again almost as husband and wife. They stood, looking blankly at one another across the sea of dead years which had rolled between and forever divided them.

Hardly knowing what she did, Letty slightly extended her hand, but it was not taken, and then she said, in a frightened voice:

"I know who you are; but how did you come here? I thought—every body thought—that you were dead long ago."

"You thought I was dead? Well, so I have been these many years. Shall I tell you who killed me?"

Mrs. Vanderdecken shrunk back, and then bethought herself that, whether he were mad or not, it was advisable to pacify him.

"I beg your pardon; I only meant that, as we are both middle-aged people now, we had better let by-gones be by-gones. Won't you shake hands, Mr. Stedman?"

At sound of that old name—the boyish name, his and Will's—the artist's name which he had hoped to make famous, and give, covered with honor, to the woman he loved—the man started, and began to tremble violently.

"Don't call me thus. I have long since dropped the name. I have forgotten I ever bore it. I told you I was dead—dead!"

Mrs. Vanderdecken looked sorry, but she was too much afraid for herself to give way much.

"Pray don't talk in that sad fashion; I am sure there is no need. You are, of course, a good deal changed, and I am grieved to see it. You must have had a hard life in India, or wherever you were. I should like to be of service to you if I could—if you would promise never to refer to youthful follies."

"Follies!"

"You know they were such," said Letty, gathering courage. "Ours was just a boy-and-girl affair. We were not suited for each other, and should never have been happy. It was really quite as much for your sake as my own that I did as I did."

"Stop!" cried Julius, fiercely, and rose up in his rags—his old coat was actually ragged now—to confront the lady—so much a lady to look at, so graceful and so elegantly clad. "Stop. You and I may never meet in this world again; so at least let us tell one another no lies. There were lies enough told by one of us fifteen years ago."

His manner was so wild that at first Letty glanced towards the door; then, rapidly calculating consequences—a new thing for her—she decided to propitiate him, if possible.

"This is not kind, or even gentleman-like, of you—and you were always such a gentleman," said she, in a soothing tone. "I dare say you were much annoyed with me at the time, for which I am very sorry, though I did all for the best. But you must have got over it now. And please don't speak so loud; people will hear you outside."

"Oh, that is all you care for still, I see—how things look outside."

His laugh was so strange, so dreadful, that Letty again doubted whether, at all risks, it would not be safer to get away from him. She looked towards the door.

"Excuse me, but since you have desired it, we will have out our 'few words.' You need not be afraid; I shall not harm you. I am not insane, though the quantity of opium I eat makes me a little queer sometimes; nor a drunkard; nor a thief, as you supposed me to be. But every thing

JULIUS AND LETTY.

else bad that a man can be—that a woman might have saved him from—I am, and it is your doing."

"My doing!"

It was fortunate for Letty that at this moment her carriage passed the window, reminding her that she was Mrs. Vanderdecken, after all. She rose in her stately height from the horse-hair sofa.

"If you talk in this way I must really go."

"Not yet; I could not allow it. But pray be seated. Though I am aware it is but poor accommodation I have to offer you."

"I can not stay, indeed. My position as—as a married lady—"

"A married lady!" repeated he, in the sneering tone of young Julius Stedman, deepened tenfold. "Fifteen years ago you were in heart and vow married to me. When you gave yourself to another man you did—what the other women do who sell themselves body and soul to any man that desire them—what your Bible calls by the ugly word—"

"I can't listen. I won't listen," cried Letty, flushing up. "Only a brute would speak in this way to me—me, a wife and a mother. Oh, my poor little girl!"

There was truth in what she said, and, maddened as he was, Julius felt it.

"I have done no injury to your little girl," said he, more quietly. "She in no way resembles you. She is a sweet little creature, and I am rather fond of her."

"You fond of her!" cried the mother, roused into courage by the one pure, unselfish instinct she had. "And what right have you to be fond of her? What is she to you that you should have gone and made friends with her, and turned her heart against me by telling her my whole miserable story?"

"I have not done so—not yet. I have never mentioned your name."

"But she will find it out when she learns who you are, as she must when you go home to your brother."

"I shall never go home to my brother. It is the last kindness I can show to him and his, to keep away from them. I have seen them all, and that is enough. To make myself known to them would only disgrace them. They will never see me, or hear of me, any more."

The voice was so hollow, so sad, and yet so resolute, that for a minute it touched Letty. Then, in her infinite relief that things were thus, she thought it wiser to leave them so.

"You may change your mind," she said, "especially if you should be ill."

"No. I am accustomed to be ill alone; it will not be much harder—perhaps less hard—to die alone."

"Ah, we'll hope not. You are too young still to talk of dying. But perhaps your plan is the best, after all."

Julius regarded her, as she spoke so coldly, so indifferently—the woman who had been his idol, into whose hands had been given, as into many another woman's, almost unlimited power over a man, to save or to destroy him; who, loving him not blindly but faithfully, might have conquered his faults, developed his virtues, and led him, like his good angel, through the world, up to the very gate of heaven. But now—

As he gazed, the last trace of softness went out of the man's heart. He was no longer her lover, but her bitterest enemy.

"You are right," he said. "My plan is best. And now we need not mention my brother again. What else have you to say to me?"

"It was about my little girl. I want you to promise never to meet my Gertrude any more."

"Why not?"

"Oh, can you not see? Only just consider."

"I have considered, ever since I saw you at the railway-station—the rich, prosperous woman, whom God would not punish. But I am juster than He—I will."

"Punish me? What do you mean?"

"I will tell you, for I like to do things fairly and openly; it was you who did them underhand. That Sunday night, by the kitchen fire in your little house at Kensington—do you remember it?—I told you that you might make me either good or bad. If you refused me at once—point-blank—I might bear it—I was young, I should 'get over it,' as you women say. But if you trifled with me, or deceived me, I should never get over it—I should turn out a vagabond and a reprobate to the end of my days. This came true. See what I am! and I repeat, it is all your doing."

"Oh, Julius!"

She said it, involuntarily, perhaps—or else to soften him—for she was growing more and more frightened, but it only seemed to harden him the more.

"Never utter that name again. I told you I had renounced it, and shall never resume it while I live, which will not be long, thank God! That is, if there be a God to thank for any thing."

"Hush! You are talking blasphemy."

"Who made me a blasphemer? Who taught me to disbelieve in every thing good, and holy, and sweet? Who turned me into a heathen, and then, as you say, into a brute? But it does not matter now; I shall be at rest soon. Only, before I die, I will make certain of your punishment."

"Oh, this is horrible!" moaned Letty. "And what do you mean to do to me?"

"Nothing that shows outside, if you are afraid of that. Nothing to make your neighbors laugh at you, and your husband ill-treat you, which, I understand, he sometimes does already."

"It is not true!" cried she, faintly.

"True or not, it is no concern of mine. I mean to be very just, very judicious. I shall not disgrace you in the world's eyes. Nobody shall discover who I am—nobody but you. But I shall stay here, close in your sight, a perpetual reminder of your falsehood towards me, as long as I live."

"You will do no worse than that? Oh, promise me."

"Promises are not necessarily kept, you know. But I always had a trick of keeping mine; so I would rather not promise."

"Only—only—" and the mother's voice grew sharp with misery, "you will not tell any thing to my child—my poor little Gertrude that loves me?"

"I can not say. It is possible I might take a fit of atonement; might make up for my various ill deeds by one good one, and prevent your daughter from growing up such a woman as yourself by giving her the wholesome

S

warning of her mother's history. It would point a moral, would it not?"

Mrs. Vanderdecken groaned. "But you can not prove it. You have no evidence but your own word."

"You forget. I showed you a letter. I have kept every one you ever wrote to me—not many—nor very brilliant—but sufficient. Suppose I were some day to inclose them in an envelope, addressed, not 'Mrs.' but 'Miss Vanderdecken, Holywell Hall?'"

In real life, people do not drop on their knees and beg for mercy, nor stand glaring at one another in fiendish malice and gratified revenge; we are too civilized for this sort of thing nowadays. So, critical as the "situation" was, the poor soldier and the fashionable lady maintained their positions; and nobody listening outside could have heard a sound beyond the ordinary murmur of conversation.

Half frantic, Mrs. Vanderdecken fell back upon the last expedient that any wise woman would have tried. She put her hand in her pocket.

"You must be very poor. I am poor too. I get but a very small allowance. Still, I would give you this—every week, if you like."

Julius took the purse, and fingered its sovereigns—truly not too many—with a half-disdainful curiosity.

"And so you are poor, after all; though you did not marry me? And you want me to accept your money? Once, you know, you might have taken all mine: by dint of working, saving, almost starving, I had gathered a good heap of it to lay at your feet—but now— Excuse me, I have no farther interest in examining this elegant purse." He closed and returned it.

"Will nothing persuade you, then? Have you no pity for me—a mother with an only child?"

"None," said Julius. "Am not I going down to my grave, a childless man, with my name blotted out upon earth? No; I have no pity for you—none."

"Yet you cared for me once. Oh, Julius, is all your love for me quite gone?"

"You must have a strange kind of love for Mr. Vanderdecken when you can condescend to ask another man that question."

The insult—and evidently meant as such—roused every womanly bit of poor Letty's nature. She started up, burning with indignation.

"Mr. Vanderdecken is a better husband to me than ever you would have been, since you can so turn against me now. And for my little girl — my poor little girl — the only creature I have left to love me — if you wean her heart from me, God will punish you—I know He will. It is a cruel and a wicked thing to do; and if you do it, you will be a wickeder man than I took you for."

And Letty burst into tears.

She had been given to weeping always — it was her strongest engine of power over Julius; but it had no effect upon him now — at least not apparently. He rose and walked to the window.

"Your carriage is still waiting, I see. Had you not better go? It is a pity to agitate yourself needlessly."

"I will go. And you may do what you choose. I never mean to speak to you any more. Good-bye."

"Good-bye, Mrs. Vanderdecken. Allow me," and on the latch of the door their hands met. Letty drew hers away with a gesture of repugnance, and passed out, never looking at him again.

When she was gone—quite gone, and even the faint perfume which her dress had left behind—Letty still liked perfumes—had melted out of the room, Julius sat down, exhausted, gazing wistfully on the place where she had stood.

"Was I right or wrong?" said he to himself. "But no matter. Nothing matters now."

And yet for hours after he wandered about the common, stricken with a vague remorse; also, in spite of himself, with a touch of something approaching respect for— not Letty, but Gertrude's mother—the woman whom, even while adoring, he had sometimes half despised.

CHAPTER XXVIII.

Little Miss Vanderdecken sat in rather a melancholy frame of mind under her yew-tree, by the pond. It was a very pleasant seat now, with the leaves all budding, and the birds singing on every side; but the little maid did not enjoy them so much as usual. There had been overnight one of those "convulsions of nature," as, with a pathetic drollery, the clever child had a habit of calling them, which shook the whole household more or less—the disputes between her father and mother, which are so sad for a child to see, and weaken so terribly all filial respect for both. The conjugal war had been violent, and lasted long; it had reached, and considerably entertained, the servants' hall, also the nursery, where Gertrude had overheard not a few remarks upon "Missis's" changeableness and selfishness, in insisting on the removal of the whole establishment at once to Brighton, and shutting up Holywell Hall entirely, for at least three months. Quite preposterous, the servants thought—giving so much trouble for nothing; and none of them wondered that master objected to it. He, being "close-fisted," was with them the least popular of the two; but here they decidedly sympathized with him, as did his little daughter.

Gertrude could not imagine what had come over her mother, to be so persistent in her fancies, since, finding all persuasion vain, Mrs. Vanderdecken had actually started that morning for Brighton, to take lodgings there on her own account, for herself and her daughter. Gertrude, hating Brighton, and loving every nook in the pretty park at Holywell, was in exceedingly low spirits at the prospect before her, of which she could not at all see the end; for her father was obstinate, too, in his way, and it was hard for him, an old man, to be driven from his comfortable home, and forced to travel daily a hundred miles by rail, as he would have to do. At seventy, he still worked at his favorite pastime of money-making as hard as if he had been twenty-five.

"I wonder how they will settle it between them, poor papa and mamma!" thought the child, dwelling on them with a sort of pity. "I wish they wouldn't quarrel so; but mamma says all married people do quarrel; if so, I'm sure I hope I may never be married," added she, kicking away a large fir-cone as contemptuously as if it had been a young lover at her feet; then stooping to pick it up again, and add it to a large heap which she had built round the root of the tree one day when she was listening to Mr. Stone's stories.

This changed the current of her thoughts, and she began to reckon how soon there might come a letter in answer to the one which, if her mamma had kept her promise, the Stedmans would get late last night, telling them that Uncle Julius was not dead.

"Mamma must surely have written, even though she did come in tired from her district-visiting. I wonder what it was that worried her so all day. Poor mamma!"

But, in spite of poor mamma, who was so often worried, Gertrude's thoughts wandered longingly to the cheerful house in Brook Street, and the good news that was coming there—nay, had come already; and it seemed to her quite a coincidence, an opportunity not to be missed, when she saw passing down the foot-path that crossed the park an old woman, whom she felt sure was Mrs. Fox. She ran forward at once. "Please tell me—I am Miss Vanderdecken, you know—how is Mr. Stone to-day?—and—has any body been to see him?"

Mrs. Fox looked surprised, but dropped a respectful courtesy. "I didn't know as you know'd him, miss; and I only wish somebody would come and see him, poor man. I was just going up to the Hall to ask your mamma if she would do so, being such a kind lady."

"I am sure mamma would—but she is gone to Brighton to-day."

"Oh dear, what a pity! What shall I do?"

"Can I do any thing—take any message?"

Mrs. Fox turned and, shrewd old body as she was, "took stock," so to speak, of the child.

"Well, my dear, I think you're a little lady to be trusted, and the servants might forget—servants in a big house often do. Would you please tell your mamma, when she comes back, that Mr. Stone is took ill, very bad, indeed; and if she'd see after him a little—she was a-talking to him in my parlor for nigh an hour yesterday morning."

"Was she?" exclaimed Gertrude, excessively astonished, and then touched to think how kind her mother had been, and how she misjudged her.

"And I dare say she had promised to be a good friend to him, as I told him she would, for I found that in his coat pocket"—handing to Gertrude a small packet, which felt like a bundle of papers, addressed, "Mrs. Vanderdecken." "It's likely certificates of character, miss; I thought I'd best bring it at once, and ask advice as to what's to be done with the poor man, for he's very bad indeed—quite off his head, and knows nobody."

"How did it all happen?" asked Gertrude, greatly shocked, and yet feeling upon her a strange responsibility. For if this poor man lost his reason, or died, what means would there be of finding out any thing about Uncle Julius? "Please tell me, Mrs. Fox; I am nearly twelve years old, though I look so small, and mamma always tells me every thing."

"I dare say she does," said the old woman, approvingly, and went on to explain how that, after the kind lady left him, Mr. Stone had gone out and wandered about all day, as he often did, returning for supper as usual; "though afterwards he asked me for pen, ink, and paper, which was the only queer thing he did. But this morning I finds him lying straight on his bed, like a corpse, only not dead and not insensible, for his eyes kept rolling about; and he seemed to know what was said to him, though he never spoke one word. I think it's brain-fever, myself, but I'd like to take advice as to what's to be done, for I know nothing of him except his name. Poor fellow!

and yet I'd do any thing for him; he lies like a lamb, and follows me up and down with his eyes;" and the old woman wiped hers with her apron before she could say another word.

"And has nobody been to see him?" inquired Gertrude, cautious through all her anxiety, for she felt that the story of Uncle Julius was a family secret not to be gossiped about in the village.

"Who was there to come, miss? he hasn't a single relative or friend as I knows of. But I thought your mamma might have heard—he might have told her something yesterday—she being a lady, and somehow I've often fancied Mr. Stone was a born gentleman. And, any how, she might have got him a good doctor."

"I know a doctor," cried Gertrude, eagerly; "I'll send for him at once; he will be sure to come; he is my"—uncle, she was going to say, but, with the painful consciousness which experience had taught her, stopped. "If I write the letter, can you find any body to take it at once to him—to London?"

"Tommy will; but would the doctor come, miss?"

"Oh, yes; I am quite sure he will come at once, if I say something to him which I shall say."

And, not without a spice of enjoyment at the romantic mystery which lurked under her compassionate errand, Gertrude fled into the house and scribbled, as fast as pen could go, her impulsive letter:

"DEAR UNCLE STEDMAN,—I write to you because mamma is not at home to write herself, as I know she would. Please will you come down here immediately, to the 'Goat and Compasses,' Holt village, where lies the poor man of whom mamma wrote to you yesterday—John Stone, the soldier from India, who knows all about your brother Julius, whom every body thought to be dead. He is very ill, Mr. Stone I mean, and if he dies, you might never find out your brother. Please come at once.

"Your affectionate niece,

"GERTRUDE VANDERDECKEN."

It was not till the letter was written, and Mrs. Fox away, in total ignorance of its contents except that it would be sure to bring Dr. Stedman at once, that Gertrude paused to consider what she had done.

No harm, certainly; a common act of charity towards a sick man—the man who had been so kind to her. And yet she was by no means sure that her mamma would like it—her poor mamma, who had shown such an unfounded jealousy of this Mr. Stone—why and wherefore Gertrude could not conceive. But, alas! the child had already, by sharp experience, learned to distinguish between what mamma liked done and what, in her keen instinctive conscientiousness, she herself thought right to be done. And why? Because the mother had herself laid the fatal foundation for all disobedience in teaching one thing and practicing another.

"Yet I have done nothing that mamma told me not to do," argued Gertrude with herself, after the letter, not the spirit; yet only as she had been brought up, poor child! "I have neither written to Aunt Edna nor gone to see Mr. Stone. And when mamma comes home to-night, of course I shall tell her every thing. And, let me see, what shall I do with this packet? I'll put it on a high shelf, and not touch it again."

And though she was dying with curiosity to know what was inside it—no doubt something relating to Uncle Julius — she restrained herself, and looked at it no more. Nay, she did what was harder still, though her little heart was bursting with sympathy and anxiety—during the whole long day she neither went herself, nor sent any of the servants to inquire how things fared with poor Mr. Stone.

* * * * * * *

Edna and her husband were taking an afternoon's stroll in the broad walk of Kensington Gardens—the place which they had haunted so much in their old poverty days—days when even the sweetness of being together hardly kept their tired feet from aching, or their anxious hearts from feeling that it needed all the love that was in them to maintain cheerfulness.

Now things, outwardly, were quite changed. No weary walking—Dr. Stedman had driven his wife to the Palace Gate—and the carriage was to meet them at the Bayswater end. She walked beside him, clad "in silk attire," and "siller had to spare," and he had earned it all. Earned, too, as he rose in the world, those bits of delicious idleness which a man may lawfully enjoy, who, having done his best for his wife and family, yet feels that life is not all money-making, and that it is sometimes wise to sacrifice a little outside luxury for inward leisure—and love.

So, with a clear conscience, and a boy-like happiness, pleasant to see in one whose hair was already gray, he daundered on, with his wife hanging on his arm, listening to every bird, and noting every budding tree, stopping continually to look in Edna's face and see if she were enjoying herself as much as he.

She did, though in a more subdued way. Women like her have natures at once lighter and deeper than men's; and no mother of five children is ever long without some anxious care or other. Still, for the time, Mrs. Stedman put her's aside; her sons were, after all, less dear to her than was their father. And as she walked along these familiar places, where she now came seldom enough not to disturb their old associations, she thought of him, not as he was now, but as William Stedman, her lover, with his love untried, his character untested, and both their lives looming before them in a dim, rosy haze, under which might lurk — what? They knew not — no lovers can know. Unmarried, a man or woman can stand or fall alone—but married, they stand or fall together. Perhaps if, before she was wed, Edna had felt this truth as strongly as she did now, she might have been more afraid. And yet not so, for she loved him, and love and suffering would have been better to her than loneliness and peace. But God had not sent her suffering—at least not more than was needed to temper her joys; or it seemed so, looking back. She, like all pure hearts, had a far keener memory for happiness than for pain.

And now her life was all clear—nay, it was almost half

done. She and William had attained — one nearly, the other quite, their half-century, and they had been married twenty years. As she walked on — thoughtful, for this spring season, which had been the time of her courtship and marriage, her eldest son's birth and her baby's death, always seemed to make her grave — Edna clung with a tenderer clasp than ordinary to the arm which had sheltered and supported her so long.

"What are you thinking about, my wife? You have been silent these fifteen minutes."

"Only five, or I am sure I should have heard of it before," said Edna, smiling. "You and the boys think something dreadful must be the matter if ever I chance to hold my tongue."

"Well, but what were you cogitating on? I like to hear. If you had put all your pretty thoughts into a book, you would have turned out a celebrated authoress by this time."

"Oh no, thank goodness! for then how could I look after you and the five boys. But seriously, I was thinking of something which I dare say some of the clever people who come to our house might find a grand subject for writing on."

"What was it?"

"Did you notice, as we drove through Kensington, a pawnbroker's shop—with a notice in the window: 'To be sold, unredeemed pledges?" It struck me how, in our human lives, so many early pledges are forever unredeemed."

"That is true," said William, sadly.

Edna hastened to change the conversation. "However, we did not come here to moralize. Tell me about the cottage at Sevenoaks."

This was a project dreamed of hopelessly for many years, and this year in a fair way of being accomplished. All her life Edna had hated London, and yet been obliged to live in it: and all his life, for the last twenty years, Dr. Stedman had determined that the first use he would make of any wealth that came to him should be to buy a cottage, where his wife, country-born and country-bred, could take refuge whenever she liked, among her beloved fields and flowers.

"Yes, I'll tell you all about the cottage by-and-by. It, at least, will not be one of the pledges unredeemed. We have not had many of these."

"Oh no. Thank God, William—no."

"Sometimes, when I look back these twenty years upon my life, and think what you have made it—"

"What God has made it."

"Yes, through you." He stopped, and loosing her arm, "eyed her over," as she called it, from head to foot. "Such a little woman she is!" said he, fondly, "but what a spirit! When we were poor, how the tiny feet kept trotting about all day long, and the small head wore itself out in ingenious contrivances! And what a cheerful heart she kept—how she met all the world and its cares without one fear!"

"There was no need for fear. I had not a single-handed battle to fight. There were always two of us. And we were always agreed."

"Not quite, perhaps," said Dr. Stedman. "Especially when we began to rise in the world—and I might have been foolish sometimes, only this grave little face kept me in my balance. Who forbade the brougham, and made me be content with cabs till I had a carriage I could honestly ride in? Who refused, year after year, to take her autumn pleasuring as many wives do, because her husband would only have to work the harder for it?"

"William!" with a laugh and a stamp, though the tears stood in her eyes, "do hold your tongue, or I shall begin to quote against you,

"'Who rose to kiss me when I fell,
And would a pretty story tell,
And kiss the place to make it well?
My mother.'

But," added she, gravely, "though we may have made many mistakes, and done many a wrong thing, perhaps even to one another, the pledge my husband gave me on his marriage-day has not been one of these melancholy 'pledges unredeemed.' I could begin and tell my tale too—of patience and tenderness and self-denial, so much harder for a man than a woman. But I'll tell nothing, unless I should happen to go up first and tell it to the angels."

"Don't talk nonsense," said William, hastily, and reverted at once to the subject of the cottage at Sevenoaks.

The plan had so delighted him, that he had entered into its minutest details with the eagerness of a boy; and Edna was a long time before she had the heart to suggest the only objection she saw to it—namely, that it was on the same line of railway as—indeed, only a few miles distant from—Holywell Hall.

"And if her husband has the objection that she says he has to the intercourse of our families, this might place my sister in rather a painful position—poor Letty!" Somehow, after her last visit, Edna had always called her "poor Letty."

"I can not see that we need modify our plans on account of either Mr. or Mrs. Vanderdecken. They have never shown us any consideration, and we owe them none."

William spoke in that formal tone, almost akin to severity, which any reference to his wife's sister always produced in him, and Edna answered, gently:

"You are quite right, and it would be foolish in us to be affected by these difficulties. Still, they do exist, and I know you will feel them far more than I shall."

"Possibly, because you only feel them for yourself, while I feel them for you. It makes a good deal of difference. But we will not discuss these matters, my dear. Whenever your sister likes to come to my house, she can, for it is your house too; but never expect me to enter hers. And I shall take this pleasant little cottage, and live in it, even were it under the very shadow of Holywell Hall."

Edna dissented no more, for she knew it was useless—her husband had a will of his own, and most often it was a right and just will. In this matter she found herself incapable of judging, especially as she was dimly conscious that, had she been in his place, she would have felt as he did—that no consideration on earth should have induced her to cross the magnificent threshold of a brother who had in any way slighted her husband. But he had no brother—oh! poor, poor Julius! So she set her mind to bear for the living lost that pain which her husband had long endured for the dead, nor wondered that William, strong in his hatreds as in his loves, shrunk with a double repugnance from every mention of her sister Letty.

She walked on silently, hoping that the thrushes would sing peace into his heart as well as her own, which felt a little sad and sore, in spite of the brightness around her. It is so easy, so blessed to see God's hand moving behind some human hand, for good; but when the same occurs for evil, or what appears to us as evil, the trial of faith is somewhat hard. It had cost her a good deal to "forgive God Almighty," as a forlorn mourner once expressed what many a mourner has thought since, for the lot of poor Julius.

And thinking of him in these pleasant places, where they had so often been together—of him far away from the world and its riot and care, gone into peace, though how and where no one knew—Edna quite started when her husband said, suddenly:

"Look, there comes Julius."

Julius their son, of course, walking quickly towards them with a letter in his hand.

"This came just after you were gone, father. A boy brought it, and said it was very important—about some one who was dying—so I hunted you up as fast as I could. I think," he added, in a whisper to his mother, "that it has something to do with the Vanderdeckens."

"Oh, William, what is it? Nothing very bad?"

"Look here," and he made her read the letter over with him—little Gertrude's letter. "What does she mean? What did your sister write to you?"

"Not one single line."

Dr. Stedman, violently agitated as he was, again perused the letter carefully. "See what it says, '*Your brother, whom every body thought to be dead.*' "

"It is possible, William—only barely possible. But we must find out. Read on."

"This man—who knows all about him—this John Stone, who I suppose sends for me—did I ever have any John Stone among my patients?"

"No," said Edna, decidedly, being one of the few doctors' wives who are trusted with all their husbands' concerns.

"A soldier, too, from India. If he had any tidings to bring, why did he not find me out? It was easy enough to do so."

"Mother," interposed Julius, greatly excited, "once, lately, an Indian soldier kept hanging about our house for a whole morning. Will and I both spoke to him. So did you."

"Yes, I remember—a thin, sickly, rather elderly man, with a long gray beard. Perhaps he was John Stone. But we must not detain papa here. William, you will start at once?"

"Certainly."

"Julius, run and look out for the carriage," said Edna, as she took her husband's arm, trying to shield his emotion even from his own son: fond and tender as the boy was, how could he understand it?

Without another word the two passed rapidly down the Broad Walk to the Bayswater gate, whence, almost as silently, they drove direct to the railway station.

Edna kept close to her husband until the train should start.

"You can not say what time you will be back, of course, but let it be as soon as possible."

"Most certainly. Julius, you'll take special care of your mother to-night?"

"That I will," said the boy, tucking her under his arm in his loving, protecting way. "Cheer up, mamma. Suppose papa should bring home some news—real news—about Uncle Julius. Or if he were to come back again alive, after all. What a jolly thing that would be!"

"Hush!" whispered his mother, and then left her son's

arm to lean forward and whisper to his father. "I wish I were going with you. Take care of yourself, William, my darling."

After Dr. Stedman reached the station he was bound for, he found he had a three-mile walk before him, and it did him good. His mind was all confused and bewildered, and the sentence in Gertrude's letter, "whom every body believed to be dead," kept running in and out of his head, awakening strange hopes, which sank the next minute into the old dull quietness which had succeeded the long suspense of pain. Julius might be alive—it was just within the bounds of probability; but how and where had he lived, in what manner had he contrived so long to hide himself from them, and what steps could be taken to discover him? Why had Mrs. Vanderdecken not written?—so like her, though—and what if this delay of hers were to make every thing too late, and John Stone should die with his secret untold?

As Dr. Stedman thought of this chance he ground his teeth together—it seemed to be the last wrong Letty had done him. He walked on fierce and fast. If he could have hated any thing so frail as a woman it would have been this woman, who, from her accursed weakness, had been the bane of his brother's life.

His brother—his own, only brother. Though William Stedman was no longer a young man by any means, and had been knocked about the world enough to make his life appear long, even to himself, still, as he walked to-day between the bursting hedge-rows, and under the budding road-side trees, his boyish days came back to him vivid as yesterday. He seemed to see the two little lads who used to go birds'-nesting of Saturday afternoons—the two youths in their teens—always together, like his own two elder boys, delighted to seize the opportunity of any stray half-holiday to ramble away for miles across country, returning, tired indeed, but, oh! so merry, with a mirth that never flagged; for Julius's light nature always stirred up his own graver and more phlegmatic one—so that they suited better than if they had been more alike. And after all the years that had rolled between, busy and prosperous, anxious and sad, Will's heart leaped back with a passionate rebound to those years that were gone forever; and he felt as if he would give nearly all he had in the world—except his wife and children—to have Julius back again, or only to see some one who could tell him how and where he died.

Dr. Stedman reached Holt Common just at twilight. A lovely spot, a heavenly evening; just the hour and place that would be sweet to die in for one unto whom death was better than life. But the doctor, accustomed to fight death hand to hand, also fully recognized the blessing of life, and the duty of preserving it. Wasting not a moment in useless delay, he hurried as fast as he could to the door of the "Goat and Compasses."

"You have a lodger here," said he, stooping his tall head to enter the bar, "a soldier, John Stone by name, ill, as I understand. Can I see him? I am a physician. My name is Stedman."

For he had determined not in the smallest degree to allude to the Vanderdeckens, or to his connection with them.

Mrs. Fox rushed forward, infinitely relieved. "Dr. Stedman, sure? The gentleman the little miss sent for? Oh, sir, I'm so glad you've come! Will you walk up stairs?"

"Stop a minute. Are you his sister, or mother, or what?"

"Only his landlady—Mrs. Fox, at your service. But I can't help feeling for him, poor fellow! and I'm sure I'd look after him as if I was his mother, for he doesn't seem to have a friend in the world."

"A young man, or old?"

"Neither, sir. Over fifty, I reckon, or may be a bit older than you are."

"Older than I am?" said Dr. Stedman, and a wild possibility that had lurked in some corner of his brain dropped out of it completely. To him his brother Julius was still a young man. "Poor fellow! I'll go to him directly; but if, as my son found out from your messenger, his brain is affected, I can not talk to you much in his room; so tell me here all you know about him."

Mrs. Fox did so; but her statement was too involved and confused for Dr. Stedman to gain much more information from it; so, afraid of losing time, he bade her take him up at once to his patient's chamber.

The good old woman had been very mindful over her charge. His sick-room was quiet and in order; he had every thing comfortable about him—clean linen, smoothly-arranged pillows and sheets, and a neat patchwork counterpane, upon which the two thin hands lay stretched, like the dead passive hands which tender friends straighten out in peace, never to work any more.

Indeed, in the darkened room, the figure on the bed looked altogether not unlike a corpse, being quite still, with wet cloths on the head, and the eyes closed. But at sound of the door-latch they opened, and met the two incomers with that strange, glassy, unseeing stare peculiar to brain disease.

"This is a doctor, my dear," whispered Mrs. Fox, soothingly. "A kind gentleman from London, who has come to see you and make you well."

"Indeed, I hope so, my poor fellow," said the doctor, kindly, as he sat down by the bedside.

At sound of his voice the sick man turned his head feebly round, and looked at him with a kind of half-consciousness; a long shiver ran all through his frame; then he closed his eyes, and clasped his hands together, as if bent upon concealing some secret which, with the last remnant of life or sense that remained to him, he was determined to keep.

"Let me feel your pulse; I'll not hurt you," said Dr. Stedman, as with his quiet, determined, professional manner he unlocked the rigid fingers, and drew the hand towards him. The face he had not recognized in the least—it was so covered with beard, so totally changed; but the hand, with its long fingers and delicate filbert nails—the true artist's hand—startled him at once.

"Doctor, what's the matter?" cried Mrs. Fox.

"Nothing," said he, controlling himself at once. "Only give me more light. I want to look at my patient."

"No, no!" A sound, hollow as if out of the grave itself, came from the sick man's parched lips. "No light—no! Send the doctor away. I want none. I want to die."

Without answering, Dr. Stedman rose and drew up the blind. But by this time the gleam of sense had faded entirely out of the poor face; it was sharp-set, and vacant with the terrible vacuity of a human face from which—temporarily or permanently—the conscious mind is quite gone.

Will stood looking at him—this utter wreck of all he had once been so proud of, so tender over, almost with the tenderness of a man over a woman. Then, stooping over Julius, with one great smothered sob, he kissed him on the forehead—softly, as he would have kissed the dead.

"Thank God! it may not be too late. Mrs. Fox, I must send a messenger to my wife at once. This is my brother."

CHAPTER XXIX.

Mrs. Stedman was sitting with all her children round her, trying to make the evening pass as usual, in reading, lesson-learning, drawing—broken by fits of play and merry chat. None of the boys, except the eldest, knew of what had occurred, or saw any thing remarkable in their father's absence; and she had charged Julius to be silent for the present. He, wise and grave beyond his years, and his parents' confidant in many things, was the only one who had been told more about Uncle Julius than that his father had had such a brother, who died abroad. And even he knew comparatively little; but it was enough greatly to interest and excite him. Besides, his mother—the one grand idol of his life, whom he worshipped with that adoring filial tenderness which is Heaven's best instrument for making noble men—his mother had been put into his charge, and he watched her with especial care—distracted the attention of the rest from her—and hovered about her with endless little caresses, listening all the while to every sound of the hall-bell, which made her start whenever it rang.

For Edna, more imaginative and quicker than her husband to put things together, could not get out of her mind a strange impression, which came very near the truth. And when her son brought her the letter, having first carefully allured her away from the rest, that she might read it unobserved, her hands shook so that she could scarcely break the seal.

The next minute she had burst out with a great cry of "Julius!"

Her boy ran to her alarmed, and took her in his arms—his dear little mother.

"Not you, my son. I did not mean you, but your uncle Julius. Papa has found Uncle Julius."

There is a belief, a feeling—Julius had had it strongly not so many weeks before, when he stood in the dark outside his brother's shut door—that if the dead were to come back to us again, they would find their place filled up, their loss mourned no longer, and the smooth surface of daily life grown greenly over them, like the grass over their graves. This is true, in degree, and Infinite Mercy makes it so; else human nature could not possibly endure its anguish to the end. But there are exceptions, and the present was one of them. Julius—poor prodigal as he might be—had fed on his own swines' husks silently, far away; he had never either disgraced or wronged any one, least of all his brother. Heavy grief though he had caused, there was mixed with it none of that aching bitterness which Edna felt in her own heart, and the mute contempt which she read in her husband's face whenever she chanced to mention her sister. Therefore, her rejoicing over the lost and found was as unclouded as her love—and she had always loved Julius.

The wonderful news could not be long hid, especially in this loving family, where the parents kept none but necessary secrets from their children. The mother was soon the centre of an eager group, asking all manner of questions, and evidently regarding the whole matter as a sort of real-life fairy tale.

"Don't bother mamma, children," said Julius, with tender authoritativeness. "Come away with me, and I'll tell you as much as I know, while she reads papa's letter."

Dr. Stedman had written, not telegraphed, that he might startle her less and give her the latest intelligence, and had sent his letter by the faithful Tommy Fox, who was to remain that night at Brook Street, and bring Mrs. Stedman back with him the first thing next morning.

"I do not want you until the morning," wrote William to his wife. "You must get a good night's rest, for I fear you may have some days, or perhaps weeks, of heavy nursing here. However, if he survives the next twenty-four hours, he will live, I doubt not. I might have sent for you to-night, but I thought it best not."

Edna felt also that it was best not—that not even his wife should share in this solemn watch which William kept so faithfully—uncertain whether, after all, his brother might not slip away, unrecognizing and unrecognized, into the next world. But even if Julius died, it would be a lighter burden to bear than that which Dr. Stedman had borne so patiently, so silently, all these years—not suffering it to darken his home-life, which would indeed have been both foolish and wrong. Still it was there; and his wife knew it. Almost every human heart has some such dark chamber in it: she had had hers too.

Now, was the grief to be lifted off or not? Edna could not tell; nor William. He had only said, in reference to the future, one thing—"If Julius recovers, will my wife take him home?" At which the wife smiled to herself. There was no need to answer that question.

So, it was necessary to prepare for possibilities; and first, by telling the children as much of their uncle's history as she thought advisable. They were not inquisitive or worrying children. Still, they had their natural curiosity, increased by the very few facts she was able to give them; indeed, little more than that Uncle Julius, whom they had supposed to be dead, had reappeared, and at last come home.

"But why did he not come home before, mamma?"

"Being a soldier, he could not do that, I suppose."

"Still, he might have written," said Julius, a little severely. "It was unkind of him to let you and papa imagine he was dead, and grieve after him for so many years."

"People sometimes do unkind things without meaning it, or, at least, without definitely intending it," said the mother, gently. "When you are as old as I am, my son, you will have learned that—" Here she stopped, hindered by the great difficulty with all young people—how to keep them sternly to the right; and yet, while preaching strict justice, to remember mercy. "In truth, my children," added she, with that plain candor which had been her safeguard all her life, and taught her sons to be as fearlessly true as herself, "it is useless to question me; for I know almost nothing, except that papa has found his brother again, which will make him so happy. You like papa to be happy, all of you?"

"Ah, yes!" and they ceased troubling her with their wonderings, but with the brilliant imagination of youth darted at once to the possibility of Uncle Julius's appearance among them, making endless speculations and arrangements concerning him. The twins, hearing he had been a soldier, brought out their favorite toy-cannon, with a man behind it, which man they immediately named "Uncle Julius." Robert, who had set his heart upon wandering half over the world, exulted in the thought of all the information he should get about foreign countries; and Will, after much meditation, leaped at once to a most brilliant conclusion.

"That folio of drawings you keep, beside the old easel in your bedroom, mamma—were they not done by Uncle Julius? You said he was an artist before he went away to India."

"Yes."

"And clever, too, to judge by those sketches, which you

have never properly shown me yet, and will not let me have to copy; very good they are, some of them," continued Will, with the slightly patronizing tone of the younger generation. "Of course, he is too old to make an artist now; but he might help to make me one."

"Perhaps," said the mother, and wondered whether Uncle Julius would recognize, as his brother and she had long since began to do, the eternal law of progression, whereby one generation slips aside, or is set aside, and another takes its place—a law righteous and easy of belief to happy parents, but hard to others, who have to drop down, solitary and childless, into the great sea of oblivion, leaving not a trace behind. As she looked on her bright, brave boys growing up around her, in whom her memory and their father's would live, long after both were in the dust, Edna thought of Julius, and sighed.

"Now, my little man, you must chatter no more, but be off to bed; for mamma has a great deal to do to-night."

Nevertheless, she was not afraid, though it was a small and already full house in which she had to make room for the wanderer; but the capacity of people's houses often corresponds with that of their hearts. And she had good servants—a good mistress usually has—and helpful, unselfish children. Her eldest, especially, followed her about the house, assisting in her plans and arrangements almost as cleverly as a daughter, and yet so manly, so wise, so reliable that for the hundredth time his mother pitied all women who had not a son like Julius.

Yet when he and she sat together over the fire, the house being silent and all preparations made, both for her temporary absence and for her return with poor Uncle Julius, if he recovered—with the reaction from her first joyful excitement over—anxious thoughts came into Edna's mind. Was she right in bringing into her household and among her young sons this man, who might be so changed—whose life for fifteen years and more was utterly unknown to her, except that he had sunk deplorably from his former estate? When her eldest son, looking at her with his honest, innocent, boyish eyes, said, earnestly, "Now, mamma, tell me all about poor Uncle Julius," Edna trembled.

But only for a moment. She knew well, her anxious life had often taught her, the plain fact that we can not live two days at once; that beyond a certain prudent fore-casting of consequences we have but to see the right for the time being, and act upon it.

"My son," she answered, cautiously, as her judgment prompted, but honestly, as mothers ought who have their children's souls in their hands, "Uncle Julius has had a very hard, sad life. It may have been not even a good life. I do not know. But papa does; and he understands what is right far better than we. He says he wishes Uncle Julius to come home—he is so glad and thankful to have him at home. So of course it is all right. We can trust papa, both you and I."

"To be sure we can," said Julius, and looked his father's very image while he spoke: so that Edna had no farther fear even for her darling boy.

It was little more than ten in the forenoon, and Holt Common was bathed in the brightest spring sunshine, when Edna crossed it, under Tommy Fox's guidance, to take the shortest cut to the "Goat and Compasses." She scarcely looked at the sweet sights around her—the green mosses, the perfumed gorse—so full was her heart, trembling between hope and fear, wondering whether it would please God to give this poor wrecked life into their hands—hers and Will's—to be made whole and sound again, even in this world; or whether, in his infinite wisdom, He would take it to himself, to do with it according to his omnipotent will, which *must* be perfect, or it would not be omnipotent.

There was a figure standing at the ale-house door—her husband watching for her. Edna looked rather than asked the trembling question, "Is he alive?" which William's smile answered at once.

He had held up bravely till now; but when he found himself alone with his wife he broke down. Edna took his head to her bosom, and let him weep there, almost like one of his own little children.

But there was no time to waste in mere emotion—the patient must not be left for ten minutes. Nothing but constant watching could save the life which flickered like a dying taper, half in and half out of the body. Julius might slip away at any moment, giving no sign, as all the night through he had given none. It was impossible to say whether he even recognized his brother, though the pressure on the brain produced stupor rather than delirium.

"He lies, looking as quiet as a baby," said Will, with a great sob. "I have cut his hair and beard; he is quite bald. You would hardly know him. I wonder if he will know you, Edna?"

"Let us come and see," answered Mrs. Stedman, as she laid aside her bonnet, and made silently all her little arrangements for the long, long sisterly watch, of which God only knew the end.

Her husband followed her with eyes full of love. "There is nobody to do this but you, my wife. You would do it, I knew." She smiled. "And I have made things as light for you as I can. Mrs. Fox will take the night-nursing. She is evidently very fond of him — but every body was always fond of Julius. My poor dear lad!"

The strong fraternal love — rare between men, but, when it does happen, the heavenliest, noblest bond, a help through life, and faithful even unto death—shone in William's eyes; and his wife honored and loved him for it.

"Come," she whispered, "perhaps, please God, we may save him yet. Come and take me to Julius's room."

For another day and night the poor brain—worn out with misery, and disordered by the continual use of opium—lay in a torpid condition, of which it was impossible to foretell the next change. Then sharp physical pain supervened, and forced into a kind of semi-consciousness the bewildered mind.

The day he had spent out on the common—(Tommy Fox afterwards confessed to having seen Mr. Stone lying for hours under a damp furze-bush) — brought back his old rheumatic torments. He had over again the same illness, rheumatic fever, through which his brother had nursed him twenty years ago. Strangely enough, this agony of body was the most merciful thing that could have happened to the mind. It seemed to annihilate the present entirely, and thrust him back to the days of his youth. He took quite naturally the presence of Will and Edna, and very soon began to call them by their right names, and comprehend, in a confused way, that he was under their charge. And in his total helplessness the great difficulty which William had foreseen, the stopping of the supplies of opium, became easier than they had anticipated. After he had been brought back, as it were, from the very gates of the grave, to some slight recognition of where he was, and what had happened to him, he seemed to wake up, as people often do after very severe illnesses, with the freshness of a child—asking no questions, but helplessly and obediently clinging to those about him, till sometimes none of his nurses could look at him without tears.

Gradually he passed out of sickness into convalescence, began visibly to amend in body, though how far his mind was alive to the things around him it was difficult to say. He noticed nothing much — neither the changes which Edna had gradually instituted in his ragged wardrobe, nor the comforts which she gathered around him in his homely room. He spoke little, and his whole intelligence seemed to be absorbed in trying to bear, as patiently as he could, his physical sufferings, which, for a long time, were very great. When at last Edna, to whose ministering care he had grown quite accustomed, proposed taking him "home," he assented, but without asking the slightest question as to what and where "home" was.

Letty, either as Letty or Mrs. Vanderdecken, he never once named.

Indeed, in the complete absorption of the time, neither Edna nor her husband thought much about her themselves. The near neighborhood of Holywell Park troubled them not; the place was half shut up, the mistress being away at Brighton. Thence she never sent, never wrote; at which they were neither surprised nor sorry.

But the night before they had settled to quit Mrs. Fox's kindly roof, the good woman brought to Mrs. Stedman, for whom she had conceived a great admiration, a note from the Hall.

"I don't know if you knows Mrs. Vanderdecken, ma'am, but perhaps you do, as it was through her little girl I heard of Dr. Stedman. And she's a kind lady — a very kind lady indeed: *he* saw her the day before he was ill. Didn't you, sir?"

Edna interposed, and stopped the conversation, but her caution seemed needless. The sick man took no notice, and she hoped he had seen and heard nothing. However, just before she left him for the night, Julius called her back.

"What was that note you had? From your sister?"

"Yes."

"Have you seen her?"

"No."

This was all he asked or was told, though, in much anxiety, Edna sat down beside him for another half hour. By-and-by Julius felt feebly for her hand.

"Are you there still, Sister Edna? I like to have you beside me. I know you now, and Will too, though at first I did not. I thought I was dreaming. I have had so many queer dreams. They all came out of that box which you never will let me have."

"No, never again."

"Does Will say so?"

"Yes."

"Then I suppose he must be obeyed. When we were lads, kind as he was to me, Will always made me obey him." Julius smiled faintly, yet more like his own smile than Edna had ever seen yet. "Where is Will to-night?"

"Gone home to get ready the house for us to-morrow, you know. Besides, he has his work to do."

"Ah yes! and mine is all done. I shirked it once; and

now, when I want to do it, I can not. Why do you and Will take me home? I would never have come of myself. I shall only be a burden upon you. Do you know, Edna, that I have not a half-penny in the world?"

"Yes."

"Except, of course, my pension as a soldier—a common soldier, which I have been—I ceased to be a gentleman years ago."

Edna smiled.

"Do not mock me; it is true. You had better not take me back. I shall only be a trouble to you—nay, even a disgrace. Will is an honest, honorable, prosperous man, while I— What will all your friends say?"

"We shall never ask them. But," added Will's wife, in reasoning not her own, for her own failed her, "it is just the story of the piece of silver—'And when she hath found it she calleth her friends and neighbors together, saying, Rejoice with me, for I have found my piece that was lost.'"

Julius turned away bitterly. "Don't talk to me out of the Bible. I do not believe in the Bible. Only"—as if he feared he had hurt her—"I believe in you."

"Thank you, dear." She often called him "dear" now, in the tone she used to her own children; for, in many ways, Julius had grown so very like a child. "And I believe in the Bible. Therefore, I came here to nurse you, and keep you alive if we could. Therefore, as soon as you are stronger, I mean to take you home, to begin a new life, and never to speak of the old life any more."

Tender as her words were, there was a certain authority in them—the quiet decision which Edna always showed, and nobody attempted to gainsay.

Julius did not, but lay quiet, with his eyelids closed, till at length he suddenly opened them.

"There was a packet—letters—which I think I made up just before I was ill. Where is it?"

"Mrs. Fox found it, and delivered it to the person to whom it was addressed."

"And that was—"

"Mrs. Vanderdecken."

"Are you sure of that?"

"Quite sure. Now go to sleep."

"One minute"—and Julius lifted himself up and caught Edna's hand. "Tell her—your sister—that for the child's sake I have forgiven her all. I will never harm her. Her daughter knows nothing—never will know. Say I forgive her, and bid her good-bye from me."

"I will," said Edna; and then, still holding her hand, Julius dropped into the quietest slumber which he had yet known.

When alone for the night Mrs. Stedman read over again the dirty-looking note, which had lain a whole day in the pocket of a small child, one of Mrs. Vanderdecken's Sunday-class, by whom it had been sent. Letty's cowardice had followed her to the last. There was in the missive neither beginning nor ending. Nothing that could identify it or its writer, or betray any fact that it was safer to conceal.

"I know all, and was glad your husband had been sent for to the poor man, you and he being the proper persons to manage the business. Give him my best wishes, and I hope he will soon get well. If I could do any thing—but it is better not—you will understand that. Only, if you like to come and talk it over with me, I shall be very glad to see you, for I am quite alone here, though I shall return to Brighton in two days."

Edna closed the letter with a heavy sigh, and sat long pondering over it, and how she should answer it; whether it would not be advisable, under the circumstances, and especially with regard to a future that was very difficult at best, to go and see Letty, as she asked, in her own house, and calmly, but not unkindly, "talk it over," as she proposed, thus closing forever the grave of a past that could return no more.

In her husband's absence Edna was obliged to trust to her own judgment, and what she knew his would be. He had said more than once that nothing should induce him to enter his sister-in-law's door, nor did his wife dissent from this. There is a limit beyond which self-respect can not pass; and charity itself changes its character when it becomes the subserviency of weak right to rampant wrong. But Mrs. Stedman, who had not an atom of weakness about her, or pride either, felt no hesitation whatever in crossing just once, and no more, her sister's grand threshold; neither humbly nor scornfully, but with a kindly, sisterly heart. If she could do Letty any good, why, well! If not, still it was well too. They would both see clearly, once for all, what their future relations to one another were to be.

So next morning, before Julius was well awake, without saying any thing to him or any body, she started off across the common to Holywell Hall.

It was a very fine house, the finest Mrs. Stedman had ever entered; for her busy domestic life and narrow means had, until lately, kept her very much out of society. She admired it extremely, for she had such pleasure in any thing orderly, fit, and beautiful. Yet, when her little feet trod on the polished black and white marble of the hall, and followed two tall liveried footmen up a magnificent staircase, stately, silent, and chill, her heart sank a little, and she was glad fate had not burdened her with her sister's splendid lot. It did not occur to her, in her utter lack of self-consciousness, that, had such been the case, the probabilities were that Holywell Hall would have been as bright as Brook Street.

The footman went before, and she was following him at once into Mrs. Vanderdecken's morning-room, when she heard her sister's voice within, and hesitated.

"Stedman is the name, Wood?—I don't know—yes, I do know the lady. Show her into the yellow drawing-room. Oh, she's here."

Rather awkwardly Mrs. Vanderdecken came forward, merely to shake hands, till, the servant having closed the door behind him, she stooped and kissed her sister, though not with much demonstration of affection.

"I am very glad to see you. It is extremely kind of you to come. You see I couldn't come to you—it was quite an impossibility."

"Certainly."

Then Letty burst out:

"Oh! Edna, do give me a little comfort. I have been so frightened—so thoroughly miserable. This is indeed a wretched business."

"I do not see that, since it has ended so well in Julius's recovery. He might have died. It was such a merciful chance that your little girl wrote to my husband."

"Yes; and I assure you I did not scold her at all for doing so. I was only too thankful to get her safe away, where she would hear no more of that dreadful story, or of him, poor fellow; he made her so fond of him. She cried her eyes out till I told her Dr. Stedman was with him, and that he was getting well. That is true, is it not?"

"Yes, thank God!"

"And nobody here knows who he is; but, like Gertrude, people think him Mr. Stone?"

"No—Mr. Stedman," said Edna, coldly. "My husband was not likely to be ashamed of his brother, or to conceal his relationship to him. But you need not be alarmed; we have carefully hidden our connection with you. No one here has the least idea that you are my sister."

"Thank you, thank you!" And then, some dim notion striking Letty that it was an odd thing to express gratitude for, she added, half-apologetically, "You see, we are obliged to be careful. In our position people do talk of us so. And he was so violent, so cruel to me—Julius, I mean. And there was something so disreputable — so dreadful—about his story. You know it, of course."

"No; he has told us almost nothing; and we are determined to inquire nothing. My husband believes less in the confession of sins than in the forsaking of them. Unless Julius speaks himself, we shall never ask him a single question about his past life."

"Well, perhaps that is your best course; any other would be so very inconvenient. I declare, when I listen to Gertrude's story—but I'll just repeat it to you, for it will relieve my mind."

And she told, accurately enough for her, Julius's whole

sad tale, which he had told to the child, and her own interview with him, which had followed it.

The facts were all new to Edna, but she said nothing: how could she? From the sick-bed beside which she had watched so long she seemed to gaze on her elegant sister, gifted with every thing that the world could give; and she understood something about the joy in heaven, not over the rich and the prosperous, but over one sinner that repenteth. The one question, Did he repent? was all she ever asked herself, and that time alone could answer.

"Was it not dreadful of him," Letty continued, "after all these years, and when I would have met him so friendly, to try to injure me thus? Ah, Edna, you don't know the agony of a poor mother who fears losing her child's heart."

"No," said Edna; "but you need have no fear now;" and then she delivered, word for word, the message Julius had sent.

Letty was a good deal touched. "Poor fellow! poor fellow!" she repeated several times, and wiped her eyes with her lace pocket-handkerchief. "But why does he bid me good-bye? Will he die, do you think?"

"God only knows. The first danger is past, but there is a weary convalescence before him. He will never be really strong, William says; and if any ill turn comes—But we will not forbode evils. I hope for the best."

"Ah, you always did. You were always the cheerfullest, bravest girl. I wish I had been more like you."

But these sudden compunctions, which ended in nothing, only made Edna sigh. She rose.

"I must go now, Letty. He will be waiting for me. I take him home to-day."

"He? Oh, I had forgotten! You mean poor Julius. I do hope he will recover; tell him I said so. Where are you taking him? to Brook Street? But of course you have no other house. Poor dear fellow, I am sure I wish him well. But are you sure he will not attempt to injure me?"

Edna smiled. It would have been a sarcastic smile

once, when she was scornful and young; now it was only sad. She did not attempt to grow grapes from thorns, or figs from thistles, any more. She only understood, though it had been bitter learning, that all human creatures were of God's handiwork, and if He had patience with them, so must she have.

"And now, Letty, good-bye; for I really must go."

Upon which Letty eagerly begged her to stay.

"Why can't you have lunch with me, Edna, my dear? I am so dull, alone here. And, besides, I should like to show you the house and the conservatory; you were always fond of flowers. Ours are considered very fine, especially our orchids. Mr. Vanderdecken has paid sixty guineas apiece for some of them."

Edna shook her head. "I have no time for orchids just at present." And then, seeing real disappointment in her sister's looks, she agreed to stay with her another half hour.

"Especially as we may not meet again for some time. You must perceive, I can not ask you to Brook Street; and as for my coming here— But we shall remain sisters, feeling very kindly to one another, I trust. And, Letty dear, if ever you are in trouble, and want somebody to help you—"

Here she quite broke down. To the last day of her life Edna would never lose this sore-wounded, ill-requited love for her only sister.

Letty kissed her, not unaffectionately.

"Thank you. We all have trouble, some time or other, I suppose. But I hope mine is far off still. I am very comfortable, and Mr. Vanderdecken is extremely kind. Then, too, I have such a pretty house. Won't you come and look at it? People say many a nobleman's mansion is not near so fine."

This was true; and Edna's innocent, generous heart admired it so warmly that her sister's spirits quite rose.

"Yes, I do think ours is a charming place, and it is a pleasure to show it to you. I am very glad you came to see me, and I only wish we could meet oftener, my dear. But I suppose that is impossible."

Edna was silent; she also felt that it was impossible.

"Gertrude will be so disappointed that she has not seen you. She thinks a great deal of her aunt Edna. And perhaps, by-and-by, when she has forgotten all about Mr. Stone, who I shall tell her is quite well, and gone away to his own relations—"

"Oh, Letty!" broke in the other, earnestly, "whatever you tell her, let it be the exact truth. With such a child as Gertrude—with any child—straightforward truth is the only way. Forgive me—it will be long before I 'preach' to you again—but I have no little girl of my own; and Gertrude is a dear child! Be careful with her."

Letty looked a little vexed. "It is hardly needful to say that to me; but, Edna, I will take care of her. She is the light of my eyes—the best little girl that ever was born! Julius said he wished my child to grow up a better woman than her mother. Tell him, I trust she may."

They had now passed out of the winter-garden, with its overpowering atmosphere of scent, into the healthy freshness of the spring morning—the delicious spring, which always brought back to Edna the days of her childhood, and, though it came late, and long afterwards, the springtime of her happy love. This was twenty years ago, and yet, at scent of violets and primroses, and singing of nest-making birds, every year it came back again fresh as yesterday. It did now, when she thought of going home to her own blessed home, from which, in all her married life, she had never been absent so long.

"I must be gone, indeed. I have not another moment to spare."

"Stay," said Letty, hesitating. "What hour do you go to the station? Let me send my carriage to take you—it would be easier than a fly—and—I should rather like to do it."

But Edna declined. Kindly as she felt towards her sister, to accept favors from her was impossible.

"Ah, well, perhaps you know best. Julius might not have liked it; and, after all, it might have looked a little peculiar. So good-bye, Edna. Remember me kindly to all at home."

So the sisters parted, indefinitely, without hinting at any future meeting. They were so different in themselves, and their lives had grown so wide apart, that much personal association would have been worse than foolish—fatal. It was far best that each should go her own way, until, or unless, the infinite chances and changes of this world should bring about a future which now seemed impossible—as impossible as that the dead should come to life again, and the lost be found. Yet this had been.

As Edna crossed the park, her heart lightened almost into mirth by the gladness of the glad spring morning, and thought of Julius, whom she was this day taking home, with a wondering thankfulness almost equal to that with which the sisters of Bethany took home their brother Lazarus—it seemed to her as if, unto Infinite Mercy, nothing were impossible.

CHAPTER XXX.

When his sister-in-law entered his room, Julius was already up and dressed, in the clothes to which they had gradually accustomed him—Edna having spirited away the old regimentals, with every thing that could remind him of his former life. To put it all behind him, and help him to begin anew, so far as there was any new life left in him, was their grand aim; and, so far, they had succeeded.

"Doesn't he look a sweet, dear fellow, ma'am, and not so very ill, after all?" said Mrs. Fox, who had hovered about him the last day or two with a tenderness indescribable.

Julius took the old woman's hand—her rough working hand—and kissed it with something of his old chivalrous air, which had made him, even under his rags and tatters, still so completely, often so painfully, "the gentleman."

"It is all owing to you, and my sister there, that the 'dear fellow' is not under ground now. Off with you, Mrs.

Fox, and cook my last dinner for me in your own perfect style. I'm so hungry."

"Bless you for that, my dear Mr. Stedman," said the good landlady as she hurried away; and then Julius turned to Edna with a keen inquiry.

"You were out this morning. Where have you been?"

She never thought of answering other than the direct truth.

"I have been across the park, to see my sister. I wanted to bid her good-bye before leaving this place, as she and I are not likely to meet again soon."

"You do not often meet?"

"No."

"Did you give her my message?"

"Word for word."

These were the sole questions he asked; indeed, it was the only time he mentioned Letty. Nay, when, on their way to the station, they met her carriage, and, to Edna's utter amazement, Mrs. Vanderdecken bent forward to bow and smile—altogether the courteous and stately Mrs. Vanderdecken—Julius returned the salute as he would have done to any other lady, and then leaned back, taking no more notice of her than if she had been a stranger.

But he did take notice, in a way that to Edna was infinitely pathetic, of every thing around them in the outside world, which seemed as fresh to him as if he had never seen it before. He examined, with that keen, artistic eye of his, every bit of landscape that Edna pointed out to amuse him; saw the primroses peeping through the roadside coppices, and the merry little birds flitting in and out—nest-building—among the hedges as they passed. And though, when they reached the railway, he seemed to shrink a little from the sight of human beings, and entreated that they might have a carriage all to themselves, still there was no morbid misery in his aspect, and no bitterness in his words. He seemed weak and weary—that was all. Only sometimes, in words he let fall—for he did not express it directly—there was the sad longing for rest, mingled with what seemed an unconscious echo of the

Psalmist's cry, "Oh, spare me a little, that I may recover my strength, before I go hence, and be no more seen!"

At the London terminus William met them, and, almost without saying a word — he seemed as if he could not speak—half led, half carried his brother to his carriage.

"This is your own brougham, I see. You are a prosperous man now, Will," said Julius, feebly smiling.

And then he lay back, exhausted, and scarcely conscious of what was passing, till Edna thought that his "going hence" was a possibility by no means far off. Still, if he died, he would die at home!

Home! A little, little word—only four letters—a thing easy to be had, and yet some never have it—never know what it means, in all their lives.

Some do not care for it, either; Edna had once thought that Julius did not—but she changed her opinion now.

When they brought him, with considerable difficulty, to the large upper chamber, once the twins' nursery, but from which they had delightedly retired, on promotion, in favor of Uncle Julius—he looked around the room with a strange, sad, wondering air.

"How pretty!" he said; and then, "How comfortable!"

It was both—having been arranged, half as a bedroom, half as a sitting-room, with all the skill that his sister could devise, and his brother carry out. But, as the sick man sank into the easy-chair by the fire, and drew close to the blaze, shivering, though it was May — Edna and William turned away, almost ready to weep. For he looked so frail, so feeble — as if, let them kill the fatted calf, and bring the purple robe as they would—the festive food might drop untasted from his lips, and the raiment of welcome be used only to wrap the pale limbs of the dead.

Things seemed dreary enough for some hours. The first excitement of his journey over—the first pleasure of finding himself in a real home — his brother's home, with all the old comforts about him, and, above all, the love that made comforts quite secondary things—Julius broke down. With a great and bitter cry about his own "unworthiness," he turned his face to the wall, and sank into a paroxysm of despair.

"It is no use—it is all of no use. I am like that wreck off the Isle of Wight, which we used to watch—do you remember, Edna, how they tried and tried to save it, but could not? You can not. This poor, ruined, wasted life of mine—you had better let it go down."

"No," said Will. "No, we'll never let it go down."

"And that wreck was not a wreck, after all, Julius," said Edna, cheerfully. "After months of labor they got her safe off, and now she goes sailing over the seas as bravely as ever."

"Does she, really?" said Julius, with a strange, superstitious feeling, that brightened him, in spite of himself, for a moment.

"Yes; for I saw her name in the 'shipping intelligence' only two months ago. She has ceased to be A 1, of course, by this time; but she is a capital ship still, and sails steadily between here and America."

"You don't say so?" cried Julius, rousing himself with a childish interest. But the momentary brightness soon faded, and he fell back into his former depression.

Will signed to his wife to go, and joined her a minute afterwards on the stair-head.

"Oh, husband, this is very hard."

"No; I expected it. We must have patience. The evil of years is not conquered in a day."

"But have you any hope?"

"While there is life there is hope. And then, we know, another and a safer Hope begins. I should not lose it, I trust, even if after all our care He took Julius out of our hands, and said, 'Give *Me* thy brother.'"

William was deeply affected; but still, his wife saw, he was determined not to yield to despair. She put her arms round his neck.

"Yes; we'll hope still, and strive on, to the last. And however it ends, you have still me and the children."

She went down stairs and collected round her her eager little flock, whom their eldest brother had cleverly contrived to keep out of the way till now. She tried to sun herself in their merry, loving faces, unseen for so long; to hear all their history since she was away; and answer, so far as she thought it well, their endless questions about her own. But in the midst of them all, half her heart went back to the lonely, childless man up stairs, whose blighted and blasted life contrasted so bitterly with her own full harvest of content. And when she looked round on her five boys, she thought, what if it were one day with any of them as with Julius, when there was no father's house to come to, no mother's bosom to shelter in? And she grew almost sick with fear and sad outlooking to the future, till William appeared. It was the blessedness of Edna's life that strength, comfort, and peace always came to her with the sight of her husband.

"How is he?"

"He is asleep," said Will. "And now let me come and sit in my old place, and let all go on as usual."

Taking up his newspaper, he pretended to read, but soon stopped to possess himself of his wife's hand, the small, soft hand, lovely still, though, like herself, it was fading a little—changing into that sweet decline which is scarcely like growing old.

"Oh, how delicious it is to have you at home! How different the house looks, boys, now your mother has come back!"

"If she had staid much longer," said Robert, indignantly, "I think we should have gone and fetched her back—from Uncle Julius or any body. If she ever goes away again—"

"Nay, I shall never go away again. Never, I hope, till—"

But when the mother saw the bright faces all fixed on hers, and looking to her for their very light of life, her heart failed her: she could not finish the sentence.

Soon all the evening routine went on as usual, broken only by those bursts of family fun, so small in repetition, so great in enjoyment; foolish family jokes, which brothers and sisters recall afterwards, when scattered far and wide, as having been the best jokes in the world. Gradually the troubled elders were won, too, from their cares, and relaxed into the pleasure of their children. The mirth was at its loudest—the boys laughing so that Edna could hardly hear herself speak—when the door opened, and there stood, in front of his brother's bright hearth and circle of happy children, Uncle Julius.

He was so pale, so haggard, his eyes so sad and wild, that the little twins gave a scream, and even Will, who was a boy given to poetic imaginings, shrunk back as if he had seen a ghost.

Julius saw this—saw them all. In a moment the door would have been shut again, and the apparition vanished, but Dr. Stedman darted forward, caught him, and brought him in.

"No, no. Let me go back again. Never mind me, Will. I am used to be alone."

And even when he was coaxed forward, and seated in his brother's own comfortable easy-chair, he shrank and shivered, like a person who has so long been out in the dark and cold that the light only dazzles him, and reviving warmth gives actual pain.

"Indeed, I'll not intrude," he said, nervously, to Edna. "You are all so merry here. I can go up to my room again. I only came down because I was restless—so restless; and I thought I should like to see you all."

"And here we all are; and every one of us is delighted to see Uncle Julius," said the mother, in her cheerfullest and most every-day tone. "Boys, come here, and let me exhibit you to your uncle."

Somewhat shyly, for they owned afterwards he was quite different to what they had expected—not at all their hero of romance, the ideal "uncle from India"—the lads came forward, one and one. He shook hands with them timidly—as afraid of them as they of him; and tried, with a great effort, to distinguish their ages, and learn to call them by their right Christian names. But his mind seemed feeble and confused, and very soon his interest in them flagged, his eyes grew dull and heavy, and he looked piteously at his brother, as if for protection against this new, old, dreadful world.

"It is all so strange, Will; I can't understand it."

"Don't try to understand it, dear old boy. Every thing will come right presently. Sit still here, and we will go on just as if you were not present. You will get accustomed to us soon."

"Shall I? But no matter, it's not for long—I hope not for long." And then, as if struck by a sudden apprehension, he called his brother back, and whispered, hurriedly, "What do they know about me—all these lads? Are you not afraid to bring me among your sons?"

Will smiled.

"I might harm them, you know. At any rate, they will be ashamed of me, and so will you. Do you remember"—half his talk now consisted of his pathetic "do you remember"—"that picture I sat for, 'In another man's garden?' You laughed at it then; but it has all come true. The poor vagabond, looking on at his brother's happiness: it's just like me now, isn't it, Edna? Nay, I beg your pardon, my good little sister. I did not see you were crying." He held out his hand, and pressed hers tenderly.

"Behave better, then, Brother Julius, or I'll not be good to you any more. And talking of pictures I think you, will not be the only artist in the family. Will, my son, come over here, and show your drawings to your uncle."

This was a grand stroke of policy on Edna's part. Julius roused himself, like a dying war-horse at sound of the trumpet, and examined keenly, first the sketches, and then the face of his young nephew, so curiously like his own.

"Sixteen are you, my boy? I was sixteen once, and people called me clever, and said I should make a great painter some day. But that is all past and gone. Ah me!"

He leaned back with a groan; and that sharp agony, perhaps the sharpest next to actual guilt that any man can know, the remorse over a wasted life, came over him heavy and sore.

Edna was sending her son away; but the next moment, in one of his strange, fitful fluctuations, Julius looked up.

"Don't disappoint the boy, if, as you said, he wants me to look over his drawings. Give me them again."

They were very good for so young a draughtsman, and well chosen, being chiefly copied from the grand old Elgin marbles. As he turned them over, the eyes of the sick man began to glow.

"Ah! this is well done, and this—all except the arm. But that bit of foreshortening is difficult. I remember how it bothered me when I drew it at the Academy. It was my best drawing, though; but I think yours is better still."

And he regarded, with his observant artist-eye, but also with a sad, half-tender interest, the little fellow who, his face hot with happy blushes, knelt at his side; then put his hand on his nephew's shoulder.

"Any thing more to show me, my boy? Any thing of your very own?"

Shyly enough young Will drew from the very bottom of his port-folio a page of heads, which, when his mother saw, she wished had been at the bottom of the sea. But it was too late.

Uncle Julius started. "What is this?"

"It is Aunt Letty. I try to draw her over and over again from memory; but I can't succeed. She has the loveliest face in all the world," added the boy, growing quite excited. "Did you ever see her?"

Edna's heart almost stopped beating.

"Yes, I have seen her."

"And do you think you could draw her? From memory? You might. No one who had once seen Aunt Letty could ever forget her."

"No."

With a calmness that almost startled Edna—only she had ceased to be surprised at any thing now—Julius took up a crayon, and eyed it tenderly as he did so.

"I don't know if I can use this. It is years since I have touched a pencil—years!"

"Please try," entreated Will, creeping up to his uncle, as if he had an especial property in him. Truly, if the younger generation sometimes "push us from our stools," they have likewise a wonderful power of soothing, and can often heal over the past, which they in their innocence annul and ignore.

The five boys all crowded round, watching, with different degrees of curiosity, the beautiful face growing under Uncle Julius's hand, which, in the eagerness of its long-forsaken labor, gradually became firm and bold. It seemed as if the artist's pure delight in work for work's sake were faintly dawning in him again. When the sketch was done, he held it at arm's-length, critically yet tenderly. It was Aunt Letty — feature by feature, as the boys at once exclaimed. Only, not Aunt Letty as she looked now. It was the face, young and fresh and sweet, of lovely Letty Kenderdine.

ONLY A FACE.

"Yes; that will do, I think," said Uncle Julius, holding it at arm's-length, and looking at it. "As you say, my boy, it is the most beautiful face in all the world — but only a face. I have drawn it many times: now I shall never draw it any more. Put it away."

Will obeyed, but shortly afterwards came and settled himself beside his uncle, to whom from that hour he attached himself with a devotedness that nothing ever altered, though it was long before it was either noticed or returned.

Yet, until the children went to bed, Uncle Julius roused himself from time to time out of his drowsy weakness and sad preoccupation, to observe them a little, with a half inquisitive, half melancholy curiosity, as if trying to fathom the mystery of these young lives, which had been growing up, as it were, on the ruins of his own, and to trace in the new faces glimpses of the old familiar ones—now fading, fast fading, as we all do fade.

"Five sons! five hostages to fortune, as people say. Will, your name is not likely to cease out of the earth."

"Our name, Julius," said Will, tenderly.

"Fine fellows they are, and, I dare say, you and their mother are very proud of them; but I thought — somebody must have told me, only my memory is so bad now —there was a little girl too—Edna, I should have liked so much a little girl of yours."

William touched his brother on the arm to enjoin silence, and glanced uneasily at his wife. But Edna had heard.

"Yes," she said, speaking in a low voice, but quite calmly, "yes, I had a little girl once, but God took her. I have learned now to be happy in my boys."

Julius looked intently at his sister-in-law, as she sat there, wife and mother, fulfilling all her duties, and rejoicing in all her joys; and saw something in her face which he had never noticed before, which showed that she, too, had known sorrow, and been taught the hard lesson which we all have to learn soon or late, in one form or other—to be content, not only with what is given, but with what is taken away. And the solitary, broken-down man, who had suffered so much, but whose suffering was always in and for himself, recognized, probably for the first time in his life, but with a force the effect of which was never afterwards obliterated, that there might be griefs of which he knew nothing, and in which he had never attempted to sympathize, yet which were in reality as sharp, or sharper, than his own.

CHAPTER XXXI.

It might have been best, according to poetical justice, and certainly as to tragical effect, that Julius Stedman should die—die in the odor of sanctity and the arms of his brother and sister, leaving to them a perpetual regret, and to his faithless Letty a perpetual punishment. But Heaven's justice is not always "poetical," and Heaven's mercy is above all. Sometimes—most often—it is shown in that blessed death which alone can retrieve all things, give to the wanderer home, and the weary rest; but in this present case it was not so.

Julius did not die. In spite of his own prognostications and his brother's still more serious fears, he began to amend; very slowly at first, with many retrogressions, still it was an amendment. The most fatal element of destruction in his career, his opium-eating, had not, happily, been of sufficiently long standing to be incurable; and after his illness he conceived a horror of it, and never touched it more. Nevertheless, his constitution was so shaken that, in all human probability, nothing except his brother's great medical skill, in addition to constant watching, could have saved him; but he was saved. At least he was gradually brought into a state of convalescence—a sort of moonlight existence, compared to the full day of health and strength—yet calm and quiet enough, so as to make his life bearable to himself, and, by-and-by, no very great burden upon other people—a condition which would have been to him ten times worse than death.

Whether he will have a long life is doubtful. Probably not; for, at best, his was a temperament in which the sword early wears out the scabbard. By fifty Julius Stedman will be quite an old man; as, indeed, he often looks now. But the value of life consists not in its length; and his is now as full as it used to be empty.

He still lives, nominally, in his brother's house, though he is frequently absent from it, for he hates London, and enjoys, with all his heart, the little cottage at Sevenoaks, which, though silently given up for one summer—Julius never learned why—was taken the next, bought by Dr. Stedman, and presented formally to his wife, to be a perpetual delight unto her and all the family.

There, in the deep peace of country life, Julius spends his days, mostly all the year round, keeping house in the absence of his brother and sister; and painting a good deal, though not at his former large subjects. Like many other people, as he grew older he grew much simpler in his tastes—humbler, too, and doubtful of his own powers; so that he contents himself with sitting at the feet of gentle Mother Nature, and reproducing her in lovely little "bits," which people call pre-Raffaelite—pictures which, unpretending as they are, have such a reality, and often such a deep pathos about them, that they are always admired, and, moreover, sold—a circumstance of no slight importance to the artist, since as long as a fragment of health and life remained in him, Julius would have been far too honest and honorable to subsist upon another man's bounty, even though that man were his own brother.

As it is, he earns quite enough money to maintain himself in the moderate way, which is all he cares for now, for his ambition has long died out, and his extremely precarious health will always prevent his working as hard as those must work who would attain eminence in any thing. He himself will never become a great artist—he knows that—but he is bent upon making one of his nephew Will.

There are few things more touching, and at the same time more ennobling, than the intense devotion of a young man to an elder one; and Will is devoted heart and soul to a passionate extent—which his father and mother, though not a bit jealous, are sometimes half frightened at —to his uncle Julius. The two are constantly together, and have been, ever since Dr. Stedman, for both their sakes, and at their earnest entreaty, allowed his son to begin, regularly and decisively, the career of an artist. So Uncle Julius and his nephew are sworn companions, delighting in one another's society, and bound together by a tie as close as that of brothers, and as reverently tender as that between father and son. In his great love for the boy, and his eager anticipations of Will's future, Julius Stedman has a life neither forlorn nor unhappy, for he has learned to place his happiness on something out of himself—to help to win for another the fame that can never be his own. When he looks at young Will, and hears him praised on every hand, he feels that his own name will not be quite blotted out, nor his memory forgotten upon earth, even though he should die an old bachelor, wifeless and childless.

He has never again seen Mrs. Vanderdecken. She lives still at Holywell Hall, in great honor and undiminished wealth, flourishing like a green bay-tree, except that—poor woman—she can not fairly be likened to "the wicked." She is not wicked, only weak. Her little daughter loves her dearly, and has unlimited influence over her, so that Gertrude has no difficulty in obtaining leave to visit Aunt Edna whenever she chooses — at whose house, of course, she meets Uncle Julius, in whom she was quick enough at once to recognize her friend, Mr. Stone. But Gertrude has tact and delicacy enough not to take notice of this, except confidentially to her aunt Edna. Nor does Julius Stedman take much notice of her; but Julius the younger does, showing as fatal a predilection for her sweet little plain face, so loving and sensible, kind and true, as his uncle did for her mother's. This new little romance may, alas! cause mischief some time; for Dr. and Mrs. Stedman dislike the idea of cousins marrying: still, they will never imagine themselves wiser than Providence, but, if any serious attachment should occur, will leave their children's choice in their own hands.

Mrs. Vanderdecken herself never comes to visit her sister. That sad cowardliness, that weak shrinking from all things difficult or painful, which had been the bane of her life—nay, of more lives than her own—haunts her still. Yet poor Letty has her good points, growing better as she grows older, through the influence of her child. She is always ready to do a kindness that does not give her very much trouble, and she is not a bad wife to her disagreeable old husband, who leads her any thing but an easy life. There is many a small skeleton hid in the cupboard at Holywell Hall, but outside her home she enjoys a good deal both of pleasantness and popularity, being a very important person in her neighborhood, where every body agrees that Mrs. Vanderdecken is not only the handsomest, but the most charming, of middle-aged women.

Every body does not say that of her sister, by any means, for Mrs. Stedman is one of those women who live so entirely within their own family, that beyond it they are little known, and not half appreciated. But those who really do know her, love her; and those who know her best love her most of all.

She and her husband are still in the prime of life, or at least only beginning to descend the brow of the hill which their children are climbing so fast. All good children—diligent, upright, affectionate, honorable; no "black sheep" has yet been found in that happy little flock, out of which the only one lost is the little one—not lost, but gone before. Very few families can say as much; but then, very few are blessed with such parents as William and Edna.

They have, to all appearance, half their life's work, and enjoyment too, still before them; but who can tell? However, they have learned not to be afraid of evil tidings; for their hearts stand fast, trusting in one another, and in the Lord. Only sometimes, when they feel—this husband and wife—how very close they have grown together, and how impossible it is even to conceive the idea of being apart, a vague dread comes over them, followed by an unspoken prayer.

Such an one was in Edna's eyes, at breakfast one morning, when she looked up at her husband, and silently pointed out an obituary notice in the *Times:*

"DIED—ISAAC MARCHMONT, Esq., merchant, aged 84; and, two days afterwards, aged 80, ELIZABETH LILIAS, his wife."

"What is that?" asked Uncle Julius—and they passed round the newspaper to him without a word.

"One can hardly be sorry," said Edna, at last. "They had such a long life together; and, except for the loss of dear Lily, it was a very happy life—I used sometimes to fancy almost as happy as our own. And this," she added, softly, as her hand sought her husband's, "this—their dying within two days of another—seems to me the happiest lot of all."

"I think so too," said William Stedman.

Julius turned, and suddenly regarded his brother and sister with those wonderful dark eyes of his—very quiet eyes now, for the fire of passion had all burned out of them—a little sad at times, though not painfully so—but bright with a strange, far-away look, such as those have to whom life has been such sharp suffering that even in their most restful seasons the other world seems sweeter and nearer than this one. He seemed to understand what they were talking about—he understood so many things now—griefs which he himself had never known, and joys in which he could never more have any part.

"Will and Edna," whispered he, affectionately, "I think I guess what you mean. You would fain go together—and I go alone. But we shall all meet there. I know that now. May God give you your heart's desire!"

He rose, and leaning a moment on Will's shoulder as he passed him, kissed Edna, and went away up stairs to his own peaceful, solitary room.

THE END.